Sue MacKay lives with her husband in New Zealand's beautiful Marlborough Sounds, with the water at her doorstep and birds and trees at her back door. It is the perfect setting to indulge her passions of entertaining friends by cooking them sumptuous meals, drinking fabulous wine, going for hill walks or kayaking around the bay—and, of course, writing stories.

Born and raised on the outskirts of Toronto, Ontario, **Amy Ruttan** fled the big city to settle down with the country boy of her dreams. When she's not furiously typing away at her computer she's mum to three wonderful children, who have given her another job as a taxi driver.

A voracious reader, she was given her first romance novel by her grandmother, who shared her penchant for a hot romance. From that moment Amy was hooked by the magical worlds, handsome heroes and sigh-worthy romances contained in the pages, and she knew what she wanted to be when she grew up.

Life got in the way, but after the birth of her second child she decided to pursue her dream of becoming a romance author.

Amy loves to hear from readers. It makes her day, in fact. You can find out more about Amy at her website: www.amyruttan.com

Karin Baine lives in Northern Ireland with her husband, two sons and her out-of-control notebook collection. Her mother's and her grandmother's vast collections of books inspired her love of reading and her dream of becoming a Mills & Boon author. Now she can tell people she has a *proper* job! You can follow Karin on Twitter, @karinbaine1, or visit her website for the latest news—www.karinbaine.com.

Heart of Courage

SUE MacKay

AMY RUTTAN

KARIN BAINE

MILLS & BOON

First Published in Great Britain 2018
by Mills & Boon, an imprint of HarperCollins*Publishers*
1 London Bridge Street, London, SE1 9GF

HEART OF COURAGE © 2018 Harlequin Books S. A.

The Army Doc's Baby Bombshell © 2016 Sue MacKay
Taming Her Navy Doc © 2015 Amy Ruttan
The Courage To Love Her Army Doc © 2016 Karin Baine

ISBN: 978-0-263-27460-8

1018

MIX

Paper from
responsible sources

FSC™ C007454

This book is produced from independently certified FSC™ paper to ensure responsible forest management.

For more information visit: www.harpercollins.co.uk/green

Printed and bound in Spain
by CPI, Barcelona

THE ARMY DOC'S
BABY BOMBSHELL

SUE MacKay

CHAPTER ONE

'WOULD YOU LOOK at that? Sex in hard boots will do it for me every time.' The female sergeant at Captain Sophie Ingram's side ogled Captain Daniels striding across the dusty compound in their direction.

He *was* drop-dead gorgeous, Sophie admitted to herself as she tried to ignore the spark of arousal low in her body. A sensation she needed to shove aside. Working in Afghanistan was not the right time or place for liaisons. On a disappointed sigh, she told the military nurse, 'I'm off sex, hunk or no hunk available.'

Kelly's jaw dropped. 'You're kidding, right?'

'Not at all.'

'I mean, look at him,' Kelly spluttered.

She did. He *was* built.

The Kiwi captain, who'd arrived in camp late last night, widened his eyes as his gaze cruised over her. That delectable mouth lifted at one corner. Guess that meant he'd heard her blunt statement.

So what? It was best put out there. Saved time and misunderstanding. He could think what he liked. She wouldn't be hanging onto his every word in the hope of scoring during the three days he was in camp, helping out in the army hospital. Her last sexual experience had been something she didn't want to remember—or repeat—and had started her considering celibacy. Except it seemed some parts of her body hadn't got that message if the tightening in her belly and beyond was any indication.

'Captain Ingram?' The overly confident man stood in front of her, his hand outstretched in a friendly, yet provocative, manner.

Sophie nodded. 'Yes.' She took his hand to shake it but ignored the challenge staring out at her from the deepest pewter eyes she'd ever encountered. Neither would she acknowledge the rising tempo of her arousal. Sex was off the menu for the duration of her posting, no matter what. In her first weeks here a certain officer—now back home, thank goodness—had wooed her, then shown exactly what he thought the role of female personnel really was. Degrading didn't come close. Joining the army for an adventure was one thing, being treated disrespectfully was another. She'd since seen enough other liaisons end messily to know sex was best avoided on tour.

But she groaned. Captain Daniels with his dark, cropped hair and knowing eyes would tempt her every time. 'Welcome to Bamiyan NZ base.'

His eyebrow lifted in an ironic fashion. 'This is my third—'

The air exploded. The rock-hard ground heaved upward, shoving Sophie's feet up to her throat. Then she was airborne, her arms flailing uselessly, her head whipping back and forth. Slam. She hit the ground, landing on her back, the air punched out of her lungs, her limbs spread in all directions.

Stones pelted her. Dust filled her eyes and mouth. Breathing became impossible. *Whizz. Bang.* The air around her was alive, splintering as objects sped past her. Bullets? Fear gripped her. Who was firing at *her*? A heavy weight crashed over her, pinning her down. A human weight. What was happening? What had caused that explosion? Her heart beat so fast it was going to detonate out of her chest. Her ribcage rose higher and higher as she strained to fill her lungs with something purer than sand and dust. Her airway hurt. Her head hurt. Every single thing hurt.

'Stay down,' a deep, dark voice snapped.

She daren't open her eyes to see who the man protecting her with his body was. Gulp. Cough. Dust scratched the back of her throat. Strong arms were on either side of her vulnerable head. Muscular legs held down her softer ones. The one and only Captain Daniels.

Around them the gunfire was sharp and loud, and dangerous. Then suddenly it stopped. But the shouting and yelling continued. Orders were barked. Screams curdled her blood. Racing footsteps slapped the ground. Fear flew up her throat, filled her mouth. Was this *it*? The end? Lying on a piece of dry, barren dirt in some place she'd barely heard of growing up in lush green New Zealand? No way. She'd fight to the last, would not die lying here defenceless and useless. Flattening her hands on the ground, she tensed, ready to push upward, to remove her human shield.

'Easy.' That voice was right beside her ear, lifting the hairs on the back of her neck. Almost seductive—if she hadn't been terrified for her life.

Sophie squirmed, felt the muscles covering her body tighten.

'Easy,' he repeated a little desperately.

'Let me up.' She'd aimed for nonchalant, got light and squeaky. Damn. She was a soldier, supposed to be fearless. A little bit, anyway.

'Wait.'

Sophie needed to know what was going on. Apart from flying bullets and a bomb exploding. Needed to assess the situation, see if she could move, find shelter, help someone. As a doctor she'd be required in the hospital unit. Squinting, she looked around to see if it was safe to move. And came eyeball to eyeball with Cooper Daniels.

Her heart stopped its wild pounding, stopped trying to bash its way out of her chest. Went completely still. Her lungs gave up trying to inhale as that intense grey gaze bored right into her, deep into places no one had been before. Places where she hid the vulnerability that directed her life. Shock ripped through her. Every muscle in her body seemed to twitch, tighten, loosen. Had she died? Been taken out by one of those bullets?

'Captains, move. Now. Sir. Ma'am.' Someone, somewhere above them, roared in a strained shout, 'Get up off the ground. We've got you both covered.'

I'm definitely alive. Sophie pushed at Cooper, desperate to get away from him, to find safety, to regain her composure and see what needed to be done. There'd be casualties for sure.

The weight lifted from her body, a hand snatched at hers, hauled her upright in one swift, clumsy jerk. 'Run towards the officers' quarters,' Cooper yelled in her ear as he tightened his grip on her hand. 'The hospital's a target.'

She ran, trusting him completely. But even as she ran she looked around, and gasped. Where the ground had been flat moments ago there was now a deep crater. An enormous dust cloud hovered above, blocking the sun's intense heat. Otherwise everything looked weirdly normal—apart from the troops stationed on the perimeter, facing outwards with machine guns at the ready.

Forget normal. A body lay against the wall of the hospital block. Sophie shouted, 'Kelly,' and veered left around the destruction, aiming for the nurse.

Cooper pulled at her, tried to prevent her going in that direction. 'Wait. It's more exposed that way. Snipers will see you.'

Sophie got it. And wasn't having a bar of it. She paused to lock her gaze on him, her heart rate steady, her lungs finally doing their job. 'We need to get to Sergeant Brooks ASAP. Move her to safety.' She had no idea where the calmness now taking over came from, but she was in control, able to do something for someone, and not be a victim being protected by this man.

His eyes widened and he shook his head as though to get rid of something. 'You're right. Let's go.'

'Kelly was standing beside me when that bomb went off,' she muttered as they reached the nurse sprawled with blood pouring from a head wound and her legs at odd angles to her body. Dropping to her knees, Sophie reached to find a pulse, holding her breath as she tried to find any sign of life. Dread rose, and she quickly swallowed on it. Now was the time to step up and be professional; not let emotions override everything else. 'Come on, Kelly. Don't do this to me.'

A faint throb under her fingertip. 'Yes.' She slumped with relief. Her friend didn't deserve to die. Sophie kept her finger in place for a few more beats, to be absolutely sure, and looked at Cooper, who was crouched beside her, gently probing Kelly's head. 'She's alive. Get a stretcher out here. We're going into surgery.' Those legs looked in need of some serious work, as did the head injury. Blood also seeped into the ground from under Kelly's right shoulder. They'd have to do a thorough assessment but she wasn't hanging around out here for some sniper to pick them off.

'Yes, Captain.' Cooper was on his feet and racing towards the hospital unit, now all business, the challenging male no longer visible. Neither was the captain, aka general surgeon. He was just one of the battalion, doing the job of an orderly because she'd told him to. Impressive.

The man who'd thrown himself over her to protect her

from those bullets. Very impressive. Sophie bit down on the flare of yearning and astonishment suddenly touching her again in that place she'd thought so well hidden. What was it about him that exposed her weak side far too easily?

'Captain Ingram, we've got two casualties from the other side of the perimeter,' a soldier called above the noise of troops clearing the area and checking on one another. 'They've been taken into the medical unit for assessment. That unit's now clear of danger.'

Nothing, nobody was ever completely out of danger, but she'd keep that gem to herself. Glancing up, she acknowledged the young man who was on his first stint overseas with the NZ Army and sometimes dropped into the hospital to talk or read to patients.

'Thank you, Corporal.' His face was chalk white. 'Did you sustain any injuries, George?'

'No, Captain.'

'Right. Captain Daniels is bringing a stretcher so we can shift Sergeant Nurse Brooks. I'd like you to help with moving her.' Shifting Kelly without doing more damage to her broken body was going to be a nightmare. Even if the unconscious woman couldn't feel a thing, Sophie knew *she'd* wince at every single movement. She hated inflicting any pain whatsoever on someone. Her fellow surgeons often gave her grief about that, pointing out that any surgery was followed by some degree of pain.

'Yes, Ma'am.'

Cooper skidded to a halt by their patient and lowered the stretcher carefully, as close as possible to her body. 'It's chaos inside. Injuries all over the place.'

Sophie swore quietly. Why? Who? How could anyone do this to another human being?

Get real, her inner voice snarled. *You're in a war zone. This is what you're here for.*

She knew all that, but reality sucked, brought everything into focus in full colour. On a ragged indrawn breath, she began organising the removal of Kelly from the hot, dusty outdoors and into the relative safety of the medical unit.

'I'll be operating with you,' Cooper informed her as they carried the laden stretcher towards the theatre section.

Sophie glanced at him. 'Surely you're needed elsewhere.'

'Orders. Kelly's the worst off by far.' Then he added, sotto voce, 'If you don't count the two deceased.'

Sophie's stomach dropped. She'd been refusing to consider some of the soldiers might've been killed. 'Do we know who they are?'

'Not yet.' Cooper locked his eyes on her. 'If you want to go find out I can take over here.'

She shook her head. 'No. Getting Kelly stable so we can evacuate her is more important.'

'I agree.' He gave her a smile that blew her heart rate into disarray again.

Suddenly Sophie felt light-headed, swaying on her feet as she stared at the floor. Reaching out for balance, her hand found Cooper's shirt sleeve and gripped tight.

'You okay?' he asked, concern flooding his voice.

Dropping her hand as though it had been scalded, she growled, 'Guess it's the shock catching up.'

'It does that.'

She was showing her inexperience in conflict situations. The past two months had been relatively quiet on the war front—near this base anyway. She'd been kept busy with small surgeries but nothing like this. Reaching Kelly, she started appraising the injuries more thoroughly.

'Multiple fractures of both legs and the pelvis. As well as that dislocated shoulder and fractured skull.' Sophie straightened up from the bed Kelly lay on, and looked at Cooper. 'She needs an orthopaedic surgeon,' which they didn't have. 'How much experience have you got in that field?'

'Enough to do the basics, but the sooner we can get her back to Darwin the better.' Cooper looked glum. 'It's going to be touch and go for her.'

'Right. Let's scrub up and do what we can.' Sophie looked around the ordered chaos, saw the commanding medical officer on the far side of the room and made a beeline for him to explain the situation.

'We've got two others needing evacuation back to Australia too,' she was told. 'A flight's being arranged for two hundred hours. Do what you can in the meantime.'

At the sink Sophie scrubbed and scrubbed her fingers, her palms, the backs of her hands. Sand and dirt and blood stained her skin and had got beneath her nails. Anger at what had happened had her compressing her mouth to hold back a torrent of expletives that'd do no good for anybody. But how could people attack others like that? Used to fixing people, making them better, it was impossible to comprehend the opposite. Her muscles quivered, whether in rage or shock she wasn't sure, but she needed to get them under control if she was going to be any use to her friend.

'Easy.' Cooper's word of the day, apparently. A firm hand gripped her shoulder briefly. 'Save the anger for later.'

Turning, she locked her eyes on those grey ones she was coming to recognise as special, or was that the man behind them? 'There's plenty of it, believe me.'

He nodded and dropped his hand to his side. 'I know. It gets me going every time.'

'Yet you keep coming back.' She'd heard that Captain Daniels was on his third tour of duty over here. Then she saw the gleam in his gaze and knew he'd picked up on the fact she'd taken note of details about him. Telling him she hadn't gone out of her way to ask anyone would only stroke his ego further so she spun away to dry her hands before holding them out to the assistant to put gloves on for her.

This whole sexual distraction was ludicrous when they were in the middle of an emergency. 'Do we even know if the attack is completely finished?' she asked no one in particular.

'Apparently so,' Cooper replied as he began scrubbing up, a smug look on his face.

He could get over whatever was causing that. They had surgery to perform, which left no room for anything else. Sexual tension included.

Uncountable hours later Sophie smothered a yawn as she leaned back against the outside wall of their little hospital and watched Kelly being transferred to the medic truck that would take her to the airfield. 'Thank goodness she's survived her first round of surgery,' she murmured to herself, suddenly wanting to hear her voice in the rare stillness of the night.

'She's got a long way to go yet.' Cooper loomed up beside her.

So much for talking to herself. 'I'm worried about her left leg. I suspect she's in for an amputation despite everything we did.'

'That patella wasn't broken, it was pulverised,' Cooper agreed.

'Kelly's a fitness freak, runs marathons for fun.' Not any more. Or not for a long time and after a lot of hard rehab. Tears threatened. 'It's so darned unfair.'

'That's war.' His tone brooked no argument and suggested she needed to get used to the idea.

'I know. But I'm hurting for a friend. Okay?' Sophie

straightened her back, hauled her shoulder off the wall, took a step away. She'd had enough of Mr Confidence, didn't need reminding why she was here.

'Don't go. Not yet.' Cooper's voice was low and, strangely, almost pleading.

She hesitated. Going inside where everyone was still talking and crying and laughing as they finally came down off the high caused by shock over the attack and continual hours of urgent surgery turned her cold. But staying here, talking to Cooper Daniels, held more danger, and she'd had her fill of that already. 'Think I'll go to my bunk.'

'I'll walk you across the compound.' When she opened her mouth to say no he talked over her. 'We don't have to talk. I'd like your company for a few minutes, that's all.'

There were no arguments to that. None that she could find without sounding like she was making a run for it to put space between them. Anyway, she suddenly felt in need of company too. Talk about being all over the place. 'Sure.' She stepped away to put space between them and rammed her hands into the pockets of her fatigues. Then tripped on a small rock.

Cooper caught her, held her until she righted herself. Left his hand on her elbow as they slowly made their way through the throng of personnel wandering almost aimlessly back and forth on the parade ground they were crossing.

Out of the blue came the need to keep Cooper with her. His hand was reassuring against her unease. Leaning into him, absorbing the warmth of being with someone as tension held her in its grip, was a tonic.

Thump. She jerked around, staring into the night, seeing nothing more than she'd been gazing at a moment earlier.

'It's okay. Some clown tossed a metal bucket at the

fence.' Cooper slipped his arm over her shoulders, drew her in closer.

'I thought…'

'Yeah. Me too.'

'Have you ever experienced anything like what went down here?' She'd known signing up to the army, even as a medic, had its dangers, but this was the first time she'd been confronted with the truth of living and working as an army officer in Afghanistan. She needed to toughen up and put it behind her, not let every little sound or bang have her leaping out of her skin.

Tension tightened the muscles in the arm draped across her shoulders. 'Once. Near Kabul.'

'Why do you keep coming back?' She'd signed up for one year and now she wondered how she'd make it through without turning into a freaked-out wreck.

'Army orders.'

So he wasn't up for personal conversation. 'Of course.' She pulled away, put distance between them again. Wrapping her arms around her body, she stared ahead at the officers' quarters. Lights blazed out over the compound and the idea of going inside to be surrounded by her colleagues became repugnant.

'Want to keep walking for a bit?' So he could mind-read. Probably as well as he could twist a dislocated clavicle back into place, as he'd done for Kelly. Or as easily as he had most upright females drooling over him without a word.

Including her, she realised. He had to be the most sexy, gorgeous, mouth-watering man she'd met in a long time. Had she drooled when Kelly had pointed him out? Couldn't have or he wouldn't have come over to see her, dribble on the chin being highly unattractive.

'I'll take that as a yes, then.'

Huh? Oh, right. Unused to women not gushing out

answers to his questions? 'I won't be able to sleep. My head's spinning and my body aches from being tossed through the air.'

'That was some landing you made.'

'Didn't you get thrown down?' she asked, suddenly remembering how quickly he'd seemed to be with her, covering her as bullets had flown past. 'Thank you for protecting me. That was incredibly brave.'

'Honestly? It's something I did without considering the consequences. You looked vulnerable and I just fell over you.'

Sophie sighed. 'That's how brave people act. They don't weigh up the consequences. Wasn't it random how the three of us standing together ended up in different places? Kelly copped the worst of the explosion and was thrown in the opposite direction from us. We're relatively unscathed.'

'Be grateful. We were needed in Theatre afterwards.'

'True.' They were heading behind the officers' quarters into comparative quiet and some darkness. Sophie looked around, saw no one in the shadows, and stopped. 'Maybe I should go back.'

'Afraid to be with me?' That earlier challenge was back, deepening the huskiness in his voice.

'Not at all,' she snapped, even as awareness of him teased her. He was large; tall and broad. It would be so easy to lay her head on that chest and wrap her arms around his waist. She knew she'd feel safe for as long as she held onto him. Shock made her gasp.

But she didn't pull away from that tiny touch of his hand brushing against her thigh as he waited to see what she'd do. She couldn't move. Hell, she didn't even want to. Right this moment she needed him. Needed reassurance that she'd survived her first bombing alive and well. Needed to get close to another human, to share the horror and the recovery from the shock. Wanted more than to be held. Wanted to feel alive in his arms.

'Sophie?' Cooper growled.

She stepped closer, so near her breasts brushed his chest. Her nipples pebbled, throbbing with longing, echoing the sensations moistening her at the apex of her legs. She had never wanted a man so badly. Never. The afternoon's attack definitely had a lot to answer for. 'Cooper,' she whispered in reply. 'Please take me.'

'Are you sure?' he asked, the softness of his voice surprising her.

'Absolutely,' she told him fiercely. 'Absolutely.' Now. Not in five minutes. Now. She leaned closer, spreading the length of her body up the length of his. She immediately felt his hardness, knew his reciprocating need in an instant. Winding her arms around his neck, she raised her mouth to capture his.

Cooper took over. His hands spanned her waist, pulling her firmly against his body, so close they'd become one. His tongue pushed through to taste her, delving deep, taking charge.

Sophie lost herself in his kiss, his scent, his strength. Her hands grappled with tugging his shirt free. The need to touch his skin, to feel his heat against her palms was urgent. So urgent she slid her hands beneath the waistband of his fatigues, her fingers seeking that throbbing heat pressing into her belly. Wrapping her hands around him, she heard his groan by her ear.

'Sophie, you are driving me over the edge too fast.'

'I want fast.' Huh? Who was this wanton woman in her skin?

Cooper obliged, shoving at her trousers until they slid to her thighs, and then he cupped her.

All the air in her lungs whooshed across her lips as his finger found her hot, moist pulse. One slide of that finger and she was clinging to him, losing all sense of reality. Or was this reality? Another slide and her legs were trembling, losing the ability to hold her upright.

So she wrapped them around Cooper, holding herself over that wondrous finger, ready for his next muscle-tightening touch. But instead Cooper slid two fingers inside her and a scream flew up her throat, caught by his mouth. Since when had she become a screamer?

And then for the second time in twenty-four hours her world exploded. Shock waves hit her. Her body was racked with spasms, her head tipped backwards, and she was only vaguely aware of where she was. Again Cooper's strong body was plastered to hers, only this time it was her weight on him, her legs around his body. Then he moved to lift her higher and she was feeling him enter her, inch by excruciating inch until he filled her.

Then he withdrew to plunge in deep again. And again. And again.

Sophie completely lost her mind as her body responded to Cooper's. All she knew was she'd died and gone to some wondrous place she'd never experienced. All energy drained from her as her response overtook her.

And afterwards somehow she made it back to her bunk and slept the sleep of the completely sated.

CHAPTER TWO

Seven and a half months later...

COOPER SWIPED AT his forehead. The Aussie heat was relentless. Darwin did not come cold. Not even cool. And this was winter. Two hours since the troop carrier had touched down and he'd already had enough, felt in need of a cold shower despite showering and changing into clean clothes less than thirty minutes ago.

He entered the Australian Army's busy medical unit and looked around for her. Sophie Ingram. No doubt she'd be another reason for a cold shower as soon as he set eyes on her. He'd never been able to exorcise the woman completely from his brain. One night, one hot act, and she now ruled his thought processes far too often. Face it, once was one time too many. But the times that really bugged him were those in the middle of the night when he was tossing and turning in desperate need of sleep. She'd sneak in, reminding him of her amazing body and that off-the-scale sex they'd shared. Only once, and yet it had been the best he'd experienced in a life of experience.

There. Leaning over a table in the far corner, reading a file, seemingly oblivious to the hustle going on around her. The breath stalled in his lungs as he drank in the sight of that tall, slight figure with perfect butt curves that even fatigues did nothing to hide. Or was that his memory filling in the details? Her coppery brown hair hung in a long ponytail down her spine. He hadn't had a chance to run his hands through that silk, hadn't kissed her as often as he'd have liked. Both things he'd regretted even when the opportunity hadn't been there. If he had, would he still be feeling there was so much more to be enjoyed? It wasn't as if he wanted anything other than a rerun of that one act. If it didn't happen it wouldn't be the end of the world, but there was no harm in finding out if she was willing while he was here.

Sophie looked as cool as an iced beer as she straightened to turn side on to place the file in a tray.

Cooper gasped, the air exploding out of his lungs. His head spun so fast he closed his eyes tight in an attempt to stop it, to remain upright. Opening them again, the picture was exactly the same. He went hot, then cold, hot again. *Thud, thud, thud* slammed his heart. He swallowed—hard—but the sourness remained in his mouth. His hands clenched at his sides as he stared at the sexy woman he'd come to see with the idea of having a meal somewhere off base, hopefully followed by an evening in the sack. He had not come to be delivered a hand grenade that the pin had been pulled from.

'Cooper?' She was coming towards him, colour spilling into her cheeks. No longer cool. Shocked. Surprised. No. Make that uneasy. Which made perfect sense given the situation. She said, 'I heard you were stopping off for a couple of days on your way home.'

He fought the urge to back away. A coward he was not, but this was…enormous. Wrong word. He could even be wrong about what he saw. No, not about that, but about his role in the situation.

'I've just flown in from the east, landed a couple of hours ago.'

Her eyes widened. So she'd picked up on the fact he hadn't wasted any time dropping in on her.

'I heard you were still here and thought I'd say hello.' *Getting yourself in deeper, bud.*

She'd reached him and stood staring, hands on hips, caution darkening those emerald eyes that had haunted him in the deep of the night. Her voice wavered as she said, 'This is my last week here before I'm shipped back home to finish my contract in Auckland.'

She was going to Auckland? So was he. The day after tomorrow. Auckland was big. They'd never cross paths. *Coward.* That's what phones were for. Contacting people. 'I guess you're looking forward to that. The heat must be playing havoc with you.' He nodded abruptly at her very pregnant belly.

She's carrying a baby. He bit down on the expletives spewing across his tongue. Dread was cranking up from deep within. He had an awful feeling about this. A dreadful sensation that his world was rolling sideways and would never be the same again.

Sophie rubbed her lower back while her gaze was fixed on some spot behind him. 'Yes, the heat's exhausting, but it's more that I want to be home before this baby makes her entrance.' Now both her hands moved onto her belly in a protective gesture, as though she was afraid of, or warding off, something. *Or someone.*

Him? His reaction? He strove to be calm, barely held onto the question hovering on the tip of his tongue. When he thought it safe to open his mouth he asked, 'You don't want a little Aussie?' Who cared? Avoiding asking what he desperately needed to know and yet was afraid to find out was only stalling, not solving a thing.

'I'd prefer to be with my friends.'

Friends, not family. Showed how little he knew about her. 'How far along are you?' His breath caught in the back of his throat as he waited for her answer. It had been over seven months since the bombing in Bamiyan, since they'd found solace in each other's bodies. Was the baby his? If it was, why hadn't she told him about it? But why should she? What would she want from him? Apparently nothing, if it was his. There'd been no contact from her since that night, which in itself was unusual in his experience of women. If the baby wasn't his, then whose?

Sophie lifted her head, her chin jutting out as she said quietly, firmly, 'Seven and a half months. She's yours.'

He reeled back on his heels. Her direct reply knocked the air out of him and had his stomach sucking in on itself. It was one thing to wonder if he was the father; completely different to learn he actually was. Again heat flooded him. 'I see.'

Huh? I do?

Goosebumps lifted his skin. According to this woman he'd spent barely half a dozen hours with in total he'd made her pregnant. Should he believe her without question? Just accept her word for it without DNA testing? They'd had sex once. Once. What were the odds? How could he trust her to be telling the truth when he knew next to nothing about her?

Sophie was standing tall, her arms now at her sides, her hands fisted, her chin jutting out further, her eyes daring him to challenge her statement.

And just like that he knew she hadn't lied, wasn't trying to tie him into anything he didn't want. The tension left him. Then it was back, gripping him harder, tightening the muscles in his gut, his legs, his arms.

I don't want to be a father.

Did Sophie want to be a mother? Obviously she did or she'd have terminated the pregnancy, wouldn't she? She didn't know he never intended being a parent, or getting into a long-term relationship. That he played the field because he was just like his father, an expert at moving on from woman to woman. Where was the relief? Why wasn't he falling over backwards in gratitude for her not involving him in this baby's life? But now she had. There was no avoiding it. 'We need to talk.'

'Why?'

'Don't play games, Sophie. I'd like to know more about this baby, and how you're keeping. What I can do for you.' There. Responsibility kicked in even before he'd thought things through. Thanks to his dad for another lesson he'd learned well. As long as it didn't backfire on him.

'That's easy. Baby and I are healthy, and there's absolutely nothing I expect from you.' Despite her determined attitude, a flicker of doubt crossed that intense gaze, and her fists clenched tighter.

Unease rattled him. She did want something. Despite her statement to the contrary, there were things she'd want from him. He'd do the right thing. Stand by her and the baby. But that was the beginning and end of it. He wouldn't be tied down. Not for the sake of a child. It wouldn't work. He and Sophie didn't know anything about each other.

You know the sex can be out of this world.

One great bonk in extenuating circumstances didn't make a long-lasting relationship. Anyway, it probably wouldn't be the same again. Want to put that theory to the test? Yeah, he did. But wasn't going to now.

Another thing against further involvement was that he didn't do love. Didn't believe in it. He'd got this far without it. One too many times watching his father's latest girlfriend pack her bags and leave when he'd been a boy had taught him that getting involved with anyone led to nothing but anguish. It'd hurt every time, watching them walk away after he'd become close and begun to think they might be there as he grew up. Sometimes it had broken him. At first he'd had to learn not to cry, then he'd learned to be stoic, and finally gruff and rude. Love wasn't anything like it was cracked up to be. Not even the mother of his unborn child was getting a look in. Telling Sophie any of that wasn't happening, though he still needed to talk to her. 'What time are you taking a break?' he snapped, louder than he'd intended.

Sophie stared at him as though searching for something.

He only hoped he could provide whatever it was. All the more reason to go somewhere private before she said anything. 'Well?'

Looking around the busy room, where heads had lifted at his question, she shrugged, which set his teeth on edge. 'I can go to lunch any time I like. Despite how it looks I don't exactly get rushed off my feet. Unless there's a forced march in the wind,' she added with a tentative smile.

'Then you get queues of soldiers with all sorts of maladies that show no symptoms.' He wanted to smile back but was all out of them right now. 'Seen it all too often.' That caution on Sophie's face was unexpected, given how she'd thrown herself at him in Bamiyan, and again underlined how little he knew her. It also softened his stance the smallest of bits.

Toughen up. Don't go all soft over this. A baby, huh? A huge responsibility even if he only kept to the outskirts of the child's life. But…he was going to be a dad.

I am not ready for this. Will never be ready. This changes everything.

He and Sophie were now tied together in some way for ever. He turned for the entrance, his legs tensing, ready to run, hard and fast, as far away as possible, to outrun this crazy situation.

The only thing holding him back was that he'd always taken his responsibilities seriously.

Haven't been dealt this hand before.

True. It was as terrifying as that bomb in Bamiyan, and the consequences were going to last a lot longer. He had another mark to step up to, one he was not prepared for and had absolutely no idea how to manage.

'We need somewhere quiet for this discussion.' Sophie probably had similar concerns. Her sympathetic tone felt like a caress even if the intent of her words was a harsh reminder of what was ahead.

How could she remain so calm? He could hate her for that. No, not fair. She'd had months to prepare for today. And his anger was directed at the shock she'd delivered, not at her personally. But she should've told him. Then he'd have been prepared. A shudder rocked him. Really? Would he ever be able to look back at this moment and say it was a good thing to have happened? His hands clenched. Not likely.

'Is there somewhere we won't be interrupted?' Cooper demanded. There were a few personnel on this base he knew and would enjoy catching up with—some other time. His best mate would have to wait too. Right now he wanted this upcoming conversation done and dusted in one sitting, though he somehow doubted it was ever going to finish, that there'd always be things to discuss about their child. Their daughter. Sophie had said, *she's* yours. Oh, hell. A wee girl. His throat clogged. His daughter. This would take some getting used to. If he even wanted to, and right now he didn't. How could a guy whose mother had committed suicide when he was six and a father who'd had an endless stream of women moving through their lives grasp the basics of good parenting?

'We could go to my quarters.' Then Sophie hesitated. 'No, we'll go off base. There's a place a couple of kilometres south where I can get a sandwich and you can have whatever you might want.'

An ice-cold beer would go down just fine about now. Sweat was rolling down his back. From the temperature or his turmoil, he wasn't sure. Probably both. 'You got a car?'

She nodded. 'I do.'

'Let's go.' The idea of that beer had his mouth watering, while the idea of talking about the baby and their future wasn't doing his stomach any favours, instead causing a tightness he couldn't loosen. So much for a quick visit and maybe a bit of sex. Sometimes life threw curveballs. Big suckers. He needed to learn how to catch them without doing any damage.

Sophie drove as fast as legally possible. Which said a lot about her state of mind. Lately she'd become ultra-cautious about a lot of things, like she was afraid to create further havoc in her life. But Cooper's sudden appearance in the medical unit had floored her. Knowing he was turning up had done nothing to prepare her for the sight of this man. None of her memories of that hot body had been exaggerated. No wonder she'd thrown herself at him in Bamiyan. But would she have if the situation hadn't been so explosive? Ha. She had to ask that when Cooper was involved?

She should've told him the moment she'd found out she was pregnant, but what would've been the point? She didn't want him thinking he had to become a part of her life. It wasn't as though they knew each other or were in love. Getting hitched or involved in any way whatsoever with a man because she was pregnant was not on the agenda. Marriage had never been something she wanted, and pregnancy hadn't changed her mind. She could support her own child, didn't need to do someone else's washing or clean up after him for the rest of her life so that her daughter could see her father every day.

Three days ago when Alistair had told her Cooper was coming he'd given her a chance to prepare what to say, yet her mind had remained blank.

She got on well with the lieutenant colonel, had managed to ignore the fact he was Cooper's close friend until now. She suspected he'd guessed who the father of her baby was right from the moment she said she'd met Cooper in Bamiyan at the time of the attack. He'd have done the sums. Was that why he looked out for her, made her life as easy as possible? Because of his friend?

The sooner they got to Harry's Place the sooner she could tell Cooper the little there was to say and then she could get away from his brooding presence. At least he hadn't erupted when she'd said the baby was his. He'd come close at one point but had managed to haul the brakes on his temper. Told her something about the man, didn't it? Controlled under fire. But of course she'd seen that before, knew how he reacted when being attacked.

'I don't suppose this rust bucket runs to air-conditioning?' Cooper looked decidedly uncomfortable as he tried to move his large body in the not-so-large car.

'See that handle? It's for the window.'

His sigh was filled with frustration, and probably had nothing to do with their mode of transport. 'I figured.'

Then use it. 'The tyres are near new, and the motor hums. It's all I need.' It wasn't as though she took it on trips out into the desert or across state.

His head tipped back against the skewed head rest. He seemed to be drawing a deep, calming breath. 'Whatever possessed you to buy it in the first place? There must've been better vehicles available in town,' he snapped. The deep breathing was apparently a fail.

She ignored the temper and its cause. Plenty of time

to talk about their baby once they got to Harry's Place. 'It's a hand-me-down that goes from medical officer to medical officer.' When his eyebrows rose she explained, liking the safer subject. 'A couple of years back some guy bought it and when he was shipped out he handed it to the incoming medic, said he wouldn't get much for it if he sold it and as most medics are never here for long it might as well become a fixture.'

For a moment Cooper was quiet and she hoped that was the end of any conversation. Silence was better than questions she found herself looking for barbs in.

But no. That was wishful thinking. 'How long have you got to run on your contract with the army?'

'Ten weeks, but I'm only going to be on call for those weeks. I don't expect to be called up. What about you?'

'I'm done. For this contract anyway.'

'You're going to sign up again?' She didn't know how she felt about that. It wasn't as though they would want to spend time together, yet he was the father of her baby. Despite her own reservations about Cooper, her daughter deserved to know her dad, to spend time with him. It would never be her fault her parents weren't together, and therefore she shouldn't suffer the consequences.

The irony had her pressing her lips together. She'd grown up having it rammed down her throat with monotonous regularity that *she* was the only reason her parents had married. Mum had been pregnant so they'd done the right thing and tied the knot. Unfortunately they hadn't liked each other and the numerous arguments had been monumental, always ending with the blame landing firmly at Sophie's feet. They'd certainly put her off getting hitched. Why bother when she was happy and free? Becoming trapped and miserable would be a rerun of her childhood. So—no tying the knot in her future. Unless she found a man she loved unconditionally and who returned the sentiment. As she hadn't been looking, she didn't know if such a beast existed.

'I think I'm over the military.' Cooper stared ahead as he answered her question.

'What next, then?'

'Hospital contract.'

'Where?' she persisted.

'Auckland.'

So he wasn't just visiting, he was stopping. Guess she should be glad they'd be in the same city. Shouldn't she? That depended on lots of things. 'That's where you come from?' When he nodded abruptly she commented, 'You're not happy with my questions.' It was like pulling teeth.

'Not particularly.'

Fair enough. 'But I know next to nothing about you.'

'That's how I like it,' he snapped.

With all his relationships? Or just the one involving her that he'd have to adjust to? Could be he thought she was working out how much she could ask for child support. She contemplated letting him stew for a while, then realised how bitchy that was. Not so long ago he'd been sucker-punched with most men's worst nightmare. Her memories of the day she'd learned about the baby were still sharp, and that had been months ago. Shock followed by excitement, followed by fear. Those emotions still rocked her some days. 'For what it's worth, I have no intention of demanding money from you to raise my daughter.'

'Our daughter.'

Kapow! So he'd accepted the fact he was a father. Or had he? Was this just a hiccup as he processed everything? Her head spun. It seemed too easy. Far too easy to be true. What was the catch? When no answers came to mind she focused on driving safely and getting to Harry's Place in one piece.

Wonder of wonders, there was a parking space right outside the main entrance. With her usual efficiency—baby brain on hold for once—she backed into it and turned off the engine.

Our daughter.

The knob came off the handle as she wound hard to close her window. 'Stupid car. Something's always falling off.' Opening the door to allow some air flow through, she couldn't stop her mind running away on her.

My baby. Our baby.

A knot formed in her gut, dread cramping her muscles. 'I don't expect *anything* of you.'

'I'm starting to get the picture. Why didn't you contact me about this? Apart from wanting nothing of me, wasn't I entitled to know?' His hand waved between them, sort of in the direction of her extended belly. As though he was struggling with the whole concept after all. Which made more sense and was a lot closer to the reaction she'd expected.

The heat was building up rapidly and making her feel very light-headed. Shoving out of the car, she slammed the door, leant against it until her balance returned. Stepping onto the pavement, she told him, 'It's not like we knew each other.' It was hard not to yell at him, to ram her words in his face.

'Which gave you the right to decide I shouldn't have anything to do with my child?' The pewter of his eyes was now cold steel. His mouth had become a flat line that dragged his face down, making her realise it was the first time she'd seen him without a hint of a smile softening his expression. No, that wasn't right. He'd looked stunned and shocked when he'd first seen her in the medical unit. No smile then either.

'I always intended telling you after the birth.' Her

cheeks were getting hotter by the second, and not from the heat slamming up from the pavement.

'Why not before?' He stepped up beside her, dwarfing her with his size as he glared down at her.

'It's personal. Private.' She so did not want Cooper hanging around for midwife appointments and examinations. No, thank you.

'That's it? Personal? Private?' When she continued to watch him, he snapped, 'It took two to tango in the first place. You can't just kick me into touch and then haul me back as it suits you.'

She gasped. She wasn't doing that. 'It's not like that. I wanted this time to myself to get used to the fact my life's changed irrevocably.' She couldn't tell him that every time she'd thought of emailing him vivid memories of being piggy in the middle of her parents' disastrous marriage rolled in, and had her shutting down her good intentions. She'd been afraid to include Cooper in case her daughter had to grow up with the same pressures. Bad enough she knew next to nothing about good parenting, let alone adding Cooper to the mix. Tossing the hand grenade back at him, she asked, 'What could you have done these past months?'

'Supported you.'

How? Money? Marriage? They were in the army, unable to move to be with someone even if they wanted to. She shuddered. 'I don't need that from you.' Her friends would be there for her if—when—she asked. Her head spun. Happened a lot lately. The sun pounded her from above. Then the ground was rushing up to meet her.

'Hey, easy.' Strong arms wrapped around her, held her safe. Too safe. She liked these arms, remembered them holding her as they'd…made a baby.

Sophie struggled to free herself of Cooper. This was another reason she hadn't wanted him on the scene throughout her pregnancy. There'd been days when she'd gone into panic mode, wondering what on earth she was doing, going through with the pregnancy. But it wasn't like there'd been any alternative. She'd never have an abortion. But the thought of raising a child was frightening. On those bad days she'd been vulnerable, and if Cooper had been around she might've clung to him, relative stranger or not. There was something about him that could easily undermine her resolve to go it alone and that was dangerous—for the three of them.

Cooper kept his hand on her waist, and began walking her inside. 'Let's get out of this sun. It's debilitating.'

'It sure is.'

So are the spikes of heat in my blood brought on by your touch.

Her knees felt as firm as a piece of string, and her breathing was shallow.

Sex in hard boots.

Kelly's words from that fateful day ricocheted around her skull. There'd been an instant attraction back then, one she'd fully intended ignoring. Seemed bombs could blow up more than the earth and buildings and people. All thoughts of staying clear of Cooper had gone AWOL when she'd leapt into his arms behind the accommodation block. Now he was with her, doing the same job to her internally as the sun was doing externally. Pregnancy had made her emotional, and this was just another example. Less than seven weeks to go and then she'd again be in charge of her hormones and everything they upset. Fingers crossed.

First there was a conversation to be had. How could she have got pregnant to a man she'd known a few hours and never seen again? A man she knew zilch about—being a sexy hunk didn't count. Except that's what had got her into this situation in the first place.

'Are you looking forward to becoming a mum?' Cooper asked as he sat down opposite her at a small table inside, after ordering their drinks and some sandwiches.

Sophie nodded slowly. 'I am now.' When she'd first seen the blue line on the stick she'd gone into denial. Being a mother had not been on her to-do list. That had ideas on it like climbing the Sydney Harbour Bridge, hiking in Greece, going to Iceland to see the Northern Lights. This…her hand touched her belly…was something she'd thought she'd consider later if and when she found the right man. Or if her biological clock switched on.

'But not in the beginning.' Cooper was studying her too intently for comfort. Looking for what? A history of madness or irresponsibility?

'I've never been inclined to settle down.' Too many things to see and do in this world to want to disappear behind a picket fence. Except that theory had slapped her across the face recently. Avoiding life was no longer an option. But Cooper wasn't going to take advantage of these uncertainties. 'Now I'm ready.' Despite the panic that occasionally overwhelmed her, she could say, *Bring it on*. She couldn't wait to meet her daughter.

Their daughter.

Eek, but this was awkward.

Thankfully her phone rang just then. Ignoring Cooper's scowl of disapproval, she answered. 'Yes, Corporal?'

'Captain, can you come back? One of the Unimogs went off a bank during the exercise and they're bringing the men in to be checked over.'

Instantly Sophie was on her feet. 'Any reports of serious casualties?'

At her question Cooper also stood up. 'I'm available if needed,' he said quietly.

'So far only two probable fractures have been reported,

but we're to see all the personnel who were on board,' the corporal informed her. 'ETA is thirteen hundred hours.'

Less than an hour away. She had to head back and make ready for the soldiers. It was a lucky escape from the conversation she wasn't ready for. 'I'm on my way.' Sliding her phone into a pocket, she turned to Cooper. 'A Unimog tipped off a bank. So far we've got a couple of likely fractures. The rest of the crew is to be given the once-over. I've got the staff to cover it.'

'In other words, you don't need me.' Was that disappointment behind his question?

'I'd have thought after a long-haul flight you wouldn't want to work.'

'You were expecting me, weren't you?'

'Yes.' She turned to the guy behind the counter. 'Can you put my sandwich in a bag? I've got to go.'

'No problem, Sophie. How's that baby doing?'

'Like a gymnast training for the Olympics.' She grinned, then saw Cooper scowling again. Didn't he like her being friendly to the locals? Tough, he was out of luck. She did friendly. Plus guys like the one behind the counter had been a part of her life for the last few months. Cooper hadn't.

The baby kicked hard.

She sucked in a breath. Her hand automatically went to the spot and rubbed gently. It was as though the baby knew her dad was here and needed to remind Sophie he'd been a part of her life ever since Bamiyan.

Cooper was staring at her hand, his throat working hard. Awe filled his eyes and softened his mouth.

'You want to feel the movement?' she asked before she had put her brain in gear.

'No.'

Relief speared her, quickly followed by disappointment. Of course he didn't, stupid. 'Fine.' She turned away.

'Sophie? I'm still getting my head around all this.'

'Sure. I understand.'

I think.

She probably wasn't being fair. The guy would be tired from that flight squashed in the back of the transport plane with a load of other men. Throw in the shock of learning about the baby and he was allowed time to accept everything, wasn't he? 'Just trying to involve you a little bit.' She turned for the exit.

'Um, can I touch? Feel her?' The new look in his eyes held hope and excitement, and stopped short her sudden need to step away from him and run.

As if running was an option with a barrel sticking out from her stomach. 'Here.' On an indrawn breath she reached for his hand and placed it where her baby was kicking. She ignored the spike of warmth that stole up her arm from where she touched him, and the sense of rightness having his hand on her belly gave her. Because it wasn't right. Never would be. They didn't belong together and this was a very intimate moment. Even if they were standing in a café full of strangers.

When ignoring Cooper proved impossible she gave in and leaned closer, breathed in his scent. Hot male with a hint of musk. Her tongue lapped her lips. This was crazy. They'd spent less time together than most people had with their dentist and yet now they were having a child and her hormones were in a spin every time he came within breathing distance.

'Wow…' Awe drew out that single word and filled his eyes so that they glittered with amazement.

Danger.

The warning flashed into Sophie's brain.

He's not going to walk away and leave you to get on with having your baby. He's hooked. Whether he knows it or not.

Pushing at his hand, she stepped backwards. 'I need to get back to base.'

'I'm coming with you.' Cooper's tone told her not to argue. He changed his moods rapidly and often. Something to remember. Now all that amazement had gone; filed away, no doubt for him to take out at his leisure.

Which worried her. Yes, he was the father. Yes, she wanted him to be a part of their daughter's life. No, he was not welcome at the birth, or any midwife sessions beforehand. He was most definitely not going to take part in deciding where she'd live, or how many hours a week she'd work, or how to bring up her daughter. Those were her decisions to make.

But there was no avoiding the fact they were inextricably tied together for the rest of their lives.

'Can't you find something to entertain yourself in town for the rest of the afternoon?' she asked, even knowing his answer. Being crammed into the car together again made her throat dry and her head spin. Cooper frightened her. Simply by demanding his rights he could destroy her independence, which was her safe haven.

'I'm coming with you, Sophie.' He already had her door open and was waiting patiently for her to clamber in, an activity no longer done with ease now that she had an enormous stomach to squeeze behind the steering wheel. 'Maybe I should drive,' he said as he watched her awkward movements.

'No way,' she shouted, and grabbed the door to slam it shut. It was so tempting to throw the car into gear and race away, leaving him on the roadside. Childish, yes. Would it relieve some of the tension tightening her muscles? Absolutely.

Cooper must've seen something in her expression because he was around the car and sliding into the passenger seat even before the key was in the ignition. Worse, he grinned at her. 'Didn't know you had a temper.'

Which cranked her *temper* higher. 'There's a lot you don't know, Captain, and I intend keeping it that way.' The car jerked onto the road as she touched the accelerator.

A hand covered her thigh, squeezed lightly. 'Easy, Sophie. Let's take this one step at a time. First being to get back to base in one piece.'

Boy. Did he know how to wind her up or what? Her first reaction was to slam on the brakes and kick him out. Literally. Her second was to slam on the brakes and ask nicely if he'd mind getting out. Finally she wound down her window for much-needed air and drove carefully, and silently, back to work. But her teeth were clenched, and her jaw ached by the time she got there.

Why had she had sex with this man in the first place? *Sex in hard boots.*

CHAPTER THREE

COOPER COULDN'T CONCENTRATE. On anything. Sophie. Baby. Both had stomped through his mind, destroying his renowned ease with most things.

She'd relented and made him part of the team to examine the men from the Unimog. He'd managed to be thorough and professional, but he was glad he'd been assigned the cases where the men said they were okay except for bruising. A matter of verification before signing them off that even he could manage while dealing with the bewilderment swamping him since Sophie's announcement about the baby.

'Get dressed, soldier,' Cooper told the musclebound specimen standing before him. 'You're in good shape.'

'Yes, Sir.' The guy might've answered him but his focus was on the woman on the other side of the room.

Sophie was busy, reading an X-ray plate of one of the less fortunate men's ribs and talking on the phone. She hung up. 'Three fractures on your right side, Corporal. With those, along with the torn ligaments in the same site, you're going to be very sore.'

Downplaying the pain earned her a grin. 'Yes, Ma'am.' He could've had his arm sawn off and he'd be happy as long as Sophie was dealing to him. It was no secret the soldiers adored her. Each and every one of them had eyes for no one else, even those in pain.

Cooper sighed. They weren't on their own. He struggled to keep his eyes away from her. She was gorgeous. Not only physically but in her style, her kindness to everyone without being overpowering, her quietness. The first time they'd been together he hadn't noticed any of these characteristics. There'd been too much going on with bombs and bullets and sex.

'Are you finished with patients, Captain Daniels?' Sophie had crossed the room to stand in front of him.

'The last soldier has gone. A few bruises to grizzle about is his lot.'

'Thank goodness we didn't get anything too serious, broken bones notwithstanding.' She was doing that belly-rubbing thing again.

'Are you aware how often you do that?' he asked thoughtlessly, and got a shy smile in return.

'Probably not. It's almost a habit.'

A cute, caring habit. 'I admit feeling the baby kick against my hand was…' A life-changing moment. Another one. The second in a matter of hours. Seemed anything to do with Sophie Ingram happened fast. Like that night in Bamiyan. Though that had made some kind of sense, given the attack and how they'd had to fight their own fears in order to help others so the moment they'd relaxed all hell had broken loose between them.

But the moment he'd seen Sophie today his world had tipped sideways. That was before he'd noticed her pregnancy. Everything he believed in as far as women and relationships went had been suspended while he'd struggled to get his head around the fact he was responsible for that bump Sophie carried so beautifully, if not a little awkwardly at times.

When she'd placed his hand on her belly and he'd felt

his daughter kick, he'd known the baby was real and not just an idea to grapple with. Scary. What he hadn't counted on was the awe that had gripped him and the instant connection with the baby—and therefore with Sophie.

Forget scary. Try terrifying.

What was he going to do? Walk away? Man up? Find a middle line that worked for both of them? *The three of them*, growled a pesky voice in his head, reminding him he hadn't really got the hang of all this yet. He wouldn't be walking away. That much he did know. He wanted to. No point denying that. But he wouldn't.

'Captain Daniels?' A corporal stood beside Sophie. 'Lieutenant Colonel Shuker requests your presence.'

'Thank you, Corporal. Can you tell me where I'll find him?' Yay, someone to talk to who had nothing to do with his dilemma.

But as he followed the soldier across the parade ground his elation deflated quicker than it had risen. Alistair Shuker, aka 'List' to his mates, was going to ask him what his plans were for the future. He was going to wave that Australian Army contract under his nose and tease him with money and a soft posting.

'Coop, good to see you, man.' List punched him lightly on the shoulder. 'How was the flight?'

'Rough, hot and boring.' Cooper returned the punch and studied his friend. They'd been together on some hairy forays in joint exercises with their respective armies. List was a man a guy could rely on to get them out of a tight spot. He was also the only man who knew him well. They'd done a lot of talking in the deep of the night while waiting for situations to go down in Afghanistan. Too much. There was nothing List didn't know about him, and vice versa. Except that was wrong. There was one snippet of information List had no idea about. One Cooper wasn't about to share.

'That why you disappeared off base with our lovely doctor? Needed a cold drink? Or great company?' List was watching him so closely he had to be able to count his whiskers even though he'd shaved that morning.

Uh-oh. Did he know about the baby after all? As in who the father was? Had known before him? Cooper shivered. He didn't like the idea. Not one little bit. The baby had nothing to do with anyone else except him and Sophie. 'You're friends with Sophie?' And that idea made him squirm with something alien—jealousy. A nasty reaction he was ashamed to admit and yet found hard to squash. Why be jealous when he had no intention of settling down with any woman? Not even an auburn-haired, svelte beauty, who right now probably needed someone in her life to support her.

'Everyone's friends with Sophie. People adore her. No one wants to see her hurt.' The warning couldn't be louder—or clearer.

All the emotions of the day balled into anger and he took it out on List. 'Don't threaten me, *mate*. Whatever's going on in that head of yours is way off the mark, so shut up. If you haven't got anything better to say then I'm heading over to the mess where hopefully I'll get some peace and quiet.' And the very cold beer he'd missed out on at Harry's Place due to Sophie being called back. His blood was boiling as he spun around to head for the door.

'Coop, stop right there.' List wasn't quite pulling rank. The words were those of a commanding officer but the tone was that of a friend. Being a New Zealand officer didn't quite let Cooper walk away in a huff from an Australian counterpart.

As much as Cooper wanted to storm off, he knew his reaction wasn't only about his friend but a combination of everything that'd gone down since landing in Darwin. Stopping his retreat, he slowly turned round. 'You wanted to talk about me signing up with your lot?'

Keep off the taboo topic, mate.

He was subjected to a long and deep perusal before List finally shrugged and sat down. 'Yes.' He nodded at the vacant chair on the other side of his desk. 'You thought about it?'

Cooper elected to remain standing, still on edge. 'A lot.'

'And?'

'I admit to not knowing what I want to do. I'm sort over soldiering, and yet going back to Civvy Street seems too tame.' Restless didn't begin to describe him. There had to be a lot more out there waiting for him, but what? Something was missing in his life. That much he got. What, how, where and why were yet to be answered. A challenge of some sort might fix whatever it was that ailed him.

A baby had to be up there as one of the biggest challenges possible.

List leaned back in his chair and placed his feet on the desk. 'Sit down, man. It's me you're talking to.'

'Yeah, I know.' All too well. As quickly as it had risen, all the tension grabbing him evaporated. This was his best pal, the guy who knew far too much about him for him to be getting antsy. Cooper dropped onto the chair and propped his feet on the opposite end of the desk, rank forgotten for now. 'So how's life treating you?'

'Can't complain.' List grinned. 'Back on the mainland where it's relatively safe, lots of women hanging around, my folks just down the road.'

'I forgot you came from these parts.'

'Born and bred Northern Territory guy. Mum and dad still live in the house I grew up in.'

'I can't begin to imagine what that's like.' Cooper again felt a spurt of jealousy. What was wrong with him today?

Never before had he thought other people, especially his pal, were better off than him. While his father was constantly on the move with work and women, never settling down with anyone for more than a year at most, Cooper felt he didn't have a home as such, but he'd got used to that. Dad always had his back and that meant a lot. He accepted that's how it was for him and that he was happier doing the same as his father than trying to be someone else. Stopping in one place with one woman for the rest of his life? He shivered. Not something he knew much about, and would probably screw up if he even tried.

Sophie sneaked into his head. Rubbing his palm where he'd felt the baby kick, he remembered the wonder that'd filled him at the thought *his* baby was in there. Not just a baby—his baby. What was he going to do now?

'You should try settling down some place,' List commented dryly. 'You never know. You might like owning a home, not a house. Having a family to come back to at the end of the day or a tour of duty.'

His house was just fine, thanks very much. 'Says the man who plays the field even harder than I do.' He'd ignore the barb List had delivered.

Or so he thought. 'Sure I do, but I'm looking, man. I want the wife and kids, the whole nine yards of snotty noses and nappies. The football in the back yard. The romantic nights under the stars when the kids are asleep in bed.'

Cooper rubbed his hands over his head. 'Thought I knew you. When did you get so staid?'

His pal laughed. 'When the plane landed here six months ago. I climbed down onto home turf and knew I was ready to settle down. I've had enough running around with the boys and not having anyone special to come home to after a particularly messy tour.'

'You're going to quit the army? And you're aiming to convince me to join up with your lot?'

'Don't put words in my mouth. I'm merely trying to get you to think things through clearly, make the right decisions with all the facts.'

There was that nudge again. This time like a bulldozer. List did know something about him and Sophie. He'd swear it. But he wasn't going to ask. A barrage of questions would follow. Questions he had yet to work out the answers to. 'Is there any other way?' he asked acerbically. Then shrugged. 'Up for a beer when you're done here?' Thinking could be highly overrated and right now he'd had more than his share of it. 'I could do with a distraction—and something cold and wet.'

And I do not want any innuendo about Sophie.

'Let's go. I'm not even meant to be here today, only came on so as I could give you a hard time.'

'Got my uses, then.' Cooper followed his mate out into the glaring sun, looking forward to catching up properly with him.

'How close are you to Sophie?' List tossed over his shoulder.

Cancel that. He should never have suggested a beer. 'Who says I am?' What had Sophie told List?

'No one. The fact that she was the first person you went to see on arrival speaks volumes. Usually it's me you're plaguing with your presence.'

Why hadn't he thought of that? 'There's no hiding anything from you, is there?'

List smirked. 'Don't forget it. One last thing and then I'll shut up.'

List didn't do shutting up very well, but what could he say? 'Go on.'

'I'd like to swap you onto the same flight out as Sophie's taking early next week. It's a long haul back to

Auckland and I'd hate for something to happen and there be no medic to help.'

Worry lifted bumps on Cooper's skin. 'Is she having problems?' Please, anything but that.

'A couple of short bouts of sharp pain. She calls them some funny name, says they're false labour pains, but I don't know. Seems strange to me.'

The worry backed off. 'Braxton Hicks contractions. They're quite normal.' He could still leave on his planned flight.

'That's them. Normal, eh? Fair enough, but I'd still like you on that plane.'

'She'll be fine.'

And I'll be at home, getting on with my next career move.

'And if she's not? What if she goes into labour between here and NZ?'

There'd be people to help her, to deliver the baby and take care of them. 'I'll be on that flight.'

Stretching out on her bunk twenty-four hours later, Sophie put her hands over her stomach and stared up at the ceiling. The heat had drained the energy out of her once again.

Kick.

'You take your toll too, little one.' Little one. Soon she'd have to decide on a name. There was a list in her drawer. Lots of names she liked but none that grabbed her. It wasn't as easy to choose as she'd have believed. A name was for life. She didn't want anything that could be shortened into an awful nickname, or something odd that might get her girl teased, but she didn't want plain and ordinary either. Her friends on base were constantly teasing her about her inability to make up her mind. Said it was a prime example of baby brain in someone who usually knew exactly what she wanted.

But then this whole pregnancy thing had been a brain mess. It shouldn't have happened in the first place, and would probably keep her celibate for a lot longer than she'd planned on.

Could just buy condoms by the ton.

Yep. That'd work.

Ha. She was only weeks away from becoming a mother. There wasn't going to be time for having fun with men. Junior here would need all her attention, and any spare time would be taken up with work. If she could find a part-time position after baby arrived. She had to. How else would they live? Babies didn't come free, and she wanted the best for hers. A cosy home—read a tiny but cheery flat. A loving mother—read one who'd never blame her daughter for holding her back from her career.

Somehow she'd find the balance between parenting and working, because one wouldn't happen without the other.

Knock, knock. 'Sophie?'

Cooper. The last person she wanted to see right now. But not acknowledging him mightn't work. He appeared to be the kind of man who'd walk right on in, and that would only make her look stupid. Struggling up off the bed, she reached to tug the door wide. 'Yes?'

Oh, but he looked good. More than good. Make that breathtaking. His white T-shirt accentuated his biceps and as for those pecs… Her cheeks reddened. They were out of this world. If she'd had to make a mistake then she'd made it with a seriously built guy. Her glance slid lower, took in the knee-length shorts that sat snugly on his slim hips.

'Sophie, can we spend some time together?'

'We worked in the same room all day.' She'd deliberately kept any conversation focused on patients or upcoming health programmes. Last night she'd seen him leave base with Alistair so had relaxed about eating in the mess, knowing he wouldn't suddenly appear at her side, full of awkward questions.

'I'd like to get to know you a little better,' he insisted.

Why so reasonable? At least she could argue with the angry version. 'It's hard to find privacy around here.' Did she really want to be alone with him when all she could think about was the outstanding features of that body his clothes did nothing to hide? A body she'd seen little of yet had known intimately.

'We could go somewhere there's air-conditioning,' he said with a tempting smile.

She made up her mind, hoping she wouldn't regret it. 'Air-con will get me every time. It's stuffy in here.' Learning more about Cooper couldn't hurt. As long as she kept it all in perspective and didn't start thinking they could have a future together. She hadn't forgotten his reputation as a playboy. Or her mum and dad's style of parenting. Which was what her baby would have if they got together. Very off-putting for her as well.

'I do have another idea. Want to go for a swim? I hear there's a nature park not far away that's safe from crocs. We could take a picnic.'

She knew exactly where he meant. 'You'd risk going that far in my car?' What would she use for a swimsuit?

Cooper swung some keys from his finger. 'Air con, remember?'

'Who have you stolen that off?'

'List.' She must've gaped at him because he explained, 'Alistair.'

'Of course.' Alistair would lend his vehicle to his mate.

Cooper jiggled the keys at her. 'Your choice. Swim or bar. Which is it to be?'

As her skin was moist with sweat due to the soaring temperatures and the additional weight she carried the idea of slipping into cold water was impossible to let pass. 'I'll change into an old shirt and some shorts.'

'Bring warmer clothes for later in case it gets chilly. I'll go get a couple of things and meet you back here in ten.'

The heat wouldn't cool down that much, and neither would she. Sophie watched him stride away, those long, muscular legs giving her heart palpitations. How could anyone be so perfect?

Aha, that's physically.

What about his personality? Couldn't be perfect as well. Probably not, but so far she hadn't found anything to make her dislike him or even be wary of him. Right now she didn't care. She was too busy enjoying the view.

Cooper waved over his shoulder at her without turning round. So he knew she was ogling him. Ego. He was so used to women falling all over him it would never occur otherwise.

Didn't help that she'd proven him right.

The water was cool and immediately brought down the heat that had plagued her all day. 'This is bliss.'

She was glad she'd come. Forget looking like a beached whale. For the first time in ages she was comfortable in the hot northern state. Auckland could be warm and muggy, but never did the temperatures reach the thirties. Which had to be a plus for when she got home.

'You're happy?' Water splashed over her as Cooper dropped down beside her.

'Very.' She sighed her pleasure.

'You're easily pleased.'

Sometimes. 'Where did you do your training?'

He went with the change of subject. 'Auckland. Qualified as a surgeon four years ago and signed up for a short stint with the army straight away. You?'

'Otago.' She'd been in a hurry to get away from home. Nothing to keep her there. 'I was four years behind you.'

'Why did you sign up for the military?'

'I love travelling and they were wanting surgeons for places I'd never been and was unlikely to visit on my own.' Travelling kept her focused and didn't allow time for the doubts and insecurities to creep in. If she didn't stay in one place for long she wasn't in danger of getting close to people.

'You wanted to see Afghanistan?'

'Why not?' It hadn't been her first pick but she'd signed up for an adventure. Not the army's fault she'd got more than she'd bargained for. 'Thank goodness it was only a twelve-month contract.' She shuddered as vivid memories of that attack in Bamiyan struck.

'Got more than you bargained for?'

'I still have nightmares about that bomb blast. Do you?'

'Often.' Cooper traced a finger over her chin. 'There are some good memories about what followed.'

Sophie's head jerked back. She had those memories too. But that had been then, while now was a whole new deal. 'I was incredibly naïve to think nothing would happen while I was there.'

I'm thinking bombs, not babies.

'I reckon every soldier who signs up is guilty of that. By the way, have you heard how Kelly's doing?'

'Really well, despite losing her leg.' They talked regularly. 'She's planning on returning to nursing on a part-time basis as soon as she gets the hang of her prosthesis. She's fallen in love with one of the medics who evacuated her to Darwin, and they've set up house together in Perth.'

'The strange twists of fate.'

Yeah. Look what fate had done for her. 'It's stopped me in my tracks, and made me reassess what's important.

Before Bamiyan my life was all about surgery and travel. Now I've got someone else to think about.'

And I still have no idea what I'm doing.

'Are you going to continue working after the baby's born?'

'I'm hoping for part time at first.' The money she'd saved while in the army would see her through till the New Year if she was careful.

'You'll employ a nanny?'

She blew air over her lips. 'Not sure yet. I don't like that idea, but I do have to earn a living.'

Cooper pushed away and began swimming. His arms cut through the water, his strength pulling him along quickly and efficiently. What had she said? It was the truth. She didn't have a wealthy family to fall back on. She didn't have any sort of family to turn to really. Mum and Dad wouldn't want a bar of her and her baby, which was why she hadn't found the courage to tell them they were about to become grandparents. She couldn't face their scorn at having made the same mistake they had. But there was a difference. She wasn't getting married for the sake of her reputation, as her parents had done.

Sophie flipped onto her back to float on the current, but the bulge that was her belly poked up at the sky and she immediately dropped back onto her feet. Sinking until the water reached her chin she relaxed into the coolness and pushed aside all her doubts for another day. It was strange how that now she'd told Cooper about the baby everything else she'd been avoiding was filling her head. Finding somewhere to live, getting furniture, baby clothes and a bassinet. Then there was telling her parents about the mistake she'd made with Cooper. Time was running out and once she was home there would be no excuse for not sorting everything out. Including the doubts and fears that followed her into sleep every night.

'Can I see you when we get back to Auckland?' Cooper appeared from behind her.

She'd been so tied up in her own thoughts she hadn't heard him splashing through the water. 'I did say I wouldn't stop you from having a part in the baby's life.' Even with his now slightly longer hair plastered to his skull he looked good. Too darned good for her heart rate, which had risen too high in a blink.

'Just checking.'

'Cooper, if I say something like that I mean it and am not going to retract it.'

He nodded slowly. 'It's weird, being brought together over something so important with someone I know next to nothing about. Allow me the odd left-field question. I'm sure you've got plenty of your own.'

'Here's one.' But not so left field. Her T-shirt clung to her outline like a second, wrinkled skin, and left nothing to the imagination. 'Will you refrain from staring at me as I waddle out of the water and wrap a towel around my waist?' Except she didn't have a waist any more.

He should've laughed at that. He didn't. Instead, he put an arm around her and began walking them towards the water's edge. 'Don't talk like that. You're beautiful and your pregnancy makes you glow: it does not make you ugly or fat or ungainly. It suits you. Please, believe me.'

How could she not when he sounded so sincere? Looked at her like she *was* beautiful? Special even. Tears sprang to her eyes. 'You say the nicest things.'

Damn you.

But of course he did. He was a playboy. A charmer. But... She'd swear his words were genuine. Not meant just to stroke her ego and win him a few brownie points. She was vulnerable at the moment. Doing this on her own was bound to make her susceptible to whatever Cooper said. Wasn't it?

Actually, no, she didn't believe that. She was strong, and, despite baby hormones tearing into things, she was managing just fine—if she didn't think about everything that could go wrong before, during and after the birth. After would be a lifetime. A lifetime of hoping she got her role as a parent right, never hurt her girl, never let her down, loved her unconditionally. How could she do that when she'd never experienced it? One thing she knew for certain—she'd never needed a man to tell her she was beautiful before, and she wasn't starting now. She'd accept Cooper's compliment for what it was, and enjoy it. 'Thanks.'

'I mean every word.'

A warm glow that had nothing to do with the sun made her skin tingle. Could be that it might help, having him around occasionally. He'd lift her spirits on the down days.

Cooper flicked a blanket out over the grass and opened a chilly bag to produce cold water for her and a beer for him. 'We've got chicken and focaccia for dinner. Basic but the best I could find in that small grocery shop down the road from the base. I didn't want to waste time going into town. You might've changed your mind about coming out with me before I got back.'

'Once the idea of a swim was lodged in my mind nothing would've stopped me coming.'

'My fatal charm had nothing to do with it, then?' He grinned at her like he couldn't care less what she thought.

Grinning back, she said, 'Nope.' This easy banter between them was good, and fun, and helped her relax a little bit more. Wrapping her towel around her, she tucked it under her breasts and ignored the steady gaze Cooper directed at her. Ignored the urgent need cranking up in the pit of her belly, tightening muscles that hadn't had a workout for more than seven months. Sinking down onto the blanket, she stretched her legs out, leaned back on her elbows to look upward and tried to ignore how he was gazing at the baby bump with something like dread in his expression.

'It will all work out, Cooper.'

'You think?' Thankfully he shrugged into a shirt.

'I hope,' she said with a rueful smile, missing the view but hoping her internal heat would cool now.

'You have doubts?'

'Who doesn't at this stage?' He didn't need to know what hers were. He'd probably hightail it out of the country without a backward glance. Despite common sense and the self-preservation she usually relied on, she wanted to spend time with him.

Cooper threw her a curveball. 'What does it feel like to be carrying a baby?'

Where to start? 'Awkward. Cumbersome. Wonderful. Exciting. Frightening.' Ouch. Why tell him that? He'd have a multitude of questions, along with doubts about her ability to be a good mother.

Cooper parked his butt beside her and reached for one of her hands, wrapped it in his larger one, making her feel delicate. 'Tell me about frightening.'

Her heart lurched. She shouldn't have said that word but he had an uncanny knack of making her say things she never intended to. If only she had the strength to pull her hand free and forget the yearning his touch evoked. 'Oh, you know. Am I going to be a good mother? How will I handle the birth? All the usual things expectant mothers apparently think about.'

'Why wouldn't you be a great mum?' His thumb stroked the back of her hand.

This was the problem with knowing nothing about each other. She had to expose herself, her vulnerabilities as well as her needs and concerns. But not all of them, or with any depth. 'I didn't have great role models growing up.'

'That could be a benefit. You'll be determined to do better, not make whatever mistakes your parents made with you.' He sounded so sure of himself, so at ease with it all. And so right.

Which annoyed her. 'Easy to say if you've had the perfect upbringing.'

'Does that even happen?' he growled, and moved to put space between them, leaving her hand cold. Delving into the bag, he passed her some crisps. 'Here.'

Seemed like she'd touched a taboo subject. He'd wanted to know about her life, so he should be prepared to reciprocate with details about his. They'd come out for some time together and she didn't want to spoil it with an argument. Her annoyance backed off too easily as she munched on a handful of crisps. It wasn't often she got off base for some fun. Fun with a man she'd never quite got over, and knew would always hold a special place in her heart for giving her a child.

While devouring bulging triangles of focaccia and chicken, they talked about things that had nothing to do with the baby—army life, their medical careers, travel. For the first time since that blue line had appeared on the stick Sophie felt completely at ease and was just thinking she could do this every day for the rest of her time in Darwin when Cooper blew the evening apart.

'Sophie.' His voice was husky and thick. 'I've been thinking. Let's get married. I can support you if you want to be a full-time mum. That way I'd always be a part of our daughter's life and you wouldn't have to take all the responsibility. What do you think?'

CHAPTER FOUR

'MARRY YOU?' *BUT*... 'I can't.' *But*... Sophie spluttered water over her front. They didn't know each other. There was certainly no love between them. *But*...

Cooper looked startled. 'Can't? You're not already married?'

Sophie shoved awkwardly to her feet as hurt lanced her. 'How dare you? You think I'd have had sex with you if I was married? Even in the circumstances you believe I'd be unfaithful? Thanks a million, buster.' She was shouting and couldn't care less that people on the other side of the grove were staring. Cooper had handed her the biggest insult he could find. Then her stomach tightened, sending pains shooting in all directions. 'Ah.' She wrapped her arms around her belly and held her breath. This hurt, big time.

'You okay?' Cooper had risen to his feet too. 'Sophie, talk to me.'

Breathe. One. Two. Three. Another Braxton Hicks contraction. Fingers crossed. She wasn't ready for the real deal. Way too soon. The pain in her belly softened, backed off. But not the hurt Cooper had inflicted. She snapped her head up and glared at him. 'No, I'm *not* okay.'

'Easy.'

'That's all you ever say when things get heated. Easy.

I'm telling you I am not going easy on you. Not after that bombshell you just delivered.'

'Which one?' His hands gripped his hips. Under his T-shirt his chest was rising and falling rapidly, like he'd run a marathon. But his gaze softened as it settled on her belly.

He was seriously disrupting all her carefully laid plans. No wonder she hadn't wanted him in on the pregnancy until after the birth. 'Both.'

'Tell me why we can't…' he flicked fingers in the air '…get married. It makes a lot of sense. We're having a child and she deserves a family to grow up in.'

'She'll have one. Mummy in one house, Daddy in another.' That sounded awful, but not as awful as Mummy and Daddy screaming that they hated each other and their daughter was the only reason they lived under the same roof. 'That's the way it's going to be. No argument.' Her lungs expelled air so fast her head spun.

Go away, Cooper.

'I don't get any say in this?' Cooper's voice was deceptively calm; that chest still moving too quickly being the giveaway to his real emotions.

Shaking her head at him, she said, 'About getting married, no.'

Why did that tug at her heart? Going solo wasn't how she'd ever envisioned raising a child, but that didn't mean she'd grab the first offer that came along. Sexy hunk making the offer or not. Sex in hard boots or not. Which made it difficult not to give in to Cooper when he turned those winning smiles on her. She fell for them every time, but so far, thank goodness, she hadn't made any major mistakes since he'd turned up on her patch yesterday.

'So we agree to live in the same city at least?' He ground out the question.

'We haven't agreed to anything yet,' she snapped back.

Where had the usual calm, happy Sophie gone? 'I'm going home to Auckland. You say you might be stopping there, or you might be going back overseas with the army. Where would you want me living if you choose to do that, huh? I'm not following you around military bases.' As if.

Calm down, girl. This is not the way to solve the differences between us.

What was the right way? Seemed they got on just fine if they kept off the subject of their child, but the moment anything to do with her and her future arose they were at loggerheads. 'Cooper…' She tried for a reconciliatory tone. It wasn't easy. 'Thank you for asking me but I will not do this for our child's sake. That's no way to start a marriage. I am open to discussions on where I live and how to raise our daughter.'

How come he was suddenly talking marriage? Alistair had warned her in an offhand way about his friend's reputation of love 'em and leave 'em. Would he be faithful when there was no love between them? And, seriously, why should he be? Another reason to stick to her guns. 'Why get hitched at all?' she asked.

Uncertainty flickered through his eyes briefly and then he was in control again. 'It's the right thing to do.'

Oh, no, it's not. Believe me.

'No one gets married because they're having a baby any more.'

'Maybe they should. I'm thinking about our child here, and how it's going to affect her, living in a single-parent family.'

'It's not uncommon these days. Not by a long shot.' If only she'd lived with one parent and visited the other she might be making a better job of her own life. Following through on his comment, she said, 'You don't really want to be married. Why should you? It would cramp your style.' When his mouth tightened she continued. 'We're all but strangers to each other. The worst possible grounds for settling down together, don't you think?'

He barked a laugh. 'To think the first time I propose I'm having to justify myself.' His fingers whitened as his grip tightened. There'd an interesting line of bruises on his hips later. 'What would make you reconsider your decision?'

'Nothing.' When he stared at her as though she'd hurt him deeply she relented. 'It's not about you. I was the only reason my parents married and I've paid for it all my life.'

The hurt dulled a little. 'That's sad.'

'It was downright cruel.' She bit on her bottom lip to prevent any more unnecessary words spilling out. She also held her breath in an attempt to hold back the tears that threatened. She never cried about her childhood. Never. The back of her hand came away from her face wet. Maybe it was time she did. Oh, sure. That would solve a whole heap of problems.

'It doesn't have to be like that between us and our girl.'

A sledgehammer might work better. 'Cooper. Listen to me. You haven't thought this through. Getting married will cramp your lifestyle so much you'll soon become frustrated and angry and want out. Then who pays? Our daughter for one.'

And me for another.

Her mouth dropped open.

Why would I care? It's not as though I love him. I mightn't have been able to forget him but that's because I'm carrying his child. I do not, could not love him.

'Sophie? You okay?' The man totally wrecking her day stood in front of her, concern plastered all over his face.

Blink. 'Yes.' Blink. *No.*

Sure, he's hot and gorgeous and even fun to be around when he's not talking about our futures, but live with him as his wife? Not likely, sunshine.

'You've gone pale.' He was studying her thoroughly. When her hand automatically rubbed her stomach his eyes dropped to watch. 'You're not having another pain?'

She shook her head. 'Let's go back to base. I'm tired.'

Annoyance replaced his concern, but he didn't argue, just began packing up their picnic. 'Fine.'

Being tired was quite normal these days for Sophie. But being bemused by the thought Cooper might mean something to her was new. How could he after so little time together? It didn't make sense but, then, none of this did. Admittedly she'd feel a little less irresponsible if she could believe she had some feelings for him. Getting pregnant by a complete stranger did not sit well when she knew how much pain an unwanted pregnancy caused those involved. Justifying it by acknowledging she might've felt something for him that night would lighten the guilt. Sometimes she wondered what she was going to say when her daughter asked about her father. Hardly going to build confidence in her when her mother told her it had been a brief encounter of the sexual kind that had carried no other meaning than to satisfy an urge brought on by a bomb exploding metres from them.

But if Cooper hung around and became a part of his girl's life then no explanations would be necessary. Would they?

The silence was thick enough to cut as Cooper drove back to the base. He was stunned at his offer of marriage. Where had that come from? Getting married would be totally wrong. It went against everything he believed in. He'd never stay in a relationship for long, even one involving a marriage certificate. He was his father's son in that respect. *Unfair.* True. Dad had never left his wife, just all the women that had come afterwards. Mum had opted to leave them—by tying a noose around her neck and hanging herself from the garage rafter.

He shivered as the hated memory slapped him. Dad's hoarse shout coming from the garage. *Mandy, don't leave me.* Was that why his dad never settled for long? He'd often wondered but had never asked. Too much hurt to be raised if he did.

Yet none of that explained why the moment Sophie had turned him down he'd hurt bad. Really bad. No one had ever turned him down for anything quite so abruptly, and his proposal had been serious, a handing over of part of himself. Her reply had been a hot lance spearing him. He hadn't planned on asking her, hadn't given it much thought except to toss the idea aside as ludicrous. Still, the words had spilled out. Gratitude should be his response to Sophie's answer. It wasn't. 'Now what?'

'We swap contact details.'

He hadn't realised he'd spoken out loud. 'You know we're on the same military flight out of here on Monday?'

'I thought you were going tomorrow.' Was that dread in her voice?

Please, no. He didn't want her keeping him at a distance. 'List changed my arrangements.'

'You're telling me you didn't have any say in the matter? You're in different armies.'

'He can be bossy at times.' Now was not the time to tell Sophie that List was concerned about her, and it especially was not the moment to be saying he agreed. That Braxton Hicks contraction had been sharp and hard, had turned her face white and her eyes wary. He wanted to be with her on the flight in case she had more or, worse, went into early labour. He did not want other men on that plane delivering their baby.

Sophie huffed something like a strangled laugh. 'You're not telling me anything new.' Then she gasped. 'He's not done that so I've got a doctor on hand? He's been nagging at me to stay here until after the birth.'

Bang on, Sophie girl. 'You got it.' But not all of it. He'd already figured that List was interfering, pushing them together as much as possible.

'Fingers crossed I won't be needing you. I'm sorry if Alistair has put you out.'

He wasn't exactly up to speed on delivering babies so couldn't argue with Sophie on that one. 'I prefer the arrangements anyway. No stopping in Sydney on that flight, just straight through to Whenuapai. Home sweet home.' Five days late meant less time getting his house sorted before taking up the temporary position at Auckland Hospital he'd signed up for while sorting out what he was really going to do.

'Have you got your own place?' she asked wistfully.

'A house in Parnell. My dad house-sat for me this trip.' And supposedly met the next great love of his life while there. Cooper's teeth slid back and forth, grinding hard. When was Dad going to learn that none of the women he thought he'd fallen in love with were right for him?

'I've got to make appointments to look at apartments to rent as soon as I get home.' She nibbled at a fingernail. 'I've never cared too much about where I lived before.'

But apparently now she did. That spoke volumes about her determination to do things right for her baby. 'Where will you go until you find somewhere suitable?' He reached across and gently tugged her hand away from her mouth. 'Don't do that. You'll regret it in the morning.' Her nails were always immaculate, resplendent in shockingly bright shades that she'd changed twice in the time he'd been here. He preferred the red to yesterday's orange.

Sophie turned her head to stare out at the passing scenery. 'I could go to my parents'.'

Her lack of enthusiasm for that idea dripped off each

word. Who could blame her? After her brief revelation about her childhood he certainly couldn't. 'They'll welcome you?'

'I guess.' Then she straightened up in her seat and turned to face him. 'Of course they will. It'd only be a temporary arrangement.'

An idea was slowly creeping into his mind. An idea that needed thinking through, required looking at from all angles before he spilled it out to Sophie. He wasn't going to blurt it out like he'd done with that marriage suggestion. Once was stupid, twice was really dumb.

But… 'You could stay with me. My house is big enough that we wouldn't be tripping over each other,' he blurted.

Damn it, Sophie. What have you done to me? I go and say the craziest things without any consideration to the consequences when I'm around you. I've never acted so impulsively in my life. Not since I was eight and told Dad's live-in girlfriend number two that I loved her and that I wanted her to stay with us for ever. That she could be my mother if she wanted.

Again silence reigned. Sophie hadn't answered and seemed to be intent on the passing scenery, dry and boring as it was. Might be for the best. Like his marriage offer—if she didn't say yes to moving in with him then he didn't have to worry about anything. Didn't have to consider that they'd be sharing his space, which wouldn't be straightforward given his reaction to her whenever they were together. She was easily the most tantalising woman he'd known. Even now his blood heated and they weren't exactly cosy with each other. His groin had been aching since arriving yesterday, and that had started before he'd set eyes on her. Anticipation had a lot to answer for. Yeah, he still wanted her, needed to make love with her again. Maybe then he'd get past this annoying niggle.

Because that's what she was to him. A persistent itch. To think he'd invited her to stay with him.

Sophie's carrying my baby.

Which gave him responsibilities, if nothing else. He'd stepped up and offered some solutions for the future, and she wasn't barrelling him over with her acceptances. Still, he had to help her in every way possible, whether she liked it or not. There were a lot of things he could do to make life easier for her as she settled into becoming a mother. Whether he liked it or not.

He'd spent his adult life playing the field with women, but he'd never been a brute or deliberately hurtful, and now he would not walk away from Sophie. Her point about a loveless marriage was valid, and in some ways he was thankful for her turning him down. It was all for the best. He wasn't the kind of guy who'd be able to live like a monk for the rest of his life, and if Sophie kept him at arm's length it could get tricky. It was doubtful that Sophie would want to stay clear of men either, but he doubted he'd be her first pick. She'd been hot for him that night in Bamiyan, had pretty much thrown herself at him. No denying he'd been ready and waiting to catch her, though. But here in Darwin she'd been a lot more circumspect around him.

Cooper pulled up outside the barracks and hauled on the handbrake. 'You've gone awfully quiet. You okay?'

'You keep knocking me sideways. First marriage, now the offer of staying with you. I never expected any of that. Thank you. Please don't think I'm ungrateful. I just happen to be a pig-headed woman who puts her independence before anything else. Except my baby, something I'm only just realising.' She finally smiled at him.

The warmth went straight to his heart, and any problems he might've thought up about sharing his home with her dissolved. 'I wouldn't take that away from you. I start at the hospital in a few days and won't be around the house very much anyway.'

Sophie shook her head at him. 'I intend finding my own place. Your home would always be yours. I wouldn't be able to change things or spread out all over the show as I'm exceptionally good at doing.' There was that smile again. 'Definitely not a tidy creature, me.'

'Don't write my suggestion off so quickly. You've got a few days before we fly out of here. Think about it.' Next he'd be begging. Did he want her living with him so badly? No. But the idea of her in a poky flat in some rank suburb was equally unbearable. She'd be comfortable in his place. He'd be able to get to know her and most likely get over the things about her that were bugging him. Living under the same roof wouldn't only show the good aspects of her character but the not-so-good ones, the things he'd struggle to put up with day in, day out. Likewise for Sophie about him.

'Cooper, you're warring with yourself, so how can I take what you say as the right thing to do? You may be trying to persuade me your way is right but you're not sure about it. It's there in your eyes every time you try to convince me you've got the perfect solution.'

Already she could read him. He found her a smile. 'Can you see that I don't give up easily when it's important to me?'

'Saw that seven months ago, pal.' She was laughing at him.

Cooper reached to draw her into his arms and held her against his chest where she fitted perfectly. His breath hitched at the back of his throat and for a moment he couldn't utter a word, so he just enjoyed the moment. What would she do if he kissed her? It would be a risk to find out. He didn't want her rejecting him completely. Not when they were having a baby.

Finally he managed, 'Crazy woman. I'm starting to really like you.' Liking her was okay. Anything stronger wouldn't work, but as that was as implausible as flying to Saturn he was safe.

'Now, there's a novel idea,' she quipped as she snuggled closer.

He swallowed hard and lowered his chin to the top of her head, breathed deep to absorb the scent of sunscreen and flowers, and relaxed against her. Felt her breasts rising and falling softly, not hard points pressing against him like last time he'd held her. Her short breaths against his shirt, her hands on his chest, everything about her made him feel complete. She took away some of the doubts that had been niggling him since he'd first seen that baby bump. Whatever the difficulties ahead, they'd manage, would sort out how to go about raising a child between them in less-than-perfect circumstances. He wasn't worried on that score. He also wasn't giving up trying to convince her to move into his house. Not yet. Though he should be. Because becoming a father still didn't sit easily with him. And having a woman on his patch permanently had him in a hot sweat of the worst kind. Yet—this was Sophie. The one woman he'd never forgotten; remembered her body as hot satin in his hands that night that had led to this situation.

Sophie pulled back, smoothed her already smooth shirt over her breasts. Then she locked her eyes on him and drew in a deep breath. 'I've got something to show you. Can you wait here?' It must be important, going by the way she held herself.

'Of course.' Glad of the distraction, he switched the ignition off and got out to open her door. Leaning back against the car, he watched her walk slowly into the building. Exhaustion tugged her shoulders downward and made her head droop. What was so important that she had to show him tonight? His mind came up blank, so he stopped trying to work it out and waited for her to return.

Then she was back, handing him a large envelope. 'This is yours to keep. If you want,' she added with uncertainty.

Which only intrigued him more. 'What is it?'

'Take a look. I kept a copy for you.'

He opened the tab and shook the contents out into his hand. One sheet of heavy paper. A photo. No, a scan. His mouth dried. His heart went into overdrive, sending his blood thudding around his body. His hand shook as he held the picture out to study. 'Our baby?' he croaked.

Sophie stepped closer. 'Yes. Look, there are her legs, and one arm. Isn't that amazing?'

He was incapable of speech. His chin jerked downward once, abruptly. Wow. His daughter. Amazing didn't begin to describe the overwhelming love for this tiny being flattening him. It filled his heart. It would be easier to chop his arm off than to walk away now. He was a goner. Over a baby. A baby he hadn't met yet. Who'd have thought?

'Gorgeous, huh?' An arm slid around his waist. Sophie. She must feel exactly as he did. Smitten.

He blinked as tears threatened to spill down his face. 'Yeah. Gorgeous.' And still downright terrifying. And so not what he'd wanted for his life, but he would not, could not give up now.

'Stop fighting it.' Sophie grinned up at him before stretching to place a soft kiss on his mouth. 'Goodnight, Cooper. Sleep well.' Then she walked inside, closing the door behind her.

He wasn't going to sleep. Not tonight. Staring at the scan, he shook his head at the enormity of what had befallen him. Yesterday he'd thought it'd take a long time to accept his upcoming fatherhood. He'd never factored in the love, the instant need to protect, the expectations of watching her grow up that were gripping him. He hadn't had a clue. Not one.

Sliding into the car, Cooper drove slowly across to the accommodation block he was staying in, barely taking his eyes off that photo long enough to see where he was going.

Sleep well, Sophie had said. Not likely. He was going to put the scan back in the envelope and store it safely in his bag, then he'd go for a run. Pound the road and try to settle the beating in his chest and find some reason for all the turmoil going on in his head.

CHAPTER FIVE

AFTER TAKING FOR ever to go to sleep, Sophie was woken by banging on her door and someone calling out. 'Captain, wake up. You're needed in the medical hut.'

Two-twenty in the morning. Must be urgent. 'Coming.' Rolling out of bed, she grimaced. Her back ached. Her head was full of cotton wool. And the baby was dancing nonstop. As for the thoughts about her baby's father that had followed her right into sleep, she was about ready to forget she'd ever met him if it meant some peace. The pillow beneath her hand was wet. Her cheeks below her eyes were puffy. She'd been crying? In her sleep? Never.

Shrugging into a shirt and pulling up her fatigue trousers, she opened the door. 'Hey, Simone, what's the problem?'

'Some of the guys have been in a brawl with civilians,' Simone told her. 'Down at McGregor's Bar.'

'So we've got drunks to contend with.' Great. 'Where did I put my boots?' She looked all around her room, came up empty-handed.

'Want me to look?' Simone grinned.

'Go ahead. Oh, no, there they are.' Feeling unsteady, she held onto the bed end as she leaned down to pull the offending boots out from under a chair.

Simone was at her elbow immediately. 'Are you all right?'

'Must've leapt out of bed too fast.'

'Captain Daniels is already at the unit, trying to quieten some of the noisier of the idiots.' The nurse was not known for her patience with soldiers who'd overindulged and got themselves into trouble.

'Who asked Coop—Captain Daniels to lend a hand?' That grin widened. 'Your friend Cooper?'

'That one.' Of course everyone on base would know she and Cooper had spent a few hours together.

'Seems he was out running when he came across the guys fighting with two locals outside the pub. Pulverising them was his summation. Something about the soldiers defending a young woman.'

Why was Cooper running in the middle of the night? Sophie shut her door and led the way outside. 'The police involved?'

'Our MPs and the state troopers. The troopers have taken the civilians to their hospital. We've got our morons to deal to.'

'Maybe not morons if they were looking out for a woman.' Any male who could go past a woman, or any one, in trouble wasn't worthy of being called a man. Unlike Cooper. Even now she could feel his body covering hers in that dirt as the air had exploded around them.

'Huh,' grunted Simone.

'Nothing too serious reported in the way of injuries, though we have a minor knife wound and a couple of black eyes,' Cooper informed Sophie the moment she stepped inside the medical unit and noted the four men waiting to be checked over. 'Noisy but not drunk,' he added.

Two MPs were trying to hold one of the men upright but he seemed determined not to use his legs for some reason.

'Wonderful,' she muttered.

I got up for this?

'I told Simone not to bother you but she wouldn't listen.' Cooper was peeved about something. Being ignored by her nurse probably. Well, Simone was never going to look at him twice. He was a male.

The noise level was rising. Standing to attention, she yelled in her best parade-ground voice, 'Soldiers, quiet.'

The room instantly became silent. Sheepish men in various states of disarray froze on the spot.

'Stand up straight. Including you.' She nodded at the man the MPs were holding. She didn't lower the decibels. Only one way to treat the soldiers when they were in this state, and that was to remind them who and what they were. Pointing to a table, she snapped, 'Form a line over there.'

'Want me to take the stab wound?' Cooper asked into the quiet.

Sophie nodded. 'All yours. Simone, who's next?'

Simone led a man across and pushed him onto a chair. 'Sergeant Dexter took a direct hit in the eye and another on the back of the head, Captain.'

Sergeants were supposed to prevent their men getting into trouble, not be in the thick of it. Unless he'd been trying to stop the fight. 'What happened, Sergeant?'

'Looking out for my men, Captain.' His mouth was a flat line.

'I meant your injuries.'

'Took a fist in the face, twice. Hit the back of my head on the kerb when I went down, ma'am.'

Sophie tilted the man's head forward and examined the wound at the back. The bleeding had stopped. 'I'm going to put some stitches in here.'

'Thank you, ma'am.'

'How's your vision? Any blurriness?'

He shook his head and winced. 'No, ma'am.'

This was not the time to be brave, but Sophie knew better than to say so. He had a reputation to uphold in front of his men. She held out a penlight torch. 'Hold this for me.'

His reaction was swift and firm.

'Good. Headache?'

'No.' Again he winced.

'Care to rethink your answer?' She stared at him for a long moment but got nothing back. His head would be thumping. Male pride could be plain stupid. 'Sergeant, you've taken a hard hit on your skull, which could've shaken your brain, resulting in a concussion.'

'I understand.'

She'd give him a concussion herself if he didn't start answering her questions honestly. Retrieving the torch, she shone it into the corner of his good eye. The man blinked rapidly. 'Sure there's no fogginess in your sight? Or your head?'

'I can see you clearly.'

Guess that was something. 'What about the other side of the room? Can you read the top line on the noticeboard?'

One side of his mouth lifted in a wry smile. 'Staff rosters for August.'

She gave up. Being stubborn was something she understood all too well. 'I want you to come and see me the moment you feel any nausea, have blurred vision or a strong headache. Understand?' When he nodded, she continued. 'About this other eye...'

It was swollen shut. Not a lot she could do until the swelling went down. After cleaning his grazed cheek and forehead with disinfectant in case he got an infection, she picked up a needle and syringe. 'I'm giving you a local anaesthetic so I can suture the back of your head. Ready?'

The sergeant turned whiter. 'Yes.'

Within minutes she'd finished and was tugging her gloves off to toss in the bin. Then she unlocked the drugs cabinet and put a few antibiotic tablets in a bottle. 'Here you go. One every twelve hours until they're finished. And some analgesics.'

Reluctantly he took them, and quickly shoved them in his pocket. 'Thank you, ma'am.' And he was gone.

Shaking her head, she called, 'Who's next?'

'Bruised ribs and a punch to the gut,' Simone informed her as she nodded to a lance corporal to approach.

'I'll check those ribs,' Sophie said. He might need an X-ray. Pressing carefully over the reddened, swollen area, she judged the lad's reactions and with what she could feel decided he'd been lucky. 'Take it easy for the next couple days.'

Cooper was finishing up suturing a corporal's knife wound, and glanced up as Sophie approached. 'This man won't be holding a rifle for a few days. The knife went nearly through to the other side at one place.'

A commotion at the unit's door had Sophie whipping around to see what was going on. The room spun. Grabbing at the nearby table, she held on until her head returned to normal.

'Sophie? Captain Ingram?' Cooper was before her, reaching for her arms.

She stepped back on shaky legs. 'I'm fine, Captain.' There was no air in the room. Her feet were leaden. 'I'm fine,' she repeated more forcefully.

'I'll see what the racket is about.' His lips were tight and his eyes were shooting daggers in her direction.

Just then an MP and a soldier pushed inside, the sergeant she'd released held between them, his head lolling forward.

'Put him on the bed,' she ordered as she focused on

work and not the pounding behind her eyes. 'What happened?'

Someone told her, 'He was halfway back to his quarters when he dropped. Out cold, he is.'

Cooper lifted the man's legs and helped manoeuvre him onto the bed. 'This the guy who hit his head on the kerb?' he asked her.

Nodding, she picked up the sergeant's arm to check his pulse. 'Concussion for sure. He was denying any symptoms, and I couldn't nail any, apart from his obvious headache. I want him sent into the city hospital for a scan. Simone?'

'Onto it,' was the reply.

Silly man. Why did he let pride get in the way of receiving the correct treatment? Even if she hadn't foreseen him losing consciousness she'd have been better prepared to treat his symptoms.

Cooper nudged her shoulder lightly with his. 'You did your best.'

'Pulse is low.' She raised the eyelid on the man's good eye. No one home.

'Respiration rate is low,' Cooper commented.

It felt good having him working beside her. 'He's coming round. Sergeant, can you hear me?'

The sergeant's eyes opened briefly.

Thank goodness. It was a start in the right direction. 'You blacked out. We're going to send you for a scan.' She spoke slowly and clearly.

He opened his eyes for a little longer.

'That knock on your head is more serious than I first thought.' Not that she'd had much to go on. 'Has your headache got worse?'

He nodded once, then put his hand up to his mouth.

'Bucket,' Cooper called loudly.

Simone returned to say the ambulance was backing up to the door.

Since Cooper was dealing with her patient Sophie filled out a form for the hospital ED. 'Simone, I want you accompanying him after we've finished checking him over.'

'No problem.'

Fifteen minutes later the unit was quiet, empty of everyone except Sophie and Cooper, who was putting the kettle on to boil.

'Want a cup of tea? Or hot milk?' he asked.

Sinking onto a stool, she felt shattered. So not up to speed. The heat and her pregnancy were taking their toll. 'I made a mistake not insisting he tell me his symptoms.'

'I heard some of your conversation. He was never going to admit things in front of his men.' Cooper dropped teabags into two mugs. 'Tea it is.'

'I should've known to take him into another room.'

'He should've known to talk to you. Are you on parade at zero seven hundred?'

The thought made her feel even more tired. 'Yes.' Four more days to go. 'Never thought I'd say this but I'm looking forward to stopping work, and I haven't even been busy in here.' She glanced at the stack of notes from their earlier patients. 'Most of the time, at any rate.'

'You could ask to be stood down.'

She raised one eye brow at him in reply.

'I figured,' was Cooper's only comment.

While she drank her tea she cruised the internet for places to rent in Auckland.

'Can't that wait?' Cooper asked with his usual bluntness.

'The sooner I set up appointments the sooner I'll find somewhere and can get my mess sorted.'

'There is an alternative, Sophie. You can bunk down at

my place for a few days if you're still determined to find your own place.' He was frustrated with her. It showed in his tone and the tightness of the hand holding his mug.

It was more than she needed right now. Shutting down the laptop, she took her tea and headed for the door. 'See you after parade.'

'Attention,' shouted the sergeant leading the parade.

Boots slapped the tarmac as rows of soldiers stood straighter than straight.

Cooper was to the side of the ground, standing at attention but not part of any unit. Sophie was at the front of the medical corps, eyes to the front. She hadn't said a word to him over a hurried breakfast in the canteen. Exhaustion had rippled off her like heat waves in the desert. Her fatigues needed straightening and her hair could do with being tied tighter but far be it for him to point that out. Someone on the parade ground would do it and cop her wrath for their effort.

List stood at the front, ready to talk to the troops. He glanced Cooper's way, and then at Sophie. A frown appeared on his brow, and he dipped his head at Sophie.

What? Cooper's gaze returned to her. She seemed to be struggling to stay upright, swaying on her feet. Her chin was pushed forward as though she was willing herself to stand erect. As he made to step out and head to her she slumped in a heap.

Cooper ran. 'Sophie.' Instantly dropping to his knees, he reached for her, felt for a pulse. It was slow but at least it was there.

Simone had been standing two away and was as quick to reach her as he'd been. 'Sophie, what's happening? Did you faint?'

'Let's get you inside out of this heat. I need to check your BP.' Low blood pressure would explain what had happened. Might explain a few incidents where she'd appeared to lose focus briefly. Like when she'd lost her balance outside Harry's on the day he'd arrived. It made Cooper think he was on the right track.

Sophie flopped against him, blinking and trying to rub her head. 'What happened?'

Cooper held her gently and looked up to growl at the man next in line. 'Get a stretcher. Now.'

'Yes, sir.'

'Sophie, can you hear me?'

'Yes. I'm fine.'

'You're not fine. When did you last have your BP checked?'

Simone answered for her. 'I did it two weeks ago. It was normal.'

'Two weeks and you haven't had a reading since?' No wonder he needed to keep an eye on her. She wasn't doing a good job of looking after herself. 'What about blood sugar?'

'Shouldn't we talk about this inside?' Simone glared at him before tilting her head towards nearby troops. 'Sir.'

List appeared, saving him having to answer. Simone was right. 'Captain Ingram? Are you all right?'

She nodded. 'I'm fine. Please continue with the parade. With your permission, Sir, I'll go to the medical unit.'

'Permission granted,' List snapped. Then he leaned down and said quietly, 'Take the morning off, Sophie. You've got to look after yourself.'

Whatever she'd been about to say was forgotten, instead her eyes widening as the soldier arrived with a stretcher. 'That had better not be for me. I'll walk, thank you very much.' Instantly she struggled to stand up.

Cooper put a restraining hand on her arm. 'No, you don't. You've just taken a tumble, and before you say a word, think about the baby.'

The look she sent him should've frozen him to the spot for eternity. At least she sank back down to the ground and muttered, 'All right.'

Cooper sighed. She had landed on her knees and tipped forward but had gone sideways just before her baby tummy could hit the ground. Still, he wanted to check her over, make sure Sophie and the baby were fine. And find the cause of these light-headed incidents she was having. This definitely wasn't the first, and he doubted it'd be the last until they knew more.

Above them List pressed his lips together, no doubt smothering a smile at Sophie's reluctant concession to Cooper's order. 'Right, soldiers.' He nodded to Simone and the soldier who'd brought the stretcher. 'Take Captain Ingram inside.'

Cooper felt for the two as they reached down to lift the stretcher once Sophie had slid across onto it. She had plenty more of those icy glares and wasn't worried about sharing them around.

List leaned close to murmur, 'Go with her. Make sure she's all right.' Then he marched back to the front of the parade.

Cooper muttered, 'Try and stop me, mate,' and strode after the stretcher bearers. Now the fun would really start.

Except Sophie surprised him. 'I'm feeling stupid. There've been a few times when I've experienced light-headedness but I put it down to the heat and lack of sleep. What sort of doctor does that make me? It's not a good start to motherhood, is it?' Her eyes lifted to him, imploring him to go easy on her.

She didn't have to ask. He wasn't about to rip into her, only wanted to make sure she and baby were safe. The sadness and worry blinking out of those green eyes hit him hard. She wasn't as confident as she made out. Yet she insisted on going it alone. Not on his watch she wasn't. Not now, not ever. They were in this together. Even if not living under the same roof, he'd make absolutely certain he was always there for her. 'I heard doctors usually made the worst mothers, always thinking of all the horrific things that can go wrong. It's cool that you're not like that.'

Suspicion clouded her eyes. 'You don't think I'm too casual?'

'No, Sophie, I don't. You look fit and healthy. I haven't seen you do anything you shouldn't, like go jogging in the heat or drink alcohol. Our baby is in perfect hands.'

She gasped.

So did Simone.

Cooper slapped a hand on his forehead. 'Sorry.' He'd forgotten they weren't alone. 'I shouldn't have said that.'

Simone was smiling as she looked at Sophie. 'Don't worry. I know nothing.' Then she leaned over to give Sophie a hug. 'Knew you were more than friends.'

Sophie looked surprised. 'Actually, we're not. Not really.'

Time he was out of there. Partaking in a discussion with the hard-nosed sergeant about their relationship was not happening. 'I'll get the sphygmomanometer and phlebotomy kit.' And some air that wasn't laced with Sophie scent and filled with words he wanted to refute. They weren't friends, not in the true sense of the word, yet he wanted to be. More than anything. He wanted to be able to spend time with Sophie and say anything he liked, help her without wondering how she'd interpret his actions. At the moment they were leery of each other, and he was past putting up with that.

Neither woman tried to stop him going, but when he returned with the equipment needed to take a BP reading and some bloods to send to the lab Sophie was on her own, looking glum.

'Hey, you're doing fine.' Cooper ran a hand over her shoulder.

Tears glittered out of the eyes she raised to him. 'You think? I'm feeling so hopeless.'

Pressure built in his chest, and the need to be there for her expanded further. This wasn't just about his responsibility towards her and the baby. This was about that friendship they didn't have yet. 'There's not a hopeless bone in your body.'

'I'd say thanks but, really, you don't know me at all.'

'I know you're stubborn, kind, fun, sexy…' Now, why had he added that? Friends and sex were a mismatch. Except sex had led to them being tied together with a child. Now the friendship had to start. Which meant sex was off the list. 'Did I mention annoying and adorable?'

Now she looked disappointed. 'It's been said before: you're a charmer.'

He'd meant every word and hadn't been trying to get his own way about anything. He'd been wanting to make her relax and stop fretting about how she was coping. That wasn't good for her or the infant. 'Let's find out what's going on.' He held up the BP cuff.

Holding out her arm, she told him, 'You can't do a glucose test. I ate breakfast.'

'We'll start with a non-fasting and if that's even slightly raised we'll follow up with a fasting blood tomorrow.' No more stalling.

Sophie sagged, her chin hitting her sternum. 'Get on with it.' There was no strength in her words, just defeat.

That unsettled him further. He preferred the fighting, stubborn Sophie to this one. Watching the monitor until it beeped, he felt out of his depth. Sure, reading BPs and taking bloods was basic medicine, but cheering up his patient when he was so involved was more complicated than he'd expected. And he was about to add to her gloom. 'BP's too low.'

'I figured.' She shook her head. 'Gestational diabetes is looking more likely by the minute.'

'They don't necessarily go hand in hand,' he argued.

'I know.' She held her arm out again and watched quietly while he drew some blood.

Three hours later Cooper found Sophie munching on a healthy salad and reading files in her office. 'Your glucose is a little too high.'

'So tomorrow I'd do a glucose tolerance test. Can we start early? I get hungry all the time.'

'I'll take the fasting sample twelve hours after your dinner tonight.' And fingers crossed the final results would be normal.

They weren't. 'I've got gestational diabetes.' Sophie put the phone down the following afternoon and stared at Cooper.

'I was hoping otherwise.' But he wasn't surprised at the result.

'You and me both. Guess I'm off the ice cream.'

'They can relax in the canteen. There'll be enough left to go round everyone from now on.'

Her smile was tired. 'Home is looking better and better all the time.'

Home meant a lot to do, if what he'd gleaned from their conversations was true. 'You made those appointments for viewing properties yet?'

'I've got four lined up the day after we touch down.'

Of course she had. Tired she may be, inefficient she wasn't. 'Anything that really excites you?' Would it be wrong to hope not? He might've got off the hook when she'd turned down his offer to live with him for a while, but more and more the need to be there with her for these weeks leading up to the birth was dominating his thoughts. She needed pampering. He was going to pamper Sophie? Yep, and why not?

'Yes, all of them,' she replied in the flattest voice he'd heard in a long time.

'Better than nothing you like.'

She didn't answer.

CHAPTER SIX

THE TEMPERATURES FINALLY *EASED*, for which Sophie was grateful. The heat had been all-consuming. By the time she boarded the air force plane bound for home she was almost sorry to be leaving.

'Thanks for everything you've done for me,' she told Alistair as she stepped up to kiss his cheek. 'You've been a pal.'

He wrapped her in a bear hug. 'Keep me posted on junior, and take care of yourself. I want a photo as soon as she arrives.'

'You'll get one.'

She was surprised to see his eyes glistening before he turned away to Cooper and said, 'Hey, man.'

Sophie watched them do the man hug and thump on the back thing, and almost laughed out loud. Guys. These two were close. She'd been a part of their camaraderie over the past few days, going with them to the pub for dinner twice. Theirs was an easy friendship grown out of hard times during active duty. She'd have liked that with someone. The closest friend she'd made in the army was Kelly, and she'd missed her every day since she'd been evacuated from Bamiyan.

'Come on, let's get on board the tin can.' Cooper took her elbow.

Sophie promptly pulled free. 'I'm not an invalid,' she said, but there was no annoyance in her words. She seemed to have run out of steam since her collapse on parade. Learning about the diabetes had knocked her sideways too, and made her ultra-careful about everything she ate.

'But you are proud.' Cooper grinned. 'Don't want anyone to see you being helped up that ramp, do you?'

She glanced across the shimmering tarmac to the plane. 'It's not Everest.' Not quite. When she got home she was not going to go for power walks ever again. Neither would she do press-ups or sit-ups or take up running once her baby was born. She was so over exercise. Though she did quite like her sculpted figure—if it was still there.

The aircraft interior was stifling. Sweat prickled her back instantly. 'Can you leave the ramp open on the flight?' she asked the young girl overseeing the last crates being loaded.

'No, Captain. That would be dangerous.'

'Fair enough.' She laughed and turned away from the serious face staring at her as though she was crazy.

Cooper led the way to two empty bucket seats. 'These'll do. I'll stow our rucksacks.'

Kick. Laying her hand on the spot, she rubbed. *Kick. We're going home, sweetheart.*

Home. A foreign word in her vocabulary. Home was apparently where the heart was. So whatever flat or apartment she rented, her heart would be there for her baby. She hadn't experienced making a home for herself, had usually rented a room in a house filled with colleagues and got on with working until the next trip. As for furniture and kitchen utensils, there was a lot of shopping coming up.

It wasn't easy lowering her butt all the way down to the seat almost on the floor.

'Hey.' Cooper was there, holding her elbow to prevent her from sprawling on her face.

'Thanks.' *Kick, kick.* 'I think little miss is aware we're off on an adventure. She's not letting me forget her.' As long as she didn't decide to make her grand entrance in mid-air. Shoving aside that fear, she asked herself if that would make her daughter an Australian or a Kiwi.

'What's causing that confused look on your face?' Cooper asked.

'When did you last deliver a baby?' Why had she asked? It wasn't what she'd been thinking at all, and she didn't really want to know the answer if Cooper hadn't delivered for a long time.

'A while ago.' He still sounded confident, but he'd been a surgeon for four years and surgeons always sounded confident.

'Define a while.'

'Sophie, are you having pains? We can get off now, but you'll have to be quick. We're due to take off in five.' He started to get out of his seat.

'Easy,' she gave back to him. 'Just passing the time with inane conversation.' But all her fingers were crossed. Having a baby on the plane, surrounded with air force personnel, was not her idea of fun. Probably wasn't Cooper's either, she realised as she shifted her butt to get comfortable.

Behave, little one.

Cooper held his breath all the way across Australia and the Tasman Sea, not letting it out until the west coast of New Zealand came into sight. Even if the ridiculous happened and Sophie started labour now they'd be on the ground within a very short time and there'd an ambulance and midwives and a hospital in case their baby needed special attention.

But even as those thoughts zipped through his head he couldn't help wondering what it would be like to be there when his daughter was delivered. He crossed his fingers he wasn't tempting fate. Sophie would hate to have her baby thirty thousand feet up in the air surrounded with people she'd never met before. She'd also intimated she wasn't having him anywhere close during the birth. Somehow he had to persuade her to change her mind.

Shock jerked him. Being at the birth would be very intimate. She'd told him a friend was planning on being there for her. That irked. He should be there. He'd got her pregnant, hadn't denied his role, so surely he could see it through to the end? The more Cooper thought about it the more he knew he had to be at the birth. Would it make her more comfortable with his presence if he promised to stay at the top end of the bed? He'd hold her hands and give her water, wipe her brow. Yeah, right. He'd never make a good nurse. But this was Sophie. A woman he was beginning to treasure: to care for as a special friend.

Friends didn't have the kind of hot sex he'd been imagining with Sophie every night in his room at Darwin.

'You'd finally relaxed, and now you're all tense again. What's up? Are we nearly home?' Sophie mumbled against his chest, where she'd been sleeping for the last couple of hours.

'There's land beneath us.' His arm had gone numb ages ago, but he hadn't moved in case he woke her. Those grey smudges under her eyes had been a dead giveaway. She was exhausted. Which meant she was in no shape to take a taxi home to her parents' and deal with explaining her situation. As far as he knew, they weren't expecting her, which could add to her problems, given there wasn't a strong bond between them all. Neither did they know they were about to become grandparents.

Nor did his father. Cooper was saving that for when

they got together over a beer and played catch up. The old man would be okay with it. Might even be ecstatic. Then again he might roar with laughter and ask what Cooper had been thinking to get a woman pregnant. The straight answer was there hadn't been any thinking going on at the time.

Sophie sat up and stretched her legs in front of her. 'You heading for your house as soon as you're through quarantine?'

'That's the plan. What about you?'

'I'm staying on the base for the night.'

No way. What if she went into labour? She'd be alone, no friends, no midwife that she'd got to know. 'Why?'

'Easier. I'll head into the city for those appointments tomorrow and decide what I'm doing after that. Probably visit Mum and Dad, suss out their reaction.'

Cooper was shaking his head at her. 'You're coming home with me.'

'No, I'm not.' But there was no substance to her words, and hope had briefly flicked through her eyes.

'No argument. It's a done deal. One night, if that's all you want. Then you can sort things out and decide what you're doing. But today, after this long, uncomfortable flight, you need a hot shower and a decent meal and then a good night's uninterrupted sleep. Something that's not guaranteed on base.' Now he was sounding condescending. But he cared, all right? Someone needed to be looking out for Sophie, and at the moment he was the only person on hand.

'Put it like that and I'm finding it hard to turn you down. One night only, right? That's the deal. I'll be out of your hair tomorrow.'

'If that's what you want.' It was for the best. They couldn't live under the same roof permanently. How could he bring a woman home knowing Sophie slept down the hall? If he wanted to, that was. Huh? Since when didn't he bring females home?

You haven't even looked at another woman since landing in Darwin and seeking out Sophie.

Get real. Sex had been non-existent since Sophie. Not even a casual hook-up. Opportunities had been endless. It had been his own interest that had been lacking. Captain Ingram had spoiled him for other women.

But that didn't mean he was making Sophie the centre of his attention. She might be gorgeous and fun, and pregnant with his child, but she wasn't the love of his life. Would never be. No one would. He enjoyed, preferred, being single and he wasn't prepared to give that up. Not even for Sophie and his child? Especially for them. They had the power to hold him down. Every decision he made would be tempered with what was best for them. While that wasn't so bad, his unreliability as a father and partner was.

He had a lot to be grateful to Sophie for. Turning him down had shocked him but she was right. They wouldn't be able to sustain an enjoyable relationship, platonic or otherwise, under the same roof for ever. It would certainly be unfair on their daughter.

His mother had opted to desert him by taking her own life, and while that was different it had set him to becoming independent, and he'd started closing his heart to loving with abandon. He and Dad had been lost without his mother, and he wasn't prepared to go through that again with anyone else, or inflict a similar loss on someone.

So thank you, Sophie, for being strong and turning me down.

The woman putting him through the wringer these days flicked him a tired smile. 'You sure there'll be hot water? Your dad won't have forgotten to leave it on?'

'If he has we'll pay him a visit.' Cooper dropped an

arm over her shoulders and tucked her close. 'Everything will be just fine. You'll see.'

'I'm looking forward to it.'

He wasn't sure what she was looking forward to, but he was happy to be taking her to his place for the night. It felt kind of right. She belonged in his life now, she and the baby. Just how much had yet to be debated. But he didn't want them there as the complete family he'd never had.

Or did he? Cooper shivered. It wouldn't work, went against everything he'd believed about himself.

Sophie stretched and rubbed her aching back as she waited for the kettle to boil in Cooper's kitchen. Yesterday's flight, sitting in that seat that had done nothing to hold her properly, had taken its toll. As for sleeping through the night in cooler temperatures? Forget it. She'd tossed and turned for hours, sleeping fitfully when her eyes had finally closed.

Kick.

'Hey, little one. You didn't get much sleep either, did you?' She rubbed her belly. At least they were home. Her daughter would be born a Kiwi.

'I like it when you do that.'

She turned to find Cooper leaning against the door jamb, his hair a ruffled mess and stubble darkening his jaw. Now her stomach tightened for reasons other than her baby pushing on it. She still hadn't been able to get past the fact she found Cooper sexy and desirable. If only she wasn't so enormous she might contemplate leaping on him and having wild sex again.

Whoa. What was she thinking? Gripping the bench, she held on and waited for that dumb idea to disappear.

'You all right?' Cooper was right there, his hand on her upper arm, his eyes full of concern.

No, not at all. What would he think if he knew what

had been going through her mind? Not once over the past few days had she seen desire or lust for her in his face. Which told her exactly what she needed to know, and must hold onto—he wasn't interested in her except as the concerned father of the baby she was carrying. 'Couldn't be better,' she lied, pulling away.

Cooper's pewter eyes locked on her. 'Really?' When she said nothing, he added, 'I don't think so.'

'I'm not going into labour if that's what you're thinking.'

'I wasn't. There was something in your eyes that makes me wonder what's going on in that sharp mind of yours.'

Wonder all you like.

But her cheeks were heating, giving her away. 'I'll have a shower.'

'What time's your first viewing appointment?' Cooper was still watching her closely.

All her skin was hot, not only on her face. There was an ache deep down, sending her blood racing and her heart thudding too loudly. He must be able to hear that. Aiming for the door, she threw over her shoulder, 'Ten o'clock in Newmarket.' Just up the road, but as it was bucketing down outside she wouldn't be walking.

'I'll be ready.'

That stopped her in her tracks. 'No need for you to come. I've ordered a taxi.'

Irritation tightened his usually tempting mouth. 'Cancel it.'

'I'm not in the army now.'

At least not where you can order me around.

'I'll drive you to all your appointments.' When she scowled at him he added, 'I've got nothing else on this morning.'

'Thought you were going to see your father and then check in with the hospital.'

He shrugged. 'Nothing that can't wait.'

Slapping her hands on her waist, or where her waist used to be, she growled, 'This is why I couldn't live here. You're so bossy and think you should have the upper hand all the time. Is this how you act when your charm doesn't work?'

He didn't say a word.

Which goaded her into saying, 'You think I can't cope? That I'm not up to looking out for myself? Next you'll be saying I can't raise my daughter on my own.'

Cooper was in front of her, in her face, instantly. 'Our daughter.'

True. But, 'Nothing's changed, Cooper. I am looking for an apartment to move into the moment it's available. I will not live with you for any longer than necessary.'

'So you're not moving in with your parents at the end of the day?'

She'd walked into that one. Losing her temper had been a mistake. 'Excuse me.' She stepped around him, careful not to let her stomach brush against him. She didn't trust her body not to get in a lather even when she was angry at him.

'Don't forget to cancel that taxi.'

Plenty of words spilled into her mind, but somehow she managed to hold onto them. Silence was best. Sometimes.

Sophie turned to the letting agent. 'How soon can I move in?' Judging by the stacks of packed cartons the current tenants were already on the move.

'A week from tomorrow.'

Her heart sank. A week living with Cooper. Or having to front up and ask her parents if she could stay with them. They'd say yes. That wasn't the issue. Being told over and over what a fool she'd turned out to be was. She hadn't learned anything from them, they'd say. Well, yes, she had. She wasn't getting married for the sake of it. A loveless marriage was never in her plans. But, then, neither had been having a baby. 'I'll take it.'

'You can't,' Cooper snapped from across the dog-kennel-sized lounge.

'Of course I can.' But she understood the shock on his face. The apartment was tiny, dark and in a less-than-desirable suburb. She was tired, and fed up with looking at places. 'It's available weeks sooner than the others I've looked at.' And it was affordable. She found a smile for the agent. 'Shall we do the paperwork?'

'I need a bond and a deposit on the first fortnight to hold it for you.' The woman dug through her bag for a key. 'I'll get the forms from my car.'

'Not a problem.' Tick. One job on her long list sorted. Tomorrow she'd start looking for furniture. Or should she buy a car first? Then she'd be independent of Cooper. She delved into her handbag for a credit card. An appointment with her new midwife came before anything else.

'Can we talk about this before you sign up?' Cooper parked his tidy backside against the bench next to her.

'No.' Why wasn't she feeling happy to have found somewhere to live? Probably something to do with it being an unexciting place. But she had to suck it up and make the most of everything. She was planning on staying put for the next year at least, and starting out miserable wouldn't be clever.

'Sophie. Are you sure? Can't we look at more places tomorrow?'

'There aren't any others. I went through the agencies' lists again this morning.' There'd been two she'd nearly asked to see but what would be the point? They were out of her price bracket and wandering around them would only increase her frustration level. *That* did not need any help. Not when she had Cooper driving her mad with need at the least convenient moments.

He didn't bother to hide his impatience. 'All right. What's wrong with the first one we saw?'

The steep rent. 'I didn't like it.' The large, sunny rooms, the modern kitchen, the small yard out the back, and the easy drive to the hospital once she went back to work: all added up to a perfect package. If she had loads in the bank.

'Sometimes I don't understand you.'

Neither do I.

'You're not meant to. Anyway, I'd swear I heard a sigh of relief when I turned it down.'

Guilt flushed his cheeks a light shade of pink. 'Even so, I'd prefer you there than here, if you still insist on finding your own place.'

So *that's* what all the less-than-helpful comments and questions at each apartment she'd viewed had been about. He'd been trying to deflect her from renting a property. Should've known. 'I get it that you want to help me—' *in ways that suit you and not me* '—and you can. By backing my decisions. If I get it wrong I'll even agree to you laughing and giving me some stick.' Lifting up onto her toes, she brushed a kiss across his mouth. 'Thank you for caring.' Whatever had precipitated that move she instantly regretted it while wanting more. Wanted to seal her lips on Cooper's, to savour him, breathe him in. To shut him up. To get a taste of what she'd known that wild night in Bamiyan.

Warning. Danger. This is Cooper.

She jerked backwards.

Hard, hot hands caught her around her middle, pulled her hungry body close to that chest she'd been ogling on and off all morning. Had he noticed? Did he understand she still wanted him? Even in her balloon-sized, less than desirable shape?

Stop with the questions. Make the most of being sprawled against him.

Good idea.

'Don't you ever forget I do care about you.' And then his mouth covered hers, possessed hers. Cooper took charge. As his tongue slid inside her mouth, the sensations caused by that hot thrust sent her mind into orbit so that all she was aware of was Cooper, holding onto him.

That hint of the outdoors that was his trademark scent. His full, masculine mouth. His firm muscles pressing against her softer ones. His erection pushing into her belly. Gulp. His erection. She moved against him, the long, hard length causing her lower muscles to contract with tension, with need, with memory.

'Oh, excuse me.' The woman was back.

Sophie leapt out of Cooper's arms, but he quickly caught her and held her in front of him. Hiding his reaction to her? Her face was flushed and no doubt her eyes would be slumberous with desire. Great. Now she'd probably have to find a new rental agent. 'S-sorry. We… It's just…' None of the woman's business.

'I understand,' the agent said, glancing at Cooper.

Any woman would, Sophie thought as she held out a shaking hand to take the forms from the amused woman. 'Let me fill these in and we can all get on our way.'

Before you decide I can't have the place.

'It's not too late to change your mind,' Cooper growled beside her ear, lifting the skin on the side of her neck in a delicious, tingling sensation.

It wasn't only her skin having a meltdown. All parts south of her baby bump were in disarray, hot and tight. Ready, willing and wanting. Why had she kissed Cooper? Why wouldn't she? It'd been a chaste touching of her lips on his, not a hot, deep kiss. No, not until he'd taken over and turned it into something off the radar. The man was so sexy it was impossible to ignore the feelings he evoked in her any longer.

And he wasn't even wearing boots of any kind.

'Have you changed your mind?' the woman asked, a hint of annoyance in her voice.

Sophie shook her head to clear the images of Cooper that had taken over her brain. 'No. I haven't,' she said, putting determination in her tone. She would not be sidetracked by anyone, least of all Cooper. She needed a home for her baby, and she needed it now so there was time to fit it out properly. Scribbling her signature across the bottom of each form placed in front of her, she waited for the calm to come at having achieved finding her future home.

But instead she found herself staring around the gloomy room, wondering what she was doing there. There was a good offer on the table if only she'd swallow her pride and take up the challenge. Cooper's house was all the things this place wasn't.

The agent was quick to put the signed papers in her bag. 'I'll be in touch when the current tenants have moved out.'

And that was that. 'I have somewhere to live,' she muttered as she sank into the front seat of Cooper's car.

'You already had somewhere if only you weren't so stubborn,' she was told sharply.

Couldn't argue with being stubborn. She'd warned him about that. 'You'll thank me for this later.'

Cooper said nothing as he drove away from the apartment.

Thank goodness, Sophie thought. She'd done enough talking to the agent that morning to last all day. Quiet was exactly what she wanted. Her hand hovered over her belly where the baby was also quiet. Too quiet? 'Baby?' Automatically her hand rubbed her tummy. Nothing. 'Move, will you?' The panic was rising in her chest, up her throat. 'Come on.'

'What's happening?' Cooper asked, already pulling off the road to stop the car. 'When did you last feel movement?'

'Not for a while.' When? She racked her brain. 'I don't know when. Before we got to the last apartment.'

'You're sure?' The worry in his eyes did nothing to allay her fears.

'No. I'm not. But she's lying very still now. She never stops moving for long. Cooper, what if…?'

'Don't go there.' His hand caught hers, squeezed gently. 'Easy, Sophie. I'm sure everything's all right. Can I try to feel some movement?'

'Yes.' She jerked her top up to expose her belly, and couldn't care less when Cooper's eyes widened. 'Hurry.'

His hand was cool on her skin, but his touch was so gentle she calmed a little. Until he stopped touching her and tugged her shirt down again. Taking both her hands in his, he said quietly, firmly, 'We should get this checked out to be on the safe side. Can you ring your midwife and tell her we're coming in?'

'I haven't made an appointment with one yet. We only got home yesterday.' The panic became a full-blown roar in her head. 'My baby. Something's wrong. I know it.'

Cooper pulled out into the traffic. 'Auckland Hospital's just down the road. We'll go to the ED.'

'Whatever. Just hurry.' Her hands clutched at her belly, while silently she begged the baby to kick as hard as she could. 'I don't care how much you hurt Mummy, I just have to know you're all right.'

Nothing.

She wanted to bang her stomach in the hope of jarring baby into action, but common sense won out—just.

It wouldn't work, and might even give the baby a shock. If she was all right. 'Hurry up,' she yelled to Cooper.

He wasn't exactly going slowly, but right now a racing car at full throttle would be too slow. Too bad if there was a cop lurking in the area. If he tried to stop them he'd get an earful from her. Or he could escort them to the hospital, flashing lights and all.

'Hold on,' Cooper snapped as he took a corner too fast.

A glance at the speedo told her they weren't going as fast as it felt—or as she'd like. But there was nothing they could do in the heavy traffic except go with the flow. Of course there was no parking outside the emergency department. Murphy's Law was working overtime today.

'Let me out,' she all but shouted. 'You can find parking without me.'

'Okay, okay. Take it easy.' Cooper pulled up beside a parked car and flicked his hazard lights on.

She wanted to shout at him for using the 'easy' word but when she jerked her head around to argue with him she saw nothing but concern and worry looking back at her. Pulling the brake on her temper, she said, 'I'm trying, believe me.'

'I know.' His smile was strained, but the finger he ran down her cheek was gentle and soft, and made her heart tighten. 'Go on. I'll catch you up ASAP. Hang on. There's a car three spaces up pulling out. Quick, out you get.'

She gritted her teeth in exasperation as she struggled to extricate herself. Infuriating how moving wasn't the same as it used to be before baby. Baby. Her hand flattened on her stomach. Baby.

Please, don't let us be too late. Please let them find a heartbeat. Please, please, please.

Sophie shoved out of the car, lurched as she fought to keep her balance.

Cooper called after her, 'Be careful. I don't want you

slipping in all that water covering the path. You'll hurt yourself and that won't do baby any favours.'

He sounded so sure baby was going to be all right, but she'd seen the worry shadowing his eyes, turning his cheeks pale. Despite everything she felt a moment of gratitude for his presence. If not for Cooper she'd still be back at the apartment, freaking out, not knowing what to do. 'Hurry.'

I need you.

Sophie ran.

Every second counted. Losing her baby was not an option.

'Hang in there, sweetheart. Mummy's getting you help.'

She skidded on the smooth concrete at the ED entrance. Teetered on one foot, regained her balance, her heart pounding.

Slow down.

She couldn't, beat the doors with her fist when they took for ever to slide open.

Bang-bang-bang.

The shots cracked through the air.

Sophie dropped to the ground hard, the air ripping out of her lungs, her shoulder taking the brunt of her fall. She cried out as pain snagged her. Rolling onto her side she curled up as tight as possible, making herself small so the shooter wouldn't have an easy target.

'Sophie,' Cooper shouted.

'Get down,' she yelled back. 'You'll be shot.'

'Sophie, it's all right.' He was there, kneeling beside her, reaching for her. 'There're no terrorists here.'

'Get down,' she repeated, stronger this time. 'There's gunfire.'

'No, Sophie, listen. That was a car backfiring. You're safe. We're safe. We're in Auckland. Not Bamiyan.'

'How can you be sure?' Her heart was thumping. How did he know no one wanted to kill them?

Cooper stood up and looked around. 'Nothing out of the ordinary going down, I promise.' He reached a hand down to her, ready to haul her to her feet. 'Do you think I'd risk your life if I had the tiniest suspicion everything wasn't all right?'

The fear backed off as she glanced left, then right. No one was running for their life. There were no shouts or screams. In fact, no one seemed worried about anything. Not even the small group gathering around them.

'Does the lady need this?' An orderly with an empty wheelchair paused beside them.

Starting to feel a little stupid, Sophie gripped Cooper's hand to pull herself upright. 'I'm fine. Just took a tumble. Thank you for your concern.'

'You're welcome,' the man said, before his gaze landed on her belly. 'You went down hard.'

'That's why I want to get her to a doctor. Now.' Cooper tucked her against his side. 'Ready?'

She nodded and took a step, wincing as her ankle protested. 'Think I pulled a muscle.' She tried again, tentatively this time, and was relieved to be able to stand on the foot. 'What an idiot. I seriously thought someone was firing at me.' Looking up at Cooper, she tried to explain, knowing he'd think she was a sandwich short of a picnic. 'For a moment there I was back in Bamiyan.'

'I figured. I've seen the same reaction in some of the guys after they've been in a battle. I'm just surprised it hasn't happened to you before.'

'It did once. But that was on base in Bamiyan. Thought I was over all that now.' Then her reason for being here slammed into her nightmare. 'The baby. I still can't feel any movement. I need to find out what's happening.' Or not happening. Sophie's heart slowed. This was turning out to be the day from hell.

Taking her hand in his, Cooper said, 'I'm with you all the way.'

Together they headed inside to the receptionist who'd stood up the moment they appeared. 'Are you all right?' she asked.

No. My baby's in trouble.

'I'm Sophie Ingram. My baby's stopped moving.' The words gushed out at about the same rate her heart was beating. She drew a breath, dug deep for calm. Felt dizzy instead. She grabbed at Cooper's arm for support, felt relief when he wound that strong arm around her again. She sank against him and drew from his strength.

'We need an urgent scan,' Cooper backed her up. 'It's been over an hour since Sophie felt the last movement.'

That long? Her heart slowed. Too long. Her knees knocked, and if Cooper hadn't been holding her she'd be in a heap on the floor. Again. 'Please, get me help,' she begged.

Within minutes Sophie heard the wonderful sound of the security door buzzing open, allowing them access to the emergency room.

A woman in blue scrubs approached. 'Hello, Sophie. I'm Dr Kate Wynn. I understand you haven't felt baby move for a while. How far along are you?'

As Sophie answered the doctor's questions they were led into a cubicle. She wanted to relax. This gripping tension would not be good for her baby. But her muscles were as tight as ever.

'You're doing great,' Cooper told her quietly.

'What if…?'

'Let's wait until we know what's going on before looking for the worst-case scenario,' he suggested with the tiniest of hitches in his voice.

'You're right.' But, but what if?

Kate told them, 'I'm getting a Doppler sent down so I can listen for a heartbeat. That way we'll know more about what's going on.'

Sophie wished she could feel half as relaxed and professional as Kate appeared, but today her doctoring persona had taken a hike. 'Hurry, please,' she whispered as Cooper helped her onto the bed.

'What's happened? You've got fresh grazes on your leg and arm.'

'Sophie slipped on the wet path outside.' At least he hadn't said she'd thrown herself on the ground and put her baby at risk of being hurt. 'I don't think she did any damage. We are both doctors,' he added with a grimace.

Being a doctor wasn't helping her baby right now. 'I'm fine, unless I've hurt my baby.'

Kate said, 'I doubt it. She's got a lot of protection surrounding her in there. Unless you landed belly first?'

'No.' One thing she'd done right. Twisting to land on her hip and shoulder had hurt her but protected her daughter.

The curtain opened to admit an orderly. 'One Doppler as required.'

'Right, let's get started.' Kate took the instrument and nodded to the orderly to leave.

Kick.

Sophie gasped. 'Oh. Ow! Do that again.'

Kate looked surprised. 'I haven't done anything yet.'

Kick.

Sophie spread her hands over her extended stomach. 'Cooper, put your hand there. She's alive and kicking harder than ever.'

His large hand slid under one of hers, and his eyes filled with relief and wonder. 'Go, girl.' His voice cracked and he stopped talking.

'Me? Or baby?' she teased through the tears now clogging her throat.

'I'll check baby's heart before giving you two a few minutes alone.' Kate smiled and said moments later, 'Listen to that. Nothing wrong with that heartbeat. Be back shortly for a full examination.' Putting the Doppler aside, she slipped out and closed the curtains tight behind her.

Cooper's hand splayed across Sophie's stomach was so large, and strong, yet gentle. So right. Like he was laying a claim on her.

What?

The question screamed into her head. It was not right. Cooper didn't have a place in her life, only that of her daughter's. But she couldn't push him away, liked the strength and warmth of his hand. Needed him at her side for now. Had needed him ever since she'd thought something was wrong with their baby. All her strength and determination to do everything properly had gone, leaving her like a jelly on the inside. But having Cooper at her side settled her jitters a little at least.

Reaching around his arm, she placed her hand over his. 'She's a busy girl in there. I'm never going to tell her to take a rest again.'

'You probably woke her up from a lovely sleep when you dived to the ground and now she's paying you back.' His smile was lopsided, filled with concern as he stared at her baby bump.

That concern would be for the baby, she acknowledged to herself. Not her. He had no reason to be worried about her. Apart from her crazy reaction to a car going past, that was. She wasn't important to him, wasn't the love of his life. Her shoulders slumped. If only they were in love and expecting their first child, together on all fronts. Not dodging around each other, trying to get along without too many arguments.

Thinking like that was dumb. She didn't love Cooper—never had, probably never would. Any feelings like that would be due to baby brain. Besides, it wouldn't work if she did. He wasn't going to fall in love with her, and a one-way relationship was as bad as her parents' hateful one.

'Right.' Cooper straightened up, stepped away from the bed. 'Let's get you sorted and then we can go home. You look whacked.'

Thanks for the compliment.

She snatched her shirt down over baby and growled, 'Tell Kate I'm ready.'

And stay out there so I don't have to see you get all excited when we get to hear baby's heartbeat again.

But she knew she could never do that. So much for keeping Cooper on the other side of the door every time she went to see the midwife. After this he was involved, and it would be petty to tell him otherwise.

Horror struck her. Did that mean he'd be there during the birth? She so wasn't ready for that.

'Let's go home,' Cooper said thirty minutes later.

Home. Yes. She needed that—somewhere to relax, unwind, forget the fears that had blitzed her today. 'Let's,' she agreed.

Then she stumbled. Home? With Cooper? No. She was going back to his house for a few days until she had her apartment fixed up. *That* would be home. Not Cooper's place.

'You okay?' he asked warily.

'Yes,' she snapped.

'I'll drop you off and head into the hospital. I need to touch base with the unit before I start.'

'I'll get a taxi.' When his eyebrows rose and his mouth tightened she added, 'I'll visit Mum and Dad.' Ask for a room.

'No, Sophie, You need to rest and put today's scare behind you, not go getting uptight about your parents.'

He was right. Of course. One more night at his house couldn't hurt. Could it?

CHAPTER SEVEN

COOPER STRODE DOWN the corridor towards the surgical unit, relieved to have left Sophie at home.

As long as she stayed there. Though he doubted she was in any hurry to see her parents. What really was going on in that family? The less Sophie told him about herself the more he wanted to know.

Talk about getting under his skin. He needed to put space between them. Needed to get back on track with being a support person for the mother of his child, no more, no less. Needed to remember he didn't do relationships of the close and personal kind, and to do so would be to the detriment of Sophie and the baby. And him.

What was he afraid of? That he'd take them in then send them packing when they got too close, and demanded more of him than he had to give? Turn Sophie into one of those women Dad had coming and going? She couldn't get close if he kept the barriers up. Couldn't hurt him if he didn't allow her in.

Under your skin already, remember?

Then there was the baby. A whole other story. He'd never walk away from his daughter. Which meant he'd never walk away from Sophie. He wouldn't feel incapable of looking after them and opt out for ever, as his mother had. The only thing he was incapable of was loving Sophie. Oh, and making up his mind about how far to press her to stay under his roof where he could do a better job of looking out for them.

When she'd dropped to the ground earlier his heart had stopped. Throw in her fears about the baby not moving and he'd come up with a dreadful scenario. Stroke or, worse, a fatal heart attack. His hands had been shaking as he'd touched her, reached to find a pulse. Even when he'd felt the steady thump, thump of blood pounding through her body it'd taken minutes for his panic to back off. He didn't want to lose Sophie. Not now. Not ever.

He wasn't making a lot of sense with this. Who would in the circumstances? If only Sophie would get out of his head, give him quiet time when he wasn't actually with her. But no. She was in there, tap-tapping away at his resolve to remain uninvolved, making him resent her for getting him in a lather over everything. She was forcing him to face up to his mother's suicide and how he hadn't forgiven her for deserting him.

If his mum had got help for her obsessive, compulsive excessive disorder his life would've been so different. All their lives would've been different. He might even be able to fall in love without thinking up a hundred reasons why that was bad for him and the other person involved.

Cooper stopped to stare out a window onto the motorway below. What if he stopped fighting this? Gave up and took things as they occurred? Dealt with imagined shootings and lack of kicks systematically? Helped Sophie move into that grot box of an apartment instead of trying to talk her out of it? Surely then he'd get past these feelings of need, of wanting to spend more time with her. Emotions that came from his desire to do the right thing, nothing else.

Get it? Nothing else.

'Cooper? That you?' a woman called from somewhere further down the corridor.

He recognised the sultry voice instantly. 'Svetlana, good to see you.' The last person he wanted right this minute.

She reached him and wrapped her arms around him. 'Where have you been? I've missed you.'

'Oh, you know. Offshore with the army.' He shrugged out of the hug. 'You're looking as lovely as ever.' Yuk. How crass. That speculative gleam in Svetlana's eyes needed a dose of cold reality fast, not encouragement. He knew how she operated, had been a willing participant in the past, but was not interested now.

Her smile widened and her tongue peeked out at the corner of her mouth. 'Army life has been good for you.' She squeezed his biceps.

Cooper took another step back. What had he seen in her? Uncomplicated sex. The only answer. They'd had some fun encounters, yet now he felt nothing, no frisson of excitement. Nothing. Just an image of Sophie shimmering in his mind. 'Can't complain.'

Svetlana followed, stepping closer, her cloying sweet perfume a thick cloud around her. 'Want to have some fun tonight, or one night this week?'

'Thanks, but I'm tied up all week.' *Come on.* 'In fact, I'm busy most of the time.'

She blinked rapidly. 'You haven't gone and got yourself all hooked up with a little wifey, now, have you?' Her smirk suggested she knew full well what his answer would be.

No, he hadn't. Wasn't ever likely to. But that didn't mean he was available for a quick romp either.

You always have been in the past.

Exactly. In the past. Not now. Not since—Sophie.

'Nice catching up, Svetlana.' He deliberately glanced

at his watch. 'I'm running late for an appointment. See you around.'

Cooper strode away, feeling guilty for his abrupt dismissal but also relieved to be away from the woman. Unfortunately there'd be no avoiding her completely since her white coat with the stethoscope hanging from the pocket suggested she worked here. Obviously she still overdid wearing the gear even when not required so as to show who and what she was.

Unlike Dr Ingram. Happy to wear fatigues or shorts and T-shirt, Sophie preferred casual in her approach to doctoring. Until she was with a patient, and then everyone knew her role. That day in Bamiyan she'd taken charge of caring for Kelly, calm despite her shock, completely cognisant of the medical details despite the fear in her eyes. Everyone who had worked on Kelly had settled into doing their jobs quickly—all because of Sophie's professional and quiet manner.

Even him. For a moment after the explosion when the bullets had started to fly he'd been terrified for his life, and for that of the beautiful woman he'd met only minutes earlier. He'd leapt to cover her body, fearful of either of them taking a direct hit, and once they had been back on their feet the shakes had set in. If not for Sophie he might've run screaming for the hills. Okay, maybe not. But it would've taken him a lot longer to settle down enough to help the wounded without leaping into the air at every loud noise.

He turned into the surgical unit and went to find Shaun Langford, the head of department and former mentor from his years specialising right here.

'Hi, Cooper. We're looking forward to working with you again,' a nurse told him, and the receptionist nodded in agreement.

'Thanks, ladies. It's good to be back.' It really was.

So much so there was a spring in his step as he reached Shaun's office. He was coming home, back to a place he'd enjoyed, where people he'd liked still worked, where he knew his role and gave it his all. Yeah, could be he'd made the right decision for his future without being aware of it.

So career move sorted. That only left his personal life.

Sophie sat back on her heels to admire the stacks of carefully folded baby clothes on her bedroom floor. 'Not bad, if I say so myself.'

'Talking to yourself is not a good sign.'

Cooper. Her skin heated at the sound of that gravelly voice. 'You're home early.' There went her quiet time. Over the last two days she'd spent the afternoons pottering around his house, pretending she lived here, as in permanently, and loving every moment of it. Cooper had an eclectic collection of furniture that made her smile. There was endless redecorating required, yet it didn't matter. The house was warm and cosy, like no place she'd lived in before.

As for all those images of the good-looking hunk standing beside her right now, they'd be the bane of her life, appearing too easily, often doing her head in. She needed to be getting her A into G and making the apartment ready to move into, but it seemed too much of an effort. Staying with Cooper was the soft option. And more exciting. There was also a certain closeness between them in the way he took her BP every morning, noted what she ate. He'd soon drive her crazy with all the attention and then she'd leave.

If she could. The sense of belonging that wrapped around her every time she came through the front door would be hard to walk away from. The essence of this house was Cooper. It said, *Take me as I am.* If that wasn't Cooper Daniels, then what was?

Right now he was reaching a hand down to help her up off her haunches. 'I haven't officially started yet.'

Pushing to her feet, not an easy or pretty manoeuvre these days, she said, 'So you go to the hospital first thing every day because I'm under your feet?' If he stayed at home she might've got to work on her list. Baby furniture was an urgent requirement. If baby made her appearance now she'd be sorely in need of just about everything. Except clothes.

His hand fell away from her elbow. 'Thought I'd go with you to the car yard, see if you can't find something half-decent to get around in.'

'That's not necessary.' She could find her own car—with the help of an Automobile Association mechanic. If she ever got around to arranging that.

'You don't want a car?' He was being deliberately obtuse.

She could be likewise, hopefully keep him a little distant. 'I'm aiming for a SUV.'

'Then let's go find you one.'

'No, Cooper. This is mine to do.' She was quite capable of finding her own vehicle, just not of doing it right away.

'Fine. Then let's go look at cots and beds and tables. At the moment your baby will be sleeping on the floor, and so will her mother.'

'Again, my problem.' Why was she being belligerent? Cooper was only trying to help. She should be pleased. In fact, why was she so reluctant to do any of the things she'd been busting to do while waiting in Darwin to come home? 'I did book an appointment with a midwife for tomorrow.' One thing off the list.

'What's up, Sophie?'

'Nothing. I bought clothes, nappies by the carton, and some cute little toys this morning.' Three hours in the mall had had her staggering under all the bags of goodies. Not practical things but adorable baby things in every colour of the rainbow. They were all that interested her at the moment. So unlike her not to be charging through the stores, picking out what she needed and getting them delivered fast.

'You bought loads of all of those yesterday.' Amusement lightened his eyes to that pewter shade she adored and turned her insides to mush.

'True.' There wasn't much space to move in this room, the floor being covered in bags from every baby outlet within a five-kilometre radius. 'Leave it, Cooper. I'm having fun.'

I am? Shopping till I drop, getting so many baby outfits that most of them will never be worn, by this baby at least, is fun?

'Think about it. I haven't been near malls since I left New Zealand nearly eleven months ago. I didn't bother in Darwin, not needing much because I wore a uniform.'

'We're going out.' His amusement had vanished.

'To the car dealer or the furniture shops?' she called after him, letting annoyance flare up. It was easier to deal with his high-handed attitude that way, and it pushed aside the sudden yearning to rip their clothes off and make wild, passionate love.

He was back at the doorway. 'My baby is not sleeping on the floor. Neither is she going without a safe car to ride in. We'll start with the furniture.'

'There's nowhere to store it until I get the keys to the apartment.' Her desire was rapidly abating.

'Then we'll put it all in my third bedroom.'

'You're taking charge,' she growled. Though it made sense. Someone had to since her baby brain was obviously incapable. But she wasn't telling him that.

'Too right I am.'

* * *

'Who'd have thought there were so many choices?' Sophie muttered as she strolled down yet another aisle in the baby furniture warehouse. 'Here I'd been thinking a bassinet was just a bassinet.'

'You hadn't figured on choosing between turned, stained wood or plain, painted wood; between pink, blue, white or every other colour under the sun. Or one with a shelf at the bottom or not.' Cooper grinned at her. His mood had lifted since they'd arrived at the massive outlet. 'And that's only the actual bassinet. Which mattress and flounces do you like?'

But she was distracted. 'How about those cute bunnies to string across the top for baby to look at?'

'She's supposed to sleep in this thing, not lie awake, staring at plastic baubles.' His grin widened, and excitement crept into his eyes.

'Right, then we'll go for the basic, no-frills version.' Not likely, but she could pull his strings. That excitement was tightening her belly and turning this into an adventure.

'I'm having the classy, stained wood one, with that pink flounce that has elephants cavorting over it.'

'You're buying a bassinet?' That had not been part of today's excursion.

'Of course I am. Where else will baby sleep when she's with me?' The excitement dimmed, and his mouth tightened. 'I need to duplicate everything you get.'

'She can't stay with you. I'll be breastfeeding.' Why hadn't that occurred to her? Of course Cooper would want his daughter to stay with him sometimes. She'd even suggested it. But that had been in the future, not until their daughter was on a bottle and no longer brand-new.

A warm hand descended on her shoulder. 'You're winding yourself up over nothing. I just want to be prepared for when my daughter does spend time with me.'

And she had promised he'd have input in her life, which meant the baby would stay with him. 'We'd better buy lots of feeding bottles, then.'

The tension instantly evaporated from his face. 'So let's really get into this. Two of everything.'

'Everything?' She choked as unexpected laughter rolled up her throat. 'You're serious, aren't you?'

'Yep.' The excitement was back, and she was glad. Then Cooper grinned. 'Starting with bassinets. I'm taking that one.' He tapped the one he'd nodded at earlier.

'But I like that one.' She laughed. 'Though not as keen on the elephants as the butterflies.'

'It's mine. I saw it first.' Then he locked his gaze on hers. 'Unless you really, really want it.'

She shook her head. 'It's yours. I've just seen another one I like better. Which baby bath do you think?'

'We need help here.' Cooper looked around for a shop assistant and soon had people following them, writing down everything they selected so that deliveries could be made to their respective homes next week.

But slowly Sophie's enthusiasm died. Why were they doing this? Sure, she needed to set up for her baby, but Cooper? He didn't need quite as many things as her. It was as though he intended having the baby living with him a lot, not for some weekends when he wasn't working.

'I see an in-depth discussion coming on.' Cooper nudged her as he slid his credit card back into his wallet after paying for everything, against her wishes. 'What's up? You not happy with me decking my house out for my daughter?'

She hadn't thought it through properly when she'd said she'd never prevent him being a part of their child's life. 'She's going to be living with me.'

'Most of the time, sure. I'm making her comfortable when she visits me, though.' His mouth tightened. 'You're not reneging on your promise of allowing me to be a part of her life?'

'No, I wouldn't do that. Never. Not after the way my parents treated me.' But... 'We need to draw up legal papers covering custody and what comes about in the event of something happening to me. Or you.' Sophie wanted to slap her forehead. She'd been very remiss not thinking about this sooner.

'You are right. We should see a lawyer.' Taking her elbow, he led her outside to his car. 'Talk about deflating the moment.'

'I'm sorry,' she snapped. 'Actually, no, I'm not. We were having fun when this is serious. We haven't thought everything through. There're so many legal ramifications about being parents it's terrifying. I've been completely irresponsible.'

'Don't go blaming yourself, Sophie. I admit none of this had occurred to me either. It would've, eventually.' His sigh was loud and despondent. 'Why today when I was enjoying myself?'

Her stance softened. 'Yeah, that was fun, wasn't it?' Then she got wound up again. 'This goes to show how unprepared to be a good mother I am.'

'We're not going there. For now we agree we'll sort out the legal stuff ASAP. In the meantime let's go home.'

Home. Again that word sank into her like a ball of warmth. If only. 'Let's,' was all she said.

'How's the body? I bet you've got some major bruises after throwing yourself on the ground.'

'One or two.' She ached in a lot of places.

'You don't think you need to talk to someone about your reaction to a backfiring car?' A load of caution laced his question, like he wasn't sure of her reaction. 'I'm thinking of the baby and what harm you could cause her throwing yourself down like that. Once she's born she'll be more vulnerable if you're holding her.'

She'd presume he cared, and wasn't about to tell her she was incompetent to be his daughter's mother. She also got that he was only concerned about the baby. Fair enough. That's how she was supposed to want it. A timely reminder that she was still on her own. 'I saw the shrink in Darwin when I first got there, and was told I did not have PTSD, or if I did it was very mild.' Despite the annoyance winding up tight inside her, she conceded, 'But a second time after eight months is concerning.'

'Maybe you need to talk to someone again. Another opinion won't hurt.'

Did that count when it came to her ability to be a good mother? 'I'll look into it.'

'I know a good guy. We were in the army together one tour. I'll give him a ring tomorrow, get you an appointment.'

Forget annoyed. Anger burst out of her mouth. 'Stop bossing me around. I'll make my own arrangements, thank you very much.' She seethed. 'Who do you think you are? Telling me what to do, who to see, where to shop? It's got to stop. Now. I was perfectly capable of looking after myself before I met you. Nothing's changed.' She was yelling, but seriously? The guy needed a bash over the head.

'No problem. Just thought I could help, take some of the strain away from you.'

What strain? Babies were delivered every day and no one suffered badly. A yawn ripped through her. She was exhausted, and Cooper wasn't helping by adding pressure to her already mounting worries. But he was here, had given her a place to stay, and helped organise furniture delivery. Tears spilled down her cheeks. What a mess she was. At sixes and sevens over everything. Another yawn dragged at her. A tired mess.

Yet the moment she walked inside Cooper's house the tension plaguing her instantly fell away.

Yes, this house was a haven. A home. The kind of place she'd love to come back to at the end of a busy day, or stay put in on days her baby was grizzly.

Her hands splayed across her belly. This had to stop. It was imperative she move into her own place—fast. Turn the apartment into something as comforting as Cooper's home, without him there. Of course she'd delayed. She didn't know where to start, how to create a home that she and baby would be safe and secure in. She'd never known that for herself. Growing up, home had been the place where she'd slept and eaten and done her homework and listened to her parents arguing. Her bedroom the sanctuary she'd hidden in when the arguing had escalated into a full-scale war. Not once had she ever walked in the front door and sighed with contentment. As she did here. Talk about being in big trouble.

'Sophie? Are you all right? You're not having pains, are you?' Cooper hovered over her, anxiety replacing the cool demeanour he'd shown since they'd talked about her supposed PTSD.

'I'm fine. No pains.' Just a crazy revelation that she had to deal with. She was not staying here permanently. Like to or not, she had to move on, set up her own life. Just as she'd planned since learning she was pregnant.

So get on with it.

'You'd tell me?' The anxiety hung between them.

'Yes.' Locking eyes with Cooper, she said with all the force she could muster, 'I will let you know the moment I think I'm in labour.' She couldn't keep him out of the picture on that score. When she'd gone into meltdown over the lack of movement from the baby Cooper had given her strength when she'd needed someone to cling to. She couldn't push him away over this.

'Good.' He tossed his car keys up in the air, snatched them and repeated the action. 'So tomorrow we'll find you a suitable car.' He wasn't easily diverted.

Something she'd be wise to remember. 'I'll do that in the morning.' While he was at the hospital.

He shook his head. 'Uh-uh. I'll do some research on the net while you tell me why you want an SUV instead of a car.'

'You can stop looking so smug. It doesn't suit you,' she growled, trying hard not to smile at him. He'd won and yet she couldn't find it in her to be cross. Not really. He had a way about him that made her feel more and more at ease. When he wasn't reminding her that there were lots more problems to add to her list than she had to tick off. Lawyers, a midwife, and now a psychologist had to be dealt with.

In the meantime, Cooper merely laughed and booted up his laptop.

'Three more ticks on my list,' Sophie sighed late the next afternoon. Things were starting to come together nicely. 'I like my new midwife. She's so enthusiastic.' When Cooper's eyebrows rose, she added, 'And professional, and competent.'

'What else is on that list?' Cooper asked as he drove through the rush-hour traffic in Newmarket on their way home from a car dealer. 'Apart from a vehicle, which it looks like we've got sorted now.'

'Dinner. Can we swing by the supermarket? I feel like pasta tonight.'

'What's with all this pasta? Seems you're always eating it. You're not of Italian extraction, are you?'

'Irish. Except I'm not fussed about spuds.' She smacked

her lips, her stomach sitting up in anticipation. 'Can't go past the sauces that go with linguine, and then there's ravioli and the delicious fillings.'

'You been to Italy?'

Nodding, she explained, 'I spent four months there after completing my internship in London. I didn't want to leave.' Not only was the food divine, the men were just as mouth-watering. Though not as delectable as the man in the driver's seat beside her. Only the car's seat? Or was he driving her life now? He definitely played havoc with her focus, which should be entirely on preparing for the baby, not on kisses. Hot kisses that swamped her mind with memories of his body against her, diverting pictures that had her longing for more.

'Why didn't you stay on in Italy?'

'I couldn't get a work permit so I returned home and saved up for the next adventure, which was in Chile.'

'We're not going to eat Chilean food, then?'

'They eat a lot of potatoes. But having said that, I did enjoy most things. Lots of seafood and meat. *Pastel do chocio* was my all-time favourite, sort of like a shepherd's pie. Haven't seen that in the supermarkets here.'

Cooper turned into the supermarket parking building. 'You might have to go back to Chile for that. From things you've said, it sounds as though you've done a lot of travelling. You got a thing against staying at home?'

More like a thing about staying still. 'My travelling days are on hold for a few years.'

'I suppose they are. But that's not what I asked.'

As a diversion she'd missed the gate. 'Travel's exciting and opens your eyes to so much more than we've grown up with here.' And it had kept her from spending time wondering if she'd ever be able to settle down in one place for long. Every time she thought about finding a place of her own she'd think about how uncomfortable her parents' home had been and known she'd had no idea how to make hers any different. Except that had bitten her on the backside this year. Settling down *was* her current goal.

As they walked inside Cooper mused, 'I haven't seen much of the world. Only the out-of-the-way and often inhospitable places the army sent me to.'

Sophie shivered. 'I'm over those. Not going back to dangerous areas again.'

'Cuts out quite a lot of the world at the moment. Hideous.' Cooper swung a shopping basket between them.

'There are definitely places to stay away from. I can't believe some of the things going on at the moment.' She paused, listening hard. Had she heard a cry? But nothing untoward reached her. Must've been imagining it. Snapping off a plastic bag, she began selecting tomatoes. 'Need some mushrooms too.'

'I'll get them.'

There it was again. A low cry, almost a groan. 'Something's not right.' Dropping the tomatoes in the basket, she headed for the next aisle.

'What have you heard?' Cooper was right with her, the empty mushroom bag still in his hand.

'Like someone's in pain.' She stared down the next aisle. Nothing out of the ordinary. Was her imagination overacting? No. There it was again. 'Hear that?' She headed for the next aisle and raced down it. Sitting the floor was a heavily pregnant girl, her face contorted with pain. Sophie reached for her hand. 'Hi. My name's Sophie. I'm a doctor. What's happening?'

'I think my baby's coming.' The young face scrunched up tight as a contraction gripped her.

The cry of pain that accompanied it cut through Sophie. 'Breathe deep, go with the pain, don't fight it.' She tried to remember everything she'd heard in antenatal classes in Darwin.

'Easy for you to say,' grunted the girl.

Cooper knelt on the other side of the distressed girl. 'Has anyone called an ambulance?' he asked the gathering onlookers.

'Yes,' replied an older woman dressed in the store's uniform. 'Just now.'

'Good. What's your name?' he asked the girl, adding, 'I'm Cooper, another doctor.'

'Melanie. It's coming,' she cried as another contraction caught her.

She might be right, Sophie conceded. Those contractions were very close. 'We need to examine her,' she said quietly so only Cooper heard. 'But it's hardly ideal here.'

'Not a lot of choice.' He stood up. 'Can you all give us a bit of privacy? Carry on with your shopping and leave us to help this girl.'

'I want some tinned corn for my fritters,' a woman said. 'If you can just step out of my way.'

Cooper sounded calm, too calm. 'Do you have to have it today?'

'It's my son's favourite dinner.'

'Make him something else,' Cooper snapped, no long holding onto his temper. 'This young lady's situation is more important.'

Sophie held onto a smile and concentrated on talking to Melanie. 'How far along are you?'

'Thirty-six weeks.'

Too early. Thirty-seven was considered safe. 'Cooper, we might need the paediatric ambulance.'

'Onto it.'

Sophie turned back to Melanie. 'Has your pregnancy been normal so far?'

She nodded. 'Blood pressure fine. No diabetes. Not even Braxton Hicks pains.'

Better than me, then.

'Have you called your…' Sophie paused to glance at Melanie's left hand '…partner?'

'He's busy.'

Really? Too busy to be here for Melanie and his baby? 'Want Cooper to talk to him?'

Melanie's face shut down. 'No.'

Something was definitely off key here, but it wasn't her place to ask questions that were obviously awkward. Not wanting to upset the younger woman any more, Sophie changed the subject slightly. 'Can I examine you?'

'Not with those people gawping at me.'

'Fair enough. Cooper?'

'Onto it.' Striding up to the nearest person still standing watching the fun, he said in a very firm tone, 'Move, sunshine. Out of this aisle. Now. And the rest of you. Where is the store manager?'

'Coming,' called a young man, scurrying towards them.

'Clear this lot out of here right now.' Did he just add under his breath, 'The guy's still wet behind the ears'?

Sophie felt her smile widen. Almost immediately they had the aisle to themselves. Cooper on the rampage was something to admire. His tone brooked no argument, like he was on the parade ground again.

'How's that?' she asked Melanie. 'We're alone.'

A contraction rippled through the girl and she didn't, or couldn't, hold back a scream.

Sophie reached for her nearest hand and held on. 'Breathe, in one, two, three, out one, two, three. And before you say anything, I'm pregnant too.'

Melanie's eyes popped open. 'So you know what this is like.'

Ah. Caught. 'No. My first time.' She squeezed Melanie's hand. 'Sorry. I'll shut up with the advice.'

'Do you want your baby?'

'Absolutely. Don't you?'

'No. Yes. I'm not ready.' Tears oozed slowly from the corners of Melanie's eyes. 'It's not fair.'

Sophie knew all about that, but it seemed she'd come to terms with her deal better than this young woman. 'I'd like to check what's going on. We're on our own now.' Where was that ambulance?

Cooper placed himself between them and the end of the aisle while Sophie took a discreet look. Melanie wasn't wrong. 'Your baby's very nearly here.'

'So I'm going to have him in the supermarket.' Her expression was wry. 'Guess that goes with everything else that's gone wrong.'

The rising and falling sound of an approaching siren reached them. 'You might get lucky and have the baby in the ambulance.'

Even before she'd finished saying that Melanie bent over her stomach, snatching for Sophie's hand as pain hit her.

Sophie used her free hand to rub Melanie's back. 'You're doing great.'

'So are you,' Cooper said from behind her. 'Like the pro you are.'

Warmth stole through her. 'Thanks.' Then she shook her head. 'Watch this space. It'll be very different when it's my turn.'

'I'll be there to rub your back. And hold your hand.'

She nodded. 'Yeah, you will be.' Decision made. She wouldn't go back on it. She'd need someone there and while a girlfriend had volunteered she knew it had to be Cooper with her. For the baby. And for him. He needed to be a part of the birth. It was his daughter she'd be bringing into the world and she wanted to be able to tell their child that Daddy had been there when she'd arrived.

A paramedic squatted down beside them. 'Hi, there. I've been told there's a baby in a hurry to make an appearance.'

'A big hurry,' Sophie told him. 'The baby's nearly here.'

'You're a doctor?'

She nodded. 'We've got minutes, so I don't know if you want to remove Melanie to the privacy of your ambulance or carry on here.' She had to hand over. It was how the system worked. But she could stick with Melanie. 'You want to try and make it out to the ambulance? There's a stretcher ready.'

'Ambulance,' Melanie grunted as she sucked in a breath and squeezed Sophie's hand. 'If there's time.'

There wasn't. Melanie's baby rushed into the world seconds later. The paramedic was instantly busy clearing the wee boy's air passage and checking his reflexes.

When the baby cried Melanie smiled and held her arms out. 'Can I hold him?'

Sophie let go the breath she'd been holding. This girl did want her baby. Whatever the situation she was facing, her baby was welcome despite her earlier denial. 'The paramedics need to take care of him for now. Let's get you onto that stretcher and shifted to the ambulance. You both need to go to hospital.'

'Will you come with me?' Melanie locked her eyes on Sophie. 'Please,' she begged. 'I don't want to be on my own.'

'Is there anyone I can call?'

The girl's head moved slowly from side to side. 'No. My parents have disowned me, and the baby's father doesn't want a bar of him.'

'Of course I'll come with you.' How could she not? Raising her eyes to Cooper, she was relieved to see his approval beaming out at her. When did she need Cooper's approval for anything? Worse, why did it feel so good? Just something else to worry about in the middle of the night.

CHAPTER EIGHT

'LET'S EAT OUT,' Cooper suggested on the phone three days later. 'There's a new Italian place just down the road.'

'That's cheating. You know I won't be able to pass on that.' But it would be fun to go out for a meal and relax, talk about things that had nothing to do with her new apartment that she'd spent the last two days scrubbing. She'd got the keys on Wednesday and should've moved in immediately. On closer inspection the place was a bit of a tip. The cold weather had also made the empty rooms uninviting.

'That's a yes, then.' He sounded exhausted.

'Are you sure you want to? I could cook eggs.'

'No eggs. Need a proper meal. We've been doing an appendectomy. I'll be home by seven.'

I'll be home by seven.

How domestic. Sophie hugged herself. Cooper had got to her in a big way. He didn't frighten her with easy comments like that one. Instead she was slowly being sucked into his life. Her barriers were coming down, one by one. To the point she almost wished she could say yes to his suggestion of living here permanently. This hesitation in everything she did at the moment was debilitating. All her life she'd leapt into things, be they work, travel or parties. She'd grabbed life with both hands and raced away.

Filling empty voids was essential, kept her sane. If she dared to stop, there was a whole load of pain and rejection waiting to pounce and knock her to her knees. This past week she hadn't run anywhere and she was still standing. No wonder that apartment remained empty.

Kick.

'Hello, in there. I hope you're up to a night out, because that's what's happening as soon as your father gets home.'

Had she really just said that? As in sounding like they were a regular family doing everyday things together? She couldn't have. But she had.

Sophie sighed. Tomorrow she'd put in a big effort to finish getting the apartment ready, so she could move in.

But first she'd shower and put on an outfit that didn't look like a sack over baggy clown's pants. The red, scoop-necked top she'd purchased yesterday would go perfectly with her black, leg-hugging trousers. Yes, she'd spruce herself up for the evening. See if she didn't get a smile from Cooper.

Cooper couldn't believe the beautiful apparition that floated down the hallway towards him when he stepped inside his house. The exhaustion dragging him down vanished in a heartbeat and his body tightened with excitement.

Steady. Nothing's happening here.

'You're looking fabulous.' Sexy as all hell. Hot. Stunning.

She did a very unlike Sophie thing. She blushed. 'Th-thanks.'

He couldn't help himself. He reached for her, pulled her close, and the baby bump tapped him at waist level. 'I mean it. You're one beautiful lady.' She smelt so tempting. And all that shining hair that she'd left free of its usual tie-back needed his fingers running through it. Her eyes were wide and welcoming and…

Cooper placed his hands on each side of her head to tilt her to one side. All the better to kiss her. His lips covered hers and he inhaled as her mouth softened under his. It wasn't enough. His tongue slid into that warmth, tasted her. He didn't need to go out to dinner. He had all the deliciousness he needed right here.

Sophie sank against him, pressing their baby into him as she moulded her breasts against his chest. Lifting her arms, she slipped them over his shoulders to meet at the back of his neck. Warm. Soft. Caressing.

His knees threatened to buckle. He held her tighter, kissed her harder, loved her more.

What? He jerked his head back. Loved her more? As in he already loved her? Absolutely not. That wasn't possible. All he felt for Sophie was compassion, concern and friendship. Responsibility. Didn't he? What about the sexual attraction?

'Cooper?' She was blinking at him, surprise piercing him from her gaze. Hopefully hurt or anger wasn't mixed in there.

'Sorry.' He jammed his hand across his hair. 'I don't know what came over me.' Yeah, right. 'I couldn't help myself.' Pathetic.

'Oh.' Her knuckles pressed against her mouth. That delectable mouth he'd just kissed. It *was* a very kissable mouth. It distracted him when he wasn't concentrating. Not how this was meant to be. Not at all.

'Give me ten to shower and change, then we'll head out.'

He didn't wait for her response, suddenly afraid she'd say no, say she didn't want to go out with him. If she had any sense that's exactly what she should do. He didn't want that. Forget the love word that had shot into his kiss-hazed brain. He was attracted to Sophie. Attracted? Try totally wanted her, dreamt of her underneath his body, making out. She was hot, even with a baby on board. Or was that because of the baby bump? Did that make her even more desirable?

Whatever. Cooper snapped the shower faucet to hot and tugged his clothes off. Confusion reigned. He wanted Sophie. Yes. Glancing down, he swallowed a smile. Too obvious, man. One kiss and his manhood throbbed with need. One kiss? Give over. He'd been excited to see her even before he'd put the key in his front door. The shower should be set on cold, not hot.

He wanted Sophie to live in his house so he could step up and be a good dad and support person. Though how he'd manage that when he physically needed her so much he didn't know.

'I went and saw Melanie again today. Jacob is ready to go home tomorrow,' Sophie told him later as they waited for their meals. Seemed she was on top of things.

A groan filled his mouth. Bad description. 'Where's home?'

'She's renting a room in a house in Ponsonby. It doesn't sound nearly as good as the suburb's reputation would suggest.'

He hadn't been surprised to learn Sophie had taken an interest in the young woman who seemed to be on her own with her baby. 'How can she afford to rent?' How could her parents have kicked her out because she was pregnant? That was when their daughter would've needed them the most. His blood had boiled when Sophie had first told him how Melanie's father had given her five minutes to pack some belongings and one hundred dollars to start out on her new life, before slamming the door behind her.

'Social welfare are helping. But this is a girl who was

doing well at school, had potential as a pro tennis player, and had lots of friends.' Sophie's eyes glittered. 'I seriously don't understand.'

'Me either.' He covered her hand with his. 'Everyone makes mistakes.' Yep, look at them.

Sophie must've been thinking the same. Her mouth lifted into a beautiful smile.

Using that word a lot tonight. But that was Sophie. Beautiful. He was about to tell her when their meals arrived. Saved by the lasagne. 'You as hungry as that plate suggests you need to be?'

'I am eating for two.'

'How do you know Junior likes pasta? She might hate it.'

'She's a mummy's girl. She'll like it.'

He grinned and finally relaxed totally. Why waste a night out with a stunning woman by being uptight and on edge about what next might come out of his mouth?

'What else did you do today, apart from visiting your new friend?'

'Had the furniture delivered and got the men to put it in the correct rooms. The apartment's starting to look a little bit like home.'

'You didn't shift anything yourself?' She could be so annoying with her independent streak. He'd told her half a dozen times that they'd get the furniture brought around tomorrow when he'd be there to help with the heavy lifting.

'Nope. Amazing how a pregnant tummy has men, even strangers, falling over backwards to help.'

Her grin caught him, made him forget to be disappointed at the fact he hadn't been the one to help her.

'Don't go. Stay with me. We can make it work.'

She gaped at him. 'We've had this discussion. Nothing's changed.'

Come on. Convince her this was the right thing to do. He reached for her hands, held them lightly in his. 'Sophie, this is important to me, to us. Definitely important for our baby.'

When she opened her mouth, he shook his head at her. 'Hear me out. I heard what you said about growing up with your parents at odds all the time, but it doesn't have to be like that with us. We'll make certain it won't. I believe that. We already like each other. Let's at least try. For our daughter's sake.'

Her cheeks whitened. 'Low blow, Cooper.'

'It wasn't meant to be. Believe me.' Drawing in a deep breath, he managed, 'Sophie, I'd like to marry you, share my home with you, bring up our child together under the same roof. I'm not asking for anything more than that.'

'Anything more?' she spluttered. 'That's more than enough. How do you honestly think this idea of yours would work out? Huh?'

'We'd have separate bedrooms.' His heart stuttered. Of course they would. How else could they manage? It had to be his manhood talking. His heart had no place in these negotiations. 'There are enough bedrooms, two bathrooms, and I'm sure we can work out ways to avoid spending too much time together in the rest of the house if that's how you—we—want it.' Sounded clinical if he was listening to himself, so he wouldn't. 'I want to be there for you and our daughter all the time. Not just have visiting rights when it suits you.'

'Back up. You want me to marry you. Sorry, but in my book marriage is the whole deal, or not at all. I'm opting for not at all. We don't love each other. Or know each other very well. Us getting together would be a carbon copy of what I grew up in—a cold, loveless environment where everyone puts themselves first. No, thank you. I couldn't wait to get away when I grew up. I never want my child feeling that way. It's horrible.' She stuffed a spoonful of lasagne into her mouth and stared at him with a dare in her eyes. Challenging him to refute what she'd said.

'We wouldn't be blaming our child for being together.' But even as he said it he knew he was wrong. If they didn't get along someone would pay the price and that would most likely be their daughter, even if she wasn't blamed for their mistakes.

Sophie spooned up more food and said nothing.

Which annoyed him. 'Okay, you might have a point.' But he needed to be doing the right thing for Sophie and the baby. It was inherent in him. 'Your parents are still together, right?'

Her head dipped in acknowledgement.

'Have you ever wondered why when they apparently hated each other so much?' She'd kill him now. No doubt about it.

But Sophie appeared stunned. After a long moment she said, 'I guess they think it's too late to go it alone.'

It wasn't much of an answer but he suspected she had no idea. Would she spend time thinking about her parents' relationship and try to see it in a different light now? He was sorry he'd put that disturbed look in her eyes. He reached across the table to take her hand. 'I was six when my mother died.' Now, where had that come from? 'She took her own life.'

Sophie blinked, but still remained quiet.

Actually, he was glad he'd told her. It felt right to explain his background, and take the focus off Sophie for a while. 'She suffered from OCD. I didn't understand what that meant for years. I just thought she didn't love me so found a way to leave so I couldn't follow.'

Sophie turned her hand over and interlaced her fingers with his. 'Your dad didn't explain?'

Mandy, don't leave me.

'I don't think he knew what I was thinking. He was a wreck himself, shocked to the core. He loved Mum and never thought she was capable of doing anything so drastic.' It had taken years for him to learn that much—his dad always ran shy of talking about the difficult years when Mum had been off the wall with her disorder.

'You must've been so lost.'

That was exactly what he'd been. 'Yes.'

The tender look Sophie gave him filled him with yearning for all the things he'd denied himself for so long.

Jerking his hand free, he leaned back in his chair. 'My dad stepped up to the mark for me. I always knew I could rely on him.' Dad had made sure he'd had everything he'd needed in the material sense, and he'd loved him. No doubt there. But he'd needed a mother too. Except his mother apparently hadn't needed him. 'It's important to me to do the same.' To bring home women and introduce them as his next great love, and then later explain how it hadn't worked out? No. Absolutely not.

Then you're going to live a celibate life?

No. Absolutely not, but he wouldn't be making rash statements about women being there for his child either.

Shoving her plate aside, meal unfinished, Sophie said quietly, 'I'm sorry about your mother. It must've been dreadful. You're lucky your dad was there for you.' Her shoulders rose as her chest expanded. 'But don't you see what you've told me? Your father brought you up single-handedly and you've done well. You and I can both bring up our child equally well without being joined by a piece of paper.'

'Not any old piece of paper.' Why wasn't he leaping with glee? Sophie had once again given him his freedom. Yes, he'd be there for his daughter, but without all the other stuff that being married would bring. It was the perfect solution. So, start leaping.

His feet were stuck to the floor, his body not up to moving with joy. This had to be the most bewildering experience he'd had as an adult. He'd put himself out there to meet his obligations, and had been turned down more than once, which had given him back the lifestyle he'd always enjoyed. A life of fun and women, and taking jobs anywhere he chose. The life he'd aimed for since he'd been a wee nipper. Yet now nothing felt right. Why? At the beginning of the week he'd applied for a permanent position at the hospital. But sorting out his personal life wasn't as easy to achieve.

Sophie stood up. 'I'll pass on coffee.'

As he waited for his credit-card payment to go through he studied the one woman capable of stirring his world with little or no effort just by being herself. Yes, she was beautiful, and that beauty was more than skin deep. The way she'd handled the birth of Jacob and his mother's distress had been little short of amazing, and now she visited Melanie every day to see how she was getting on. She cared, deep down, for people. Were strangers replacements for family and friends? If that was true, his daughter would still be in good hands. So would he if he ever needed her help, or even just her company.

'Can you remove your card, sir?' the waitress asked.

'Sorry, daydreaming.' He slid the card into his wallet and followed Sophie out to his car. Daydreaming about this woman who'd got his boxers in a twist. Unfortunately only mentally. He'd like nothing more than for her to be tugging them off his butt and dealing with him—after he'd sent her over the edge with an orgasm that would brand her as his.

Sex like they'd shared in Bamiyan. Off-the-scale sex. Typical. He was back to thinking about the physical with Sophie. Was that his problem? If they spent one hot night in the sack would all this turmoil disappear? There'd be no need to propose marriage, or suggest they share his home? Sex was the answer? If so, great. Bring it on. But he had a sinking feeling in his gut that he was so far off the mark he wasn't in for a good night's sleep this side of Christmas.

Rubbing her forehead, Sophie wished her headache away and snatched up the keys to the SUV Cooper had found for her yesterday. The mechanic had just given the all clear to buy it. 'Thanks, Graham. I'll head to the car lot and hand over the money.' A lot of money that would make a sizable hole in her savings. She'd spent more than she'd intended. Reliability and safety were top priorities, and Cooper had talked her into a newer model than she'd budgeted for. He'd offered to pay the extra, which had only got her back up and had her refusing his gesture.

She was doing a lot of that at the moment. Marriage. A home. And now money for the SUV. No one had ever made her so many kind offers before. In the end that's all his marriage proposals were. Kind. Generous. Considerate. Not binding in terms that would keep them together in a loving relationship. He didn't want a noose around his neck, and she had no doubt that's how he'd see her after a while.

Did *she* want that noose? It wouldn't be a snare if she loved Cooper. But it would be a one-way street and that she couldn't tolerate. Better to be in love and lonely but standing strong than to be wishful and despairing as her love got trampled on.

'Drop by any time if you need help attaching the baby seat.' Graham held the driver's door open for her to clamber in, bringing her back to reality and what she needed to do.

'Thanks.' What a kind man. He'd already gone out of his way to pick up the SUV for her. He'd had his office girl make her a mug of tea while she'd waited, and had filled in the change of ownership papers. Why couldn't she fall in love with a man like that? Not that she'd fallen in love with any man yet. Who was she kidding? Not even she was believing that line any more.

She had fallen for Cooper. It had happened when she hadn't been looking. Drip by drip, wearing down her resistance. What was there not to love about the guy? Throw in that he supported her and the baby already and she was toast.

But loving Cooper didn't mean marriage. He certainly didn't love her. His proposals had been all about obligations, nothing else. Cleverly worded, but obligations none the less. At least he had accepted he was the father and hadn't done a bunk. Not by a long shot. Better than she'd hoped for in those months before he'd found out.

The few kisses they'd shared had been devastating, undermining her every time. Sizzling. Demanding. Earthshattering.

Her phone rang from somewhere in the depths of her handbag. Pulling over, she put the gear shift into park and finally managed to find the phone just as the ringing stopped. The number on the screen was familiar, and one she'd avoided for too long. Her mother. She'd avoided Cooper's left-field query about why her parents were still together too. The answer could tip her off balance. Her belly tightened. She couldn't put off telling her parents about the baby any longer. Might as well get it over with. Then she could get on with her real life.

Back on the road she changed direction to head for the harbour bridge and the north shore. Her heart began a heavy pounding and her mouth dried. At every major intersection she had to fight not to turn around and head back to Parnell and Cooper's house. Her safe haven. Whatever her parents had to say when they learned about her pregnancy, it wouldn't be good. Worse, they were going to be hurt she'd kept it to herself for so long.

Then she was turning into the street she'd grown up in and there was no more time for prevarication.

'Mum, you're looking different.' Sophie stood back from hugging her mother. It wasn't the hairstyle or the chic clothes. No changes there. But there was a subtle difference she couldn't put her finger on.

'*I'm* looking different?' Her mother's gaze was fixed on the baby bump.

That's it.

'You're smiling.' Truly? Warmly. At her. Or at her extended stomach.

'Oh, Sophie, you're pregnant. That's wonderful.' Wonder filled her mother's eyes.

And shocked Sophie to the core. Her world lurched and she had to put a hand on the wall for balance.

'Jack, get in here and see what Sophie's brought us.'

Pardon? 'I didn't know Dad was at home. What about work?' How could her mother be pleased about that? It didn't make sense. Her mother only relaxed around the house when he was at work.

'I'm fully retired as of…' Her father stopped in the doorway. 'You're pregnant.' He stated the obvious.

'Yes.' Now that everyone was aware of the impending baby Sophie's tight muscles relaxed, allowing her stomach to push further out. 'Phew, that's hard work.' Then she thought of the explosion that would surely come as her parents got to grips with the situation, and her stomach tightened again.

'Sit down, darling, and tell us everything. When is the baby due? Who's the father? Anyone we know? Where is he?' Her mother hadn't taken her eyes off Sophie's tummy once.

Everything? I don't think so. You also don't know anyone I'm friends with.

She sank onto the couch and immediately her mother sat beside her, again shocking her, while her father took the armchair opposite. 'I'm due in five weeks.'

'You're tiny for being so far along.'

'I don't feel small, Dad. The midwife doesn't think so either.'

'So you've got that organised already.' Her mother settled back against the cushions, looking like she was there for the long haul.

She'd fill them in on some of the details and get on her way. 'I met my midwife last week, a few days after I got back. I apologise for not coming to see you sooner but I've had to find somewhere to live, buy furniture, a vehicle, and a hundred other things.' In other words, she'd been too busy. It was the standard excuse in this family and everyone understood it for what it was—easier to stay away and avoid the arguments.

'You're here now. That's what's important.'

Huh? Was this a dream? Would she wake up soon and find she was still in her SUV about to descend upon her parents and this was all wishful thinking? Put there by Cooper's crazy suggestion that her parents might not dislike each other? 'I'm currently staying with a friend.' Get it over with. 'He's the baby's father. I'm dossing down at his place until my apartment's ready to move into, which looks like being the day after tomorrow.'

'You're not going to live with this man?' her dad growled. 'He doesn't intend taking full responsibility for you and the baby?'

'Jack, that's enough.'

That's more like it. 'I'm not moving in with him. My choice. Not his.' If anyone should understand it would be her parents.

'He wants you with him?' her dad asked.

No, not really. He only thinks he does. 'Cooper's proposed and I've declined.' Before either parent could rant about that, she added, 'He's also suggested I live permanently in his house, if not as his partner then as a friend, so as he can be there for the baby. Again I said no.' Sophie sat back and waited for the eruption.

All she got from her mother was, 'You've always known your own mind. If this is what you think is right then we're behind you all the way.'

Her dad added, 'As long as you understand how hard it's going to be on your own with a baby.'

Things were getting stranger and stranger. Her father agreeing with her mother? Over something she'd done? They were even smiling at each other. How weird was that? 'Um, are you both all right?'

Do you like each other?

'Yes, darling. Why wouldn't we be?' her mother asked.

'You've brought us the most wonderful news. We didn't expect to become grandparents for a long time, with you so busy dashing off to exotic places around the world or working your tail off at the hospital.'

Dad said all that without a scowl.

Suddenly Sophie started laughing. This really was a dream. Had to be. There was no other explanation.

'Sophie? What's so funny?' Her mother looked worried.

She had no idea. Not really. Spluttering as she tried to control her hysteria, she managed, 'It's just baby brain.'

'It was totally odd,' Sophie told Cooper that night. 'I was with Mum and Dad for a couple of hours and not once did they as much as glare at each other, let alone give me a hard time. It was as though they like each other.'

'Maybe they do.' He looked smug.

'How's that possible after thirty-four years of disliking one another?' Why now? Because she didn't live with them any more? Couldn't be. She'd left years ago. Sophie shook her head. 'I *think* they were my parents.'

Cooper grinned. 'You want to get DNA done on them?'

It wasn't funny. It hurt. 'They seemed happy together, and that's an alien word in their relationship.' Or was that only when the three of them had been together? Her stomach sucked in on itself. She'd known she was the problem with their marriage, and now that she'd gone they were starting to find each other again. Ouch.

'Maybe they've woken up to the fact they've wasted a lot of years arguing, and now it's time to enjoy life together.'

'That would be too easy to accept.' But she wanted to. She was done with the pain her parents could inflict. Would love to let it all go and move on. Move on instead of racing away as though chased by an angry bull.

Cooper placed his hands on her shoulders. 'Give it a try. Take what they offer and forgive them for the past.'

Her eyes filled. 'Forgive them?' She choked. 'After a lifetime of pretending everything was fine? Of bearing the brunt of their unhappiness?' She shuddered.

'Yes, Sophie, exactly that.' Cooper's eyes were locked on hers. 'What's to lose?'

'My reasons for everything I do.' Gulp. She'd like to let it all go, she really would. But how?

'Our baby replaces that, surely?'

Hot tears spilled down her cheeks and she let them. 'Yes,' she whispered. Her daughter was her reason for living. Undeniable. She'd put her life on the line for her. Click, click went her spine. 'You're right. Thank you.'

For telling me how you see it.

Cooper's lips brushed her forehead. 'I'm here for you. Always.'

'Dad asked me to move home. As in he meant every word and was genuinely disappointed when I said no.' Which had blown her theory out of the water. Was it possible her mum and dad had fallen in love? Had the attraction that had resulted in her birth always been there but overshadowed by the responsibilities thrust on them by their upright, rigid families?

Cooper's face tightened. 'Nice to know I'm not the only one being turned down at the moment.'

Sophie waved a finger at him. 'I've done the right thing for all of us.'

I think. But then I am suffering from baby brain a lot. Could be I've got everything wrong. Even the bit about not loving Cooper.

Huh? No. She loved the man. No doubts. And that's where it stopped. She'd be strong, take this new twist in her life on her own, work it out day by day.

Everything was so complicated these days. What happened to just being a surgeon who worked hard to save money to go on exotic trips? *That* woman knew exactly what she wanted from life and didn't get sidetracked by cute little dresses with teddy bears romping all over them. Or by men built for sex. Or by a man with the biggest heart she'd come across, and a body she wanted to spend more time up close and personal with. A man who'd offered her more than she was able to deal with, was afraid to accept in case her heart was stomped on.

A man who'd just steered her in a completely different direction from any she'd gone in before.

Her blood moved faster as a thread of excitement sprang to life in her veins. She was going to be a mother— a loving, caring, happy mother. She would not bring her own childhood into this relationship with her daughter.

She would not argue and fight with Cooper when things didn't go her way.

She'd embrace her love for him and hope that it would set her free.

CHAPTER NINE

'TELL ME MORE about your childhood,' Cooper urged. After her revelation about her parents he wanted to know why Sophie felt so adamant about not marrying. Their lack of love, or inability to show it, didn't seem reason enough for Sophie to avoid marriage.

'What's to tell?'

Everything. He'd start slowly, ease his way around to the big questions—if he got the chance. 'You've never mentioned siblings. I take it you're an only child.'

'Mum and Dad didn't want me. Why would they have had more kids?'

The pain in her blunt reply churned his gut. He obviously hadn't understood how deep her anguish went. It had been wrong of her parents to have been so unloving. How could anyone not love Sophie?

He'd been busy in Theatre most of the day, yet all he'd been able to think about was how he needed to get home to see what Sophie had been doing. Had she done too much heavy lifting or moved some of that furniture by herself? Knowing she wouldn't hesitate worried him, yet the moment he'd walked in his front door all the tension had gone. Just like that. He'd come *home*. Home was where Sophie was. So he'd be without a home very shortly.

'Do *you* want more children?' The question popped out.

Her eyes widened. 'Let me get used to this baby first.'

'I always wanted a sister when I was growing up. Thought I'd have someone to share my thoughts about Dad's girlfriends with. But that probably wouldn't have worked out anyway, boys and girls seeing these things differently.'

Her chin lifted. Her eyes fixed on him. Sizing him up? Or deciding how much to say? Finally, 'I wanted a sister so that someone would love me and not blame me for everything.

'Someone to share the blame.' Sophie's eyes returned to normal size, the green beginning to sparkle. 'I think I would like another child in a couple of years. But I'm getting ahead of myself.'

'You might be, at that.' Cooper's gut squeezed tight. He didn't want to think of her having other children. Unless he was the father. What a strange picture that brought to mind. Two people, unmarried, not living under the same roof, having more than one child together. Not right. Neither was Sophie having this one on her own. He had to be there, be a part of their child's life all the time, not every second weekend.

Her shoulders lifted in an eloquent shrug. Then, thankfully, her mouth tipped upward in a cheeky smile. 'Relax. It's not happening—unless we're in the same place and a bomb goes off.'

'You need a bomb to fire you up into a wildly hot woman?' he asked before putting his brain into gear.

Her cheeks flushed an endearing shade of red. 'Only to leap into a complete stranger's arms.'

'For the record, we'd known each other five hours.'

'Exactly. Strangers.' She was looking everywhere but at him, that red shade deepening.

'I don't regret a moment of that amazing time.' A very short encounter he'd never forgotten. The surge of longing, the heat of her body around his, the intense release. The calm that had followed. 'Do you?'

Her hand patted her belly as her brow furrowed. When she looked directly at him it was as though he'd been hit with a stun gun. 'Me neither. Not at all,' Sophie whispered.

'Because you got a baby out of it?' His heart paused, his lungs holding onto the last breath he'd taken.

Coppery hair slid across her shoulders as she shook her head. 'That was a bonus.'

Not a regret. Neither was making love, if he'd interpreted correctly. The air hissed over his lips. His heart got back to normal, though still a little loud. 'I thought you were hot the moment I first saw you standing with Kelly.'

Surprise widened her eyes again. 'Sex in hard boots.'

'What?'

'You strode towards us like you owned the world, all lean, hard muscle and completely at ease with yourself. A man used to getting his own way.'

'You labelled me sex in hard boots?' Laughter was building up inside him. He'd never have guessed. 'I always believed if it hadn't been for the high level of tension we were feeling brought on by the bombs and bullets I'd never have got close enough to make love to you.' She hadn't been putting it out there to him.

'Kelly said it first and I couldn't deny she was right. Later, I knew it for a fact.'

She wasn't being coy about that night. Neither had she been at the time, throwing herself into his arms and wrapping those legs around him.

Cooper stood and crossed to lean down so that his face was close to hers. His arms were either side of her head, his hands splayed on the back of the couch she sat on with her legs tucked under her butt. 'You were sex in fatigues. Those boring old army outfits should've been banned from your wardrobe.' He'd never thought any woman looked great in them until he'd seen Sophie that day.

Tilting her head back, she locked her eyes on him. Amazing how bright that green was. Like highly polished emeralds. Her tongue did a quick lap of those full lips he'd taken a fancy to. *They're only lips.* Hot ones.

'I've still got a set somewhere.' She grinned.

'Are you suggesting we get dressed up?' To get undressed in a hurry if past experience with Sophie was anything to go by.

She leaned closer, her mouth brushing his. 'No.'

Cooper pushed nearer, his mouth on hers. Kissing Sophie was rapidly becoming his favourite pastime, and he'd happily take it further if she was willing. The edginess he'd felt from the moment he'd seen her in Darwin had got more intense over the weeks since. His manhood often ached with longing for her, keeping him awake for hours every night. 'I want you,' he whispered, afraid she'd leap up and go lock herself in her room. Not that she'd been backing off with their kiss.

Sophie placed her hands around his neck, pulled him down over her, her lips not leaving his mouth. Her legs straightened out and somehow she was nearly on her back. Actions were speaking louder than any words she might've said.

Cooper followed through, lying beside her, not quite covering her body, cautious of knocking that baby bump too hard. His hands sought her bare skin, sliding under the blouse and up to those heavy breasts. When his fingers found her nipples she drew a quick breath.

'Oh, yes, more,' she groaned.

Happy to oblige he slid further down to place his mouth over one tight nipple and ran his tongue back and forth until Sophie's back arched under him and her hands gripped his head. Holding him there. A groan poured through him as every part of his body tensed in sweet anticipation.

'We need to shift,' Sophie murmured by his ear.

Really? 'Not far,' he replied between licks.

'Easier if I'm on top.'

'No problem.' With Sophie in his arms he flipped them over. Immediately she straddled him, her moist centre touching, teasing, tempting him.

I've died and gone some place out of this world.

His hands roamed the stretched skin of her tummy and his lips trailed kisses down over the wondrous baby bump. Then Sophie was gripping him, rubbing against his body slowly, and he was lost.

Sophie woke smiling. Her body ached pleasurably. Her muscles were loose, sated for the first time in a long time. In more than eight months. That first time hadn't been enough.

Cooper's arm lay across what used to be her waist, and his regular breathing touched the back of her neck, making her warm and cosy. Happy even. She was with Cooper, in his bed, and she didn't want to be anywhere else. Everything was right in her world. Waking up next to this man was new to her. To do it again would be wonderful. After another night like the one they'd just shared. To do it every night would be incredible—and impossible. Reality would hover outside the door, ready to pounce if she got too complacent.

Kick, kick.

'Ouch.' Talk about a timely reminder.

Kick.

'You're hurting Mummy.' Though to be fair, baby would've been bounced around at times throughout the night.

'Good morning, beautiful.' Cooper propped on one

elbow to lean over her. 'How's our girl? We didn't wear her out, did we?'

Sophie took his hand and placed it where the baby was doing her morning warm-up routine. 'I wish.'

'Whoa. She's really going for it.'

'Have you thought of names for her?' Asking about names had never been on her list of things to discuss with Cooper. It should've been. No names that she'd first written down were making her smile.

Taking her chin between those fingers she remembered doing amazing things to her body during the night, Cooper forced her to turn so he could eyeball her expression. 'Thank you for asking. There are a couple I like but didn't think you'd want my input.'

She hadn't for a long time. But after all they'd shared over the past ten hours it was time to let go some of the fear of sharing that kept her alone. Besides, she was moving on now. If she and Cooper could spend a night together like the one she'd just woken from, then there was a lot more they could do together. The only reason they weren't was that she was still holding back, tying down her independence because to let any of it go terrified her. Her independence had been born of necessity, a way to survive the brutal onslaught of her parents' tirades. It had been the light she'd focused on, the future she needed to escape to. Despite deciding to let go of the past, it wasn't happening so easily. There were habits to break here. 'I said I'd never stop you having a part in baby's life. That includes choosing a name for her.'

He nodded, so she continued. 'I've got a list that's getting shorter by the day. I keep thinking I'll find something better. What names have you chosen?'

'Lily and Emma.'

'Lily. I like it.' Emma was on her list, but not Lily. 'Lily Ingram. That works.'

'So does Lily Daniels.'

Sophie winced. 'Ingram-Daniels. Bit of a mouthful.'

Cooper sat up. 'We know how to fix the problem. My offer's still on the table.'

A chill lifted the skin on her arms. They could share a night of mind-blowing sex. They could even agree on a first name for their child. But they would never agree about marriage. Rolling over awkwardly, she stood up from the bed, and immediately felt at a disadvantage as Cooper's gaze cruised her big, extended body. It was one thing to make love with him, but to stand here while he studied her was too much. Snatching up a pillow to hold against her, she headed for the door. 'I need to shower.'

'You are very beautiful, Sophie. Don't hide from me.'

She hesitated. Cooper hadn't watched her growing slowly, inch by inch over the months. He was getting the full-blown picture and not cringing. That said a lot for the man. It also told her that she needed to put a stop to this before she got in too deep. They were not having an intimate relationship. Despite spending the night in his bed exploring each other's bodies. Despite the warmth expanding through her even now when her legs were tense, ready to run.

No more running, remember?

'Nothing's changed. I can't marry you.' Okay, so some things would take for ever to change.

'Are you sure that's because of how your parents treated you growing up?' Determination was lighting up in his eyes. 'Or is there a deeper reason?'

Sophie wasn't sure at all any more. But one thing she'd swear was that she would not marry a man who did not love her. Even looking forward, that was non-negotiable. 'Whatever the reasons, they're mine. You need to get it into your head once and for ever that we are not tying the knot.'

Not waiting for his reply, she headed for the bathroom. Cooper was capable of talking her into making decisions that were wrong for her. She had to be strong as she worked out her future. Had to hold out for what was important to her, because that was important for her child. She couldn't accept the first offer that came her way. Even if it came from the only man who'd managed to rattle her with his caring ways, his kindnesses and his humour.

Don't forget his determination to see something through.

Exactly. That was why she was taking a shower and not another round in bed.

The sex in hard boots image had a lot to do with her wanting more of him. Her lungs expelled overheated air. But it went further. Behind that stunning face and hard body was the man who had her longing for a life she'd never believed in.

It's not possible, no matter that you love him.

'Sophie?' Cooper called down the hall. 'If you're that certain, why did last night happen?'

A very good question, and one she had no answer for except, 'I like sex. I like you. Why not?'

Her flippant words would sting him, but this was about keeping the wall erected between them.

The first step towards that was to move into her apartment.

'Then rest assured it won't be happening again. Neither will I propose again.' His voice was heavy with pain, the words silent hits against her heart.

She'd done a number on him, and for that she was very sorry. His pain cramped her stomach. Guilt made her squirm. She should've gone about it in a softer, kinder way, but he never took notice of anything she said. Until now. Harsh words had made a difference. Sometimes the sledgehammer approach was all there was. He'd finally got the message. He'd said so. No marriage. No sex.

Life was looking up.

She sank against the bathroom wall and pressed her fist against her mouth. From the mirror desolation stared her in the face.

Cooper glared out through the rain at his overgrown lawns. What did people do on a Saturday afternoon in weather like this? He'd spent the morning at the hospital, visiting his patients, talking to them about their surgeries and when to expect they might go home.

He'd even had a coffee with Svetlana as a delaying tactic against coming back to this empty shell of a home. The instant they'd sat down in the cafeteria he'd regretted asking her to join him. She'd read his invitation differently from how he'd meant it, and turning her down again hadn't sat comfortably with him. He didn't like deliberately hurting anyone. But what was a man to do?

There was no excitement within these walls. Since Sophie had moved out, not even leaving behind one piece of clothing or a book for him to hold, the place was back to being a house, not a home. She'd made the difference. Had made it warm with her personality, vibrant with her enthusiasm for their impending baby. Typical. The moment he'd realised how much he'd had with her she'd done a bunk.

So go grovel. Ask her to come back.

It wouldn't work. When Sophie said no she meant no. Changing her mind was mission impossible. Besides, there were only so many times he could handle being turned down. When she'd said she liked having sex with him his body had sat up but his heart had slowed at the reminder they wouldn't be getting married.

It went to show that other parts of his body were wiser than his heart and brain. Sex with Sophie was hot and, apparently, uninvolved. The only kind of sex he'd ever gone for. Now that his heart had decided to get in on the act everything was skewed. But he'd soon quieten that down. Had to. No other way to survive life post-Sophie.

Couldn't she see he was only trying to do right by her and the baby? Grinding his teeth, he held back the oath threatening to emerge.

His phone vibrating in his pocket was a welcome distraction. 'Hey, Dad, how was your trip?' he asked.

'Hello, son. Queenstown's got to be the best place to visit in winter. We visited Arrowtown, went tobogganing on Coronet Peak without breaking a leg, and I won't mention the fabulous waterfront restaurants.'

We. Cooper sighed. *Here we go again.*

Dad had another young woman to trot out and about. At least *he* didn't go for ridiculously younger females. 'When did you get back?'

'Last night. Which is why I'm ringing. You at home, by any chance? Thought I'd drop by and catch up on what you've been doing.'

'Sure thing.' His afternoon wouldn't be so dull any more. Spending time with his father was never boring, even if it was sometimes uncomfortable, depending on his latest conquest.

'I'm bringing someone with me I'd like you to meet.'

Nothing new in that. 'I'll make sure there's a bottle of wine in the fridge.' Make that two. Might as well enjoy the afternoon and drown out thoughts of Sophie for a few hours.

'It's a pleasure to finally meet you, Cooper,' the woman his father had introduced as his 'special friend', Gillian, held out her hand.

Knock me down.

Cooper took the proffered hand, trying to hold his

mouth from falling open. 'I have to say the same.' A special friend was nothing new. But Gillian was lovely in a completely different way from Dad's previous encounters. Dressed in simple black trousers with a blouse that didn't expose acres of flesh, she was refreshing. *And* she'd definitely left her thirties decades ago. 'Delighted.'

'I'm not staying long,' Gillian told him as she accepted a glass of wine. 'I need to hit the supermarket, and I'm sure you both have plenty to talk about without me butting in all the time.' She gave him a knowing wink before turning to his father. 'Don't forget to ask Cooper if that date suits him.'

His father smiled softly. 'Not likely to, am I?'

Something was up. Cooper's gut had begun churning and turning sour in an old familiar way. At thirty-eight years old his stomach should know it was wasting acid. Whatever his dad did he did, and that was that. The only hope he could come up with was that his father hadn't decided to sell up and invest his money in some offshore scam. Though that was highly unlikely, the old man being shrewd with his money, if not with women.

The churning continued, but Cooper refused to ask any questions. He knew they only brought answers he wouldn't like. He'd wait until his father came out with it.

Which he did before the front door had closed behind Gillian. 'We're getting married, son. Next month. Eighth of October, to be exact.'

Kapow! Dad was settling down. With a woman his own age, and who didn't look like she'd promise the earth and leave anyway. 'Dad.' He choked up. He spun a chair around and straddled the seat. The back rest was essential for his arms, which in turn held his head up.

'You'd never have guessed, would you?' If anyone wondered what a smile from ear to ear really looked like, they only had to look at his father right now.

'You care about Gillian that much?' Role reversal here. Not that his father had had the opportunity to quiz him about any particular woman becoming a permanent fixture in his life. *Sophie*. Yeah, right. No need for questions when she wasn't interested.

'Yes, I do. I want to give her everything. I want a proper relationship and I know I'll have it with Gillian.'

This could be good for the old man, who'd been lonely since his mother had left them. He was a man who didn't like his own company too much and filled the empty gaps with women. Until now completely unsuitable women.

A man just like me.

Gasp. Give over. Not true at all. Then why did he move around a lot? Join organisations like the army where time alone was a rarity? Because he wanted to give something of himself to his country. Sure. That came into it, but it was hardly his primary motivation.

'Cooper? Are you not happy for me?' His father sounded worried, annoyed even. 'I assure you Gillian is a wonderful woman, and you won't change my mind.'

'I'm thrilled. Seriously.' He stood and reached to wrap his arms around his father. 'I can see she's lovely.' Why had it taken this long for the old man to find someone more suited to him?

Stepping out of the hug, his father sat down and stretched his legs out. 'I just wish I'd met her twenty years ago.'

Cooper sprawled over the couch. 'Guess them's the breaks, eh?'

'You'll be at the wedding? It's going to be small, just Gillian's daughters and their husbands, and grandchildren, and you.'

'Try keeping me away.' For something as huge as this he was accepting it too easily. His stomach had returned to quiet mode, his arms no longer felt tingly and useless.

'I've always wanted this for you.' And thereby for himself. Then his tongue got away from him, which only went to show he hadn't quite accepted his father's news yet. 'You're not rushing this?'

His father beamed contentedly. 'Neither of us is getting any younger. There's a reason why that's a cliché.'

'Come to think of it, I haven't seen you so relaxed in years.' If ever. Which wrapped it up for Cooper. 'You're happy. I'm thrilled.'

'Yes, son, I am. Gillian makes me feel calm—about everything.' He raised an eyebrow. 'And we both know how stressed I usually get about anything and everything.'

'True.' Something he'd inherited to some extent but did better at controlling than Dad.

'It's not what she does but how she comports herself, dealing with situations in an orderly, quiet manner.'

'I know what you mean,' Cooper muttered.

'You do?'

'Yeah.' Shock rippled through him. 'I do.' Sophie did that for him. The first time had been when that bomb had blown their world apart. She'd got back on her feet and immediately began assessing the situation from a medical point of view, giving orders, saving lives. That calm ability to prioritise and make sure Kelly and the others had got the absolute best care while chaos had reigned around them had settled his pounding heart and put his fear on the backburner. He knew he'd looked in control, but internally he'd been a mess.

Since then there'd been other instances where a look or word from Sophie and his worry settled. 'I totally get you.'

'Who is she?' his dad asked, with a knowing gleam in his eye.

'Sophie.' Oh, hell. The baby. Reality clanged into his head. 'What date did you say you're getting married?'

'October the eighth. Is there a problem?' His dad's mouth tightened. 'I want you there.'

Cooper stood up and paced across the room. Turned, came towards his father. Be calm. How could he?

Sophie, where are you when I need you? I'm about set off another grenade.

His chest rose on an indrawn breath. Think of Sophie and how she calmed him.

Sophie.

'Dad.' His fingers rammed through his hair. 'How do you feel about becoming a grandfather?'

CHAPTER TEN

'HELLO, JACOB.' SOPHIE took Melanie's baby and held him close. 'How's my favourite wee man this morning?' Tears threatened. That had been happening a lot today. Baby brain? Confusion over her relationship with Cooper? Waking up alone in her cold apartment? All of the above and more.

'Grizzly, hungry and tired,' Jacob's mother retorted. 'But I wouldn't change a thing if it meant being without him.' Her face lit up with love.

Sophie sat on the second chair in the kitchenette of the tiny flat supplied by social welfare that Melanie had moved into with her help. 'I can't wait to hold my baby now.' Since Jacob's arrival the birth of her daughter had become very real. After talking with Melanie, so were the sleepless nights, the constant crying and disgusting nappies. None of which dampened her excitement. Bring it on. Bring her on.

'Counting down the days, are you?' Melanie asked, with a worried look at Jacob. 'I didn't do that. I was so afraid of the pain, as well as worrying what I'd do afterwards.'

I bet you were.

'I don't want her coming too early. But I'm so ready it's hard waiting.' She wouldn't wish health issues on her child just for the sake of a few days, but she'd had enough of carrying this bulge around.

'I had a visitor today,' Melanie said quietly. 'My mum.'

The mother who'd kicked her daughter out of her home months ago. 'How did that go?'

'She wants me to have Jacob adopted so I can get on with my life. She says I have no idea what it's going to be like, giving up everything for a child, and I'm going to regret it for the rest of my life.'

A chill slid up Sophie's spine. Hadn't her mother complained often about how she'd given up everything for her? How she'd had to stop her nursing training, how she'd married the wrong man, how her life had become dull and pointless. All because of her daughter.

Thanks, Mum.

'She won't budge on her stance?'

A fat tear slid down Melanie's face as she shook her head. 'I thought she loved me, but she won't listen to what I want. I'm supposed to make something of my life. Being a mother doesn't count.'

The bitterness appalled Sophie. But she also understood it—because she'd been there. Was sometimes still stuck there, but now she was slowly edging her way ahead. Listening to Melanie's tale only strengthened her resolve to do what was right for her baby and not what her heart wished. She'd been right to turn Cooper down about marriage and even about sharing his house. 'Don't let them beat you. You are strong, and on the days you don't think you can cope you've got my number.' She'd come to care a lot for this tough young woman in a very short time. 'We'll work our way through your problems.'

'Thanks for the *we*. It means a lot. Now, I'd better feed Jacob before he screams the roof down and the neighbours complain.'

He had become very vocal in the short time Sophie had

been holding him. 'Hey, wee man, talk nicely to Mummy. She's the drinks trolley.' Standing up, she stretched and rubbed the small of her back. 'I'd better get cracking.' Cooper had asked if he could visit her on his way home from work.

Of course she'd said yes, because she hadn't found the strength to do otherwise. She missed him. Her apartment was cosy but nothing like Cooper's comfortable home where she'd loved curling up on the sofa with a book and coffee. She wanted to say that the difference was in the size of the apartment, but it wasn't. It was in the lack of Cooper's company. She'd enjoyed sharing a meal with him, and discussing surgery, and the army and life in general, in finding socks on the bathroom floor. Just knowing he lived there had put her at ease in a way she'd never experienced.

'You're looking tetchy.' Cooper grinned at her when she opened her front door to his knock. 'Will these cheer you up?' He held out a bunch of daffodils. 'First of the season, though it doesn't feel like spring today.'

A gust of cold wind underlined his words. Shivering, she took the bright yellow bundle. 'They're lovely.' Moisture dampened the corners of her eyes. Cooper had brought her flowers? He'd rung her each day since she'd moved out nearly a week ago, always friendly and chatty, always asked if there was anything she needed doing. Not once had he made a comment about them being together for the baby's sake. She didn't know this Cooper, and wasn't sure how to take him.

'I thought so.' He looked as pleased as he sounded.

'Come in so I can shut the not-so-spring-like weather out.' Heading into her small lounge, she suddenly stopped. 'I don't own a vase.'

'Not used to getting flowers, then?' He chuckled.

'Ego.' No, she wasn't. 'I'll put them in the coffee

plunger.' It was the only tall, narrow container that came to mind. Put on shopping list one vase. Just in case. 'Want a wine?'

'Got bourbon, by any chance?'

Add bourbon to the list. 'Sorry. Since I'm not drinking I haven't filled the cupboard with spirits.' And she was saving on the dollars that had dwindled far too rapidly since returning from Darwin.

'Wine will be fine. Shall I get it while you're arranging those daffodils? Oh. Very classy.'

She'd pulled the paper from around the stalks and dropped the flowers into the plunger. 'There. Arranged.' She added water and placed the colourful bunch in the middle of her new table. 'They brighten the place up heaps.'

'How was your day? Did you see the midwife again?' He leaned that delectable butt against the bench, bottle in one hand, glass in the other.

'Yes, and all's good. My BP's hovering on borderline low but that's better than where it used to be.' Thank goodness. That had been scary.

'And your glucose?'

'No change.' She'd been meticulous in avoiding sugary foods from the moment she'd learned she had diabetes. No way was she hurting her baby, neither did she want the diabetes to continue after the birth. 'I paid Melanie a quick visit. Jacob's a treat. I'd swear he's growing already.'

'How's Melanie coping?'

'She's awesome with Jacob, considering she's only eighteen and on her own. Her mother's paid a visit, apparently pushing her to put the baby up for adoption. Even said she knew a couple who'd take him.' At least her parents hadn't done that to her, though she might've been loved better if they had. She'd never know, and she didn't think the answer had been for her to be adopted out. They were *her* parents, and she did love them in an oddball kind of way. And since visiting them to drop her news in their laps she'd begun to think they might reciprocate that love after all.

'Sophie? You're looking sad when moments ago you were all smiles.'

'Why are some parents so assertive? What's wrong with asking Melanie what she wants and trying to help her achieve that?' Her own doubts flooded in, cooling her skin and making her shiver. What if she couldn't be the mother she hoped to be, the mother she'd have adored as she'd grown up?

'Come here.' Cooper wrapped his arms around her. 'You're going to be the best mum yet.'

She should pull away from this man, who was becoming very adept at reading her, but it felt so right being held by him, leaning against that hard body. She needed his strength today. Her own ability to stand strong had gone on holiday, leaving her prone to pointless tears. Even better, though, Cooper apparently believed in her. That was gold. Tipping her head back to look at him, she said, 'You sound so sure. Thank you. It makes a difference.'

'Only speaking the truth.'

Even when he didn't know her well. Breathing deeply, she pulled away before it became impossible to leave him. 'What have you been up to today?' She flipped the conversation onto him and away from all her insecurities. Enough of them for one day.

He picked up his glass, his soft, caring gaze still on her. 'The usual follow-ups with patients, appointments with new ones, and an emergency gall-bladder operation.'

'That sounds like fun. I'm envious.'

'Fun is not the word I'd use, though, yes, I still get a kick out of performing surgery. Why the envy?'

'I'm bored.' More tears threatened, which was ridiculous. What was wrong with her to be acting like a spoilt brat? Looking around the apartment, the answer was obvious. 'Now that I've got everything ready here and have bought more clothes and toys than baby will ever use, I'm missing work.'

'You're restless. Find me a thirty-seven-week pregnant woman who isn't. When did you last perform an operation?'

'Two days before you turned up in Darwin. An appendectomy.' Serious work had been referred to the local hospital.

'Nothing too taxing, then.' He sipped his wine. 'Make the most of this time. I bet once the baby comes you won't have a moment to spare.'

'Yeah, yeah. I know all that. But I've never been one to sit around, and I've already had my fill of the malls.'

'And I was sure you're a female.' Cooper gave her one of his delectable smiles.

The kind that went straight to her libido. Damn him. Sex was not happening. Not now, not ever again. So a distraction was needed. 'Want to grab something to eat and take in a movie?'

As distractions went it worked—sort of. Sophie managed to tamp down her libido as she ate her burger and chips. It helped that while he ate his second burger Cooper annoyed her by pointing out that fast food was not healthy. Then the movie enthralled her and all thought of sex was forgotten.

Until she climbed into her lonely, cold bed and tried to go to sleep. Big fail. Wrapping her arms around herself to find some warmth, all she could think was what if Cooper had come in instead of dropping her off at the door? Would they have ended up in bed, making out? Would he now be kissing hot, slick trails over her breasts and down to where she throbbed with need? Would she have given in to her longing? Or would she have fought it, pushing him away once again?

You're never going to know.

Right now she had to snuggle tighter and forget Cooper. Forget she loved him, and focus on her own life and how everything was now about the baby. Starting with getting some sleep.

Not happening. Deep breathing didn't work. Swapping from her left side to her right was no better. Even when her body warmed, sleep remained elusive.

Rolling onto her back, she stared up at the dark ceiling.

Cooper brought me flowers.

The last time anyone had done that had been in her third year at med school and she'd been going out with one of her fellow students. It had been her twenty-third birthday and he'd taken her to dinner at his father's restaurant. That's when she'd understood he'd been far too serious about her and she'd pulled the plug on their relationship. Somehow she didn't think Cooper was about to walk away from her. Not when he'd proposed twice. She had done her darnedest to push him away, but it seemed he didn't know when to give up.

You're not being fair. If you don't want to settle down with Cooper then don't keep him on a string.

She hadn't known she was.

You went out with him tonight, didn't you? You accepted those flowers.

The warmth left her body. Had she been a bitch? Using Cooper when she was out of her depth with this pregnancy? As if anyone could keep him dangling. He was in charge of his own life. But one thing was true. She'd been unfair. All because she loved him, and at the moment needed his steady presence.

So why the flowers?

* * *

The doorbell rang as Sophie was just about to throw something at the wall in boredom. 'Coming,' she yelled in relief.

But when she yanked the door open and was confronted with two burly guys, leaning against what appeared to be a large chair wrapped in padded plastic wrap, disappointment tugged. 'I think you've got the wrong address.'

'Sophie Ingram? This isn't Apartment Three, The Willows?' One of the guys deliberately stared at the bronze three on her doorframe.

'Yes, but that's not mine.' Her finger stabbed in the direction of the chair.

The other guy tugged a packing slip from his pocket and read it. 'Yes, it is. Bought and signed for yesterday by a…' He squinted. 'Cooper Daniels.'

Her jaw dropped. Cooper had bought her a chair? Whatever for? She had two reasonably comfortable ones in her lounge and there was no room for another, even if she needed it.

A chair is bigger and says more than daffodils.

'You know this dude?' one of the men asked.

'Yes.'

I thought I did. But he's buying me things. Gifts. Hadn't expected that.

'You'd better come in.' She glanced at her doorway. 'How are you going to fit the chair through this gap?'

'No problem. We're instructed to put it in your bedroom.'

Clang. Her jaw was behaving badly this morning. 'My bedroom?' She'd be needing to knock a wall down to make space. 'I think you should put it in the lounge.'

'It says here that we've got to put the chair in your bedroom.' The guy squinted at the docket again and grinned.

'And that we're to take no notice of the lady if she insists otherwise.'

'You'll have to shift my bed,' she acquiesced.

'Not a problem.' Grin-face chuckled. 'You don't look in any state to be moving heavy furniture, if you don't mind me saying.'

Did she have a choice?

Just you wait, Cooper Daniels.

But after the men had managed to fit the chair into a corner of her room by manoeuvring the dresser to one side and the bed in another direction, and had gone away, she'd removed metres of plastic wrap to find a leather rocking chair that matched her furniture perfectly. No denying the gift was thoughtful and caring. Like Cooper. A nursing chair was exactly what she wanted and hadn't been able to justify spending money on.

'Last weekend I met someone whom I quite like,' Cooper told Sophie on Friday night when he turned up at her apartment after work.

Sophie's heart stopped. Cooper had met a woman? One he liked? What about…? Her? Their baby?

'Her name's Gillian and she's in love with my dad. They're getting married.'

Sophie's knees sagged in relief. Leaning against the table for strength, she said, 'Married? I'm glad you like her.' Phew. But she shouldn't have been worrying. If she wasn't marrying him then she had no right to be disgruntled.

Cooper pulled a chair out from the table. 'Sit down. You look ready to drop. Ah, not as in about to have the baby.'

Sinking onto the chair, she leaned her elbows on the table and lowered her chin into her shaky hands. 'Tell me more.'

And divert me from the shock of that sudden stab of jealousy.

Cooper twirled his bourbon glass between his finger and thumb. 'Dad started dating within a year of Mum's death. I guess he was lonely.' His throat worked as he sipped his drink. The silence stretched out between them. A shudder jerked through him. 'Dad had a succession of young women, none staying long. Though the second one did hang around for nearly a year and I thought at the time she might become my stepmum. It didn't happen.' He put his glass down with a bang. 'Anyway, this isn't about me. Gillian's close to Dad's age and they're in love. It's so odd seeing Dad tripping over himself to please her. Not that Gillian takes advantage. She's just as busy making him happy.'

Sophie wished she could have a drink too. Seemed everyone was fixing up their lives lately. Maybe there was hope for her one day.

Cooper continued, 'The thing is, I told Dad about the baby, and he and Gillian want to meet you. You're also invited to the wedding, though there's a problem there. It's on the same day as Junior is due.'

Sophie's head was whirling. 'Slow down. I can't keep up.' She didn't want to. This was too much. Cooper's father and soon-to-be wife wanted to meet her, presumably as grandparents-to-be. Why had she never considered this? Cooper had hardly ever mentioned his family so she'd not thought it through. It wasn't all bad. Not bad at all really. 'Our baby will have four grandparents.' A smile began lifting her mouth as her heart warmed. 'That's wonderful.'

'Agreed. Did you hear the rest of what I said?'

'No. Wait. The wedding date. It's the same as our girl's expected arrival.' Her buoyant mood sank. Naturally Cooper would want to attend his father's nuptials. Until this moment she hadn't realised how much she was depending on him being with her for the birth.

'How many babies arrive on their due date?' Cooper asked with a smile. 'Let's wait and see what happens. I am going to be there for the birth, Sophie. Our baby comes first.'

Hope flittered through her, to be followed by pain. 'I can't ask you to forego your father's wedding.'

'You didn't. I'm telling you. I am not missing my daughter's birth.' His smile was so soft and intoxicating it made her want to curl up on his lap.

So she remained on her chair and waited for this particular brain fade to settle back to normal.

'Feel like going round the corner for Thai?' he asked before she'd got herself under control.

Thai, Indian, burgers. She didn't care what she ate. She'd be with Cooper for another hour or so. The sigh that escaped her was full of excitement.

So much for restraint around this man.

Glad of the mask covering his lower face, Cooper relaxed into a smile as he began the final layer of sutures on Jason Mowbray's abdomen.

Last night Sophie's face had been a picture when she'd heard his father wanted to meet her. There'd been no doubts whatsoever about Dad becoming a grandfather—he'd embraced the whole situation in an instant. Sophie had been just as accepting of his father's place in her baby's life.

She'd kill him if she knew how hard he was trying to get her to rethink her stance on getting married. Getting her to meet his father and Gillian was all part of the plan.

The chair had been a huge hit. For a moment when she'd first rung after it'd been delivered, he'd wondered if he'd gone too far. He had been prepared to argue his case, which was that as the baby's father he was entitled to look out for the baby's mother. The argument hadn't eventuated, Sophie being ecstatic about the chair and forgetting to be annoyed at his interference.

Cooper dropped the suture needle into the kidney dish and straightened up, rubbing his lower back with one hand. 'Right, that's done.' Nodding at Becky, the anaesthetist, he added, 'Let's bring him round.'

'That tumour wasn't as large as you'd predicted,' the senior registrar on the other side of the table commented.

'Something to be thankful for.' Jason still had a rough time ahead, with chemo and radiation as soon as today's wounds healed. The guy was only thirty-five. Far too young to be dealing with cancer.

Cooper had seen it all before, often, and always wondered what was ahead for him. Life was unpredictable, was meant to be grabbed with both hands. He knew it. Yet he'd been so restless for so long, not knowing what he wanted to be doing—to be grabbing.

You haven't been restless since landing in Darwin last month.

Because of Sophie. Yeah, he got it. Seeing that she and the baby wanted for nothing, were safe and cared for, was his focus at the moment.

There were more ways of proving to her that he could be a good father and ideal partner than by putting his future in her hands with marriage proposals. Empty proposals. If only he'd known his true feelings for her before putting them out there, he might've convinced her he meant it. Might've told her he loved her. He froze. His hands clenched. No, he would not have done that.

It had taken his father's comment about how Gillian calmed him, centred him, for *him* to realise Sophie did the same for him. She was the centre of his universe. He was still reeling with accepting what that meant. That he loved her—with every cell of his body. Now he had to show her. He wouldn't think about what he'd do if she never came round. Probably go back to the army and transfer offshore. No, he wouldn't. He had a daughter to factor into any moves he made now.

'Cooper? You all right?' Becky was peering at him with a worried look.

'Yes.' The bones in his fingers cracked as he unclenched them one by one. Couldn't be better. 'How's Jason doing?'

'Coming round slowly.'

As per normal, then. Air huffed from his lungs. Thank goodness. He still needed to know his patient had come through the anaesthesia before he fully relaxed after every procedure he performed. A leftover from the very first operation he'd performed as a consultant when the woman had had a fatal cardiac arrest as she'd been coming round. Not his fault and yet he'd carried the guilt ever since. 'Right, take him through to Recovery.'

Becky nudged him. 'Got time for a coffee before going to talk to Jason?'

He always tried to have a moment with his patients in Recovery, hopefully reassuring them as they fought their way through the post-anaesthetic haze. 'Put the kettle on. I'll grab my phone.'

Urgency drove him to his locker. He'd been out of communication for two and a half hours. What if Sophie needed him? The blood was racing around his body as he tapped the screen. No new messages. He sagged against the locker in relief.

'That baby's certainly got you in a twist.' Becky was shaking her head at him. 'Like all first-time dads.'

'That obvious, huh?' Hauling himself upright, he shoved the phone in his pocket and slammed the locker shut. 'There's less than three weeks to go. I'm going to be shattered by the time she does make an appearance.'

Becky just laughed. 'That's only the beginning.'

Not really. But she didn't know he wouldn't be dealing with the interrupted sleep, the midnight feeds and dirty nappies.

But the days were speeding past. By the time the baby arrived he hoped he'd have made inroads with getting closer to Sophie. He loved her. No argument. Winning her over was proving to be a hurdle.

Proposing for a third time was not an option. He couldn't take rejection again. Not when he finally understood how much he loved her. Hearing Sophie say no now would break his heart into so many pieces he doubted his ability to put them back together. He just had to continue spending time with her, helping her get prepared for the birth and doing the little things with the hope she'd begin to appreciate having him around.

'Here, get that into you.' A mug of murky coffee appeared before him.

A train whistle sounded from his pocket. *Sophie?* Coffee slopped on the floor as he fumbled for the phone. His ear hurt where the phone hit. 'Hello? Sophie? What's happening?'

'We're on.' A breathless gurgling sound followed her sentence.

'Are you laughing?' Couldn't be in labour, then.

'Sort of,' she gasped around a groan. A long groan that had nothing to do with laughter and everything to do with pain.

His stomach clenched, his jaw tightened. Sophie was in pain.

Sophie's in labour.

And he was here in the hospital, doing nothing to help her. 'Where are you?' The coffee mug hit the table. His scrubs flew across the room in the general direction of the laundry basket. 'I'm on my way.'

Erratic breathing came from the phone. 'Cooper.' His name was ground out. 'I need you. Now. At the maternity unit.'

'On my way.' Yeah. She needed him. He slumped forward. Was he up to speed with this? Could he help or would he be a hindrance?

'Cooper? Is the baby coming?' Becky was wiping up spilled coffee.

His head jerked. Pulling himself straight, he looked the anaesthetist in the eye. He was strong, he did not flinch at the first sign of trouble. He would be there with Sophie, for Sophie, all the way through the birth. 'Yes. I've got to go. Can you see Jason, explain and tell him I'll be in to see him later?'

He didn't wait for her reply.

He barely waited for the traffic lights to turn green.

As for the lift up to the maternity unit? Forget it. He took the stairs two at a time.

'Which room?' he yelled as he charged towards reception. 'Sophie Ingram.'

'Right behind you.' A midwife chuckled.

The door banged against the wall as he tripped over his own feet and fell through it. 'Hey, Sophie, I'm here.'

'I think everyone on this floor is aware of that.'

Cooper stared at the woman standing by the window, looking for all the world completely relaxed, like she had nothing pressing to do. 'Why are you so calm?'

Because she's Sophie, that's why.

'You didn't sound composed on the phone.' Not at all.

'That's because—' Sophie gasped, leaned forward to wrap her arms around her belly, the muscles in her neck cording as a contraction seized her.

'Hey…' Cooper stepped up, wound his arms right

around her. 'I'm here, sweetheart.' She was tense, her whole body contorted with pain. How could he take that away from her? Take the pain into his body for her?

She sank against him, her body now limp. 'That was the worst yet.'

Using his palm, he rubbed gentle circles over her back. 'When did you start labour?'

'About two hours ago. I couldn't find my phone to call you. It was in my bag all along.' When she lifted her head she gave him a watery smile. 'It's happening. Our baby's coming. I can't believe it.'

Cooper's heart crunched at the sight of her misty eyes filled with awe. Leaning down, he brushed his lips across her mouth. 'You look beautiful.'

Those emerald orbs widened, and she gave him a sweet smile. 'You're delusional.'

Then the smile snapped off, the eyes tightened into slits and she was gripping his shoulders, hanging on grimly as her body took another hit.

'Remember to breathe.' The midwife appeared beside them. 'You're doing fine, Sophie.'

'There wasn't long between the last two contractions,' he noted.

The midwife nodded. 'I think this wee girl is in a bit of a hurry. Time for another examination, Sophie.'

Um, should he disappear for a few minutes? But he wanted to be with Sophie all the way. She shouldn't be on her own at all. The midwife didn't count as a special support person. He locked eyes with her. 'I can wait outside.'

Warmth stole through him when she shook her head. 'Not necessary. Stay and hold my hand.'

So calm. So Sophie.

Cooper wanted to retract those words later when Sophie cried out with pain and squeezed his hand to breaking point. All semblance of calm had taken a hike.

'You're doing great,' he told her as her body tensed under the power of another contraction.

'Huh. Like you'd know.'

'You've got me there.'

'Don't be smart. Shut up and hold me.'

Yes, ma'am.

Catching her around the waist, he tugged her gently so she was draped over him. Putting his hands to good use, he began softly massaging the knots in the muscles around her shoulders.

Knots that returned within minutes as another contraction took over.

Cooper started again. Stopped to hold her as she worked through the pain gripping and squeezing at her. Started massaging, stopped to hold, massage, hold. Time became a blur.

Until the midwife told Sophie, 'Time for another examination.'

Then he held Sophie's hand while they waited for the verdict.

'Baby's crowning. We're almost there. You're doing really well, Sophie.'

Cooper kissed the back of Sophie's hand. 'You're amazing.'

Emerald became sort of green-grey as Sophie's eyes turned misty. 'I'm glad you're here with me. With us.'

Who knew what colour *his* eyes were now? They were certainly wetter than normal, and his voice croaked as he said, 'We're a family.' One way or another.

Surprisingly he didn't get slapped for saying that. Instead, Sophie pulled his head down to kiss him. A full lips-on-lips kiss that spoke of happiness and love and exhaustion.

The kiss finished abruptly as Lily Ingram-Daniels

rushed into the world, giving her mother one last, long grip of pain.

When Lily eventually obliged the midwife with a cry Sophie reached for her baby, all trace of pain gone from her face, replaced with love so strong and fierce Cooper had no doubt his daughter was in the very best of hands.

Cooper's body was racked with relief and love, with amazement and fear as he gazed at his daughter. He would love this wee girl for the rest of his life, would do anything to protect her and keep her happy. He feared what could happen to her and knew that was never going to leave him. He'd become a father.

Slashing his hand over his eyes and across his cheeks didn't stop the flood of tears, just as others streaked down Sophie's cheeks. If he hadn't loved her before this moment then he'd have fallen for her right now. Her sweat-slicked skin glistened, her damp hair clung to her face, and she was the most beautiful sight he'd ever seen. *They* were. Mother and daughter.

'She's got your colouring,' Sophie said without taking her eyes off her girl.

'As long as she's got your nature.' He grinned.

Then Sophie did look up at him. 'Sit on the bed.' She held her precious bundle out to him. 'Come on, Dad, meet your daughter properly.'

His knees buckled, depositing him beside Sophie with a thump. His arms were reaching for Lily even before he'd shuffled his butt further onto the bed. And then his arms were full of the sweetest, softest little girl he'd ever known. He stared at her, drinking in the cutest little nose, the few strands of dark hair, the clenched red fist that had pushed free of the blanket.

'Here.' Sophie leaned forward with a tissue to mop his face. 'You're going to drown her at this rate.'

The midwife cleared her throat. 'The paediatrician wants to see Lily to make sure everything's fine.'

Sophie's chin shot up as she asked, 'What are you concerned about?'

Cooper's heart stopped.

Please, no. Pick me, leave my daughter alone.

'Nothing's wrong. Around here it's routine to have babies checked over by any specialist who's hanging around the joint.'

Sophie sighed. 'That's good. Thank you.'

Cooper knew he was grinning like a loon but didn't care. 'Baby brain eh? And you thought it would be gone the moment little miss here put in an appearance.'

She whacked his arm softly. 'Thanks a lot.' Her eyes followed Lily as the midwife took her away. That perpetual smile faded.

'Hey…' He wrapped both her hands in his. 'Relax. She's going to be fine. So are you. Hopefully you'll get some sleep tonight.'

Her nose screwed up in annoyance. 'Whatever's best for baby, I know, but I'd prefer to be going home now.'

'You have to learn to feed Lily first.'

'Why, isn't it as easy as it looks?'

'You're asking me?' He grinned. It might be weeks before his mouth returned to normal. 'But I can hang around to keep you from getting bored.'

And watch over his girls.

CHAPTER ELEVEN

SOPHIE COULDN'T BELIEVE she'd fallen asleep. Not when her baby was in the crib right next to her bed. How could she not have stayed awake to watch over her? She pushed up onto an elbow and peered into the crib, marvelled at the sweet face and the tiny body wrapped in a blanket.

I produced that?

Pride filled her before worry took over.

I went to sleep. How could I?

'I've been keeping an eye on you both,' Cooper said softly from the other side of her hospital room.

Thank goodness someone had. 'How long have I been out?'

'An hour. And relax. You needed it. Lily's been sleeping the whole time but I think the nurse will be in shortly to watch you feed her.' He looked so at ease with all of this.

Sophie felt her heart lift as she studied him. 'I couldn't have done any of this on my own and there's no one else I'd have wanted there for the birth.' Not even her friend who had intended being her birthing partner.

'I wouldn't have missed it for anything.'

Unless she'd been an idiot and not allowed him in the room. But she hadn't. At least she'd had the sense to see he had every right to be there, and in return she'd had the best partner imaginable. 'You were awesome. Didn't know you could massage like that.' His hands on her back and shoulders had been firm, yet soft, as he'd worked out the knots in her muscles. He'd soothed and calmed with his hands and his quiet words of encouragement.

The wicked grin that lit up his face told her exactly what he was happy to oblige her with. 'You only have to ask.'

If she had the courage to do exactly that, she doubted she'd be able to hold out against him any longer. He might love his daughter, but he didn't love her, and that was the bottom line. 'Asking is not my strong point.'

'Don't I know it?' The grin didn't dim.

Neither did the tightening sensations low in her belly. That grin would get the man anything. Two days after giving birth and she wanted Cooper? She could want all she liked, but she wasn't getting him. Even if her body was ready—*no, body, you're not*—she would not give in to the heat that rose through her far too often whenever Cooper was near. Heck, he only had to look at her and she melted.

'You've gone quiet.' Finally he stopped grinning, his mouth tightening as he crossed to look down at his daughter. 'About this afternoon…'

They were going home. Pounding began behind her eyes. The fun was about to start. She'd have to manage without nurses popping in to check up on Lily, without help at the press of a button, no more grumpy little lady banging less-than-tasty meals down on the bedside table. 'I'm looking forward to it,' she fibbed.

'I'm taking you home with me.'

They'd agreed it would be best if Cooper picked them up rather than her trying to cope with a taxi. He'd even taken the latter half of the afternoon off work. 'I know… Oh.' She finally heard what he'd really said. 'No, we're not going to your house. I've got the apartment ready.'

Her hands were enfolded in large warm ones. 'You can leave any time you like. But you've been so snug in here and my house is toasty warm. Not to mention I can cook dinner every night, save you having to worry about what to have.'

Her apartment was chilly, the heat pump never quite getting up to speed despite the fix-it man working on it twice. 'I can manage my own meals.' That's what can openers were for.

'I'll get up to change Lily's nappies during the night.'

'Sold.'

The grin returned. 'Should've said that first and saved myself the trouble of having to cook dinners.'

Cooper's house was as warm as Sophie's hospital room had been because he'd loaded up the log burner before going to pick her and Lily up. He'd made up the bed in the room she'd been using before she'd hightailed it to her apartment. He'd put a bassinet where it would be easy to reach. There was a change table and stacks of nappies and wipes and singlets and little bodysuits. All things he'd purchased last night after leaving the hospital. They'd come in useful whenever Lily was with him.

Sophie stared around, then choked up. 'You make everything seem so easy.'

'Happy to help.' *Tick*. Another point in his favour. He was probably making an idiot of himself, but how else could he entice her to move in permanently? His little bundle of joy flexed an arm, diverting his attention away from Sophie. His heart swelled.

Doubt trickled into Sophie's face.

'You're overthinking things again.' Cooper laid Lily in the bassinet. 'One day at a time, okay?' He held his hand out, his mood suddenly serious. Wrong. Not serious. Vulnerable.

'You really want us here, don't you?' A pulse beat in her throat.

'Yeah, Sophie, I do.'

More than you can believe.

He'd do anything to change her mind about living alone, put as much energy into winning her over as he used to put into keeping women at a distance. Hard to believe he was the same man. Maybe he wasn't. All because of this wonderful woman.

'I love you,' said Sophie.

Cooper blinked one eye open. The lounge was in semi darkness and no one was standing by the couch he'd fallen asleep on. No Sophie. He must've dreamt those three little words. Because he wanted to hear them so much?

Soft warmth held his arm against the back of the couch. Glancing down, he took in the tiny dark head tucked against his chest. Of course. He'd taken Lily to change her after a feed.

When he'd returned with the baby to her bedroom Sophie had been comatose. Pulling the covers over her, he'd beaten a hasty retreat and settled here with Lily until such time as one or other female woke.

He hadn't meant to fall asleep. Guess the birth and a full operating schedule every day this past week had finally caught up. No wonder he'd imagined he'd heard Sophie saying the impossible.

His eyes drooped shut. Ping. He stared across the room to where he thought he'd heard something. 'Sophie?'

'Who else?'

His blood heated some more as the full effect of her smile touched him. If only that hadn't been a dream. 'Last time I saw you...' Her face had been soft and devoid of worry, her mouth curved upward and her cheeks flushed rosy pink. 'You looked so relaxed I couldn't wake you.'

'You should've. I don't have four surgeries scheduled for tomorrow. Or is it today?'

If only it was Saturday. The alarm wouldn't go off at six. His patients wouldn't be lying in wait after a sleepless night. His daughter and Sophie would be with him all day. 'What is the time?'

'Time I took over so you can go to bed and get a proper rest.' She was there, reaching down for their daughter, those full breasts spilling forward inside her pyjama top.

Sexy. Beautiful. But most of all a woman in love with her infant. If only she had enough for him as well. 'How long have you been watching us?'

The rosy pink in her cheeks intensified. 'I woke in the dark and panicked. Tore out here looking for Lily. Seeing you holding her like she's precious, even in your sleep: it's a picture I'll never forget.' She turned her head away.

Snatching at her hand, he brought her hand to his lips, brushed a soft kiss across her palm.

'Cooper.' Her voice sounded lower than normal, and strained. Slowly her head came round so she faced him, apprehension tightening her mouth.

Thud, thud inside his chest. She was going to drop a bombshell, he could see it in her eyes. He tried to deflect her. 'Go back to bed. I'll bring Lily to you when she wakes.' Coward.

'I— You—' She closed her eyes and drew a long, slow breath. Then she locked her gaze on him. 'I love you.'

What? Was he still asleep? The beating going on against his ribs told him, no, he was wide awake. That he'd heard the one thing he'd been wanting to hear for days. But he needed to be sure. 'I dreamt of you telling me that.'

Her smile was shy. 'It wasn't a dream. I did say it while you were lying there.'

He wanted to leap to his feet and punch the air, shout

out the window, wake the whole street. He needed to hold Sophie, tell her his feelings. But he was holding his daughter. Without taking his eyes off Sophie, he slowly eased upright. 'You love me.'

The wonder filling him, wiping away all the doubts, was turning him into a puddle of love and desire.

Her eyes were wide, filled with worry. Where had his strong, brave woman gone? 'Yes,' she whispered. 'Yes.'

'Don't be afraid,' he said softly against the continuous thumping still going on in his chest. 'I needed to know that.'

'You did?' Her teeth were gnawing at her bottom lip.

Carefully placing Lily on the baby rug spread on the floor, he reached for Sophie's hand, tugged gently. 'Come here.'

The moment she lowered herself onto the couch he shuffled sideways so they were touching from shoulder to hip to thigh. With his free hand he took her chin to turn her to face him. Locking his eyes on hers, he told her the truth. 'No one has ever told me that before.'

'No one? What about your father?'

'Men in my family don't use the L word. The one and only time I told someone I loved her I was eight and she was twenty-eight. She left Dad the next day.'

'You don't say it, but you certainly show it. I've seen how much you care about me since you first learned we were pregnant.' The nibbling stopped. Hard to continue when those full lips were lifting into a smile. A smile that was quickly dampened with a stream of tears.

'I will always look out for my own.' A road block in his throat kept him from saying anything else.

'I don't want to be a responsibility. I want to be someone you share your life with.'

His jaw slackened. The road block became thicker.

And the knots in his gut loosened. 'That's what I want too.' He'd known it for weeks now, had probably felt it since the day their world had exploded in shrapnel, bullets and dirt. But he'd been afraid to voice it in case Sophie turned him down again. Coward. Love was worth laying his heart on the line for. He'd been wrong to deny himself. But… His lungs expanded on a new breath. Could he say the L word?

Unaware of what he was trying to say, Sophie continued. 'I'm glad I told you. In fact, I'll tell you again. Cooper Daniels, I, Sophie Ingram, love you from the bottom of my heart. And…' Her hand came between them, palm up. 'And I always will.'

Absolutely. 'And I love you, Sophie, most sexy, beautiful woman on the planet.' Go for it. Risk all to gain all. 'Mother of my child, filler of my dreams, I have to ask you. Will you marry me?'

The baby shrieked.

Sophie laughed.

And he held his breath.

'Bad timing, little one,' Sophie spluttered. 'Guess that's what a mother's life's all about.'

His lungs were about to burst.

Sophie?

Stunning emerald eyes locked on his as she leaned in close and trailed a soft kiss over his mouth. 'Yes,' she breathed. 'Yes for the first time you asked. Yes for the second, and definitely yes today.'

Lily shrieked again.

'There's no denying that,' Cooper said as he handed their daughter to her mother. 'Did I really say I loved you? And did you agree to marry me at last?' His head was spinning. It had taken thirty years to tell someone he loved them and this time the result was unbelievable. No, make that amazing, wonderful. Perfect.

'All of the above.' Sophie nestled the baby against her nipple and grinned at him. 'Didn't hurt a bit, did it?'

'No. Funnily enough, it didn't. I should've tried it years ago.'

Sophie's grin dipped.

'Only in practice to make me better at it.'

Her lips tipped upwards again.

'You are so easy to please.' He grinned back.

'Don't get complacent already.' Then she looked down at their daughter. 'You don't know how lucky you are, darling, having Mummy and Daddy together, and loving each other.'

Cooper's heart swelled. 'I'm the lucky one around here.' He'd found love, learned to give love, and all many years before his old man had. 'All because of you,' he whispered against Sophie's lips. Just before he claimed them in their most passionate kiss yet.

EPILOGUE

'MERRY CHRISTMAS, MY *LOVELIES.*' Cooper swept into their bedroom with coffees in one hand and two small gifts perfectly wrapped in Christmas paper and with red ribbons in the other.

Sophie pinched herself. The most gorgeous man on the planet—even with that ridiculous Santa's hat on his head—and he was hers. 'Enjoying your honeymoon, are you?'

Yesterday they'd married in the rose garden at the Auckland Domain with a small group consisting of their parents and friends there to support them and share in the special moment.

'You bet. Here, let me take little one while you open this.' Cooper swapped present for baby in one deft move. Leaning in, he kissed her softly. 'I so love you, Sophie Daniels.'

'And I you, Mr Sex-in-Hard-Boots.'

'Love it when you talk dirty.' He grinned and tickled his daughter's tummy. 'Guess what I've got Mummy for Christmas? A pair of hard boots for me to wear to bed.'

Sophie spluttered into her coffee. 'Just as well I bought you sexy red lace knickers, then. In my size, of course.'

'Open your present, will you?'

'Patience not being your strong point, I guess I can do that.'

'I have better strong points.' He grinned.

'Not in front of the children.' She grinned back and tore the paper off the small jewellery box. Flipping the lid, she gasped at the silver charm bracelet lying on white satin. 'It's beautiful.' She'd wanted one for so long, but had thought it pathetic to buy her own. Picking the bracelet up, she rubbed her fingers over the charms Cooper had added. 'Aw, shucks, a heart. You really can be romantic when you try.'

His hand tapped his heart. 'She wounds so easily.'

'And a baby's bootie. For Lily.' Tears clogged her throat until she looked at the third charm, and then laughter cleared the blockage. 'A work boot.'

'A *hard* work boot. Cool, eh?' He looked so pleased with himself. 'I had that one made specially.'

Sophie slipped the bracelet onto her wrist, her fingers lingering on the hard boot. 'It's beautiful. Thank you.' Then she leaned closer to thank him properly. Married kisses were just as exciting as previous ones.

Of course Lily interrupted, not liking to be left out of most things her parents were doing.

Cooper sighed. 'Yes, my girl, there's a present from Santa for you too, but I don't think it's going to distract you long enough for me to give your mother her real Christmas present.'

'Santa, you're a bad influence.' Sophie opened the second present and a similar, though smaller bracelet glittered at her. 'I'm glad you chose different charms.' Her heart filled with love for this man who'd become such an essential part of her during the last year. When she'd seen the New Year in at a party last January she'd no idea what was in store for her. Just went to show life was full of surprises. 'I'd better get up. Everyone will be arriving soon.'

'Melanie's already phoned. She's running late. Jacob's being difficult this morning.'

'We will hold off opening presents until they're here.

My parents are always late anyway.' She reached for Cooper's hand. 'I can't believe we're having a real Christmas, as in family and friends and parcels and a big, eat-too-much lunch.'

'A proper one with parents, or grandparents, depending who you are.' His eyes were moist. 'Thank you. I never had this and thought I never would. I owe you for ever.'

Now Sophie's eyes filled, and she shook her head at her husband. 'No, you don't. We are not beholden to each other. Not when we love each other so much. Our daughter is so lucky to have us, and everything we can give her, like a perfect Christmas Day.'

'I'll go put that turkey in.'

'We're not eating for hours. It'll be dry.'

'Turkey's take hours, slow cooking and plenty of basting. Trust me, it will be perfect.'

Sophie laughed. 'I trust you with most things, but cooking the turkey?' She shook her head at him. 'I'm going to ring Gillian and ask her.' Darn, but that sounded like they were part of a family. Of course they were. That had brought it home to her, that was all. That was everything. There were people in her life she could ring and have inane conversations with about how to cook the turkey or what to do when Lily was grizzly. It had taken time but now she had the life she'd once dreamed of. Everything had come together. Sinking back into the pillow, she beamed at Cooper and Lily. 'Wow.'

'That's it? Wow?'

'Yeah. I am so happy.'

And when Cooper kissed her again she knew for real how lucky she was. Especially when Lily didn't interrupt this kiss. *Wow.*

* * * * *

TAMING HER
NAVY DOC

AMY RUTTAN

This book is dedicated to all of
those men and women who give the ultimate sacrifice.
Thank you.

PROLOGUE

IT WAS PITCH-BLACK and she couldn't figure out why the lights were off at first. Erica moved quickly, trying to shake the last remnants of sleep from her brain. Not that she'd got much sleep. She'd come off a twenty-four-hour shift and had got maybe two, possibly three, hours of sleep. She wasn't sure when the banging on her berth door roused her, telling her they needed her on deck.

What struck her as odd was why had the hospital ship gone into silent running.

She'd been woken up and told nothing. Only that some injured officers were inbound. She hadn't even been told the nature of their injuries. When she came out on deck, there was only a handful of staff and a chopper primed and waiting.

Covert operation.

That was what her gut told her and the tension shared by those waiting said the same thing.

Top secret.

Then it all made sense. She'd been trained and gone through many simulations of such a situation, but in her two years on the USNV *Hope* she'd never encountered one.

Adrenaline now fueled her body. She had no idea what

was coming in, or what to expect, but she knew she had to be on her A-game.

Not that she ever wasn't on her A-game. Her two years on the *Hope* had been her best yet and she'd risen in the ranks finally to get to this moment, being trusted with a covert operation. She had no doubt that was what it was because it must be important if their mission to aid a volcanic eruption disaster zone in Indonesia was being stalled. As she glanced around at the staff standing at attention and waiting, she saw it was all senior officers on deck, except for a couple of on-duty petty officers.

"How many minutes did they say they were out, Petty Officer?" Erica had to shout over the sound of waves. It was unusually choppy on the Arabian Sea, but it was probably due to the fact that the ship was on silent running. Only the stabilizers on the sides kept USNV *Hope* from tipping over. She couldn't see Captain Dayton anywhere, but then she suspected her commanding officer was at the helm. Silent running in the middle of the Indian Ocean at night was no easy feat.

"Pardon me, Commander?" the petty officer asked.

"I asked, how many minutes out?"

"Five at the most, Commander. We're just waiting for the signal."

And as if on cue a flare went off the port side and, in the brief explosion of light, Erica could make out the faint outline of a submarine. The chopper lifted from the helipad and headed out in the direction of the flare.

"Two minutes out!" someone shouted. "Silent running, people, and need-to-know basis."

Erica's heart raced.

This was why she'd got into the Navy. This was why she wanted to serve her country. She had fought for this moment, even when she had been tormented at Annapolis about not having what it took.

Dad would've been proud.

And a lump formed in her throat as she thought of her father. Her dad, a forgotten hero. She was serving, and giving it her all helping wounded warriors, and being on the USNV *Hope* gave her that. She had earned the right to be here.

The taunts that she'd slept her way to the top, telling her she couldn't make it, hadn't deterred her. The nay-saying had strengthened her more. Even when her dad suffered with his PTSD and his wounds silently, he would still wear his uniform with pride, his head held high. He was her hero. Now she was a highly decorated commander and surgeon and it gave her pride. So she held her head up high.

The better she did, the more she achieved the shame of her one mistake being washed away. At least, that was what she liked to think, even if others thought she'd end up with PTSD like her father: unable to handle the pressures, her memory disgraced. Well, they had another think coming. She was stronger than they thought she was.

The chopper was returning, a stretcher dangling as it hovered. Erica raced forward, crouching low to keep her balance so the wind from the chopper's blades wouldn't knock her on her backside.

With help the stretcher unhooked and was lifted onto a gurney. Once they had the patient stabilized they wheeled the gurney off the deck and into triage.

It was then, in the light, she could see the officer was severely injured and, as she glanced down at him, he opened his eyes and gazed at her. His eyes were the most brilliant blue she'd ever seen.

"We're here to get you help," she said, trying to reassure him as they wheeled him into a trauma pod. He seemed to understand what she was saying, but his gaze was locked on her, his breath labored, panting through obvious pain.

There was a file, instead of a commanding officer, and she opened it; there was no name, no rank of the patient.

Nothing. Only that he'd had gunshot wounds to the leg three days ago and now an extensive infection.

Where had they been that they couldn't get medical attention right away? That several gunshot wounds could lead to such an infection?

Dirty water. Maybe they were camped out in the sewers.

"What's your name?" she asked as she shone a light into his eyes, checking his pupillary reaction. Gauging the ABCs was the first protocol in trauma assessment.

"Classified," he said through gritted teeth. "Leg."

Erica nodded. "We'll take care of it."

As another medic hooked up a central line, Erica moved to his left leg and, as she peeled away the crude dressings, he let out a string of curses. As she looked at the mangled leg, she knew this man's days serving were over.

"We'll have to amputate; prep an OR," Erica said to a nurse.

"Yes, Commander." The nurse ran out of the trauma pod.

"What?" the man demanded. "What did you say?"

"I'm very sorry." She leaned over to meet his gaze. "Your leg is full of necrotic tissue and the infection is spreading. We have to amputate."

"Don't amputate."

"I'm sorry, but I have no choice."

"Don't you take my leg. Don't you dare amputate." The threat was clear, it was meant to scare her, but she wasn't so easily swayed. Being an officer in the Navy, a predominantly male organization, had taught her quickly that she wasn't going to let any man have power over her. No man would intimidate her. Something she'd almost forgotten at her first post in Rhode Island.

"Don't ever let a man intimidate you, Erica. Chances are they're more scared of you and your abilities."

She'd forgotten those words her father had told her.

Never again.

"I'm sorry." She motioned to the anesthesiologist to sedate him and, as she did, he reached out and grabbed her arm, squeezing her tight. His eyes had a wild light.

"Don't you touch me! I won't let you."

"Stand down!" she yelled back at him.

"Don't take my leg." This time he was begging; the grip on her arm eased, but he didn't let go. "Don't take it. Let me serve my…" His words trailed off as the sedative took effect, his eyes rolling before he was unconscious.

His passionate plea tugged at her heart. She understood him, this stranger. She'd amputated limbs before and never thought twice. She had compassion, but this was something more. In the small fragment she'd shared with the unnamed SEAL, she had understood his fear and his vulnerability. It touched her deeply and she didn't want to have to take his leg and end his career.

If there'd been another way, she'd have done it. There wasn't.

The damage had been done.

If he'd gotten to her sooner, the infection would have been minor, the gunshot properly cared for.

It was the hazard of covert operations.

And her patient, whoever he was, was paying the price.

"Let's get him intubated and into the OR Stat." The words were hard for her to say, but she shook her sympathy for him from her mind and focused on the task at hand.

At least he'd have his life.

* * *

"Petty Officer, where is my patient's commanding officer?" Erica asked as she came out of the scrub room.

"Over there, Commander. He's waiting for your report." The petty officer pointed over her shoulder and Erica saw a group of uniformed men waiting.

"Thank you," Erica said as she walked toward them.

Navy SEALs.

She knew exactly what they were, though they had no insignia to identify themselves. They were obviously highly trained because when she was in surgery she'd been able to see that someone had some basic surgical skills as they'd tried to repair the damage caused by the bullets. Also, the bullets had been removed beforehand.

If it hadn't been for the bacteria which had gotten in the wound, the repair would've sufficed.

At her approach, they saluted her and she returned it.

"How's my man?" The commanding officer asked as he stepped forward.

"He made it through surgery, but the damage caused by the infection was too extensive. The muscle tissue was necrotic and I had to amputate the left leg below the knee."

The man cursed under his breath and the others bowed their heads. "What caused the infection? Couldn't it be cleared up with antibiotics?"

"It was a vicious form of bacteria," Erica offered. "I don't know much about your mission."

"It's classified," the commanding officer said.

Erica nodded. "Well, you obviously have a good medic. The repair was crude, but stable."

"He was our medic," someone mumbled from the back, but was silenced when the commanding officer shot him a look which would make any young officer go running for the hills.

"If it hadn't been for the bacteria getting in there…

Depending on whatever your situation was, it could've been caused by many factors," Erica said, trying to take the heat off the SEAL who'd stepped out of line.

"Like?" the commanding officer asked, impatience in his voice.

"Dirty water?" Erica ventured a guess, but when she got no response from the SEALs she shook her head. "I'm sorry, unless I know the details of your mission I can't help you determine the exact cause of how your man picked up the bacteria."

The commanding officer nodded. "Understood. How soon can we move him?"

"He's in ICU. He has a high temperature and will require a long course of antibiotics as well as monitoring of his surgical wound."

"Unacceptable," the commanding officer snapped. "He needs to be moved. He can't stay here."

Erica crossed her arms. "You move him and he develops a post-op fever, he could die."

"I'm sorry, Commander. We have a mission to fulfill."

"Not with my patient, you don't."

"I'm sorry, Commander. We're under strict orders. I can give him eight hours before our transport comes." The commanding officer nodded and moved back to his group of men as they filed out of the surgical bay.

Erica shook her head.

She understood the protocols. It was a covert operation, but she didn't agree with all the regulations.

Their medic was useless. He needed medical care for quite some time and as a physician she wanted to see it through.

When that young SEAL had blurted out that the man she'd operated on was their medic, her admiration for her patient grew. He'd operated on himself, most likely without anesthetic, and probably after he'd removed the bullets from the other man they'd brought on board after him. That man didn't have the same extent of infection but, from what she'd gleaned from a scrub nurse, the gunshot wound had been a through-and-through. It hadn't even nicked an artery.

The man was being watched for a post-op fever and signs of the bacterial infection but would make a full recovery.

Her patient on the other hand had months of rehabilitation and, yes, pain.

I wish I knew his name.

It was a strange thought which crept into her head, but it was there all the same, and she wished she knew who he really was, where he was from. Was he married? And, if he was, wouldn't his wife want to know what she was in for as well?

Her patient was a mystery to her and she didn't really like mysteries.

She headed into the ICU. He was extubated, but still sedated and now cleaned up. There were several cuts and scratches on his face, but they hadn't been infiltrated by the bacteria.

Erica sighed; she hated ending the career of a fellow serviceman. She grabbed a chair and sat down by his bedside.

She had eight hours to monitor him, unless she appealed to someone higher up about keeping him here for his own good. At least until he was more stable to withstand a medical transport to the nearest base.

USNV *Hope* was a floating hospital. It was not as big as USNV *Mercy*, but just as capable of taking care of his needs while he recovered. And it wasn't only the physical wounds Erica was worried about, but also the emotional ones he'd have when he recovered.

She knew about that. There were scars she still carried.

Her patient had begged for his leg because he wanted to serve. It was admirable. Hopefully, he'd get the help he needed. The help her father hadn't had.

She reached out and squeezed his hand. "I'm sorry," she whispered.

He squeezed back and moaned. "Liam?"

Erica didn't know who Liam was but she stood so he could see her. "You're okay."

His eyes opened—those brilliant blue eyes. "What happened?"

"You had a bacterial infection. Your leg couldn't be saved."

He frowned, visibly upset, and tried to get up, but Erica held him down.

"Let me go!" He cursed a few choice words. "I told you not to take it. You lied to me. You lied to me, Liam! Why the heck did you do that? I'm not worth it. Damn it, let me out of here."

Erica reached over and hit a buzzer as she threw as much of her weight on him as possible, trying to keep him calm as a nurse ran over with a sedative.

It was then he began to cry softly and her heart wrenched.

"I'm so sorry."

"It was your life, Liam. My life… I have nothing else. You left me. We promised to stay together. I need my leg to do that."

Erica didn't know who Liam was, but she got off of him as he stopped fighting back. "I'm sorry." She took his hand once more. "I'm so very sorry."

He nodded as the drugs began to take effect. "You're so beautiful."

The words caught her off guard. "I'm sorry?"

"Beautiful. Like an angel." And then he said no more as he drifted off to sleep.

Erica sighed again and left his bedside. She had to keep this man here. He couldn't go off with his unit.

He needed to recuperate, to get used to the idea that his leg was gone and understand why. He was a medic; he'd understand when he was lucid and she could explain medically why she'd taken his leg.

Pain made people think irrationally. She was sure that was why her father had gone AWOL during a covert mission, endangering everyone. That was why he had come home broken and that was why he'd eventually taken his own life.

"Watch out, she's going to go AWOL like her father!"
The taunts and jeers made her stomach twist.
Block them out. Block them out.

"You need to get some sleep, Commander Griffin. You've been up for over thirty hours," Nurse Regina said as she wrote the dosage in the patient's chart. "Seriously, you look terrible."

Erica rolled her eyes at her friend and bunk mate before yawning. "Yeah, I think you're right. Do you know where Captain Dayton is?"

"He's in surgery now the ship isn't on silent running," Regina remarked. "Is it urgent?"

"Yeah, when he's out could you send him to my berth? I need to discuss this patient's file with him."

"Of course, Commander Griffin."

Erica nodded and headed off to find her bunk.

She was going to fight that man's unit to keep him on the hospital ship so he could get the help he needed.

There was no way any covert operation was going to get around her orders. Not this time. Not when this man's life was on the line.

He deserved all the help she could give him.

The man had lost a leg in service to his country. It would take both physical and mental healing.

He'd paid his price and Erica was damn well going to make sure he was taken care of.

CHAPTER ONE

Five years later, Okinawa Prefecture, Japan

"CAPTAIN WILDER WILL see you now, Commander Griffin."

Erica stood and straightened her dress uniform. She'd only landed in Okinawa five hours ago on a Navy transport and she was still suffering from jet lag. She'd flown from San Diego after getting her reassignment from the USNV *Hope* to a naval base hospital.

Another step in her career she was looking forward to, and the fact that it was in Japan had her extremely excited.

It was another amazing opportunity and one she planned to make the most of. Hopefully soon she'd get a promotion in rank but, given her track record, it seemed like she had to fight for every promotion or commendation she deserved.

It's worth it. Each fight just proves you can do it. You're strong.

Captain Dayton taking a disgraced young medical officer under his wing and letting her serve for seven years on the *Hope* was helping her put the past to rest.

Helping her forget her foolish mistake, her one dumb moment of weakness.

Erica followed the secretary into the office.

Dr. Thorne Wilder was the commanding officer of the

general surgery wing of the naval hospital. They wouldn't see as much action as they'd see in a field hospital, or on a medical ship, but she'd be caring for the needs of everyone on base.

Appendectomies, gall bladder removals, colectomies—whatever needed to be done, Erica was going to rise to the challenge.

Dr. Wilder had requested her specifically when she'd put in for reassignment to a Naval hospital. She'd expected some downtime in San Diego while she waited, but that hadn't happened and she didn't mind in the least. She'd spent almost a year after her disgrace at Rhode Island in San Diego, waiting to be reassigned, and then she'd been assigned to the *Hope*. Perhaps her past was indeed just that now.

Past.

It also meant she didn't have to find temporary lodging or, in the worst-case scenario, stay with her mother in Arizona where Erica would constantly be lectured about being in the Navy. Her mother didn't exactly agree with Erica's career choice.

"You're in too much danger! The Navy killed your father."

No, the Navy hadn't killed her father. Undiagnosed PTSD had killed her father eventually, even if his physicians had had a bit of a hand in it by clearing him to serve in a covert mission.

Her mother wanted to know why she hadn't gone in to psychiatry, helped wounded warriors as a civilian. Though that had been her intention, working in an OR gave her a sense of satisfaction. Being a surgeon let her be on the front line, to see action if needs be, just like her father. It was why she'd become a medic, to save men and women like her father, both in the field and in recuperation.

"Commander Erica Griffin reporting for duty, sir." She stood at attention and saluted.

Dr. Wilder had his back to her; he was staring out the window, his hands clasped behind his back. It was a bit of an uneven stance, but there was something about him: something tugging at the corner of her mind; something she couldn't quite put her finger on. It was like when you had a thought on the tip of your tongue but, before the words could form, you lost it, though the mysterious thought remained in your head, forgotten but not wholly.

"At ease, Commander." He turned around slowly, his body stiff, and she tried not to let out the gasp of surprise threatening to erupt from her.

Brilliant blue eyes gazed at her.

Eyes she'd seen countless times in her mind. They were hauntingly beautiful.

"You're so beautiful... Beautiful. Like an angel."

No man had ever said that to her before. Of course, he'd been drugged and out of his mind with shock, but still no one had said that to her. Not even Captain Seaton, her first commanding officer when she'd been a lowly and stupid lieutenant fresh out of Annapolis. Captain Seaton had wooed her, seduced her and then almost destroyed her career by claiming she was mentally unstable and obsessed with him after she'd ended the relationship.

She was far from unstable. She had a quick temper, but over time she'd learned to keep that in check. Her job and her status in the Navy intimidated men, usually.

So his words, his face, had stuck with her. As had the stigma and that was why she'd never date another officer. She wouldn't let another person destroy her career.

Dating, if she had time, was always with a civilian. Though she didn't know why at this moment she was thinking about dating.

"Like an angel..."

As Erica stared into Captain Wilder's blue eyes, a warmth spread through her. She'd always wondered what had happened to him. Since he'd been moved against her wishes, she'd assumed he hadn't made it.

She'd apparently been wrong. Which was good.

Five years ago when she'd woken up, she realized she'd slept for eight hours. So she'd run to find Captain Dayton, only to be told that, yes, her request had been heard, but had been denied by those higher up the chain of command. When she'd gone to check on her patient, he was gone.

All traces of him were gone.

It was like the covert operation had never happened.

Those men had never been on board.

Even her patient's chart had gone; wiped clean like he'd never existed. She'd been furious, but there was nothing she could do. She was powerless, but she always wondered what had happened to that unnamed medic.

The man who had begged her not to take his leg.

The man who'd cried in her arms as the realization had overcome him.

Now, here he was. In Okinawa of all places, and he was a commanding officer.

Her commanding officer.

Dr. Thorne Wilder.

Captain Wilder.

She'd never pictured him to be a Thorne, but then again Thorne was such an unusual name and she wasn't sure many people would look at someone and say, "Hey, that guy looks like a Thorne." His head had been clean shaven when he'd been her patient, but his dark hair had grown out. It suited him.

The scars weren't as visible because he wasn't as thin, his cheeks weren't hollow, like they'd been when she'd treated him and his skin was no longer pale and jaundiced from blood loss and bacterial infection. She hadn't realized how tall he actually was—of course when she'd seen him he'd been on a stretcher. She was five foot ten and he was at least three inches taller than her, with broad shoulders.

He looked robust. Healthy and absolutely handsome.

She couldn't remember the last time she'd seen such an attractive man. Not that she'd had much time to date or even look at a member of the opposite sex.

Get a grip on yourself.

He cocked his head to the side, a confused expression on his face. "Commander Griffin, are you quite all right?"

He didn't remember her.

Which saddened her, but also made her feel relieved just the same. Erica didn't want him blaming her for taking his leg or accusing her of something which would erase all the work she'd done over the years to bring honor back to her name and shake the venomous words of Captain Seaton.

It was the pain medication. The fever. It's hardly surprising that he doesn't remember you.

"I'm fine… Sorry, Captain Wilder. I haven't had a chance to readjust since arriving in Okinawa. I'm still operating on San Diego time."

He smiled and nodded. "Of course, my apologies for making you report here so soon after you landed at the base. Won't you have a seat?" He motioned to a chair on the opposite side of his desk.

Erica removed her hat and tucked it under her arm before sitting down. She was relieved to sit because her knees had started to knock together, either from fatigue or shock, she wasn't quite sure which. Either way, she was grateful.

Thorne sat down on the other side of the desk and opened her personnel file. "I have to say, Commander, I was quite impressed with your service record. You were the third in your class at Annapolis."

"Yes," she responded. She didn't like to talk about Annapolis—because it led to questions about her first posting under Captain Seaton. She didn't like to relive her time there, so when commanding officers talked about her achievements she kept her answers short and to the point.

There was no need to delve in any further. Everything was in her personnel file. Even when she'd been turned down for a commendation because she was "mentally unfit".

Don't think about it.

"And you served on the USNV *Hope* for the last seven years?"

"Yes."

He nodded. "Well, we run a pretty tight ship here in Okinawa. We serve not only members of the armed forces and their families but also residents of Ginowan."

"I look forward to serving, Captain."

Thorne leaned back in his chair, his gaze piercing her as if he could read her mind. It was unnerving. It was like he could see right through to her very core and she wasn't sure how she felt about that.

Everyone she'd let in so far had hurt her.

Even her own mother, with her pointed barbs about Erica's career choice and how serving in the Navy had killed her father. Her mother had never supported her.

"The Navy ruined our life, Erica. Why do you want to go to Annapolis?" Erica hadn't been able to tell her mother that it was because of her father. Her mother didn't think much about him, but to Erica he was a hero and she'd wanted to follow in his footsteps.

"I'm proud to serve my country, Erica. It's the ultimate sacrifice. I'm honored to do it. Never forget I felt this way, even if you hear different."

So every remark about the armed forces ruining their life hurt. It was like a slap in the face each time and she'd gone numb with her mother, and then Captain Seaton, who had used her. She shut down emotionally to people. It was for the best.

At least, she thought she had, until a certain Navy SEAL had crossed her path five years before. He'd been the only one to stir any kind of real emotion in her in a long time.

"I have no doubt you'll do well here, Commander. Have you been shown to your quarters on base?"

"Yes."

"Are they adequate?"

"Of course, Captain."

He nodded. "Good. Well, get some sleep. Try to adjust to Okinawa time. Jet lag can be horrible. I'll expect you to report for duty tomorrow at zero four hundred hours."

Erica stood as he did and saluted him. "Thank you, Captain."

"You're dismissed, Commander."

She nodded and placed her hat back on her head before turning and heading out of the office as fast as she could.

Once she was a safe distance away she took a moment to pause and take a deep breath. She'd never expected to run into him again.

Given the state he'd been in when she'd last seen him, she'd had her doubts that he would survive, but he had and he was still serving.

Even though he was no longer a Navy SEAL, at least he hadn't been honorably discharged. It had been one of his pleas when she'd told him about his leg.

"This is your life, Liam. My life... I have nothing else. I need my leg to do that."

The memory caused a shiver to run down her spine. It was so clear, like it had happened yesterday, and she couldn't help but wonder again who Liam was. Whoever he was, it affected Captain Wilder.

It doesn't matter. You're here to do your job.

Erica sighed and then composed herself.

She was here to be a surgeon for the Navy.

That was all.

Nothing more. Dr. Thorne Wilder's personal life was of no concern to her, just like her personal life, or lack thereof, was no one else's concern.

Still, at least she knew what had happened to her stranger.

At least he was alive and that gave her closure to something that had been bothering her for five years. At last she could put that experience to rest and she could move on with her life.

After Erica left, Thorne got up and wandered back over to his window. From his vantage point he could see the walkway from his office and maybe catch a glimpse of Erica before her ride came to take her back to her quarters on base.

She'd been surprised to see him, though she'd tried not to show it. She hid her emotions well, kept them in check like any good officer.

Erica remembered him, but how much else did she remember?

Bits and pieces of his time on the USNV *Hope* were foggy to him, but there were two things he remembered about his short time on the ship and those two things were losing his leg and seeing her face.

He remembered her face clearly. It had been so calm in the tempestuous strands of memory of that time. He remembered pain.

Oh, yes. He'd never forget the pain. He still felt it from

time to time. "Phantom limb" pain. It drove him berserk, but he had ways of dealing with it.

At night, though, when he closed his eyes and that moment came back to him in his nightmares, her face was the balm to soothe him.

A nameless, angelic face tied with a painful moment. It was cruel. To remember her meant he had to relive that moment over and over again.

And then, as fate would have it, a stack of personnel files had been piled on his desk about a month ago and he'd been told to find another general surgeon to come to Okinawa. Her file had been on the top as the most qualified.

It was then he'd had a name for his angel.

Erica.

As he thought about her name, she came into view, walking quickly toward an SUV which was pulling up. He thought he adequately remembered her beauty, but his painful haze of jangled memories didn't do her justice.

Her hair wasn't white-blond, it was more honey colored. Her skin was pale and her lips red. Her eyes were dark, like dark chocolate. She was tall and even taller in her heels. He was certain she could almost look him in the eye.

She walked with purpose, her head held high. He liked that about her. Mick, his old commanding officer in the Navy SEALs Special Ops, had told him a month after his amputation that the surgeon who'd removed his leg wouldn't back down. Even when Mick had tried to scare her off.

He'd been told how his surgeon had fought for him to get the best medical care he needed. How she'd sat at his bedside. She'd seen him at his most vulnerable. Something he didn't like people to see.

Vulnerability, emotion, was for the weak.

He'd been trained to be tough.

He'd been in Special Ops for years, even though he'd started his career just as a naval medic like Erica.

And then on a failed mission in the Middle East they'd become cornered. He'd thrown himself in front of a barrage of bullets to save Tyler from being killed. Bullets had ripped through his left calf, but he'd managed to stop the bleeding, repair the damage and move on.

Only they'd been surrounded and they'd had to resort to the old sewer system running under the city to make their escape and meet their transport.

The infested and dirty water was where he'd probably caught the bacteria which had cost him his leg, but it was his leg or his life.

For a long time after the fact, he'd wanted to die because he couldn't be a Navy SEAL any longer. He'd almost died. Just like his twin brother, Liam, had on a different mission. He remembered the look of anguish on Liam's wife's face when he'd had to tell her that her husband was gone. It was why Thorne wouldn't date. Seeing the pain in Megan's eyes, the grief which ate at her and her two kids… It was something Thorne never wanted to put anyone through. It was best Thorne severed all ties. He wasn't going to stop serving and it was better if he didn't leave behind a family.

And it was his fault Liam was dead and that Megan was a widow. One stupid wrong move, that was what Thorne had done, and Liam had pushed him out of the way.

Liam had paid with his life and Thorne would forever make penance for that mistake.

Thorne had enlisted in the Special Ops and was accepted as a SEAL. It had been Liam's passion and Thorne planned to fulfill it for him.

And then he'd lost his leg saving another.

He didn't regret it.

Though he was ashamed he was no longer in the Special Ops. When he'd taken that bullet for Tyler he'd been able to see Liam's face, disappointed over another foolish move.

Thorne had returned to serve as a medic ashamed and numb to life.

He wasn't the same man anymore, and it wasn't just the absence of his leg which made him different.

At least he still had surgery. When the assignment to command the general surgery clinic in Okinawa had come up, Thorne had jumped at it—and when he'd seen that Erica, a highly recommended and decorated surgeon in the Navy, was requesting reassignment to Okinawa Prefecture, Thorne had wanted the chance to know more about the woman who'd taken his leg and saved his life.

Had she?

His mother didn't like the fact he'd gone back to serving after he lost his leg.

"I lost your brother and almost lost you. Take the discharge and come home!"

Except Thorne couldn't. Serving in the Navy was his life. He might not be an active SEAL any longer, but he was still a surgeon. He was useful.

He was needed. If he couldn't be a SEAL and serve that way, in honor of his brother he could do this.

Thorne scrubbed his hand over his face. His leg was bothering him and soon he'd head back to his quarters on the base and take off his prosthetic. Maybe soak his stump in the ocean to ease the pain. He couldn't swim, but he could wade.

Water soothed Thorne and aided him with his phantom limb syndrome. Seeing Erica face-to-face had made his leg twinge. As if it knew and remembered she'd been the one to do the surgery and was reacting to her.

Perhaps bringing her here was a bad idea.

She knew and had seen too much of his softer side. He'd been exposed to her, lying naked on her surgical table, and Thorne was having a hard time trying to process that.

Perhaps he should've kept her away.

A flash behind him made him turn and he could see dark clouds rolling in from the east. It was typhoon season in Okinawa, but this was just a regular storm. The tall palm trees along the beach in the distance began to sway as the waves crashed against the white sand.

A dip was definitely out of the question now.

The storm rolling in outside reflected how he felt on the inside and he couldn't help but wonder if he was losing his mind by bringing her here.

When had he become so morbid and self-obsessed?

He couldn't reassign her without any just cause. It would damage her reputation and he wouldn't do that to Erica.

No, instead he'd force her to ask for a reassignment on her own terms.

Though he didn't want to do it, he was going to make Erica's life here in Okinawa hard so that she'd put in for the first transfer to San Diego and he could forget about her.

Once and for all.

CHAPTER TWO

"YOU'VE BEEN HERE a week and you've been getting some seriously crummy shifts."

Erica glanced up from her charting at Bunny Hamasaki, a nurse and translator for the hospital. A lot of the residents of Ginowan knew English, but some of the older residents didn't. Bunny was middle-aged, born and bred on Okinawa. Her father was a Marine and her mother a daughter of a fisherman.

She'd been born at the old hospital down the road and seemed to know everyone and everything about everyone.

"I could say the same for you," Erica remarked.

Bunny snorted. "I'm used to these shifts. This time of night is when I'm needed the most. Plus I can avoid my husband's snoring and bad breath, working the night shift."

Erica chuckled and turned back to her charting.

Bunny reminded her of her scrub nurse, bunk mate and best friend Regina. Truth be told, she was a wee bit homesick for the *Hope* and for her friends.

This is what you wanted. You'll make captain faster this way.

And that was what really mattered—proving herself.

"I don't think I'm getting crummy shifts."

Bunny snorted again. "Commander, with all due respect, you're getting played with."

Bunny moved away from the nursing station to check on a patient and, as Erica glanced around the recovery room, she had to agree.

Since her arrival a week ago all she'd been getting was night shifts.

Which seriously sucked, because by the time she'd clocked out she was too exhausted to explore, socialize or make friends in Okinawa. Then again, she was here to work, not to make friends. After her shift, she'd return to her housing on base and collapse.

Maybe she'd unpack. Though she didn't usually do that until she'd been on-site for at least a month.

No. She'd probably just crash and sleep the day away. Except for the first day she'd arrived and met with Dr. Wilder, she hadn't seen Okinawa in the daylight.

He's putting you through your paces.

That was something she was familiar with.

Even though she was a high-ranking officer, she was positive the other surgeons were having fun initiating her, seeing how their commanding officer was doing it.

"Stupid ritual," she mumbled to herself.

"What was that, Commander?"

Erica snapped the chart closed and stood to attention when she realized Dr. Wilder was standing behind her. "Nothing, sir."

Thorne cocked an eyebrow, a smile of bemusement on his face. "You're not up for formal inspection, Commander. At ease."

Erica opened her chart again and flipped to the page she'd left off at, trying to ignore the fact that Dr. Wilder was standing in front of her. She could feel his gaze on her.

"I heard the whole conversation with Bunny," he mentioned casually.

"Oh, yes?" Erica didn't look up.

"I'm scheduling you for the night shift deliberately. You do realize that?"

"I know, Captain Wilder."

"You know?" There was a hint of confusion in his voice.

Erica sighed; she was never going to finish this chart at this rate. She set down her pen and glanced up at him. "Yes. Of course you are. I'm not a stranger to this treatment."

"I bet you're not." He leaned against the counter. "You think it's a stupid ritual?"

"I do." She wasn't going to sugarcoat anything. She never did.

His eyes widened, surprised. "Why?"

"It's bullying."

"You think I'm bullying you?" he asked.

"Of course. I'm new."

"And it doesn't bother you?"

"The ritual bothers me. I think it's not needed, but it's not going to dissuade me from my job."

There was a brief flash of disappointment. Like he'd been trying to get her to snap or something. She was made of stronger mettle than that and he'd have to do a damn lot more to sway her. She was here to stay for the long haul, or at least until she made captain—and then the possibilities would be endless.

"Well, then, you won't mind working the night shift again next week."

So much for unpacking.

"Of course not." She shrugged. "Is that all you wanted to talk about, my shift work?"

His gaze narrowed. "You're very flippant to your commanding officer."

She wanted to retort something about him being on

her operating table five years ago, but she bit her tongue. The last time she'd lost her cool, when she'd forgotten about the delicate and precise hierarchy, she'd lost her commendation. Of course, that had been a totally different situation with a former lover. Captain Wilder wasn't her lover. He was just a former patient and now her commanding officer.

She was used to this macho behavior. Erica could take whatever he had to throw at her. As long as he didn't bring up what happened during her first post, but she seriously doubted he knew all the details about it because he would've mentioned it by now.

Everyone always did.

"Sorry, sir." Though she wasn't. Not in the least.

"It won't last forever." He was smirking again.

"Can I be frank, Captain Wilder?"

He shrugged. "By all means."

"Perhaps we should go somewhere privately to discuss this."

"I don't think so."

"Fine, suit yourself." The recovery area was usually quiet, but it was even more so now, and it felt like everyone was fixated on her and Captain Wilder. "If this is your way to try and make me crack, you won't succeed."

Thorne crossed his arms. "Really? You think this is a means to drive you away?"

"I do and you won't succeed. If there's one thing you'll learn from my file, Captain, it is that I don't give up. I won't give up. So I'll take whatever you have for me, Captain, and I won't complain. So, if you're looking to see me break, you won't. If night shifts are what you want to give me, so be it. I've done countless night shifts before. It's fine. If your plan is to ostracize me, well, then, you won't succeed unless I'm the only one working and there are no patients. I'm tougher than I appear, Captain Wilder."

* * *

Thorne was impressed. He didn't want to be, but he was. She barely saw the light of day, yet she came in and did everything without a complaint. When he'd heard her mumble something about stupidity, he'd been planning to swoop in and make his kill. Push her to the breaking point.

Only she'd risen to the challenge and basically told him to bring it on.

Yes, his goal with the numerous night shifts was to ostracize her, but it wasn't working. He admired that. He didn't want to, but he did. She was right. It wouldn't work unless she was working by herself out in the middle of a desert somewhere. He was so impressed.

So she'll take whatever I give her.

It was time to throw her off.

"Tell you what. You're on days as of Saturday. Take tomorrow off and readjust your inner clock. I'll see you at zero nine hundred hours. Get some sleep. You obviously need it."

He didn't give her a chance to respond; he turned and walked away, trying not to let her see his limp, because his leg had been bothering him today, and maybe because of that he'd decided to be a bit soft on her.

No, that wasn't it. At least, that was what he told himself.

Just as she wouldn't back down, he wouldn't either.

Thorne would make sure she left the hospital and that it would be her idea. Even though he kept his distance he was always aware of what she was doing and when he was around her he felt his resolve soften because she impressed him so.

He was drawn to her.

No woman had affected him like this in a long time. Even then he wasn't sure any woman had had this kind of hold on him.

Don't think about her that way.

Only he couldn't help himself. He'd been thinking about her, seeing her face for years.

She haunted him.

Why did I bring her here?

Because he was a masochist. He was taunting himself with something, someone he couldn't have.

A twinge of pain racked through him. He needed to seek the solace of his office, so no one saw him suffer.

Erica had to go before things got out of hand.

He pushed the elevator button and when it opened he walked in. Thankfully it was empty at this time of night and he could lean against the wall and take some weight off his stump. Even if it was just a moment, he'd take it.

He waited until the doors were almost shut before relaxing, but just as the doors were about to close, they opened and Erica stepped onto the elevator.

Damn it.

He braced himself. "Can I help you, Commander?"

"Excuse me, Captain, but I don't understand why you've suddenly changed your mind about my shifts. Didn't you understand what I was saying to you?"

"I do understand English," he snapped.

Go away.

"Why did you suddenly change my shift? Especially so publically. Others will think you're being easy on me or that I'm a whiner."

"Weren't you whining?"

"No. I don't whine. You don't have to give me a day shift."

"I thought that's what you wanted."

Erica pushed the emergency stop and the elevator grinded to a halt. "I want you to treat me like any other surgeon, like any other officer. I'm not green behind the ears, or however that saying goes."

"It's *wet* behind the ears," Thorne corrected her.

"Well, I'm not that."

No. You're not.

Thorne resisted the urge to smile and he resisted the urge to pull her in his arms and kiss her. Her brown eyes were dark with what he was sure was barely controlled rage, her cheeks flushed red. She was ticked off and he loved the fire in her.

His desire for Erica was unwelcome. He couldn't have a romantic attachment.

I don't deserve it.

Emotions were weakness.

Compassion for his patients, he had that in plenty, but these kinds of feelings were unwelcome. Still, he couldn't stop them from coming, and as she stood in the elevator berating him he fought with every fiber of his being not to press her up against the elevator wall and show her exactly what he was thinking, that he'd fantasized about her for five years.

"Well?" she demanded and he realized he hadn't been listening to a word she'd been saying. He'd totally zoned out, which was unlike him. He rarely lost focus, because if you lost focus you were dead.

At least that was what he'd picked up in his years in the Navy SEALs Special Ops and on the numerous dive missions.

Tyler had lost focus and that was why the sniper would have finished him off, if Thorne hadn't thrown himself in the path. Just like the stupid mistake he'd made when Liam had thrown him out of the way and paid with his life. Thorne had only lost a leg saving Tyler's life.

Just thinking about that moment made his phantom limb send an electric jolt of pain up through his body and he winced.

"Are you all right?" Erica asked, and she reached out and touched his shoulder.

He brushed her hand away. "I'm fine." He took a deep breath.

"You look like you're in pain."

"I said I was fine!" He straightened up, putting all his weight on his prosthetic and working through the pain. "I won't give you an easy ride, but I also won't be so cruel. I realize that my actions are detrimental to your mental health."

The words "mental health" struck a chord with her. He could tell by the way the blood drained from her face. He knew they would hurt. In her file he'd read that her first commendation had been turned down due to her being unfit emotionally. Though he didn't have the details as to why, that was unimportant. His barb worked and he regretted it.

"My mental health is fine," she said quietly.

"Is it?"

She didn't glance at him as she slapped the emergency button, the elevator starting again. The elevator stopped on the next floor and the doors opened. She stepped out. The confidence, the strength which had been with her only a moment ago, had vanished.

And, though he should be pleased that he'd got to her, he wasn't. Thorne hated himself for doing that to her.

It's for the best. She's dangerous to you.

"Thank you for your time, Captain. I will see you on Saturday at zero nine hundred hours." The doors closed and she was gone and Thorne was left with a bitter taste in his mouth. His small victory wasn't so sweet.

CHAPTER THREE

"AHA!" ERICA PULLED out her sneakers from the box. "It's been a long time."

Great. You're talking to sneakers now.

Maybe she was overtired. As she glanced around the room at all the boxes she realized how disorganized her life had become.

It wasn't many boxes, but she didn't really like living in a state of chaos. She'd gone from the USNV *Hope* to San Diego and within forty-eight hours she'd been posted to Okinawa.

If she kept busy she didn't notice it so much, but now that she had some free time it irked her.

She'd rather be busy than not. Relaxation was all well and good, but she had a job to do. She stared at her bright-blue sneakers with the neon yellow laces. Although she loved running, it was not what she wanted to be doing today.

Erica would rather be in the hospital removing a gall bladder. She'd even take paperwork.

This was a new posting and she had a lot to prove.

Not only to herself, but to her comrades.

Damn Captain Wilder.

Questioning her mental health like that. How dared he?

Are you surprised?

He was probably just like Captain Seaton—threatened by her. She cursed Captain Seaton for being a major *puenez*, or "stinkbug", as her *mamère* often said about men who were scared of strong women. She was also mad at herself for being duped by Captain Seaton and letting him affect her career.

And then she chuckled to herself for condemning her superior who had given her the day off. Most people wouldn't be complaining about that and she found it humorous that she was condemning the man again.

Hadn't she done enough damage when she'd had to take his leg after it had got infected?

The guilt about ending his career as a SEAL ate at her, but not her decision to take his leg. There was no help for that. He would've died.

Perhaps he would've preferred death?

"Your father wanted to die and the Navy gave him the means to do so."

Erica shuddered, thinking about her mother's vitriol, because it made her think of that last moment she'd seen her father—the haunted look in his eyes as he'd shipped out.

"Be good, Erica. You're my girl."

He'd held her tight, but it hadn't been the same embrace she'd been used to. Three days later, he'd gone AWOL. Two weeks later, after a dishonorable discharge, he'd ended his life.

You did right by Thorne. Just like the surgeons saved your father's life the first time he was injured. You saved Thorne's life.

It was her job to save lives, not end them. His desire to die was not her concern any more. She'd saved his life and they'd taken him away. Captain Thorne Wilder was no longer her concern.

She'd done her duty by him and that was how she slept at night.

Erica sat down on her couch and slipped on her running shoes, lacing them up. There wasn't much she could do. She wasn't on duty today, unless there was an emergency, so she might as well make the best of it. Besides, running along a beach might be more challenging than running laps on a deck.

She stretched and headed out to a small tract of beach near her quarters. Though the sky was a bit dark, the sea wasn't rough, and the waves washing up on shore would make her feel like she was out on the open sea. Back on the *Hope*.

As she jogged out toward the beach she got to see more of the base. It was pretty active for being on such a small island far off the mainland of Japan.

The hospital was certainly more active than being on the *Hope*. Unless they were responding to a disaster, there were stretches at sea where they weren't utilizing their medical skills. Those stretches were filled with rigorous drills and simulations.

As she headed out onto the beach, she followed what appeared to be a well-worn path along the edge so she wouldn't have to run in the sand.

Erica opted to go off the path and headed out onto the sand. It slowed her down, but she didn't care. It would work her muscles more.

Besides, even though it was a bit overcast, it was still a beautiful day on the beach. The palm trees were swaying and the waves lapping against the shore made her smile.

As she rounded the bend to a small cove, she realized she wasn't the only one who was on the beach at this moment and it made her stop in her tracks.

Thorne.

He was about fifteen feet away from her, in casual

clothes, his arms crossed and his gaze locked on the water. She followed where he was looking and could see swimmers not too far out in the protected cove.

I have to get out of here.

She turned to leave but, as if sensing someone was watching him, his gaze turned to her. Even from a distance she could feel his stare piercing through her protective walls. A stare which would make any lesser man or woman cringe from its hard edge, but not her.

Of course, now she couldn't turn and leave. He'd seen her, there was no denying that. He walked toward her fluidly as if there was no prosthesis there. So different from yesterday when he'd moved stiffly, his chiseled face awash with pain.

His face was expressionless, controlled and devoid of emotion.

So unlike the first time she'd met him, when he'd begged her not to take his leg and made her heart melt for him just a little bit.

"Commander, what a surprise to find you here," he said pleasantly, but she could detect the undertone of mistrust. He was questioning why and she had the distinct feeling her appearance was an unwelcome one.

"It's my day off and I thought a run along the beach would be nice."

It was nice until I ran into you.

"Never heard someone mention a run as nice." He raised an eyebrow.

Erica gritted her teeth. "I haven't seen much of the base since I first arrived. I'm usually sleeping when the sun is out."

Ha ha! Take that.

He nodded, but those blue eyes still held her, keeping her grounded to the spot as he assessed her. No wonder he'd been a Navy SEAL; apparently he could read people, make them uneasy and do it all with a cold, calculating calm. Even though it annoyed Erica greatly that it was directed at her at this moment, she couldn't help but admire that quality.

It was why it made the SEALs the best of the best.

Only, she wasn't some insurgent being interrogated or some new recruit. There was a reason she'd been one of the top students in her class at Annapolis.

She wasn't weak. She was tough and stalwart and could take whatever was dished out. She'd told him as much.

This she could handle. It didn't unnerve her. When he'd shown that moment of weakness, begging for his leg, that had shaken her resolve.

"No," he finally said, breaking the tension. "I suppose you haven't seen much of the base."

Erica nodded. "No, I haven't, but I'm not complaining."

A smile broke across his face, his expression softened. "I know you're not."

"What's going on out there?" she asked.

"SEAL training," he said and then shifted his weight, wincing.

"I didn't know this base was equipped for that."

"Yes. It's where I did my training." He cleared his throat. "I mean…"

"I knew you were a SEAL." She held her breath.

He feigned surprise. Captain Wilder might be good at interrogating and striking fear into subordinates, but he wasn't much of an actor. "How?"

Erica wanted to tell him it was because she'd been the one who'd operated on him—that he'd been on her ship— only she didn't think that would go over too well. He was obviously hiding from her that he had a prosthesis, as if such a thing would make her think differently of him.

Did he think it was a sign of weakness? If he did, he was foolish, because Erica saw it as a sign of strength. A testament to his sacrifice for his country. Only she kept that thought to herself. She doubted he'd be overly receptive to it right now. The last thing she needed was to tick him off and have him state she was mentally unstable or something.

So instead she lied. "I looked up your record before I shipped out. I wanted to know who my commanding officer was in Okinawa."

His gaze narrowed; he didn't believe her. She could tell by the way he held himself, the way his brow furrowed. Only he wasn't going to admit it. "Is that so?"

"How else would I know?" she countered.

"Of course, that would be the only way you'd know." Thorne crossed his arms and turned back to look at the ocean. "Aren't you going to ask me why I'm not out there swimming with them?"

"No," Erica said.

He glanced over at her. "No?"

"With all due respect, Captain Wilder, that's not my business."

"Yet knowing I am a former SEAL was?"

"Any good officer worth their salt tries to find out who they're serving under. The reasons you left the SEALs or aren't active in missions any longer is not my concern. Some things are better left unsaid."

His cheeks flushed crimson and she wondered if she'd pushed it too far.

"You're right. Well, I may be retired from the SEALs, but I still oversee some of their training. Anything to keep involved."

Erica nodded. "A fine thing to be involved with."

Thorne smiled again, just briefly. "Well, I don't want to keep you from your run. If you continue on down the beach, there's another nice path which wraps around the hospital and forks, one path leading into the village and the other back to base. If you have the time, be sure to check out the village and in particular the temple."

"Thank you, Captain."

"When we're off duty, you can call me Thorne."

Now it was Erica's turn to blush. It came out of the blue; it caught her off guard.

Maybe it was supposed to.

"I'm not sure I'm comfortable with that."

"What harm is there in it?"

She didn't see any harm. When she went on shore leave with other shipmates or was off duty she didn't address them so formally. What was the difference here? The difference was she was never attracted to any of them, had never seen them so vulnerable and exposed.

"I'll think about it."

He cocked an eyebrow. "I have to say, I'm hurt. Am I so monstrous?"

"No." Erica grinned. "I only address my friends so informally."

"I'm not your friend?"

Now it was her turn to cock an eyebrow. "Really? You're asking me if we're friends?"

"I guess I am." He took a step closer to her and her pulse raced. She'd thought he was handsome when she'd first seen him, but that was when he'd been injured. Now he was healthy, towering over her and so close. She was highly attracted to him, she couldn't deny that. He stirred something deep inside her, something she hadn't felt in a long time.

Yearning.

There had been a couple other men since Captain Seaton, but not many, and none in the Navy. She didn't have time or interest.

Until she met Thorne.

Thorne was dangerous and, being her commanding officer, he was very taboo.

"We barely know each other, Captain. How can we be friends?"

"Easy. We can start by using our given names. I'm Thorne." And then he took her hand in his. It was strong and sent a shock of electricity through her.

Get a grip on yourself.

She needed to rein this in. This was how she'd fallen for Captain Seaton. He'd wooed her. She'd been blinded by hero worship, admiration, and she wouldn't let that happen again.

"We're not friends," Erica said quickly.

"We can be." His blue eyes twinkled mischievously. He was playing with her and she didn't like it. Thorne ran so hot and cold. He was trying to manipulate her.

"I don't think so, Captain." She suppressed a chuckle of derision and jogged past him, laughing to herself as she continued her run down the beach and perfectly aware that his eyes were on her.

Thorne watched her jog away and he couldn't help but admire her. Not many had stood up to him. He had the reputation of being somewhat of a jerk, to put it politely. He'd always been tough as nails. As Liam had always said. Yet Liam had gone straight into Special Ops and Thorne had become a medic. He wasn't without feelings.

He hadn't always been so closed off, but when you saw your identical twin brother lying broken on the ground after an insurgent attack, after he'd pushed you out of the way, then pieces of you died. Locking those parts of him away, the parts which still mourned his brother, was the only way to survive.

The only way to continue the fight, so that his brother's death wasn't in vain.

Thorne had hardened himself and, in doing so, had driven so many people away. They kept out of his way, they knew not to mess with him or challenge him. It was better that way. No one to care about. He didn't deserve it.

Erica was different.

You knew that when you approved her request to come to Okinawa.

His commanding officer still talked about the courage it had taken to stand up to him during that covert operation. How Erica had been adamant that Thorne was to remain on the USNV *Hope*. It had impressed Mick and that was hard to do.

Perhaps in Erica he'd met his match?

She's off-limits.

He needed that internal reminder that Erica was indeed off-limits. Thorne couldn't let another person in. There was no room for someone else in his life, so he had to get all these foolish notions out of his head.

Except, that was hard to do when he saw her, because those hazy, jangled memories from that time flooded his dreams—only now she wasn't just some ghost. The face was clear, tangible, and all he had to do was reach out and touch her to realize that his angel was indeed on Earth.

"Captain!" The shouts from the water caught his attention and he tore his gaze from Erica and out to sea.

The few men who had been doing their training were trying with futility to drag one of their comrades from the water, but the waves were making it difficult and the crimson streak following the injured man made Thorne's stomach knot.

Shark.

It was one of the dangers of training in the sea, though attacks were rare.

His first instinct was to run into the fray to help, but he

couldn't step foot into water. His prosthesis had robotic components and it would totally fry his leg. He needed his prosthetic leg to continue his job.

He was useless.

So useless.

He pulled out his phone and called for an ambulance, then ran after Erica, who wasn't far away.

"Erica!" he shouted, each step causing pain to shoot up his thigh. He hadn't run in so long. "Commander."

Erica stopped and turned, her eyes wide and eyebrows arched with curiosity. Without having to ask questions, she looked past him to the blood in the water and men struggling to bring their friend safely ashore.

She ran straight to them, whipping off her tank top to use as a tourniquet, wading into the surf without hesitation to aid the victim, while all he could do was stand there and watch in envy.

Only for a moment, though, before he shook off that emotion.

He might not be able to help in the same way as Erica, but he'd do everything he could. As soon as they had the man out of the water and on the beach, Thorne dropped down on one knee to survey the damage to the man's calf.

"What happened?" Thorne asked, not taking his eyes off the wound as Erica tightened the tourniquet made out of her Navy-issue tank top.

"We were swimming back in and Corporal Ryder fell behind. It was then he cried out. We managed to scare the shark off," one of Corporal Ryder's comrades responded.

"My leg!" Corporal Ryder screamed. "My leg is gone."

Thorne's throat constricted and his phantom leg twinged with agony, which almost caused him to collapse in pain.

You're fine. Your leg is gone. There is no pain.

"Your leg is there, Corporal," Erica responded. "You hear me? Your leg is there."

Corporal Ryder howled in agony and then cursed before going into shock.

"Lie him down, he's going into shock." Thorne reached out and helped Erica get Corporal Ryder down.

Erica was helping the other recruits assess Corporal Ryder's ABCs, the water still lapping against them as they worked on the leg, and Thorne stood there useless because he couldn't get his prosthetic leg wet; the corporal was still half in the water.

"How bad?" Thorne directed his question to Erica.

"We can probably salvage the leg. We won't know until we get him into surgery."

The ambulance from the hospital pulled up in the parking lot. Two paramedics were hurrying down the hill to the beach with a stretcher.

"Well, Commander Griffin, it looks like we're both scrubbing in. I don't know how many shark attacks you've seen…"

"Enough," she said, interrupting him, her expression soft. "Thank you for letting me assist you, Captain Wilder."

Thorne nodded and stood, getting out of the way as the paramedics arrived. "Commander, you go with the paramedics in the ambulance. I'll be there shortly."

There was no way he could keep up with the stretcher. He'd get there in enough time.

Corporal Ryder needed all the help he could get.

Erica nodded and, as the ABCs of the corporal's condition were completed, he was on the gurney, headed toward the ambulance.

Thorne stayed behind with the other men, his stump throbbing, phantom pain racking him as his own body remembered the trauma he'd suffered.

He needed a moment to get it together.

To lock it all out, so he could be of some use to the corporal and help save that man's leg, where his own hadn't been.

CHAPTER FOUR

"MORE SUCTION."

Erica glanced up from the corporal's leg wound, but only briefly, as she carefully suctioned around the artery.

"Thank you, Commander," Thorne responded.

Their eyes locked across the surgical table. Even though she'd been here two weeks she had yet to operate with Thorne. When he had stitched his own leg, Erica had admired the work, given the condition and the crude tools he'd used. Now, watching him in action in a fully equipped and modern OR was something of beauty. She was so impressed with his surgical skill. There was a fluid grace with his hands, like a fine musician's, as he worked over the corporal's calf.

It was a simple wound to the leg, if you could call a shark bite simple. It didn't need or require two seasoned trauma surgeons, but Thorne had requested she be in there with him.

"You triaged him in the field. You have the right to be there too, Commander."

Even though she wasn't needed and it was her day off, Erica went into surgery with Captain Wilder against her better judgment. He'd been accommodating, but she still had a feeling that she was being scrutinized, manipulated, and that one wrong move and he'd send her packing. Well, maybe not personally send her packing, but she was sure he'd expedite it.

He probably wants to make sure you don't hack off Corporal Ryder's leg like you did to his.

Erica *tsked* under her breath, annoyed she'd let that thought in.

"Is something wrong, Commander?" Thorne asked.

"No, nothing. Why?"

"I thought you might have been annoyed about working on your day off. I know I've been pretty hard on you since you've arrived."

"No, I'm not complaining—far from it."

"You were huffing."

Erica glanced up again. Thorne's blue eyes twinkled slightly in what she could only assume was devilry.

What was that old saying her grandma had had? *Keep away from men who are* de pouille *or who are* possede. *They're just as bad as* rocachah.

Or, *keep away from men who are a mess or mischievous children. They're like beach burrs.* Erica had thought at the time her *mamère's* advice was a bit nuts, but Captain Seaton certainly had been a *peekon* in her side and Thorne had the look of a *possede* for sure.

Great. I'm now channeling Mamère.

"I wasn't huffing over the work. The work, I love."

"Yet something rankled you."

"Why are you being so *tête dure*?" Then she gasped, realizing some of her Cajun had slipped out.

"So what?" Thorne asked, amused.

"*Tête dure* is stubborn, persistent and hardheaded. I'm from Louisiana."

"Really? I wouldn't have guessed it."

Erica rolled her eyes. "Don't judge a bed by its blanket."

"You mean a book by its cover?"

"Whatever."

"So why are you huffing?"

"Why are you being persistent?" she asked.

"Why not? I am the commanding officer of Trauma. I want to make sure those under my command…" He trailed off and Erica's stomach twisted. Was he alluding to her past in Rhode Island again?

Not everyone is out to get you. Just because one commanding officer accused you based on what happened to Dad doesn't mean they all will. Captain Dayton hadn't.

Then why did he keeping hinting at it? Maybe it was some kind of psychological warfare. Not that Thorne was at war with her. Perhaps it was some kind of SEAL training? It probably was and she shouldn't take it personally.

Erica cleared her throat. "If you want to know the reason I'm *tsking*, which is totally different from huffing, the reason is the wound. He's pretty mangled."

Thorne sighed. "His dreams of being in the Special Ops are over."

"He's lucky it didn't sever his femoral artery or we would have lost him on the beach." Erica continued to work, her hands moving as fast as Thorne's, working to repair the damage. It was an automatic process, one she didn't have to think too hard about. "More people die being trampled by hippos than by shark attacks."

"Hippos, Commander?" There were a few bewildered looks in the OR.

"Twenty-nine-hundred people annually."

"You're joking. That can't be right."

"It is. Look it up."

"Hippos?"

Erica chuckled. "I know, right?"

"Do you think the leg is salvageable?" Thorne asked, changing the subject.

"Yes." Their gaze locked again for a brief instant. The intensity of that shared moment made her think he wanted to ask her why his, which hadn't been as mangled, hadn't been saved.

She'd wanted to save his leg, but the infection had been too virulent.

Still, she'd always thought about him. What had happened to him, that gorgeous, brave Navy SEAL who had begged her. Who had called her beautiful.

"Like an angel."

Erica tried not to let those memories back in, but it was a failure. Hot flames of blood rushed up into her cheeks and she was thankful for the surgical mask. She broke the connection, her pulse racing.

You can't have this. He'll turn on you like Seaton did.

"I think Corporal Ryder, barring any post-op infection, will keep his leg," she said.

"Infection. Yes." His words were icy. "Well, look at this."

Erica glanced up and in his forceps there was a milky-colored sharp object, which looked like a bone fragment.

"What is that? Did it come off his femur?"

"It's a shark's tooth." The corners of his eyes crinkled with a smile obscured by his mask. He placed the tooth in the basin. "That will be something the corporal will want to keep."

"Like a badge of honor," Erica chuckled.

Thorne laughed quietly. "That, or he'll be out hunting the shark that ended his career prematurely."

"You don't think so?"

Thorne nodded. "Corporal Ryder has it in him. He had a passion to be in Special Ops; he's going to be annoyed."

"His life was saved. The animal didn't do it on purpose."

"It doesn't matter," Thorne snapped. "You don't know what it's like to be in such an elite force, protecting your country. Nothing else matters. You endure endless hours of torment to train, to make your body ready for the most treacherous conditions, and you gladly do it. You'd gladly lay down your life for a chance to keep your country free."

"Very patriotic," Erica said, trying to control her annoyance. "I may not be part of that elite crew, but what I do serves my country as well. I feel the same way."

"It's not the same. He'll have a bone to pick with that shark. You mark my words."

"So, would you?"

"Would I what?" Thorne asked, not looking at her.

"Go after the person or animal that ruined your career."

Thorne cleared his throat. "I did."

There was something in his tone which made her shudder, like she was in danger, but probably not in the same kind of danger as the shark.

This was something different. This kind of danger made her heart beat a bit faster, made her skin hot and made her feel like she was already the cornered prey animal with its throat exposed, waiting for the predator to make its kill. She didn't think Thorne wanted to kill her, far from it—but what he wanted from her, she didn't know.

Get revenge on her? Bring her to her knees?

She had no idea.

It was the kind of danger which excited her and terrified her.

It was the kind of danger she didn't run from. It was the kind she stood up to and she was ready for whatever was to come.

Thorne watched Erica as she checked on Corporal Ryder's vitals. Ryder had developed a post-op fever and had been in the ICU since he'd come out of surgery. He hadn't even fully come out of the anesthetic.

"My leg. My leg. Oh, God. Please, no!"

That was what Ryder had been screaming as they'd

pulled him from the water. He'd been screaming at the top of his lungs. Even though they'd all assured Ryder that his leg was still there, that it was attached and could be saved, it was like the young man had made up his mind that it wasn't going to happen.

Thorne had seen that before—when the spirit just wanted to give up and no amount of modern medicine would help that patient recover. It was like the soul was already trying to escape.

"Hold on, Liam. Just hold on."

"I can't, Thorne. Let me go."

"Why did you step in front of the IED for me?"

Thorne had read his own records, the ones which had been taken by his commanding officer from the USNV. He'd developed a post-op fever, no doubt from the virulent infection coursing through his body.

In his brief memories, when he could recall that moment, he remembered the feeling of slipping away, but something pulling him back.

An angel.

Erica.

Seeing her face hovering above him had grounded him.

Sometimes when the pain was bad, when it felt like the amputated leg was still there and he couldn't take it any longer, he hated Erica for saving his life.

Then again, after he'd been shot and they'd spent those days holed up in the sewers, he hadn't thought he was going to get out of there. He'd thought he was going to die in the sewer, which would've been better.

One less body in a casket for his mother to weep over.

No, don't let those memories in.

He didn't want to think about his twin's funeral, because when he thought of Liam he inevitably thought about how he'd tried to save his life.

"You're crushing me, Thorne."

"I'm applying pressure. I'm the medic, you're the hero. Remember?"

Liam had smiled weakly. *"I'm past that point. Let me go."*

That moment of clarity, when you felt no pain and your body was just tired of struggling on. You weren't afraid of death any longer. Death meant rest.

Thorne glanced back at the ICU. He saw that look of resolution on Corporal Ryder's face and he hoped the young man would fight.

Ryder still had his leg.

Thorne didn't and if he hadn't been in the medical corps of the Navy, if he hadn't had so many commendations and something to fall back on, he would've been discharged.

Ryder has to live.

Thorne clenched his fists to ease the anger he was feeling, because if he marched in there now to do his own assessment of the situation, to ease the guilt and anguish he was feeling over Corporal Ryder, he was likely to take it out on Erica.

The surgeon who had taken his leg. Only, she'd tried to save it. He'd seen the reports. It was the infection from the dirty water he'd been forced to live in.

There was nothing to be done at that point. There had been no one to blame but himself. He was the one who'd decided to step in front of that bullet to protect Tyler.

He didn't blame Erica—only, maybe, for saving his life.

He'd thought about her countless times, about kissing those lips, touching her face. Of course, those had been fantasies as he'd recovered. He thought those feelings of lust would disappear when he met her in person.

Thorne was positive that he'd built her up in his head. That it was the drugs which had obscured his memories.

No one could be that beautiful.

He was wrong. Even though his memory had been slightly fuzzy, his fantasies about her didn't do her justice.

When she'd rushed into the fray to give Corporal Ryder first aid on the beach, he knew why she was one of the top trauma surgeons in the medical corps.

The real woman was so much more than his fantasy one. Which was dangerous, because he felt something more than just attraction…

It was dangerous, because he did feel something more than just attraction toward her. He wanted to get to know her, open his heart to her, and that was something he couldn't do.

He wasn't going to let in any one else.

There was no room to love. He wouldn't risk his heart, and if something happened to him, well, he wasn't going to put any woman through that. He'd seen what had happened to his brother's wife and children when Liam had died. And, make no mistake, it was his fault Liam had died.

Thorne couldn't do that to anyone else.

So these emotions Erica was stirring in him scared him.

He'd been alone almost a decade and managed. What he needed to do was get control of himself. Then he could work with her.

No problem.

Yeah. Right.

He headed into the ICU, sliding the isolation door shut behind him. Erica glanced up at him briefly as she continued to write in Ryder's chart.

"Captain," she said offhandedly, greeting him.

"Commander," Thorne acknowledged, moving to the far side of the bed to put a distance between them. "How's he doing?"

"Stable." She said the word in a way that made Thorne think being stable was sufficient and in some cases—especially this one, where it wasn't even as serious as other wounds—stable should've been enough.

"Any sign of infection?"

"No." Her cheeks flushed briefly.

"Well, that's good. If the wound becomes infected and he doesn't respond to antibiotics we'll have to amputate."

She looked at him. "You have an obsession with amputation."

"Can you blame me?" And even though he knew he shouldn't, and even though he knew she already knew his leg was gone, he bent over and rolled up his scrub leg. "Titanium."

Their gazes locked and his pulse was pounding in his ears. He waited to see if she would admit to it. On one hand, he hoped she would and on the other hand, he hoped she wouldn't, but how long could they keep up this facade?

"I know," she said quietly without batting an eyelash, before she turned to her chart.

Thorne was stunned she admitted to it. When they'd first met again here in Okinawa she'd acted like she didn't remember him, just as he'd pretended he didn't recall her.

He smoothed down the scrubs over his prosthetic leg and then straightened up. The tension in the room was palpable. Usually, tension never bothered him and he thrived in high-stress situations, but this was different.

Against his better judgment, and under the guise that he wanted to see Corporal Ryder's charts, he moved behind her. Which was a mistake. Her hair smelled faintly like coconuts. He was so close he could reach out and touch her, run his fingers through her short honey-colored hair. He resisted and instead took the chart from her, flipping through it.

"Just a fever, then?"

"Y-yes," she stuttered. "Yes, a fever. There shouldn't be

a reason why his vitals are just stable, because they were just that. One small change…"

Thorne stepped away from her. "I understand. As long as there isn't infection."

He didn't look at her, but he got the sense she wanted to say more, and he wanted her to say more.

"You know," she whispered, her voice shaking a bit with frustration.

Good. He wanted her to hate him. It would be easier. *Hate me.*

"Yes." He handed her back the chart. Thorne knew she was annoyed. It was good that she was, maybe then she'd avoid him. If she hated him, then he'd be less tempted to want her. There would be little chance of them ever being together, which was for the best.

Yeah. Tell yourself another lie, why don't you?

"Looks good, Commander Griffin. Keep me updated on any changes in the corporal's status." He turned and left the ICU, trying to put a safe distance between the two of them.

The hiss of the isolation room's door behind him let him know she was following him. Why did he think she wouldn't follow him? From the little he knew of Commander Erica Griffin, he knew she wasn't the kind of officer to take anything lying down.

He was in for a fight.

She grabbed his arm to stop him. "I don't think we're done talking, Captain Wilder."

They were standing right in front of the busy nurses' station, where a few nurses stopped what they were doing. Even though they weren't looking their way, he could tell they were listening in earnest.

Not many officers stood up to him.

"Commander, I don't think this is the time or the place to bring it up."

"Oh, it's the time and place." She glared at some of the nurses and then grabbed him by his arm and dragged him into an on-call room, shutting the door behind her, locking it.

"Commander, what's the meaning of this?" he asked, trying to keep his voice firm. He didn't like the idea of being locked in a dark on-call room with her.

Especially when his blood was still thrumming with wanting her.

"I think you know exactly the meaning of this. Why did you pretend you didn't remember me?"

"You did the same."

Her eyes narrowed. "Only because I thought you didn't remember me for the last two weeks."

He cocked an eyebrow. "So that justifies lying to me?"

She snorted. "I never lied to you. However, you lied to me."

"Why didn't you say anything to me?" He took a step toward her, though he knew very well he should keep his distance.

"Why would I? If you weren't going to mention the traumatic experience, I wasn't about to bring it up again."

"Perhaps you felt guilty." He was baiting her, pushing her buttons.

Hate me. Loathe me.

She advanced toward him. "I don't feel guilty for saving your life. I did what had to be done. You would've died if I hadn't taken your leg. You're a doctor, and I'm sure you've had access to the chart which magically disappeared off the ship when you were taken, so you know I had no choice—I don't regret what I did. Given the choice again, if it meant saving a life and having someone hate me for the choice I made, I would cut off your leg to save your life."

Thorne took a step back, impressed with her, but also

annoyed that he was even more drawn to her and her strength.

He didn't know how to reply to that.

Didn't know what to say.

Suddenly there was someone pounding on the door.

"Commander Griffin, it's Corporal Ryder... He's crashing."

Suddenly there was nothing left to say. Erica flung open the door and both of them sped toward the ICU, the sound of a flatline becoming deafening, and everything else was forgotten.

CHAPTER FIVE

ERICA FLIPPED THE tooth over, like it was a poker chip, staring at it morosely as she sat at a bar, which reminded her of *Gilligan's Island*, complete with bamboo huts, tikis and coconut shells. It was like a throwback to something from the sixties.

Normally, she wouldn't occupy a bar or pub, but tonight she needed company.

She needed a drink and this was the closest place to her quarters.

Besides, she'd never had a whiskey and cola adorned with a pink umbrella and glittery streamers before. Her drink reminded her of her first bike, which had had the same streamers. At least her drink didn't have spokeydokes. The Bar Painappurufeisu, which she believed translated to "Pineapple Face," served alcohol and that was all that mattered at the moment.

"Scooby, hit me again," she called to the barkeep.

Scooby nodded and smiled, probably not really understanding what she was saying, and said, "No problem," before heading down to the other end of the bar.

Erica giggled again.

She definitely needed to lay off the liquor. She rarely indulged and this was what she got for that. She was a lightweight and laughing at everything.

At least if she was laughing she wasn't thinking about what had happened to Corporal Ryder. Then she glanced down at the shark's tooth in her palm and slammed it against the counter.

"To hell with it, Scooby. I need another drink."

"No problem," Scooby answered from the end of the bar.

"Don't you think you've had enough?"

Erica glanced over and saw that Thorne had sat down beside her.

Just what she needed. Someone else whose life she'd ruined. She wasn't a surgeon—she was apparently no better than the grim reaper.

"Scooby will let me know when I've had enough."

A smile twitched on Thorne's face. "The only English Scooby knows is what kind of drink you want, monetary value and 'no problem'."

Scooby looked up and gave a thumbs-up. "No problem."

Erica moaned and rubbed her forehead. "Great. I've been rattling off to him about various things."

Thorne shrugged. "He's a good listener. It's his job. Although, he was a fisherman before the base sprung up."

"I thought most Okinawans knew English."

"Most do. Scooby doesn't; he only learned what he needed to know."

Erica narrowed her eyes. She didn't believe a word Thorne was saying, though that could be the liquor talking.

"You don't believe me?" he asked, his eyes twinkling.

"Why should I? Since I arrived you've questioned me, *lied* to me and generally have been a pain in my butt. No offense, Captain."

"None taken, Commander."

Erica turned back to her drink, playing with the many

glittery decorations. Her body tensed, being so close to Thorne. It wasn't because he was her commanding officer; that didn't bother her in the least. It wasn't because she'd taken his leg; she knew she'd made the right medical decision. It was because she was drawn to him and she shouldn't be. Captain Wilder was off-limits and it annoyed her that she was allowing herself to feel this way. That he affected her so.

Especially today.

"What do you have there?" Thorne asked, though she had a feeling he already knew.

She set it down on the countertop anyway: the shark tooth, gleaming and polished under the tiki lighting.

"Why do you have that?" he asked.

"I didn't think it should go to medical waste. I know we were saving it for…" She couldn't even finish her sentence. She was a doctor, a surgeon and she was used to death. People did die, and had died on her, but usually only when they were too far gone.

Thorne had been worse, yet he was here, beside her. Alive.

Corporal Ryder's death shook her because his death shouldn't have happened. It boggled her mind. She cupped the shark tooth in her palm again, feeling its jagged edge against her skin.

Thorne reached over, opened her fingers, exposing her palm, and took the shark tooth from her.

His touch made her blood ignite. A spark of electricity zipped through her veins.

Pull your hand away.

Only, she liked the touch. She needed it at this moment.

"Let me see that," he said gently. Erica watched him, watched his expression as he looked over the tooth carefully. "Can I keep it?"

"Why?" she asked.

"I knew him—he has a younger brother. Perhaps I'll send it to him if he wants it."

"Sure." She picked at the paper napkin under her drink. It was soaked with condensation and came apart easily. "Did you get a hold of Corporal Ryder's family?"

Thorne nodded slowly. "I did."

"I don't have any siblings." Erica wasn't sure why she was telling him that.

"That's too bad."

She nodded at the tooth again. "Do you think that's something his family would want? I mean…under the circumstances."

"I think so. Though, the flag at his state burial will mean more."

Erica sighed sadly. "There was no reason for him to die."

"He was attacked by a shark."

"It was a simple wound. It didn't even sever the artery."

"You know as well as I do that sometimes there are things beyond our control as physicians. If he gave up the will to live… I've seen it so many times. Even if you fight so hard to save a life, if that person has decided that they're going to die there's nothing you can do."

Erica nodded.

It was true. She knew it. She'd seen it herself so many times, but Ryder's death was so senseless. He would've made a full recovery. Sure, he wouldn't have been able to continue his training to become an elite member of the SEALs, but he also wouldn't have been discharged from the Navy.

Was that worth dying over? Was that what had driven Ryder just to give up?

Was that why Dad just gave up? How much pain had he been in?

She sighed, thinking about him. Her father had had a

loving family; he'd often told Erica she was the light in his life. Yet it hadn't been enough.

She hadn't been enough.

"Did they say what caused his death?" she asked, hoping Thorne could give her a more tangible answer.

"No, but there will be a postmortem, and maybe then we can get an answer. I'm thinking that the drugs, the shock of the attack and surgery was just too much of a strain on him. It's rare, but it does happen."

Erica nodded. "Well, why don't you join me and drink to Corporal Ryder's memory."

"Is that what you're doing?" he asked.

She nodded. "Oh, yeah."

"Then I'd love to join you, but you made it clear we can't be friends."

Erica winced. "I overreacted. I'm sorry. We can be friends."

"Okay." He motioned to Scooby who brought him a stubby-looking bottle.

"What's that?" she asked, because she couldn't read the Japanese on the label.

"It's beer. I don't know what kind, but it's damn good."

"I didn't know the Japanese brewed beer."

"You should've done your research before you took a posting in Okinawa prefect, then."

Erica snorted. "I did my research, I just somehow missed that."

"Okay, what do you know?"

She looked at him strangely. "Are you testing me?"

Thorne shrugged. "Why not? You said you studied."

Erica shook her head and pinched the bridge of her nose. "What part of 'pain in my butt' didn't you get?"

"Haven't you ever heard of a pub quiz before?"

"Really?"

Thorne chuckled. "Okay, fine. Although the prize would've been totally worth it."

"Prize?" Erica asked. "Now I'm intrigued. What would be my prize?"

He grinned. "Play and find out."

Just walk away.

The prize was probably something not worth it. Or something totally inappropriate—not that she would mind being inappropriate with Thorne, if he hadn't been her commanding officer; if they didn't have a history as surgeon and patient. Yet here she was, falling into this sweet trap again.

He's not Seaton. They're not all Seaton.

Which was true, but after a couple of drinks she was willing to let her guard down. *It's the booze.*

And maybe it was completely innocuous. Perhaps he was just being kind and just trying to get her mind off the fact that they'd lost someone today. Someone who shouldn't have died.

Since when has Captain Wilder ever been nice to you?

That was the truth. He hadn't been overly friendly or warm since she'd arrived at the base. Even when he'd been her patient he'd called her names and told her not to take his leg.

He didn't have the sunniest disposition.

"Like an angel."

That blasted moment again, sneaking into her mind, making her thoughts all jumbled and confused. She should just walk away, but she was too intrigued not to find out what the prize was. Besides, when was the last time she'd backed away from a challenge? If it was something inappropriate she could tell him where to go; they were off duty.

Still, she wasn't here because of a lark.

"I don't think it's appropriate."

"Because of Corporal Ryder?" Thorne asked.

"Yeah. Maybe I should just call it a night." She got up to leave, but he reached out and grabbed her arm, stopping her from leaving.

"Don't go," he said.

Erica sat down. "Okay, but I have to say I'm not in much of a jovial mood. Prize or not."

Thorne chuckled. "Tell you what, you'll still get your prize."

"And what would that be?"

"A tour around Ginowan and the countryside. You could test your knowledge."

Erica couldn't help but smile. When Thorne wanted to be, he was charming. "I don't think that's wise."

"Why?"

She didn't know how to answer that truthfully.

Because I don't want to be alone with you. Because my career is more important.

Because I'm weak.

"I don't think that's wise. You're my commanding officer."

Thorne's face remained expressionless. "You're right. Of course you're right."

Even though he didn't show any sign of anger, there was tension in his voice and possibly a sense of rejection. She knew that tone well enough from other guys she'd turned down, because there just wasn't time for romance.

And because you're frightened.

Erica stood. "I should go. Good night, Captain Wilder."

Thorne nodded but didn't look at her. "I'll see you in the morning, Commander Griffin."

Thorne watched her leave the bar; even though he shouldn't, he did. It was good that she'd turned him down. He didn't know what had come over him.

Probably the beer.

"You're looking for trouble with that one," Scooby said.

Thorne snorted. "I'm not looking for trouble."

"Good, because that one is strong willed. Why did you tell her I can't speak English?"

Thorne chuckled. "I was playing with her."

"Ay-ay-ay. Perhaps I should warn her off of you, Captain Wilder. Perhaps you're nothing but trouble." Scooby smiled and set another bottle of beer down on the counter. "I'm sorry to hear about the corporal. He was a good man."

"He was."

"I would like to send something to his family." Scooby reached behind the bar and pulled out a picture. "This was from last month. Corporal Ryder led our bowling team to victory."

Thorne smiled at the picture of Scooby, Corporal Ryder and some other officers in horrific bright-orange bowling shirts holding up matching color marble balls.

"I'm sure they'd like that."

Scooby nodded and walked away. Thorne carefully placed the framed picture down and then set the shark tooth on top of it.

Damn you, Ryder.

"You hold on, Liam. Do you hear me?"

"I hear you."

"It's not as bad as you think. You can live."

Liam shook his head. "No, little brother."

"Stop calling me little. I'm three minutes younger than you."

Liam chuckled, his pupils dilating, his breathing shallow. "You'll always be my little brother, Thorne. Remember that."

Thorne cursed under his breath and finished off his beer. He didn't want to think about Liam right now.

When do you ever?

It was true. Since Liam had died in his arms, he didn't like to think about him.

But then, who would want to think about a loved one they couldn't save?

One who could've been saved.

One that would still have been alive if he hadn't made such a foolish mistake.

CHAPTER SIX

DAMN AND DOUBLE DAMN.

Erica turned on her heel and tried to walk away as fast as she could, even though the little voice inside her head told her that she couldn't avoid Captain Wilder for the rest of her life. She was his second in command.

Needless to say, she was damn well going to try.

"Commander Griffin—a word, if you will."

Erica grimaced and cursed under her breath.

Damn.

She turned around slowly as Thorne walked toward her. He wasn't wearing his usual scrubs; he was in uniform. Not the full dress and not the fatigues—the service khaki and it didn't look half bad on him.

The khaki brought out the brilliant blue color in his eyes.

Damn.

"Of course, Captain Wilder. How can I help you?"

He shook his head. "Not here. Let's go to my office."

Erica's stomach knotted. Oh, great. What was going to happen to her now? Last time she'd been involved with a commanding officer she'd been sent packing. That was why she didn't mix work and relationships.

They walked in silence to his office. He opened the door for her.

"Please have a seat."

"I prefer to stand, if you don't mind, Captain."

Thorne frowned. "Why are you standing at attention, Commander?"

"Aren't I being called up on the rug?"

"It's called 'out on the carpet'. I think that's what you mean."

Erica sighed. "Right."

"No, Commander. You're not being scolded. At ease."

She relaxed, but not completely. This time she wasn't going to be caught unawares. This time she'd be ready for whatever Captain Wilder had for her. Erica planned to keep this commission. She wasn't going to be run out of another one. Not this time. Since her Rhode Island posting, when her reputation had been left in tatters, she'd worked damned hard to get it back. It was her prize intangible possession. Her reputation was at stake and that was all she had left.

"You can sit, Commander."

"I still prefer to stand, Captain."

"I'd prefer it if you'd sit."

"Why?" she asked.

"I never sit in the presence of a lady who remains standing. It's how I was raised. So if you would sit, then I could sit—and I'd really like to sit because my leg has been bothering me something fierce today."

Erica could see the discomfort etched in his face, the barely controlled pain. His knuckles were white as he was gripping the back of his chair and there was a fine sheen of sweat across his brow. It wasn't about nicety; he was suffering.

"I'm sorry, Captain."

He shook his head. "Don't be sorry, please just have a seat."

She nodded and sat down on the other side of his desk.

Even though he told her she wasn't being reprimanded, she was still ill at ease. She had no idea why Thorne wanted to see her.

Performance review?

One could only hope. She'd been at the job for a month now.

"Commander, I called you up here because I want to apologize."

What? "I'm sorry...what, Captain?"

"Apologize, Commander. It's not an easy thing for me to say, but that's why I called you up here."

"I'm not sure I quite understand."

"For making you feel uncomfortable at the bar two weeks ago and on the beach. I know the corporal's death affected you and it looked like you needed a friend. I'm sorry if my actions were out of line."

"Thank you, Captain." Erica was stunned. She'd never had a superior apologize to her before. It surprised her. There were many things she'd been expecting him to say, but an apology had not been one of them. "I'm sorry too."

Thorne cocked an eyebrow. "For what?"

"For avoiding you."

A smile broke out on his face, his eyes twinkling. "I knew you were."

"You did."

"You're not that aloof, Erica. May I call you Erica now?"

She nodded. "Yes. I think we've established that when we're alone that's acceptable."

"So, why have you been avoiding me?"

"I thought it was for the best. I'm here to prove myself. I'm not here to make friends."

"Everyone needs a friend."

"Not me." And she meant it.

"Really? I'm intrigued—you have no friends?"

Erica rolled her eyes. "I have friends, just not here. At home and not in the service." Well, except for Regina, but he didn't need to know that.

"I'm talking about friends here. You need a friend."

"And what about you?"

Thorne leaned back in his chair, tenting his fingers. "What about me?"

"Who are your friends, if you don't mind me asking? You work just as much as I do, if not more. I've been to Scooby's bar a couple of times and two weeks ago was the first time I saw you there."

"Scooby knows English, by the way."

"What?" she asked.

"I was pulling your leg, but he warned me that I should tell you the truth."

She rolled her eyes. "I don't know why I fell for that. I knew he knew English. He's been living around the base his whole life."

Thorne shrugged. "It's a bit of an initiation."

"I thought my crazy shifts at the beginning were that."

"Partly." He grinned. "It's true, I don't have many friends here, being the commanding officer of the trauma department and being involved in Special Ops training. Well, as much as I can be with my prosthetic. I can't do much in the way of water training."

"We can be friends." Erica was stunned when the words slipped out of her mouth and she could tell Thorne was just as surprised.

"Really? After that whole rigmarole you just gave me about being here to prove yourself and not make friends?"

She smiled. "Perhaps you're wearing me down. Perhaps I do need a friend."

Their gazes locked and she could feel the blood rushing to her cheeks; hear her pulse thunder in her ears.

You're weak. So weak.

"I'm glad," he said, finally breaking the tension which crackled between them. "Very glad. So I can assume my apology is accepted."

"Yes."

"Good. So were you really avoiding me because you didn't want to be friends or was it something else? You know, I used to interrogate people in the Special Ops. I know when someone is lying to me." He got up and moved toward her, sitting on the edge of his desk in front of her. Their bodies were so close, but not quite touching.

Get a grip on yourself.

"Fine. I was avoiding you because I thought perhaps you might've been coming on to me."

"And if I was?"

Flames licked through her body.

"Then it would be inappropriate," she said, meeting his gaze. "It would be unwelcome."

No. It wouldn't.

Thorne nodded and moved away. "Good, because I wasn't—and I wanted to make sure you weren't avoiding me because you thought I was being inappropriate with you, Commander."

She should be glad, but she wasn't. If Thorne wasn't her captain or her former patient…if she hadn't seen him at his most vulnerable… Well, there was no point in dwelling on the past. The past couldn't be changed and there was no possible hope or future with Thorne. None. He was off-limits.

"I'm glad to hear that." She stood. "May I get back to my duties? I was about to start rounds."

"Of course. But, look, my offer still stands about taking you around Ginowan. As friends. I think it would do you good to get off the base and see some sights. I know you're used to working on a ship where there weren't many escape options."

"Thank you. I would like that."

He nodded. "It'll do you good to get out there. We'll meet tomorrow at zero nine hundred hours. You're dismissed, Commander."

Erica saluted and left his office posthaste. Not because she was late for rounds, but because once again she found she had to put some distance between her and Thorne. Why did he have to be her commanding officer? Why was she even thinking about him in that way? She'd lost her prestigious posting in Rhode Island because she'd dated a commanding officer and when it had gone south she'd been thrown under the bus.

"Lieutenant Griffin is mentally unfit to become a commander. Look what happened to her father."

Men couldn't be trusted.

She didn't need this, yet he was right. Erica was lonely and, even though she tried to tell herself otherwise, she wanted the companionship Thorne was offering.

She wanted the friendship and maybe something more.

And that thought scared her.

Thorne pulled up in front of Erica's quarters in his tiny Japanese-made turbo. She had to suppress a giggle when she saw him because the car was so small and he was so tall.

He rolled down the window. "I'd open the door for you, but once I get behind the wheel it's a bit of a pain to get out and back in with my leg."

"No worries." She checked to make sure her door was locked and then headed for the car. She climbed into the passenger seat. She was five-ten and it was a squeeze for her too. So she could only imagine that Thorne might've needed a shoehorn to get his big Nordic frame into this little hatchback.

"I thought you would've driven an SUV or something," she said.

"Not in Okinawa. Some of the roads are narrow. I do have a nice, big gas-guzzling truck on my mom's farm back in Minnesota."

"Minnesota. That doesn't surprise me, given your Viking name."

He grinned. "Yes, my family is from Norway. Your name, though: it's hard to figure where you're from."

"I was a Navy brat, but my *mamère*—my grand-mother—lived in the bayous of Louisiana and I was born there."

"A Southern girl."

"Yes, sir. Though don't ask me to do a Creole accent or drawl or whatever. I don't have one. I was born in New Orleans, but I didn't live there very long. I was raised on the East and West Coasts. Except for a three-year stint in Arizona."

"Yet you blurt out some Cajun every once in a while."

"A bit. I spent a lot of summers with Mamère."

"You've been all over."

"Yes and working on a medical ship helped with that."

"I bet." He put the car into drive. "You haven't seen Okinawa yet."

"No. I haven't."

"You're in for a real treat, then."

He signaled and pulled away, down the road to the base's entrance. They signed out with the Master of Arms on duty. Once the gate lifted they were off down the road toward the city of Ginowan. The wind blew in her hair and she could smell the sea. She took a deep breath and relaxed. It was the first time in a long time she'd actually sat back and relaxed.

"Where are we headed?" she asked, not that she really

cared where they were going. She was just happy to be off the base and seeing the sights.

"There's a temple in Ginowan that's pretty. Thought we'd stop there first. Maybe we can spot some Shisa dogs."

"What are Shisa dogs?"

"They guard the island. There are stone carvings of lion dogs hidden everywhere."

"Neat."

Thorne nodded. "Not much of the original architecture remains. Most was destroyed in 1945 during the Battle of Okinawa in World War II."

"I did know that. My grandfather fought during that battle, actually."

"With the Navy?"

"No, the Marines."

"Did he survive?"

Erica chuckled. "Of course, or I wouldn't be here talking to you today. My father was the youngest of seven children and he wasn't born until 1956."

Thorne laughed. "Good point."

"Did any of your family serve?"

Thorne's easy demeanor vanished and he visibly tensed. His smile faded and that dour, serious face she was used to seeing around the halls of the base hospital glanced at her.

"Yes. My brother."

"Navy?"

"Yes." It was a clipped answer, like he didn't want to say anything further, and she wasn't going to press him, but she couldn't help but wonder where his brother was. Did he still serve? Was Thorne's brother in the SEALs? Maybe that was why it was a bit of a sore spot for him.

Either way, it wasn't her business.

Just like her past wasn't his business.

"So, tell me about these dogs."

Thorne's expression softened. "I'm no expert on Oki-nawan history. Your best bet is to ask Scooby."

"Oh, yes? The man who supposedly doesn't know English? 'That'll be no problem'," she air-quoted.

Thorne laughed with her. "Again, sorry about that."

"I know, I know. It was all a part of my initiation. I've had several now; I should be used to them."

"Scooby wants to warn you off of me and vice versa."

"Vice versa?" she asked. "Why? What have I ever done to him?"

"He thinks we're both too pigheaded and stubborn to get along well."

Erica chuckled. "He could be right. I am stubborn, but not without just cause."

"So I've heard."

Now she was intrigued and a bit worried. "From who?"

"My commanding officer. He said you were quite ada-mant that I not be removed from the ship, even if the or-ders came direct from the White House."

She laughed. "That's true. When it comes to my patients. Some find it annoying."

"Not me," Thorne said and he glanced over at her quickly. "It's the mark of a damn fine surgeon. Which you are."

Heat flamed in her cheeks. "Thank you."

"There's no need to thank me. I'm speaking the truth. I don't lie."

"That's funny," she said.

"What?"

"That you don't lie, when you *clearly* did." She regret-ted the words the moment she said them.

Good job. You are finally starting to make friends and you insult that one and only friend.

Instead of giving her the silent treatment he snorted. "I didn't really lie per se."

"How do you figure that?"

"I just withheld the truth."

Erica raised an eyebrow. "Right. And the definition of lying is…?"

Thorne just winked at her. "Here we are. I hope you wore socks. No shoes in the temple." He parked the car on the street and they climbed out. It was good to stretch her legs. The little temple was built into the side of a hill surrounded by an older part of town, which was bustling. The temple was overgrown with foliage and the stairs up to it were crumbling.

"It's beautiful." And it was. Erica had traveled around the world, and had seen many places of worship, but there was something about this temple which struck her as different and captivating. Something she couldn't quite put her finger on.

"Shall we go in?"

"Are we allowed to?" she asked.

"Sure." And then without asking her permission Thorne reached out and took her hand, sending a shock of electricity up her spine at his touch. He didn't seem to notice the way her breath caught in her throat when she gasped.

Instead he squeezed her hand gently and led her through the packed streets toward the temple. What was even weirder was that she didn't pull away.

She let him.

She liked the feeling of her hand in his. It was comforting, and in the few past relationships she'd had, she could never recall sharing such a moment of intimacy. There had been lust, sex, but hand-holding? Never. Such a simple act gave her a thrill.

Don't think like that. It means nothing. You're just friends.

Right. She had to keep reminding herself of that.

They were just friends.

That was all there was between them and that was all there could ever be.

CHAPTER SEVEN

THORNE DIDN'T KNOW why he reached out and took her hand to lead her across the busy Ginowan street. It was instinctive and a gentlemanly thing to do. They were halfway across the street when he realized that he was holding Erica's hand, that he was guiding her through the maze of people, whizzing motorbikes and cars toward the temple.

She didn't pull away either like she had before.

Erica let him lead her to safety. It was an act of trust and Thorne had a feeling that trust didn't come too easily to her.

Not that he blamed her. People couldn't always be trusted. He'd learned that well enough both in his service as a SEAL and a surgeon.

"Yes, Dr. Wilder. I quit smoking."

"No. I know nothing about threats to your country."

Thorne could usually read people like a book. It had been one of his strong suits when he was in the Special Ops. Erica was hard to read though and maybe that was another reason why he was *so* drawn to her.

He did like a challenge.

You shouldn't be thinking this way. She's your second in command. She made her feelings quite clear to you the other day.

She was a puzzle. One he wanted to figure out. He was

a sucker for puzzles. Thorne cursed himself. He couldn't be involved with her or any other woman.

He couldn't emotionally commit to someone.

Not in his line of work.

Not after seeing what it had done to his brother's widow, to his mother.

When he'd lost his leg and woken up in that hospital in San Diego, unaware of where he was and how he'd got there, his first memory besides Erica's face haunting him had been seeing his mom curled up on an uncomfortable cot, a few more gray strands in her black hair, dark circles under her eyes.

It had almost killed his mother when Liam had died.

No. He couldn't do that to someone else and he couldn't ever have kids either. He didn't want to leave his children without a father should something happen to him.

You're not in Special Ops anymore. What harm could happen here?

A shudder ran down his spine. What harm indeed? Corporal Ryder probably hadn't thought his life would end during a simple training exercise. That it would end because of a shark bite.

Take the risk.

It was a different voice in his head this time, one that he thought he'd long buried, and it wasn't welcome here now.

No. She's off-limits.

"I think it's going to rain," Erica said, glancing up at the sky.

"What?" Thorne asked. "Sorry, I didn't hear you."

"Rain. It became overcast quite quickly."

Thorne didn't look at the sky; he glanced at the delicate but strong hand in his. It felt good there, but it didn't belong. He let it go and jammed his hands into his pockets.

Her cheeks bloomed with pink and she awkwardly rubbed her hand, as if wiping away the memory of his.

"Maybe we should go inside," Thorne offered, breaking the tension between them.

"Sure," she agreed, but she wouldn't look at him. "Lead the way."

He nodded and led her up the walkway toward the temple entrance. This had to stop. She was affecting him so much. Usually he was so focused on his work. Now he was distracted and he knew he had to get control of this situation before it escalated any further. She'd agreed to be friends. They could be friends.

Who are you kidding?

He watched her as she made her way to the small, almost abandoned Ryukyuan temple. It was made of wood and stone and embedded in the side of a hill. It was more a tourist attraction than it was a functional temple, as most Okinawans practiced at home in honoring their ancestors.

She paused and touched the stone at the gate, glancing up, and her mouth slightly opened as she marveled at the architecture. It was old, mixed with new, as parts of the small temple had been destroyed during the battle of Okinawa.

"Beautiful." She smiled at him, her eyes twinkling and her honey-blond hair blowing softly in the breeze. She was weaving some sort of spell around him. He just wanted to take her in his arms and kiss her. The thought startled him because, even though it wasn't new, he'd been trying to ignore the desire, the lust which coursed through him. He didn't recall ever having this urgency before with women he dated in the past.

This need.

This want.

"I thought you wanted to get out of the rain?" Thorne asked.

"Right." She blushed and stopped at the door to take off her shoes and Thorne followed her, glad he was wearing slip-ons so he wouldn't have to struggle with laces and his leg.

"Welcome. You're welcome to look around; we just ask that there be no photography," the guide said from behind the desk as they entered the temple.

"Thank you." Thorne paid a donation to allow them in and explore the history of the temple. Erica was wandering around and looking at the carvings and the paintings on the wall.

"Are these the lion dogs you were talking about, Thorne?"

"Ah, yes," the guide said, standing. "The Shisa is a protective ward to keep out evil spirits. They're often found in pairs."

Thorne nodded and then moved behind Erica, placing his hand on the small of her back to escort her further into the temple, where a few other tourists were milling about, reading about the history and photographs on the walls.

Erica leaned over and whispered, her breath fanning his neck. "I really know nothing about Okinawa history."

"I know a bit."

"What religion do Okinawans practice?"

"There are several forms, but it all falls under the Ryukyuan religion. A lot of the worship has to do with nature."

Erica smiled. "Pretty awesome."

"I have some books for you to read, if you're interested."

"I don't have time to read." Then she moved away from him to look at some old pictures after the battle of Okinawa. "Crazy. They say it was the bloodiest battle of the Pacific War."

"It was and 149,193 of those lost were Okinawan civilians."

"Such a loss of life."

"It is," he said. "It's a hard line we walk as surgeons who serve. We don't like to see death, but yet we serve something bigger and greater. Something that helps innocents remain free."

Gooseflesh broke out over her at his eloquent words. She often felt at war with herself and her beliefs. Even though she was in the Navy she wasn't one who went out to fight. Though she'd learned about armed combat as part of her training during Annapolis, she hoped she'd never have to be in a situation to use it.

Thorne was different.

He'd actually served in combat situations.

He carried a gun and as a SEAL had undertaken covert operations that she couldn't even begin to imagine. She wanted to ask him if he'd ever killed someone before, but she could tell by the pain in his eyes when he read the names on the list, the names of those who had fallen during the Battle of Okinawa, that he had.

And it pained him.

Besides it wasn't her business to ask him that and she was enjoying his company; the last thing she wanted to do was drive him away by prying.

The moment he'd mentioned his brother he'd put a wall up.

"It is a hard line to walk," she said. She moved away from him into a hallway, which was carved. They were heading under the hillside and she could hear water running. When they got down at the end of the hallway there was a hole in the ceiling letting the light filter through and in the center was a pond where pots of incense were burning.

Misty rain fell through the opening, causing smoke to rise from the incense. It was beautiful, and the smell was spicy but welcoming.

"What's this?" Erica asked as she moved closer.

"It's called a Kaa, I believe. Water is holy, hence the incense."

"It's beautiful."

Thorne nodded. "It is."

They stood in companionable silence for a while around the Kaa. There was no one else in the room with them and suddenly she was very aware of his presence.

It was like there was some sort of spell being weaved here in this moment, next to the water and with the incense thick in the air, and for a moment she thought about kissing him.

It had been a long time since she'd kissed a man and the thought of kissing him here made her pulse race and her body ache with anticipation.

"It's pretty damp in here. Why don't we go find somewhere to have a cup of tea and maybe lunch?" He didn't wait for his answer, but turned and walked down the hall back to the entrance.

Erica followed him.

The spell was broken, for now.

After the temple and that moment in the Kaa, they drove back toward the base. The drizzle was making it impossible really to enjoy anything. Thorne did suggest heading over to the American village, but Erica didn't really feel like shopping.

Half the stuff she could or would buy, she couldn't even wear on a day-to-day basis anyway. She was either in scrubs working in the hospital, in fatigues or in dress uniform when she was on duty and that was what she was most comfortable in. It was no big loss.

Shopping had always been a luxury in her youth.

With her mother on a widow's pension, there hadn't been much money to go around.

After high school she'd gone straight to college and then Annapolis to help pay for her medical career.

Regina, her one close friend on the *Hope,* had always teased her about being tight with her money. When they would go on shore leave she would be the only one who didn't buy a lot of things.

Things were hard to transport.

Things took up space. Erica was a bit minimalist.

So they headed back to the base and found themselves at the Painappurufeisu.

"Isn't it a little early to drink?" Erica teased, though she was really ready for a drink. The ride back to the base had been silent and awkward.

"Scooby runs a full-service pub. He's got the best pizza near the base."

"Really?" Now she was intrigued.

"Do you like pizza?"

Erica shrugged. "It's okay, but then I really don't have a lot of experience with pizza besides the offerings of chain restaurants. The *Hope* didn't sail in the Mediterranean, so I didn't even get to experience any real Italian pizza. I'm not sure that pizza is my thing."

Great. You're rambling about pizza.

Thorne looked at her like she was crazy and she didn't blame him. She was saying the word "pizza" a lot. Instead he surprised her by asking, "How can pizza not be your thing?"

She chuckled. "I don't know?"

"Pizza has to be everyone's thing. Well, in moderation."

She rolled her eyes, but couldn't help but laugh. "I take it pizza is your thing?"

"And beer."

"Right. You have a taste for the local brews."

"They're good. You'd be surprised. They can have more of a kick than some American beers."

"I can give you a kick if you'd like."

He laughed. "No thanks. I'll take my chances with the local brew. So, are you up for trying some of Scooby's pizza?"

"Sure, but I have to tell you that sounds inherently weird and kind of sacrilegious to my childhood."

Thorne laughed. "His real name is Sachiho, but he actually prefers Scooby. Back before we were ever serving in the Navy, a drunk airman couldn't say his name and called him Scooby instead and it stuck."

"Sachiho…what does that mean?"

Thorne shrugged. "No idea. You could ask him. He would be impressed that you knew it."

"Or he'll just answer me, 'no problem'."

Thorne shook his head. "Again. I'm sorry for that little farce."

"Sure you are."

He pulled in front of the Painappurufeisu. Rock music was filtering through the open windows. The neon sign was flashing, letting everyone know the bar was open for business.

"You know, I was hoping you would take me to eat at a local place. Somewhere authentic."

Thorne held open the door to Scooby's. "Trust me, the pizza here is authentic."

"I don't know whether I should be eager or worried about that."

"You'll have to wait and find out."

As soon as they entered the bar Scooby waved at them. "Hey, Captain Wilder and Commander Griffin, it's a pleasure to see you again."

Thorne waved and then led them to one of the bamboo booths, which was upholstered with a jungle theme material. It was then Erica noticed the wall beside their booth was lined with a green shag carpet.

"I think I've fallen into a time warp." She reached out and touched it to make sure that it was really green shag.

"Why's that?"

"This reminds me of Elvis's jungle room at Graceland."

"Have you been to Graceland?"

"Yes. A couple of times. My *mamère* was an Elvis fan." It was only about four hours from her home in Louisiana to Graceland.

"Ah, I like Elvis too," Scooby said, interrupting. "The King of Rock and Roll. I've been to Graceland too. It's where I got the idea for my jungle-themed dining room."

"Well, Elvis lined the ceiling of his jungle room. Why did you line the walls?"

Scooby shrugged. "I wanted to go all out."

"That you did."

"I told Erica that your pizza was the best around these parts," Thorne said.

Scooby beamed with pride. "This is true. Would you like a pizza?"

"Your house special."

Erica's eyes widened in trepidation. She hoped the special didn't have some kind of delicacy she'd never heard of or something like eel or other sea creature that she had no stomach for.

"No problem—and two beers?" Scooby asked.

"Please." Thorne grinned.

Scooby glanced at her. "You look concerned, Commander."

"I'm not a big fan of pizza."

"No problem, Commander. You will be." Scooby nodded and left.

"He's a man of many layers," she remarked. "Elvis, Graceland and pizza?"

Thorne nodded. "Don't forget bowling. He loves bowling. He loves all things American."

"I can see that, but why didn't he move there?"

Thorne leaned across the table, his eyes twinkling. "His wife wouldn't let him."

Erica rolled her eyes, but she couldn't help but laugh, and she couldn't remember the last time she'd let loose like this. This was better than the tense silence, which had fallen between them at the old temple in Ginowan.

"You know, I would really like to go see the Cornerstone of Peace in Itoman one day," she said, but then realized she was somewhat angling for another date when that was the furthest thing from the truth.

Was it?

Even though the drive to Scooby's had been a little tense, when Thorne had put up his walls again, she was enjoying herself.

Besides, maybe she wasn't *exactly* angling for another date, but another outing with her friend, because that was what they were.

That was all they could be.

"It's impressive. I think everyone should see it once in their life."

"Have you been, Thorne?"

"I have. It lists everyone who died during the battle. Civilian, allied forces and axis powers."

"I'd like to see it."

"We can go after lunch if you want."

"S-sure." And their eyes locked across the table. His was face unreadable as they sat there, that tension falling between them again.

"Here we go. Two beers," Scooby said cheerfully, breaking the silence between them as he set down two dark bottles of beer.

"These have Shisa on them." Erica winked at Thorne.

"Ah, you learned about Shisa today, Commander Griffin?" Scooby asked.

"I did. I also learned your name isn't really Scooby but Sachiho."

Scooby grinned. "Aye."

"What does it mean in Ryukyuan?"

"It's not native to Okinawa. It's more common in Japan. My mother was from Japan. But, in answer to your question, it means 'a charitable man'."

"You're very charitable, Scooby," Thorne teased.

Scooby's eyes narrowed. "You're not getting a free lunch out of me again, Captain."

They all laughed.

"I'll go grab the pizza." Scooby hurried away.

"Did this drunk soldier try to get out of a tab and felt that Sachiho maybe didn't suit Scooby at the time?" Erica asked.

"I never thought of that, but I'm not going to ask him."

Scooby returned and set the pizza down in front of them. "Specialty of the house."

Erica breathed a sigh of relief. "The specialty of the house is pineapple?"

Scooby looked confused. "Painappurufeisu means 'pineapple face'. What did you think my specialty would be?"

Erica laughed. "I have no idea, but I have to learn not to trust Captain Wilder."

Thorne took a swig of his beer, amusement in his eyes.

Scooby *tsked*. "Captain Wilder, you should be nicer to your second in command. Don't listen to a word he says, Commander."

"I'll take that to heart, Sachiho. Thank you."

Scooby grinned and left them to eat.

"Is this why this posting was vacant with hardly any applicants? Do you drive your commanding officers away, Captain?"

He smiled. "Possibly."

"Well, I think I'll take Sachiho's advice and not trust you. Unless we're working in the OR."

"Probably best."

"I've never had pineapple on a pizza before," she remarked.

"Well, then, I wasn't totally off base. It is a delicacy and something you've never had before."

They dug into the pizza and Erica really enjoyed it. While they ate they chatted about life on base and about some of the more colorful characters.

When they were done, she leaned against the back of the booth, staring at the green shag carpeting, chuckling to herself.

"What's so funny?" Thorne asked.

"My *mamère* would really like this place. Hawaii was her favorite vacation spot, the second place being Graceland."

"How many times have you been to…where is Graceland, exactly?"

"Memphis, Tennessee."

"Really?" Thorne asked. "I thought that's where Beale Street was—you know, the birthplace of rock 'n' roll, home of the million-dollar quartet, where Cash got his big break."

Erica cocked an eyebrow. "And who do you think was part of that million-dollar quartet? It was Cash, Perkins, Lewis and Presley."

"I only know about Cash," Thorne said. "Cash was awesome."

"Well, Memphis is home to Beale Street and Graceland. Who do you think invented rock 'n' roll?"

Thorne grinned. "You have me there. That would be interesting to see one day, but don't let Scooby know I have any interest in going to Graceland."

"Why?"

"He'll start the slide show."

Erica laughed and then her phone began to vibrate. She glanced down and saw it was from the hospital. When she looked up she could see that Thorne was looking at his phone as well. "Incoming trauma."

"I know," he said. "Accident on trawler."

"We better go."

Thorne nodded. "Agreed."

They slipped out of the booth and he paid Scooby. As they headed outside Erica could hear the choppers bringing the wounded from the trawler out at sea. The chopper was headed straight for the helipad at the hospital. Several vehicles whizzed by as on-call staff raced toward the hospital.

As she opened the door to Thorne's car a large chopper zoomed overhead. It was loud and nearly ripped the door from her hand, it was flying so low and so fast toward the hospital. It reminded her of the chopper which had brought Thorne aboard the *Hope*.

Only this time it wasn't night, they weren't on a ship in the middle of the ocean, which had gone into silent running and it wasn't a covert operation. This was what she was used to, though she couldn't even begin to fathom the kind of emergency, which would've happened on a trawler off the west coast of Okinawa.

"Let's go, Commander."

Erica nodded and climbed in the passenger seat.

"You know," Thorne said as he started the ignition. "I had every intention of taking you to the Cornerstone of Peace today."

"You did?"

He nodded. "I did."

"Well, maybe another day, then."

Thorne nodded. "Another day."

CHAPTER EIGHT

"WHAT HAPPENED?" THORNE asked the nearest nurse as he came out of the locker rooms, his casual attire abandoned for scrubs. Once they'd pulled up to the hospital Erica had left, running ahead into the fray. Thorne couldn't keep up with her and when an emergency like this was called it was all hands on deck.

He grabbed a trauma gown, slipped it over his scrubs and then grabbed gloves.

"There was an explosion on a trawler. It burned a lot of men and then the trawler started to go down. We have some men with hypothermia and water in their lungs."

"Okinawan?"

"Some. Most of the men are Indonesian, but the trawler was registered to several different countries off the east coast of Africa."

Thorne frowned. "They're fishing far from home."

"You said it, not me."

Thorne nodded at the nurse. Maybe the trawler hadn't been fishing exactly and maybe the men had been up to something else. Either way it didn't matter and it was out of his jurisdiction. Right now he had lives to save. He headed out to meet the gurneys as they came in.

It wasn't long before the doors opened and the rescue team wheeled in a burn victim, who was screaming.

"Male, looks to be about twenty. Indonesian, doesn't speak a word of English."

Great. It was going to be tricky to get any kind of history.

"Get me a translator that knows Indonesian here, stat!" Thorne demanded.

"Yes, Captain!" someone in the fray shouted. He didn't know who, but it didn't matter, as long as his order was taken care of. He needed to know if this boy was allergic to anything and he needed to know what had caused his burn.

Was it fire? Was it chemical? These were the questions he needed answered before he could help his patient. He wanted to make sure if it was a chemical burn that any trace of the chemical was washed from his skin.

"I've got it." Thorne grabbed the gurney and wheeled it to an open triage area. "Don't worry, I'm a doctor, and you're in good hands."

The young man just whimpered, his brown eyes wide with fear and pain. It was obvious that the boy was in shock by his pale complexion, his shaking and his shallow breathing. Thorne slipped nose cannula into his nose.

The boy started to freak out, but Thorne tried to calm him down.

"Breathe, just breathe. It's oxygen."

The boy began to shake, but his breathing regulated as he inhaled the oxygen.

"We need to start a central line." A nurse handed Thorne a tray and he moved into action. The boy reached out and gripped his arm. His eyes were wild as he watched Thorne in trepidation. "I'm sorry, this will hurt—but only for a moment and then it will help."

The boy shook his head, not understanding. He took one look at the needle and started to cry out in fear.

"I need that translator now!" Thorne barked.

"I'm here. I can help." Erica stood in the doorway.

"You know Indonesian?"

"I know a few languages and we helped out in Indonesia quite a lot when I was on the *Hope*."

"Good. Could you tell him that this will help with the pain?"

Erica nodded and leaned over the patient. *"Hal ini akan membantu."*

"Ask him what kind of burn he has."

Erica asked the boy how he'd got his burns.

"Api."

"Fire, Captain."

"Okay. Then we know how we can proceed. Tell him we'll help him, that this will ease his pain and we'll take care of him."

Erica gently spoke to him. The boy nodded and calmed down. Erica continued to hold his hand.

Thorne inserted the central line as Erica continued to murmur words of encouragement to the frightened boy. Soon he was able to feed the boy medication to manage the pain and the grip on Erica's hand lessened until she was able to let it go.

"You should go back out and lend a hand."

Erica nodded but, the moment she tried to leave, the boy reached out and grabbed her.

"Silakan tinggal."

"What's he saying?" Thorne asked.

"He wants me to stay with him."

"We have other trauma."

"And other surgeons. I can stay for a while. At least until he passes out. He's scared."

Thorne frowned. "I understand your compassion, but this boy's burn will require hours of debridement. Your presence as my second in command is required on the floor."

"I'm sorry, Captain. I have to stay here."

"Are you disobeying me, Commander?"

Erica's eyes narrowed and he could tell she was angry. Heck, he was too. He wished he had the luxury of keeping her in the same room as him as he did his work, but he needed her out there helping, not catering to this boy.

Bunny poked her head into the triage room. "The translator showed up."

"Thanks, Bunny." Thorne turned to Erica. "The translator is here. Go back to the floor, Commander."

Erica bent over and whispered some words to the boy, who nodded and let go of his hold on her. Once he did that Erica moved out of the triage room without so much as a backward glance at him.

Thorne didn't want to annoy her, far from it, but she was a valuable asset to the trauma floor. He couldn't have her playing translator to a scared young man.

"Captain Wilder?"

Thorne glanced up to see a young lieutenant standing in the doorway. "You the translator?"

"Aye, Captain."

"Good. I need to explain what I'm doing to this young man and reassure him that this will help. Nurse, will you gown our translator?"

"Of course, Captain."

Thorne turned back to his instruments while the nurse put a gown and mask on the translator. He glanced out into the trauma floor and saw Erica assessing another patient who had just been brought in. The paramedics had been working on him, giving him CPR as they wheeled him through the hospital doors.

Only now Erica had taken over, shouting orders as she climbed on the gurney to administer CPR, nurses and intern surgeons racing to wheel her away from the oncoming traffic and to a triage room.

Thorne knew he'd made the right decision booting her out of the room. She was a surgeon and a damn fine one.

One that he was proud to have on his team.

Erica stretched. It felt like her back was going to shatter into a million pieces and her feet were no longer useful appendages that she sometimes liked to apply the occasional coat of red nail polish to. No, they now were two lumps of ache and sweat.

"How long was that surgery?" she muttered under her breath as she scrubbed out because she'd lost track of time in there.

"Eight hours," a scrub nurse said through a yawn. "Good work in there, Commander." The nurse left the scrub room and Erica stretched again.

Yeah, she'd believe eight hours for sure, though it felt like maybe that surgery had lasted days. There were a few times she hadn't been sure if her patient was going to make it. She placed her scrub cap in the laundry bin and headed to her locker.

"I heard you had a piece of the trawler's engine embedded in your patient's abdomen?"

Erica groaned, recognizing Thorne's voice behind her. She'd been angry with him for forcing her away, for not letting her comfort that young man, but Thorne had been right.

She needed to be out on the trauma floor, practicing medicine and not translating. If she'd disobeyed orders she wouldn't have been able to operate on her patient and save his life. Her back might've liked that, and definitely her feet, but she was glad she was in the OR doing what she loved.

Saving a life.

Damn. He was right and he probably wasn't going to let her live it down.

"Yes. Part of the engine decided my patient was a good resting place."

Thorne winced. "The prognosis?"

"So far so good. He's in the ICU. How's your patient?"

"Resting comfortably in the burn unit. From what he was telling the translator, that trawler was not fishing off the coast of Okinawa."

"I thought as much."

Thorne crossed his arms. "What made you think that?"

"There were traces of methamphetamine in my patient's blood stream. We had a few close calls on the OR table. A few codes."

Thorne nodded. "The proper authorities have been called. Since they weren't in international waters, we've called the Japanese officials. I'm sure several patients will be interrogated."

"I wouldn't doubt it."

Thorne hesitated, as if he wanted to say more, but couldn't.

Or wouldn't.

Though she barely knew him, Erica recognized a stubborn soul. Sometimes it was like looking in a mirror, because she was stubborn too. Stubborn to the point it had almost cost her her commission a few times.

"You did good in there, Commander."

Erica nodded. "Thank you, Captain."

"Go rest." Thorne turned to leave, but then stopped. "I heard the *Hope* will be in port in a week."

"Really?" she asked.

"Does that make you happy?" he asked.

"It does bring some cheer. Yes. It'll be good to catch up with some old friends."

A strange look passed over his face. "I thought you didn't make friends. I thought you were something of a lone wolf. Like me."

"I had a select few on the *Hope*. It's hard to be confined in close quarters and not make friends, Captain."

"You're right." Then he turned to leave.

"What about our rain check?" she asked, not really believing that she'd asked that. "The Cornerstone of Peace?"

He glanced over his shoulder briefly. "Maybe some other time."

And with that he walked away. He never once brought up her insubordination to her. How she'd almost disobeyed his orders in that triage room. Nor did he apologize for ordering her out. Not that he had to. Captains rarely apologized.

Especially when they were right, and he'd been right.

She'd been the fool. The one in the wrong. And it had probably cost her the friendship.

And more.

Erica closed her eyes and took a deep, steadying breath before turning and heading back toward the locker room. Really, she should be glad that it was such a quick break. That nothing awkward had come between them, which would make it impossible to work with him and would result in her eventual transfer.

This was better.

A working relationship. That was all she wanted from him. He was her commanding officer and she'd do her duty right by him, this hospital and her country.

Still, it stung when he walked away from her and she hated herself a bit for that because, despite every lie she told herself, she really enjoyed their day together.

She liked being around him.

For that one brief moment, it was nice to have a friend.

It was nice to go on a date.

CHAPTER NINE

SHE DIDN'T KNOW he was watching her and Thorne didn't really know why he was watching her. From the research room, he could see out onto the trauma floor. After the trawler accident he'd put her back on some night shifts just so he could get some space from her.

With the *Hope* coming into port, well, it reminded him of when she'd taken his leg. It reminded him of his pain, of his vulnerability, and that she had seen him so exposed.

It was an easy way out, but he hadn't seen her in a week.

Erica had the next two days off while the *Hope* was docked in port.

Still, he didn't know why he remained after hours to do research.

So you could see her. Who are you kidding? He liked to torture himself, apparently.

The research room had a one-way window. You could see out, but not in. He'd really intended to catch up on some work, but the trauma floor was quiet tonight and she was spending a lot of time working on charts at the nurses' station. Again he acted irrationally and avoided her. It was easier than dealing with the emotion she was stirring inside him.

He knew that she was breaking down his walls, ones

he'd had up for ten years since Liam had died. He didn't deserve to be happy again. He'd been the foolish one who'd cost his brother his life.

So he hated himself for wanting Erica, for enjoying the time they spent together. He hadn't realized he was so lonely.

Focus.

Thorne tore his gaze from her and returned to his work. There was a knock at the door.

"Come."

The door opened and Captain Dayton of the USNV *Hope* opened the door.

Thorne stood, saluting the other captain. "Captain Dayton, I wasn't expecting you until tomorrow."

"We got in a bit early and I wanted to check in at the hospital and visit with an old colleague of mine."

"Commander Griffin?" Thorne asked.

Captain Dayton smiled. "Yes. She was a formidable surgeon. I took her under my wing, thought of her like a daughter."

Thorne nodded toward the trauma floor. "She's out there charting if you want to speak with her. I'm sure she'll be pleased to see you."

Captain Dayton smiled. "I will. Thank you. And thank you for accommodating some of my nurses and surgeons. It's very important we have this simulation training to keep us up to date. After this we head back to San Diego to get some retrofits and some much-needed shore leave."

"No problem, Captain Dayton. Your staff has free run of facilities here."

"My thanks, Captain Wilder."

"I hope your staff can have a bit of off-time here in Okinawa. There is a lot to offer."

Captain Dayton cocked an eyebrow. "Is that so?"

"Yes. In fact, I know Admiral Greer was planning on

throwing a bit of a social while the *Hope* is in port. Though that's supposed to be a secret."

Captain Dayton laughed. "I'll keep that secret safe. That sounds like fun. Well, after my crew completes their simulation training, I think they'll have earned the right for a bit of rest and relaxation before heading to San Diego. I'm very much looking forward to your simulation course, Captain Wilder."

Captain Dayton extended his hand and Thorne shook it.

"I look forward to presenting it."

"I think I'll go visit with my former prized officer."

Thorne sat back down as Captain Dayton left the research lab and headed over to Erica. He tried to look away, to give them their privacy, but he couldn't. Something compelled him to watch.

When Erica saw Captain Dayton her face lit up as she saluted him and then embraced him, kissing his cheek. A surge of jealousy flared deep inside him as he watched Erica being so intimate with another man. His jealousy was misplaced. He had no right to feel this way.

He had no claim.

Erica wasn't his.

She could be.

He cursed under his breath and turned back to the computer, but his curiosity got the better of him. Even though he knew he should keep away from Erica, he couldn't help himself.

Despite the warnings he watched the interplay between the two. Captain Dayton was old enough to be Erica's father, but what did that matter? Age was meaningless.

As she talked to her former commanding officer Thorne saw her eyes twinkle. Her smile was genuine and as they talked she reached out and touched him.

When Thorne and Erica talked there was no touching.

When they were together it often felt tense at best because Thorne was too busy trying to keep Erica out.

Thorne sighed. His leg was aching. It was time to get back home, have something to eat, a shower and then bed.

He didn't have time to worry about Commander Griffin. There wasn't enough emotion in him to invest in her.

At least, that was what he kept trying to tell himself.

He went to log off when the door to the research lab opened again.

"Captain! I'm sorry I didn't know you were in here." Erica's face flushed pink, but only for a moment.

"I was just leaving for the night, Commander."

She nodded and stepped into the room, shutting the door behind her. "Are you prepping your simulation for the crew of the *Hope*?"

"I am. It's how to deal with some common medical issues and emergencies Special Ops have to face. Wounds... infections."

Erica sat down at the computer next to him. "Infections like yours?"

"And more. Communicable diseases as well."

"Sounds like a potpourri of fun that you have planned."

He chuckled. "I try my best. I see Captain Dayton found you."

"Yes," she said quickly. "He was a good commanding officer, but a bit suffocating."

Now he was intrigued. "Suffocating? You looked pleased to see him."

"Were you watching me?"

"For a moment."

"For someone who has been ignoring me the last week and giving me endless night shifts again, you're very observant about who I associate with."

"Is this how you usually talk to your commanding officer?"

"No." She grinned. "Just you."

He rolled his eyes. "Thanks. I do appreciate that, Commander Griffin."

"So, you wanted to know how he suffocated me— well, he wouldn't let me do anything without clearing it with him first. At least, for the first year I served under him."

"Everything?"

"Everything. I have to say it's a nice change being under your command, Captain."

"Why's that?" he asked, secretly pleased to hear it.

"You let me do my work."

"I expect nothing less from members of my surgical trauma team. I pick the best of the best."

She blushed. "And I'm the best?"

"One of." He had to get out of here. When he'd moved Erica to some night shifts it was to get some distance between the two of them. This was not distancing himself from her, but Erica had this way of drawing him in.

He both loved and hated that.

"I better go. My shift ended hours ago." He stood. "Have a good night, Commander."

"Thank you, Captain."

Erica had seen many men turn tail and run from an uncomfortable social situation. Usually she thought it looked a bit ridiculous. So much so that it amused her. But this actually made her feel a bit of hope again.

Hope that maybe Thorne hadn't completely washed his hands of her. That maybe, just maybe, he would tear down his walls to let her in.

You're not tearing down any walls.

Which was true.

She wasn't exactly an open book either.

Scooby had called them both stubborn and thought that

Thorne and her together would be volatile. She thought maybe Scooby was right in this instance.

Still, she was drawn to him.

She was attracted to him.

She wanted him.

Get a grip on yourself.

She couldn't want him. She couldn't have him.

Keep lying to yourself.

Erica didn't know he was still in the hospital. She'd come in early to see if she could catch a glimpse of him, but he'd stayed holed up in his office for the entire week. She had heard from some of the nurses that he was dealing with the aftermath of the trawler explosion with the authorities as well as protecting those who were on board the ship and were innocent.

Like the burn victim, Drajat.

He was only eighteen and had had no idea that his uncle, the patient Erica had saved who'd had part of the engine in his abdomen, was drug running.

Drajat had told the authorities that he thought they were actually on a fishing trip. He thought he was earning money so he could attend school; the trace amount of methamphetamines in his system was equal to that of an innocent bystander being around the drugs, but not using them.

Meth was easily absorbed into the skin.

As soon as Drajat was stable enough he would be flown back to Jakarta.

As for Drajat's uncle… He was progressing well, but was still in ICU. Once he was able to be interrogated, well, Erica wasn't sure what the Okinawan police would do with him. This was an international issue as the trawler had crossed into Japanese waters.

"Commander?"

Erica turned in the swivel chair to see that Thorne had returned.

"Yes, Captain? Is there something I can help you with?"

He opened his mouth but then shook his head. "No. It's nothing."

"It's obviously something. I thought you were leaving for the night."

Thorne scrubbed his hand over his face. He looked tired and she didn't blame him in the least. There was also pain behind those eyes. His whole body was clenched tight, taut like a bowstring. It was the leg again.

"I'm sorry for bothering you, Commander. It's nothing." He turned to leave, but hissed through his teeth and reached down.

The last time she'd seen him suffering like this had been when she'd first arrived at the base. When she'd tried to help him he'd bit back at her, lashing out in anger and humiliation.

"You're in pain."

"I've been here too long. It's nothing."

"It's not nothing." She stood and went to the research lab door. Locked it.

"What're you doing?" he asked.

"You're going to sit down and I'm going to massage your leg."

"I don't think so," Thorne snapped. "That's highly inappropriate."

"Do you have a massage therapist who does it for you? Or how about physical therapy?"

Thorne glared at her. "I don't need either. I've been managing well with this prosthesis for some time now."

Erica rolled her eyes. "Sit down, Captain, and that's an order."

"You're ordering me now?"

She crossed her arms. "I am. You should have weekly

massage therapy or physio appointments for your leg. It might have been five years since you lost it, but a prosthetic leg can be hard on the muscle. It's painful."

"I know it is," he growled.

"Thorne, I can help relieve some of your pain. You can barely move, so I can't even begin to imagine how you'll get back home."

She stared him down.

With a grunt of resignation he sat down in an office chair. "So how are you going to help me? Are you going to give me a shot of morphine or some other analgesics?"

"No, I'm going to massage you myself." She slipped off her lab coat and set her phone down on the counter with her stethoscope.

"You're...what?"

"I'm going to massage you. Drop your pants, Captain Wilder."

CHAPTER TEN

THERE HAD BEEN many times since he'd first met Erica when he'd pictured her telling him to drop his pants and in all those scenarios it involved her in a bed, underneath him.

Not once had he ever fantasized about being locked in the research lab, in pain and having her ordering him to take his pants off so she could rub his stump. This was not perfection at all. This was far from it. He didn't want her seeing him like this.

In pain.

Exposed.

"I don't think I heard you correctly, Commander Griffin. You want me to take off my pants?"

She nodded. "Yes. You're wearing suit trousers; it'll be impossible to roll up the leg of said trousers over your prosthetic. Besides, you need to remove your prosthetic so I can massage where it hurts."

"I don't think that's appropriate." He tried to move away, but she blocked him.

"With all due respect, Captain Wilder, I've seen that leg before. I know that leg. I know what was done to it and I know how to relieve your pain."

Though he didn't want to, Thorne took a deep breath and then stood, unbuckling his pants and slipping them off. He tried not to let it bug him that she was seeing him like this: vulnerable. He didn't let any woman see him with his pants off. He didn't let any woman see him with just his prosthetic, let alone the remains of his leg.

Erica did have a point, though. She was the one who'd performed the surgery. She was the one who'd removed his leg, fashioned the stump which had left minimal scarring and a good socket to work a prosthetic in.

The surgeon side of him knew it was a damn good amputation.

The other side of him saw it was a fault. An imperfection. The absence of his leg reminded him that a piece of him was missing and how was that desirable to any woman?

What does it matter? She's off-limits.

And that was why he did as she asked.

He sat down and unhooked the prosthetic, embarrassed that she was there. Their eyes met as she knelt down in front of him, helping him remove the prosthetic and the wrappings underneath, which helped prevent the chaffing.

Her touch was gentle as she ran her hand over his thigh. The simple touch made him grit his teeth as he held back the intense pleasure he was feeling. Her hands on him made his blood burn with need.

It had been so long since he'd been with a woman, but this was not how he'd pictured it. Not even close. The way he fantasized about Erica had nothing to do with his stump, of massaging the knots out of his muscles.

"It healed nicely," she remarked, which kind of shattered the illusion.

"What?" he asked.

"The wound healed really nice. Barely any visible scarring."

"It did. It was a good job."

"I didn't know. You were taken out of my care hours

after surgery and then I never knew what became of you. You had no name, no record."

Thorne shrugged. "Special Ops."

"I know." Her brow furrowed. "Do you have a lot of chaffing?"

"Only when I work long hours. Lanolin helps."

She nodded. "Good. I'm glad to hear it. Let me know if I hurt you."

"It'll hurt no matter what you do, but I'm sure it will feel good after a while. It always does."

"I thought you didn't get a regular massage?"

"I don't—well, not by someone else. I usually handle it on my own."

Erica glanced up. "You should have someone else do it."

"Don't have time for that." He winced as she touched him.

"Am I hurting you?"

Far from it. He loved her touching him.

"Get on with it," he snapped.

"Just try and relax." She began to rub the muscle in his thigh, which was hard as a rock and tense from the pain.

He let out a string of curses.

"Do you want me to stop?" she asked.

"No. It does feel good."

"Your muscles are so knotted."

He nodded and tried not to think about the fact that Erica was kneeling on the floor between his legs, touching him. If he thought about that, then he wouldn't be able to hide anything from her.

So he focused on the pain, but that made it worse.

"Thorne, are you okay?"

"Fine," he lied.

She deepened the massage and beads of sweat broke across his brow. His mind began to wander to that moment when Tyler had been lying in a pool of dirty water. The bullet had grazed him, but Thorne's leg was on fire.

Still, he was the unit's doctor first and foremost. He'd done his duty to make sure Tyler survived.

"You're bleeding, man," Tyler had said as he'd knelt down to tie a tourniquet around his leg.

"I'm fine," Thorne had said. "It didn't nick the artery. Just a bit of bleeding. It'll be fine."

"It's an open wound in the sewer, Wilder."

"I have antibiotics." Thorne had dug through his first aid kit and pulled out a syringe of morphine and a needle and thread.

"What the heck are you doing, Wilder?" Tyler had asked in trepidation.

"Stitching. We still have to swim out to the sub waiting for us. It's shark-infested water. I'm closing up the open wound now."

"It'll get infected that way."

"It doesn't matter. We'll get back to the submarine and it'll be fine. You'll see, Tyler."

Thorne had injected the painkiller and then threaded the needle…

He relaxed, as the pain from his stump seemed to be dissipating. He looked down at Erica working the muscle in his thigh and rubbing around his socket. It was a firm touch, but soft. Her hands were incredibly soft.

Don't think about that.

"Tell me about the surgery," he demanded.

"What surgery?"

"Mine," he said. "Tell me about it. How bad was the leg?"

"Didn't you read your report?"

"There wasn't a lot of information. So tell me. How bad was it?"

"Bad. I won't lie. Your leg was highly infected."

Thorne nodded. "It went down to the bone?"

"Into the tissue," she said. "You did a good repair job on yourself, but…"

"You don't have to say it. I was trapped in an old sewer system for days. If we had been able to get out of there faster and get back to the sub I wouldn't have lost it. I would've been able to stop the spread of the infection."

"Yes. Most likely you could've."

Silence fell between them. It all came back to that moment. She was the one who'd taken his leg and he'd lost it.

"I don't blame you."

She snorted. "Really?"

"I did maybe at first, just a bit."

"You had some pretty choice words for me when you heard me talking about taking it."

"I was a bit fevered by then. My apologies."

"I'm glad to hear you don't blame me. I was worried you did," she admitted, not looking at him, but he could see the pink rise in her cheeks.

"No. If the roles were reversed, and I was given no choice but to amputate or let you die, I would've done the same."

"Does that help?" she asked gently as her ministrations softened.

"It does."

She smiled. "I can tell. Your muscle isn't so knotted. It's relaxing."

"You're good with your hands," he murmured and then gasped when he realized what he'd said. "Erica…I didn't mean…"

Erica was stifling back a giggle and then he couldn't help but laugh as well. It broke the tension that had fallen between them.

Smooth move.

"Well, I suppose I was due for something like that. I

did order you to take off your pants." She wiped a tear from her eyes and then stood. "I would hate for someone with a key to open that door and see me kneeling between your thighs without your pants on."

"Good point." He reached over and began to put on his prosthetic.

"No, let it breathe for a moment. Wearing your prosthetic for so long without a break is why your muscles were so tense."

"So you want me to sit here in the research lab without pants."

Erica grinned, her eyes twinkling. "For another ten minutes and then you can make yourself respectable and head for home. You need rest."

"You do too."

Her smile wobbled and she ran her fingers through her hair. "I have another eight hours on this shift and somehow during my day off I have to study for your intensive simulation."

"You're attending my simulation? I gave you two days off."

"I'm not missing a chance to train with a former Special Ops Navy SEAL. Especially one who performed first aid on himself in the field."

"That was nothing. That was survival."

"I know."

They smiled at each other. It was nice. He'd forgotten how much he missed being around her. His stupid avoiding tactic had cost him.

"Why don't you find a nice on-call room and crash?"

"I think I'll do that. I'll leave you to put your pants on by yourself."

"One leg at a time... Right—I only have one." He winked at her.

"That's a terrible joke."

"I have more." He grabbed his prosthetic. "Go. Rest. You have to rest while you can when you're doing these long shifts."

"I will, but promise me you'll head for home and do the same. I am your second in command here; I can relieve you of your duty."

"Would you get out of here?"

She smiled, grabbed her things and left. Thorne leaned back in the chair, closing his eyes.

He was relaxed for the first time in a long time. When he'd been at the San Diego hospital recovering in a private ward until he'd been able to be debriefed he'd balked at the idea of physiotherapy and massage therapy.

He was made of tougher mettle than that. He only did what was necessary to survive and any physiotherapist who got in his way didn't last long. When he'd lost his leg, he hadn't wanted anyone touching it. The pain was penance.

Erica was right. He needed more help. He needed someone who knew how to massage an amputee. He needed pain relief that wasn't in the form of a pill.

He needed to learn how to manage his pain.

He wrapped his stump, put on his prosthetic, then pulled on his pants, making sure everything was presentable. When he put weight down on his legs, they ached, but they weren't as bad.

A nice, hot shower and bed would help.

He left the research lab and, as he passed an on-call room, he saw Erica was passed out on a cot. She was lying on her side, with her hands curled up under her head. She looked like an angel.

Heck, she was an angel, and he was the very devil himself, because he wanted to join her. He wanted to curl up beside her, wrap his arms around her and lose himself. Only he didn't deserve happiness. One wrong move had cost him his brother. Since he'd cost his brother a life of happiness, he couldn't have what he'd taken from him.

He was unworthy.

You deserve it. It wasn't your fault.

He ignored that voice.

He shut the door to the on-call room and headed out to his car, trying not to think about her between his legs, her hands on a part of him no one had seen in a very long time. He tried not to think about *her*.

Only, that was foolish.

He was a doomed man.

After her shift Erica showered, changed into some casual, comfortable clothes and headed down to the docks. The white hospital ship could be seen blocks away and she couldn't help but grin when she saw it.

She'd served on the USNV *Hope* for so long it was home to her. It felt like she was going home and as she approached the docks, crew members and staff were filtering down the steps off the ship for a brief shore leave before the simulations started tomorrow.

Erica waited on the other side of the barricade, anxiously scanning the crowd for Regina. Of course, her people-watching was constantly interrupted by other colleagues and former crew members who were happy to see her.

When she'd served her time on the *Hope* she'd flown out of Sydney, Australia. *Hope* had been returning out to sea to start a three-month voyage of the South Seas and aid a tsunami disaster.

She hadn't gotten a chance to give a lot of people a proper goodbye. Including Regina, who was very angry that Erica had left in such a rush, but when you were called by the Home Office there was little chance to say proper farewells. There were no gold watch ceremonies in the Navy. One day you were here, the next you could be reassigned and off somewhere else.

Regina was a nurse, but she wasn't part of the Navy, and didn't quite get all the nuances or strict rules which Erica was bound by.

"Erica!"

Erica turned and saw a short, ebony-haired girl pushing her way through the throng of people toward the barricade.

Erica waved at her friend and waited while the Master of Arms cleared Regina for entrance. It only took a few minutes and then that ball of energy was running toward her and throwing her arms around her.

"Oh, my goodness. I've missed you, you crazy lady," Regina said, shaking Erica slightly. "Why the heck did you have to go and get reassigned, and to Okinawa of all places?"

Erica chuckled. "It's good to see you too, Regina. And for your information I quite like Okinawa Prefecture. It's very laid-back here."

"A Naval base laid-back?" Regina asked in disbelief. "I find that laughable."

"Okay, the base may not be laid-back, but the feeling around the island certainly is. Wait until you meet Scooby. He runs the Pineapple Face."

Regina wrinkled her nose. "Please tell me that's a bar?"

"Yes. It's awesome. It's like something out of old sixties sitcom reruns, and the proprietor Scooby is a huge Elvis fan. Huge."

"Oh, I like him already!" Regina slipped an arm through hers and they walked away from the docks. "So I'm being put up in your quarters, eh?"

"Yes. I hope you don't mind that I made those arrangements."

"Are you kidding me? Of course I don't. My new bunk mate on the *Hope* is a bit loony and she snores. Loudly."

"Sorry to hear that, but I talk in my sleep. You used to complain about that."

"I'd rather hear you spout off about elves, turkeys and whatever other nonsense you're dreaming about than Matilda's snore conversations with herself. It's horrible. I suggested she hit the hospital and the sleep apnea clinic. Seriously, there were a few times I thought she was going to inhale her pillow."

Erica laughed until her sides hurt. "So what else is happening on the ship?"

"Same old same old. There's nothing new to report other than Captain Dayton has a new protégé. His name is Lieutenant Clancy and he's really good-looking."

"How good-looking?" Erica asked, having an inkling where this was going. Regina was married to an officer who worked in San Diego, but just because Regina was married it didn't seem to stop her from scoping out gorgeous guys and potential husbands for Erica.

"It's my hobby," Regina had remarked once.

Regina scanned the crowd and then subtly pointed ahead of them. "There. That's how good-looking he is."

Erica glanced over, trying to be nonchalant. Regina was right; he was handsome. Tall and broad-shouldered from the rigorous training. His officer ranking meant he was probably fresh out of Annapolis: Captain Dayton only picked protégés who came from his alma mater. It also meant that he was most likely a trauma surgeon, as was Captain Dayton.

As she was looking at him, he glanced their way and smiled at her. One of those smiles that made Regina swoon and Erica want to put up her defenses.

"He's coming this way," Regina hissed in Erica's ear, barely containing her excitement.

"Hi, there," he said.

"Lieutenant Clancy, this is my friend, Commander

Erica Griffin." Regina could barely contain her excitement.

Lieutenant Clancy came at attention and saluted. "I'm sorry, Commander. I didn't realize who you were."

"At ease. It's okay, Lieutenant. I'm not wearing my uniform. How would you know?"

Clancy smiled. "Are you assigned to this base, Commander?"

"I am. My previous assignment was the *Hope*."

"Really? So you're the surgeon who Captain Dayton has been gushing over since I arrived on board."

She chuckled. "One and the same."

"He didn't mention how beautiful you were, Commander."

Erica tried not to roll her eyes. She really didn't have time for this kind of come-on. And, no matter how cute the lieutenant was, he was Navy and off-limits. All Naval men were.

Except one.

If Thorne had come up to her and given her that cheesy pickup line she might've fallen for it, but then Thorne would never do anything like that. He had pride—an alpha male through and through.

A hero.

"Well, it was a pleasure to meet you, Lieutenant, but Regina and me have some catching up to do and it's my day off." Erica gripped Regina by the arm and forcibly marched her away from the docks at a quick pace.

"Are you crazy? He's really into you."

"Regina, we've been together for what…five minutes?…and you're already up to your old antics."

Regina laughed and squeezed Erica's arm. "And you love it. Come on, admit it, you've missed me."

Erica chuckled. "I've missed you and possibly your tomfoolery."

"Tomfoolery? Easy there, Shakespeare, or I may start up with my buffoonery or clownery."

They laughed together.

"I have missed you," Erica admitted.

"What's it like on the base?"

"Good. It feels odd to not be at sea. When I was back in San Diego before this assignment it was hard to get my land legs back."

Regina grunted. "I know. Every time I have leave and I'm in San Diego with Rick, for two days I swear I'm walking around like I'm drunk."

"You don't have the best land legs."

"Don't even get me started." Regina glanced around. "It's pretty here, though. How far are we away from mainland Japan?"

"Well, you have to take a twenty-four-hour ferry to get to Kagoshima."

"Wow. That's far. I guess living it up in Tokyo is out of the question."

"Yes. You seriously suck at geography."

Regina stuck out her tongue. "So, what else is interesting about this base? You're holding something back. Something you're not telling me."

"What're you talking about?"

"I know when you're hiding something from me."

"I'm not hiding anything from you." Erica let go of Regina's arm. Damn, she hated that Regina was so intuitive. It was what made her a good nurse; she could always glean that little nugget of information out of a patient. "Are you hungry? I'll take you to that pub I was talking about."

"What are you hiding from me?"

"Nothing! I'm just trying to feed you." Then Erica spied exactly what she was trying to hide. Thorne was walking their way.

Regina had been there, working with Erica when

Thorne had come in. She'd been his nurse for the few brief hours he'd been on board. Of course, he hadn't pleaded with her about his leg; he hadn't reached up and kissed her and called her beautiful.

"Angel."

"Oh, my God!" Regina froze. "Look who it is."

Erica grabbed her and pulled her behind a shrub. "Get down!"

"What?" Regina smiled then. "That's what you're hiding."

"Shut up!"

They crouched behind the bush until Thorne walked past and was out of sight. Erica let out a sigh of relief.

"That's that SEAL from…what…five years ago? The one who you were fighting so hard to keep on the ship. I thought for sure he would've died."

"I thought he did too."

Regina crossed her arms. "So why are we hiding from him, then?"

"We're not."

"Please. What was with the 'get down!' then?"

"I thought I saw a bug." Erica was not the best liar in the world, especially when she tried to lie to Regina; she didn't even know why she bothered with it.

"Please. Since when have you been afraid of bugs? Remember when we stopped in Hong Kong? You were the only one who tried those fried bugs. Which, by the way, still freaks me out to this day."

"There's nothing to tell."

"Who is he?"

"Captain Wilder is my commanding officer," Erica responded. There was no point in hiding that aspect. Regina would find out.

"Does he know?"

Erica shook her head. "I'm not talking about this. I'm going to get something to eat."

"Well, first can I drop my duffel bag off at your quarters?"

"Okay. Then eat."

"Yes. Then eat." Regina rolled her eyes. "In time you'll tell me. You always do."

Not this time, Erica thought to herself. She wasn't saying anything more, because there was nothing to tell. Absolutely nothing.

Except undeniable chemistry.

She cursed silently to herself. It was happening again and she didn't want it to.

Yes, you do.

No. There was nothing secretive or gossip-worthy in nature about her and Thorne. All Regina needed to know was that Thorne was her commanding officer and that he would be running the simulation tomorrow. That was it. End of discussion.

CHAPTER ELEVEN

WHY IS HE TOUCHING HER?

It was ticking him off because he should be focusing on the simulation lab, which was about to start. He'd been collected and ready to start at zero nine hundred hours, until some young lieutenant had come in and sat down next to Erica.

She was smiling at him as they spoke quietly to each other and then the lieutenant put his arm on the back of her chair. He wasn't totally touching her, but it was close enough.

Why should you care?

He shouldn't. He had no prior claim to Erica. She was off-limits. She wasn't his. Though he wanted her. He desired her. There was no use denying it anymore, to himself, at least. That was where those feelings were going to stay, buried deep inside.

Thorne cleared his throat and shuffled his papers, trying to ignore Erica and the lieutenant, but he couldn't.

Just like he hadn't been able to keep his eyes off of her last night at the pub. She'd been laughing and having a good time with a friend from the *Hope*. The lieutenant had been there, joking and smiling with them.

Thorne's only company had been Scooby.

"She doesn't laugh like that with you."

"Thanks for pointing that out, Scooby. I appreciate it."

Scooby had shaken his head. "That's not what I mean. It's all fake."

"I find that hard to believe, Scooby."

"It's fake. When she looks at you, that's something more. It's better."

Though Scooby hadn't been able to elaborate on how it was better.

Thorne found that hard to believe. She didn't look at him *different*. Not that he could tell. Then he uttered a few oaths under his breath, mad at himself for thinking about Erica and thinking about looks and lieutenants.

He glanced at the clock on the wall. It was nine. Time to start.

"Welcome everyone to my simulation lecture today." He moved around the other side of the podium. "Today we're going to be using robotic simulators and your tools would be the general tools that could be used in battle or emergency situations. There will be very basic tools, because in extreme circumstances you have to think with your head and improvise. I will be breaking you off into teams and each team will be given a different scenario."

"How long do we have, Captain?" a young ensign asked.

"I will start the timer. The first team to finish successfully, well, I don't have a prize." He grinned. "But perhaps I can be persuaded."

There was a bit of laughter and his gaze fell on Erica. She was smiling at him warmly. The same way she'd looked at him when they'd had pizza together at Scooby's place and, though he should just ignore it, he couldn't help but return her smile.

Concentrate.

"Okay. Organize yourself into teams. I want a mixture

of levels of command. Not all surgeons with each other. I want to see a true team of medical professionals."

As they organized themselves into teams, he got his cards ready and Erica came up beside him.

"I think your prize should be one of Scooby's house pizzas."

"That might appeal to some, but really, what's so special about a pineapple pizza?"

"That it's one of Scooby's," she said matter-of-factly.

He chuckled. "Well, if I'm offering that, I don't think it's very fair that you're participating in this simulation. You've already had a taste of the prize. It might drive you to cheat."

"Are you calling me a cheater, Captain Wilder?"

"If the shoe fits."

"I'll have you know…" She trailed off and then the joviality disappeared. "Well, I better get to my team."

He watched her walk away, and then turned back to see that friend of hers watching them with a strange look on her face, like she'd caught them doing something naughty. What the heck was happening to his hospital?

Since when had he reverted back to high school? Because that was what it felt like and he was not happy about that.

"Can I help you…?"

"I'm a nurse, Captain." She stepped forward. "My name is Regina Kettle. I'm a nurse on the *Hope*."

Thorne nodded. "And is there something I can help you with? Do you have a question about the simulation?"

"No, not at all. My apologies for staring, but I think I know you."

So that's why she was staring and why Erica was acting weird. Did this nurse remember him as a patient? Had this nurse seen him when he'd been so vulnerable? That thought made him nervous.

"I don't think so."

She narrowed her eyes. "Well, maybe not, then."

"We're about to get started."

"Sure thing, Captain." She moved past him and returned to her team.

Don't let her shake you.

It didn't matter if she remembered him. It didn't matter if she'd been there when he'd lost his leg. It didn't make him less of a soldier or a surgeon.

Something it had taken him a couple of years to deal with himself when he could no longer be a part of the Special Ops.

So why is it bothering you so much?

He silenced the niggling voice in his head. When he looked over at Erica she was on the lieutenant's team and he was leaning over her, whispering in her ear while they went over what supplies they had.

"Lieutenant!" he snapped.

The lieutenant in question looked up, his cheeks flushing with color. "Yes, Captain Wilder?"

"What's your name, seaman?"

"Lieutenant Jordan Clancy." He saluted.

"Tell you what, I'd like you to switch places with the Ensign Fitz over here. I think the ensign would benefit more from working with Commander Griffin."

The blush remained. "Of course, Captain."

Lieutenant Clancy and Ensign Fitz switched places. Thorne felt a little inkling of satisfaction and then he noticed the nurse was smiling smugly to herself, as if she'd uncovered some kind of secret.

He was not handling this well.

Pathetic.

And he was angry with himself for being so petty. This was what Erica did to him. She made him think and act irrationally. Before she arrived he'd led a relatively quiet existence. He didn't wrestle with his guilt every day.

What existence?

"All right, I'll be handing out your scenarios. Do not look at them until I start the clock." He passed cards to all the teams and then pulled out his timer. "Okay, go!"

The teams began to move quickly, moving through the scenarios and working together with the minimum equipment they had.

There were some promising officers, surgeons and medical personnel training in the simulation today. Erica handled her team efficiently as they dealt with the trauma to the chest wall. She immediately reached for the plastic bag and tape to stop the wound and the patient from bleeding out so they could properly assess them.

It gave him a sense of pride to watch her.

She was incredibly talented, beautiful, poised and a commendable second in command and officer.

And totally off-limits.

At least that was what he kept trying to tell himself, but he wasn't sure if he wholly believed it anymore.

"Are you sad your team lost?"

Erica was startled to see Thorne taking the seat next to her at the bar.

"No, not at all." She took a sip of her drink. "We would've won except for Ensign Fitz's blundering mistake."

"You mean when he killed your patient?" Thorne asked.

She laughed. "Yes. That does put a damper on the contest."

"He needed to learn."

"I could've won had you not taken Lieutenant Clancy from me."

His expression changed just slightly and he shifted in his seat. "Were you mad at my decision?"

"No, other than I lost." She leaned over. "I hate to lose, by the way. Just for future reference."

He smiled and nodded. "Noted."

"So why did you pull the lieutenant from my team?"

"I thought you said you weren't mad," he replied.

"Not mad. Just curious. I want to know what drove you to your decision."

"Ensign Fitz has a lot to learn and you're a damn fine surgeon."

Somehow she didn't believe him. Regina had suggested that Thorne had moved Lieutenant Clancy because he was jealous and possessive at the time. Regina had said she saw the way Thorne looked at her and, the moment Jordan had begun to whisper sweet nothings in her ear, Thorne moved him.

Erica thought the whole thing was preposterous.

Although the "sweet nothings" wasn't totally off; Lieutenant Clancy had been flirting with her, telling her how good she looked and asking her out for a drink later—which Erica had promptly turned down, much to Regina's chagrin.

"It's Captain Wilder, isn't it? You have the hots for him."

"I don't have the hots for him, Regina. I just have no interest in dating a superior or any officer."

Regina had rolled her eyes. "Then who are you going to date?

"No one."

"You're hopeless."

This was why Erica didn't date. Maybe she was hopeless, but there was good reason. Her career was too important.

She would never risk that for anything. Even a stolen moment with Thorne.

"Thank you, Captain. I appreciate the compliment."

"Thorne, remember? We're off duty."

"Right." She began to peel at the label on her domestic beer. The happy-looking squid was starting to lose tentacles as Erica nervously shredded the label, which was soft as the water was condensing on the outside of the bottle.

Don't think of him that way.

"So what did you think of the simulation today?" he asked.

"I thought it was good. Better than some other simulations I'd been involved in. Some are just endless lectures."

"I don't lecture."

She laughed. "I saw you tear down Ensign Fitz when he killed our robotic patient."

"That's a stripping down. It's not a lecture."

"It sounded like one of my father's." She took another swig of beer.

"Your father served, didn't he?"

"He did. He was a good officer, but I'm not like him." She didn't want to talk about her father. Not because she wasn't proud, but because people's condemnation and their scrutiny of her father cut her to the quick.

"How do you mean?"

She shook her head. "I'm not as strong as he was."

"You're just as strong. I see it."

"He wasn't called mentally unstable while he served."

It was only after.

She sighed. "Sorry."

"No, it's okay. I apologize for that. It was uncalled for."

"I'm used to it. It seems wherever I go I'm judged on that. Judged for making one mistake. I've had so many psychiatric evaluations and understanding conversations…"

Thorne held up his hands. "Erica, I was just making conversation. I don't think that at all."

Had she just heard him right?

"You don't?" she asked in disbelief.

"Why would I? Why I would judge you on the mistakes another made? You're a totally different person—I think, perhaps, stronger with all you've had to deal with. Was your father a medical officer?"

"No."

"Well, then, I don't know how you can be held to the same standard as him and vice versa. Serving as a medical officer is totally different than a plain officer."

"And being a Special Ops SEAL is so much more." She reached out and squeezed his hand. "Did you deal with PTSD when you returned home?"

"That's classified." He winked.

"I can always request your medical record as your surgeon."

He leaned over and she felt his hot breath as he murmured in her ear. "You can't. You're not on my record. It was wiped. I have never been on board the *Hope*."

"That's terrible! So who did they say did the surgery, then?"

He shot her a wicked grin. "Me."

"You?"

"Me. I was the medical officer with the unit."

"So you amputated your own leg, in the field in a very neat and dare I say brilliant way?"

His blue eyes twinkled. "You got it."

"You're not serious, are you?"

"Would I lie to you?"

Erica laughed. "Really, we're going to head back into *that* territory, are we?"

Thorne shrugged. "I'm absolutely dead serious. According to my official medical file out of San Diego where

I recuperated, I was the chief medical officer in my unit, and I alone amputated my own leg."

Erica muttered a few choice curses that were quickly drowned out by an inebriated seaman shouting for music.

"No problem!" Scooby got up and selected music on his tiny digital jukebox, blasting a song at an obnoxious level as people crowded the dance floor.

Thorne laughed. "Do you want to dance?"

"Are you insane?"

"No, I'm serious. Come on; this is a fun song."

Erica shook her head in disbelief as a weird, drunken crowd formed on the small dance floor in front of them.

"I can't believe what I'm seeing."

"What, the dance or the crowd?" Thorne teased.

"Both." Erica took a swig of her drink. "I'm surprised that no one is filming this. This is going to end up on the internet."

"Good idea." Scooby scurried away.

Erica gave Thorne a sidelong glance. "You don't think he's going to get a camera, do you?"

"Don't put it past him. He might actually still have a camcorder back there."

Scooby returned and held up his phone. "Come on, Captain Wilder and Commander Griffin. Get out there and dance."

"She said no, Scooby."

Scooby frowned. "Why?"

"I don't dance in such an organized fashion." She winked at Thorne, who was laughing.

"Bah, you're no fun. I'll film you anyway."

"I have to get out of here," Erica shouted over the din. She set the money down on the counter. "Do you want to get out of here, Thorne?"

"What?" he asked, wincing.

"Let's go!" she shouted and took his hand, pulling him

out of the bar. They managed to avoid Scooby's camera by disappearing in the throng of people that was now gathering around the edge of the dance floor.

She hated really thick crowds in small spaces. So it wasn't that she was afraid of dancing, or being caught on Scooby's video and ending up online, she just knew it would be a sudden crush of people and she didn't want to have a panic attack in front of Thorne.

When they were outside Erica took a breath of fresh air and began to laugh. "That was crazy. I didn't think Scooby had that repertoire of music."

"He has all kinds."

"I thought he only liked Elvis?" she asked.

"He's a man of many layers. Like an onion."

They began to walk along the sidewalk. The stars were out and a large full moon was casting an almost near-perfect reflection on the water of the bay. The *Hope* loomed up out of the darkness. The white color of the ship caught the light from the moon and the bridge was lit. She knew Captain Dayton was up on his bridge overseeing some of the minor works before they set back out on the ocean again the day after tomorrow. The major retrofit would happen when they docked in San Diego.

"Do you miss serving on the ship?" he asked, breaking the silence.

"Sometimes," Erica said. "I wanted a change. I like the different opportunities. I'm pretty blessed to do what I love to do."

"I get it."

"Do you miss being a part of Special Ops?" she asked.

He cocked his eyebrows.

"Yeah, I know, a dumb question. Of course you do." She sighed. "It's a beautiful night; do you want to walk down to the beach?"

"No, my leg isn't so good on the sand at the best of times. I don't want to be stumbling at the moment."

She didn't know what he meant by that, but they kept on the main path toward the officers' quarters.

"What do you remember of that day?"

"What day?" she asked.

"I guess I should say *night*, but I'm not really sure if it was night when you took my leg."

"I didn't take your leg, Thorne."

"I know—when you operated," he said, correcting himself.

"I remember everything."

"You do?" he asked, surprised.

"I do. I wondered what happened to you for so long."

"So it was just curiosity about my well-being?"

"No, there was more to it." They stopped in a small green, which was between the hospital, the docks and the officer quarters. Suddenly she was shaking and she didn't know why; she was falling fast and she was so scared about taking the step.

What if I get burned again?

"What else?" He took a step toward her, his hands in his pockets, like he was trying to stop himself from something.

"Your eyes." Then she reached out and lightly touched his face. "You were scared, but I don't think it was fear. It was something else. Your eyes haunted me."

"So my eyes haunted you?"

"You mentioned someone: Liam. Who was he?"

Thorne stiffened at the name. "Someone I knew a while ago."

It was apparent that the topic of Liam was off-limits.

"You said I was as beautiful as an angel." Her cheeks burned with heat; she couldn't look up at him and when she did he ran his thumb over her cheek.

"You are," he whispered. His eyes sparkled in the dark; her pulse was thundering between her ears and her mouth went dry. Thorne's hand slipped around her waist, his hand resting in the small of her back. He was so close, they were so close, and all she wanted him to do was kiss her again.

You're so weak.

She couldn't let this happen again but she wanted it too. She was so lonely.

"Thorne, I don't know... This isn't right."

He took a step back. "You're right. I'm sorry."

"No, don't be sorry. I want to, trust me, but...I can't. I don't have room for anyone in my life but me."

"Neither do I, Erica. I can't promise you anything."

"I don't need promises. I've had promises made before and they were always broken. I don't rely on them." This time she was the one who closed the distance between them. "I don't expect any promises."

"Then what do you want?" he asked as he ran his knuckles down her cheek.

She wasn't sure what she wanted. She wanted to be with Thorne in this moment, but what would it do to her reputation? Could she just have one night with him?

That was what she wanted.

Just one night of passion.

Perhaps, if she fed the craving she had for him, then it would burn him from her system and she could move on. It would clear the air.

You're weak.

"What do you want, Erica?" His voice was husky as he whispered the words into her ear.

"I want you to kiss me." She reached out and gripped his shirt.

He leaned forward and she closed her eyes as he kissed her. And then it deepened and she was lost.

CHAPTER TWELVE

ERICA WASN'T SURE how they got to Thorne's door. All she knew at that moment was she had him pressed against the door, was melting into him. His kiss made her weak in the knees, senseless, and she didn't want it to end.

He gently pushed her away and she moaned.

"What?" she asked.

"I have to open the door," Thorne answered, his voice husky with promise.

"Good; I thought you'd changed your mind."

"No, never." And then he pulled her into another kiss, which seared her blood and made her swoon against him.

"Open the door." Erica let him go for just a moment as he unlocked the door. Once it was open he scooped her up, causing her to shriek.

"What're you doing?"

He shut the door behind him with a kick from his right leg. "Carrying you to my bedroom."

"You can't."

Thorne kissed her. "Watch me."

And he did carry her to his bedroom, then set her down on her feet. She slowly slid down the length of his body, feeling the heat of him through seemingly many layers of his clothes. Clothes she wanted gone as soon as possible.

"You look good enough to eat," he whispered against her neck.

Her pulse quickened. "Pardon?"

"You heard me. I've been fighting it all evening. Seeing you in the bar by yourself… I've been fighting the urge to take you in my arms from the moment you landed in Okinawa."

"Tell me more."

Thorne moaned and held her tighter. Her body was flush with his and Erica wanted the layers separating them to be gone. She wanted them to be naked, skin to skin.

"Do you want me to tell you or do you want me to show you?"

Erica didn't respond to that, instead she used her mouth to show him exactly how much she wanted from him. She was tired of being alone and for once she wanted to feel passion again, even if it was only fleeting. Thorne was worth it.

The room was dark except for a thin beam of light through the curtains and she was aware how close they were to Thorne's bed. She was suddenly very nervous. It had been so long since she'd been with a man. It felt like the first time again.

"What's wrong?" Thorne asked, brushing her hair from her face. "Are you having second thoughts?"

"No. No, I'm not having second thoughts. It's just been a long time since I've been with a man."

"It's been a long time for me too."

"I want you, Thorne. All of you." And she wanted it. She wanted him to possess her. For once she didn't want to be the woman men were afraid of because of her rank and her training. Tonight she was just Erica. She was just a woman and he was a man.

He kissed her again, a featherlight one, then buried his face against her neck. His breath caressed her skin, making goose pimples break out. A tingle raced down her spine and she sighed. She couldn't help herself.

"Take off my clothes," he whispered.

Erica did just that. Unbuttoning his shirt and running her hands over his chest, it was mostly bare except for a bit of hair, which disappeared under the waist of his pants. Next she undid his belt, pulling it out and snapping it. He slid his hands down her back and cupped her butt, giving her cheeks a squeeze.

"Don't be naughty," he teased.

"I swear I won't." And then she undid his pants, crouching to pull them down. He kicked them off and then moved to the bed, sitting down to remove his prosthetic leg. "Let me."

His body stiffened as she ran her hands over his thigh again and undid his prosthesis, setting it against the nightstand. She started to massage his thigh; he moaned.

"That feels good, but I don't want you to massage me," he said.

"Oh, no."

"No." He pulled her close, kissing her. "Now it's your turn. Undress."

Erica stood and began to take off her clothes. His eyes on her excited her, making her heart race. She'd never done anything like this before. It was usually lights-out, under the covers. She'd never stripped for a man before.

"You're so beautiful. Like an angel," he murmured. He reached out and pulled her down to him. "So beautiful."

"Thorne…" She trailed off because she didn't know what else to say to him. His hands slipped down her back, the heat from his skin searing her flesh and making her body ache with need. She was so exposed to him; it thrilled her. She'd never felt like this before. He cupped her breasts, kneading them, and she moaned at the sensation of his hands on her sensitized skin.

He pinned her against the mattress, his lips on hers, their bodies free of clothing and skin to skin.

She was so ready for him. Each time his fingers skimmed her flesh her body ignited. He pressed his lips against her breast, laving her nipple with his hot tongue. She arched her back. She wanted more from him. So much more.

Erica wanted Thorne to make her burn. To make her forget everyone else. His hand moved down her body, between her legs. He began to stroke her, making her wet with need.

"I want you so bad."

Erica moaned as he moved away and pulled a condom out of his nightstand drawer.

Thorne moved back to her. "Now, where were we?"

He pressed her against the pillows and settled between her thighs. He shifted position so he was comfortable. The tip of his sex pressed against her. She wanted him to take her, to be his.

Even though she couldn't be.

Thorne thrust quickly, filling her completely. She clawed at his shoulders, dragging her nails down his skin as he stretched her. He remained still, but she urged him by rocking her hips. She wanted him to move. To take her.

"You feel so good." Thorne surged forward and she met every one of his thrusts.

She cried out as he moved harder, faster, and a coil of heat unfurled deep within her. Then it came, pleasure like she'd never experienced before. It flooded through her and overwhelmed her senses, her muscles tightening around him as she came. Thorne's thrusts became shallow and he soon joined her in his climax.

His lips brushed her neck as she held him against her and then he rolled onto his back, pulling her with him, so she could hear his heart beating. She lightly ran her fingers across his skin while his own fingers stroked her back.

"I'm sorry that was so fast. I needed you so bad, I couldn't hold back."

"It was amazing," she whispered. "No apology necessary."

Erica settled against him, the only sound was that of the ocean outside and his breathing and then she tensed as she realized what she'd done. She'd fallen in with another commanding officer, something she'd sworn she'd never do again. As the euphoria melted away, she was angry at herself for being so weak.

How could she have let this happen again?

Thorne isn't like Captain Seaton. You didn't make any promises.

Captain Seaton had been angry that she'd been the one to reject him ultimately and that was why he tried to ruin her career.

She didn't think Thorne was like that. He seemed to have a good head on his shoulders. He was rational, but a bit of niggling self-doubt ate away at her. Trust was a big issue for her. She wasn't sure if she could trust Thorne.

She wasn't sure if she would honestly trust another man again.

Thorne watched her. He wasn't sure if she was sleeping. Her eyes were closed, but her breathing wasn't deep, as if she was in sleep. He knew he'd promised her that nothing had to happen out of this, that was the way she wanted it and that was what he wanted. Wasn't it?

Of course that was what he wanted.

They'd made no promises; if promises had been exchanged he wouldn't have gone through with it, because he was never going to have a relationship. He'd been weak and forgotten that he couldn't have her.

He rolled over onto his back and scrubbed his hands over his face, staring up at the fan slowly rotating on his ceiling. What had he done? The guilt ate at him.

"What's wrong?" Erica murmured.

"Nothing." He turned to his side again. "Just watching you sleep."

"Why are you watching me?" she asked, moving onto her side and tucking her hands under her head.

"I couldn't help it. It was relaxing."

"That groan you gave out didn't sound like you were at ease."

"Perhaps not."

She smiled and then frowned. "So, what happens now?"

"What do you mean?"

"I mean when we're back on duty." Erica leaned on an elbow. "I don't want any awkwardness. I'd like to act like nothing happened between us."

"We'll just go on as normal. Nothing has to change; I think we both made our intentions clear."

"We did." Then she got up, holding the sheet against her.

"Where are you going?"

"Back to my quarters." She bent over, picking up the pieces of her clothing scattered all around the room.

"I'm not kicking you out, Erica. You don't have to leave."

"I do." She sat down on the edge of the bed and began to dress. "If I stay, then it might mean more."

"I won't think that. Come back to bed."

Erica chuckled. "Is that your best 'come hither' look?"

"I wasn't aware I was doing one." He leaned across and pulled her back down against the mattress to place a kiss on her lips upside down. "Stay."

"I can't. Remember, I have Regina staying with me. If

I don't come back to bed, she's going to wonder and then start poking around. She might even get a transfer until she figures it all out."

Thorne shuddered. "Okay, you better go, but know this—it's against doctor's orders."

She rolled her eyes, got up and finished dressing. Then she came around to his side of the bed and kissed him.

"Thanks for tonight."

"Anytime." He wanted to say more things. He wanted to tie her down in his bed and never let her go, but she was right. If she came out of his quarters the next morning and someone saw her, there would be gossip. She didn't want any more gossip about her, which was fair.

He didn't want the gossip either. Thorne didn't want to get her in trouble or transferred. Losing her would be detrimental to the welfare of the base hospital.

And you too.

Yeah, he'd miss the comraderie. She was the only second in command he'd ever met who'd stood up to their commanding officer. Who worked alongside him as a team. They were equals.

She was strong.

Thorne had thought being with her once would flush her from his system, instead he found himself wanting more.

So much more.

Erica tried to sneak back into her quarters. The television had been flickering in the window when she approached and she was worried that as soon as she walked through the door she'd be bombarded with questions, but when she peered through the window she could see that Regina was passed out in front of the TV.

Maybe dancing at Scooby's had exhausted her.

One could only hope.

Erica shut the door behind her as quietly as she could, locked it and then slid off her shoes to creep along the tiled hallway to her bedroom.

She was almost home free.

"Where were you tonight?"

Darn.

Erica turned to see Regina sitting upright, no sign of being asleep or having been asleep. "You were awake when I came home, weren't you?"

"I was. I saw you peek through the window."

"You're a pain." Erica tried to escape again, but she was up against a pro.

"Where were you?"

"I'm an adult. You're not my mother."

Regina crossed her arms. "I was worried when you disappeared from the bar. It would've been nice if you had told me where you were going."

"You're so good at guilt."

A small smile played around Regina's lips. "I'm sorry, but it's true. I was worried."

"You were worried? You were too busy dancing." Erica mimicked Regina's terrible but endearing moves.

Regina rolled her eyes. "Come on. I don't get out much."

"It's apparent."

"I still don't know how that song started."

"Some poor seamen who had had too much to drink." Erica set her purse down on the counter in her kitchen and went to get a glass of water. Regina laughed. "And why didn't you jump in?"

"Oh, I was in the middle of talking to Thorne." And then she cursed under her breath, realizing she'd said "Thorne" to Regina instead of calling him Captain Wilder. Dang.

"Who?"

"Captain Wilder."

"So we're on a first-name basis with Captain Wilder, now, eh?"

"Shut up." Erica took a big swig of water, trying to ignore Regina who was smugly dancing around the kitchen.

"I knew it. I knew something was up. You were with him, right?"

"Yes."

"You are such a bad liar!" Regina exclaimed. "I so *knew* you two had chemistry floating around. Why else would you dive behind a bush to avoid someone? You've never hid from anyone or anything before. Tell me everything!"

"There's nothing to tell."

Liar.

There was a lot to tell, but it was stuff she wasn't sure she wanted to share at this moment because she wasn't exactly sure of how she was feeling herself. When she'd come here and seen that her commanding officer was Thorne, she'd been worried that she would be too weak to resist him. She didn't want another relationship. That was what she kept telling herself. It became a broken record in her head.

And, just like any song you heard over and over, the broken record had become nothing more than background noise when Thorne took her in his arms and kissed her. Now she didn't know what to do with all these emotions swirling around inside.

She was torn and frightened.

"Come on, there has to be something going on. You're sneaking into the house in the middle of the night." Regina looked her up and down. "You reek of guilt."

Erica rolled her eyes. "How can I reek of guilt?"

Regina leaned forward and sniffed. "Okay, not guilt,

but cologne or something very manly. Unless you've taken to wearing men's deodorant."

"You know what? I have." Erica set the glass in the sink. "I'm kind of tired. I think I'm going to hit the hay. I have a long duty-shift tomorrow."

"Erica, it's okay to admit you like this guy."

"No, it's not. You know my story. You know what happened to me before. I was in a relationship with my commanding officer before the *Hope,* and I thought he loved me, but he didn't. Not the way I loved him and so I broke it off. I was the one that was isolated. I was the one who was getting the crummy shifts. I was the one passed up for commendation and promotions. I was the one he reported as mentally unstable. It's why I left."

"I thought you didn't want a relationship because of your mom losing your dad."

Erica sighed and leaned against the counter. "That's part of it, but not really. I saw what my father's service did to his marriage and his family, but that didn't stop me from serving. That didn't stop me from proving to everyone that I was a good officer too. I stepped out of my father's shadow long before my relationship with Captain Seaton."

Regina nodded. "Okay, so your holdup is not your parents' marriage, but being burned by a lover?"

"I guess so. See, before I was hurt I thought my perfect match would be someone who served in the same capacity as me. My mother was not in the Armed Forces."

"Erica, you had one bad relationship. Who doesn't?"

"Has a former lover almost ruined your reputation and career by calling you mentally unstable?"

Regina bit her lip. "Well, no."

"Then you're not an authority."

"Look, we've all been hurt by love before we found that perfect someone. I think that Thorne is your perfect someone."

"And how would you know that? You've met him once."

Regina shrugged her shoulders. "I just know. I'm quite intuitive and you've said that countless times. I have it on record."

Erica chuckled. "Intuitive in your job."

"Well, it counts for knowing good relationships too."

"There's no relationship. He doesn't want one either."

"How do you know?"

"He told me."

Regina frowned and pursed her lips together. "I don't buy that. I think you should talk to him about your feelings."

"What feelings?" She would have got away with that except she blushed. There were feelings there; she just wasn't sure she was ready to admit those feelings. Not yet.

When?

And that was the conundrum she was in. She was being a coward and she hated that. Erica wasn't a coward.

"I don't know why you're trying to deny them." Regina sighed. "Whatever you do, you have to tell him."

"I'm telling you, he doesn't want anything more than what we had tonight, Regina."

"Do you know that with one-hundred-percent certainty?"

No, she couldn't. She really didn't know how Thorne was feeling. Maybe he'd just been saying those things to get her between the sheets, maybe not. Damn it, she didn't have time for this. A relationship was not on the cards for her.

She wasn't going to put her heart on the line again.

Career was all that mattered. She just wanted to keep advancing until she commanded a posting of her own.

Relationships, love, family: they just tied you down.

You're lonely.

Lonely or not, it wasn't an excuse to go out and just

marry the first guy you came across so you could get those two kids you'd secretly been longing for, which would put a strain on the marriage, which would eventually result in divorce because that significant other didn't get your passion, your drive.

Her head began to pound.

"I'm going to bed. Good night, Regina." Erica turned to leave, but Regina stopped her. "Regina, I'm really tired."

"I know. Look, I'm sorry." Regina gave her a hug. "I just want you to be happy. I saw the way you two looked at each other, and I think it's mutual, but until one of you opens up nothing is going to happen. I know you don't want to hear it, but I think you two are perfect for each other."

I think so too.

"I can't open up, Regina. I just can't." She gave her friend another hug. "I'm going to get some sleep. Should I wake you to say goodbye before I go to work?"

"Yes," Regina said. "Or I'll kick your butt."

Erica grinned. "Just think, in a few days you'll be on a leave with Rick in San Diego."

"Not just a leave."

"Oh?"

"I'm going to take a job at a private clinic in San Diego. Rick and I are trying."

"For a baby?" Erica asked surprised.

"Yep."

"So you won't be going back on the *Hope*?"

Regina shook her head. "Nope. This was my last run."

"So that's why you're trying to fix me up. You're trying to make sure I'm taken care of before you head for the public sector."

"You got it. I will succeed."

"Keep thinking that."

"I'm glad I got to see you. Perhaps Rick will get stationed in Okinawa. If not, I'll come visit."

"You better."

Regina smiled. "Go sleep. I'll see you tomorrow."

Erica nodded and took herself off to bed, but she doubted she'd get any sleep, and she was right. As soon as her head hit the pillow, she rolled over on her right and stared at the empty spot beside her.

The emptiness had never bothered her before, but now it did. She was very aware how empty her bed was and she was mad at herself for caring.

She was mad at herself for wanting something she knew she couldn't have.

CHAPTER THIRTEEN

"GOOD MORNING," THORNE WHISPERED, his breath fanning against her neck. She didn't even hear him come up behind her. She was busy charting after an early-morning shift in the ER. Even though they were alone, she felt uncomfortable that he was so close, making the butterflies in her stomach flutter.

She cleared her throat and rubbed her neck, shifting away slightly. "Good morning, Captain."

"Formalities?"

"Yes." Her cheeks flamed with heat. "We are on duty, after all."

"Good point. My apologies, Commander. What happened while I was off duty?"

"There was a motor vehicle collision. Minor. One went to surgery with Lieutenant Drew." She handed the chart to Thorne.

"Why?" he asked, flipping through the pages.

"Spleen was bleeding too much. Lieutenant Drew is performing a splenectomy as we speak." She glanced at his watch. "Barring complications, he should be finished soon."

Thorne nodded. "Anything else?"

"Seven people with a cold, and a couple crewmen of the *Hope* stumbled in for help easing their hangovers before they boarded." She shook her head. "It was like a flash mob last night at Scooby's, a really inappropriate flash mob."

Thorne pulled out his phone and pulled up the web. "It was, in fact."

Erica leaned over to see the video from Scooby's, the choreographed movements to the song. "Pretty impressive for a bunch of drunkards."

"I know. Scooby was quite happy he got to film it." Thorne's eyes twinkled.

Erica laughed. "I bet he was. That man is obsessed with pop culture."

"Who?" Bunny asked, appearing behind the charge desk.

Erica jumped back from Thorne and cleared her throat again as she stared at the chart. "Sachiho."

Bunny cocked an eyebrow. "Who?"

"Scooby," Thorne interjected. "There was a bit of a scene of the weird kind last night at Scooby's bar."

Bunny chuckled. "When isn't there?"

"Is there something I can help you with, Bunny?" Erica asked, hoping that she could throw herself into busywork.

"Nope. I'm just about to head out. My shift is over." Bunny put the last of her charts away. "Have a good day, Commander and Captain."

Bunny left the two of them standing there at the charge desk alone.

"Why did that feel awkward?" Thorne asked.

"I have no idea."

Only she did. Well, at least she knew why she was feeling awkward, because she didn't want to be alone with Thorne again. Only, that was ridiculous. She was going to be alone with him again. Sex had changed it.

Your feelings for him, too.

"I thought you were going to watch some SEALs train

down at the aquatic center?" she asked, trying to sound nonchalant and failing.

"I might yet."

"What test is it?"

"Drown proofing. The next week there will be several rounds of it."

"Oh, that test looks brutal. I've seen it."

"It's hard-core. Though, I can't really demonstrate it anymore. I was pretty darn good at it, though." He smiled to himself.

"I'm sure you were. You swam in open water with an infected leg wound."

The smile disappeared. "Yes."

"I'm sorry. I didn't mean to bring it up. You don't like talking about it, do you?"

He shrugged. "I don't like to dwell on the past. I can't change it. Just got to keep one foot in front of the other and move forward; the future hasn't been written."

"So you don't believe things are predestined?"

He shook his head. "Nope and, if they were, I'd have to have some words with someone about the rough end of the stick I got a few times—and I'm not just talking about my leg."

Erica smiled. "I understand."

"Well, I better check on the lieutenant's surgery. Make sure the splenectomy is going smoothly and we don't lose the patient."

"I'll see you later."

"I hope so." He turned and left her standing there with her charts. She watched him walk away. There was just a slight limp to his gait, but he was still that strong, Navy SEAL Special Ops officer who had begged her not to take his leg.

There were so many admirable things about him. Also there were many annoying things about him. Maybe

Scooby was right. They were too volatile together. That was what Scooby had told Thorne and Thorne had told her.

What does Scooby know? He has green shag carpet on his ceilings and walls.

"*I saw the way he looked at you and the way you looked at him.*"

Erica shook Regina's words from her head. They were the last words Regina had said to Erica before she'd walked back up the gang plank to board the *Hope*. Erica had had a break and had gone outside to watch as the *Hope* sailed east towards the States. She'd wished for a moment she was back on the ship headed for San Diego.

Not that she knew any one besides Regina and Rick in San Diego, but it was the gateway to a new port of call. Headquarters. It was one thing she'd loved about serving on the *Hope*. Every day was something new and exciting, but she'd only been able to go so far on the ship.

Here in Okinawa or another similar base she could rise above her current rank. That was, if she didn't mess it up by sleeping with her commanding officer.

Oh, wait: she had done that.

Erica pinched the bridge of her nose and shook her head. No, she couldn't let this escalate any further.

They'd shared one night of passion and that was all it could be.

Keep telling yourself that.

Her phone pinged with an email. She glanced down and saw it was from Admiral Greer. Confused as to why the admiral would be emailing, she opened it, reading it quickly. She almost dropped her phone and had to read the email again, her hands were shaking so bad.

All her hard work was about to pay off as her dream post was offered to her.

All she had to do now was tell Thorne she was leaving.

* * *

You're here to see SEAL training. That's it.

It was the end of the week of SEAL training and she was coming to watch that and not tell Thorne that she'd accepted a new posting at Annapolis in Maryland.

The email from Admiral Greer had been to promote her from commander to captain and offer her a position at the prestigious school. Her dream position. She'd said yes without a second thought. Now she had to tell Thorne and she was positive he'd understand.

At least that was what she kept trying to tell herself, but she wasn't a good liar. Even she didn't believe herself.

She'd always wanted to go and work at the United States Naval Academy. She'd be training medical corp recruits. It was something she'd always dreamed of, but the opportunity had never presented itself. After that fiasco in Rhode Island she'd never thought it would, to be honest.

Now it had, she had to jump at the chance. Even if it meant leaving Thorne behind.

He didn't make any promises. Neither did you.

This was her career. Love had screwed it up before and she couldn't let that happen again. No matter how much she wanted to stay with him.

The last time she'd chosen love over career it had burned her. Seriously burned her. And that hadn't even been love. That had just been lust.

With Thorne it was different. They connected.

And now she was leaving.

He'll understand.

If the situation was reversed, he would jump at the opportunity.

She snuck into the aquatic center and took a seat in the bleachers. The trainees were in the water doing their drown proofing, which consisted of bottom bouncing, floating and various retrievals. The test usually exhausted the swimmer, but also prepared them for rigorous missions.

Thorne was walking along the edge of the pool with another instructor. She could tell by the way he paced on the deck that he wanted to be in there with them, but couldn't.

He turned away from the testers and looked up at her. *Damn it.*

She wasn't ready for this. Blood rushed to her cheeks as he headed in her direction, up the few stairs to where she was sitting.

"Erica, what're you doing here?"

"I've never witnessed this particular test. I thought it might be interesting to watch."

He smiled and then sat down on the bench next to her. "You just came off an extremely long shift. I know because I scheduled it. You should be at home sleeping."

"I'm a bit tired, but I had to come see this." She looked closer. "I thought their hands are tied?"

"They will be; the instructor is just acclimatizing them, getting them ready for the test. These guys are pretty green. Besides, the instructor will pull them out of the water, freeze them out a bit."

"I bet they'll freeze."

"Get them used to hypothermia, but not really. This is a controlled environment and they won't be out of the water that long." And just as he said the words a whistle echoed and the trainees clambered out of the water as fast as they could. When they were standing to attention, that was when the instructors begin to tie the trainees' hands together.

"I thought my training at Annapolis was difficult," she muttered under her breath.

"You have to be tough to go on the kind of missions these men could go on."

"I don't doubt that. It's why I never even contemplated

becoming a SEAL. I just wanted to be in the Medical Corp. Going the officer route helped pay for that training."

"That's how I originally started," Thorne said a bit wistfully as he stared down at the group of ten seamen, dripping and trying not to shiver on the pool deck.

"What made you go into the SEALs?"

"The death of my twin brother." There was a sadness to his voice. One she was familiar with. One she had used herself when talking about her father. It was pain.

"I knew you had a brother, but I didn't know he was your twin. I'm sorry," she said and she placed a hand on his knee, at a loss for words. "How did you...? How did he...?"

"Die?" he asked.

"You don't have to tell me. I didn't mean to pry."

"It's okay."

Thorne ran his hand through his hair. "He died in service. He showed up at the field hospital I was stationed at. I was called off my ship to assist. In the field hospital there was an IED. There was an explosion and Liam died in my arms."

She took his hand in hers and squeezed it. "I'm sorry. So sorry."

"I appreciate the sentiment, but it was my fault."

"How?" she asked, confused.

"I don't want to get into it."

"I get it."

He glanced up at her. "Do you?"

"I do. I don't like talking about my father to many people."

Thorne nodded. "Did he die in service?"

Erica's stomach knotted. "No. He didn't."

She didn't talk about her father, not to anyone.

She sighed again. "He died as a result of service. He was wounded on a mission, came back home and the doctors cleared him—but I think the wound and losing most of his unit caused PTSD. He went back when he healed and was on a covert operation when he went AWOL, blowing the mission, and he was dishonorably discharged. It was then he killed himself."

"I'm sorry to hear that."

"He was my hero. If he could've got the help he needed..."

"I understand." He stared down at her hand, tracing the back with his thumb, which made her blood heat as she thought of his hands stroking her body.

"I better go." She took her hand back, feeling uncomfortable, and stood. She'd opened up to Thorne too much. It was dangerous letting him know that about her.

He opened up to you.

And that was a problem. She was scared.

"I'll walk you back to your quarters."

"It's broad daylight, Thorne. I think I can manage."

"I don't mind." The tone of his voice implied that he wouldn't take no for an answer. He was going to walk her back whether she liked it or not. She didn't mind it, except the fact that she might not be able to resist asking him inside.

Remember how Captain Seaton hurt you. Don't do this to yourself.

Only Thorne wasn't Captain Seaton. Thorne was different. He wouldn't report her as mentally unstable because she was taking a new position and leaving him.

At least that was what she kept trying to tell herself, but it was so hard to open up and trust again. She'd resigned herself a while ago to the fact that love was not to be a part of her life and then she'd met Thorne.

He limped slightly as they walked to her quarters.

"Why don't you go back?" Erica asked. "You don't have to do this. I am a big girl."

"It's not a bother. I needed to stretch my leg. The moisture actually bothers me sometimes. Phantom leg pain."

"I'm sorry you have to go through that."

"Most people do. With the trauma inflicted, the brain can't really understand why the nerves aren't there any longer. Besides, I was hoping you can give me another massage sometime."

She laughed. "Oh, really? So that was your master plan—take me home and, instead of letting me sleep, I'm supposed to massage you?"

"Well, we could do something else."

Heat bloomed in her cheeks. "Thorne, I don't think it's wise. Do you?"

Then he pulled her close to him. "No, it's not wise, but I can't resist you. Believe me, I've tried. I want to resist you."

Her pulse thundered in her ears. She was pressed against his chest and very aware of how close they were.

"Thorne," she whispered, closing her eyes so she wouldn't be drawn into his eyes, which always seemed to melt her. "I can't. I just…I can't."

"Why?"

"I thought we were going to be friends?"

Thorne let go of her. "I'm sorry, Erica. I wanted to respect your wishes. I did, but when I'm around you I can't help myself. I didn't… I don't want a relationship. I can't give you a relationship."

"And I can't give you one either." She reached up and touched his cheek. "I can't be with another commanding officer. The last time I got involved with someone I work for it almost cost me my career. Unless you can promise me a lifetime, unless you can promise me that our relationship won't affect my career, then I just can't. I can't."

Because I'm leaving.

Only she couldn't verbalize those words.

Chicken.

She tried to turn and leave, because she was embarrassed she'd admitted it to him. Embarrassed that he knew she'd been foolish enough once to believe in forever with someone who wasn't worthy. She made it to her quarters and opened the door. Just as Thorne came up behind her.

"Erica, I would never jeopardize your career. I hope you know that."

"I know. I just wanted you to know why… I couldn't really hide it any longer. I thought for sure you knew. I was pretty sure it was on my service record."

"No, why would it be? If you were passed up for commendation or a promotion in rank, do you really think those responsible for denying that would record it on your service record?"

She was a bit stunned.

"You look surprised," he commented.

"Captain Dayton knew why I was passed up for promotion. I don't even know why he actually picked me to come aboard the *Hope.*"

"Captain Dayton is a smart man. He saw talent. Just like I did." Thorne rubbed the back of his neck, frowning, as if he was struggling to tell her something and she was expecting him to tell her why he couldn't be with someone.

What was holding him back?

What's holding you back?

Still she waited. She waited for him to open up to her, waited pathetically for a sign that maybe it would be worth a second thought. Only he said nothing to her and she was angry at herself for even thinking for one moment that she'd give up on her dreams for a man. When had she become so weak?

Her career mattered. Her life mattered.

"Thorne, I have something to tell you."

"Erica, don't say something we'll regret."

"I'm transferring to Annapolis."

The blood drained from his face and his brow furrowed. "Pardon?"

"I'm transferring to Annapolis, Maryland. I was offered a position as Captain and I would be working with medical corps recruits. It's a chance of a lifetime and I couldn't turn it down."

"No, of course not." He smiled, but it was forced. "Who gave you the commendation?"

"Captain Dayton actually recommended me."

He chuckled, but it was one of derision, not mirth. "Is that a fact? When do you leave?"

"In a week."

Thorne nodded slowly. "Well, of course you have to go."

"I do." Only part of her was screaming not to go—the part of her that wanted to stay with Thorne, marry him and settle down. But he couldn't give her any promises and neither could she. If he didn't want her, she didn't want to settle down with a man who would resent her down the road or, worse, she would resent him for making her give up on her career.

No, she had to go.

"I'm sorry I'm leaving you without a second in command."

"I'll make do until a replacement can be sent." He wasn't looking at her as he backed away from her door. "I better put in a request now."

"Do you still need me to look at your leg?"

"No," he snapped. "It's fine. I'll see you tomorrow, Commander Griffin."

Her heart ached as she watched him walk away quickly and she tried to tell herself it was all for the best.

This way she wouldn't get hurt.

* * *

It was her last day. She was shipping out tonight, but this was her last day working at the base hospital. Her last day working with Thorne.

Things had been awkward since she'd told him that she was accepting a post in Annapolis. They spoke, but barely, and it was about work. She waited for the other shoe to drop. She waited for him to report her as unfit or something.

And when the conversation drifted from work or the duty roster it became tense. It was like he was mad that she was leaving. But it was part of life in the Navy. Officers took postings, left postings.

Her promotion to captain was something she couldn't give up but, anytime she went to talk to him about it, he turned and walked away from her, making it blatantly obvious that he was avoiding her.

She'd even gone to Scooby's a few times, trying to catch him. Only he hadn't been there and Scooby was even concerned he hadn't seen Thorne in a while.

"He shouldn't be alone, Commander. He thinks he can handle it. He can't. I know he's not the only one around here."

Erica was sure that last part was a jab at her. Scooby didn't understand her circumstances. He didn't get why she couldn't be with someone again. She couldn't tether herself to another person and Annapolis was the dream.

It had been since she'd graduated there.

Only, being around Thorne had made her think for a moment that maybe it might be good to be with someone. She wanted it to be him, but he didn't seem to have an interest in letting her past his barriers.

"Commander!" Bunny shouted from the charge desk, a phone in her hand. "Commander Griffin."

Erica rushed over. "What's wrong?"

"It's a code black," Bunny whispered. "You're to go out to the helipad. The west part of the trauma floor is being cleared. Need to know only."

"Tell them I'm on my way." Erica started running toward the helipad. The wing in question was being cleared quickly and Masters of Arms were beginning to block off the entrances and barricade people from that section of the trauma floor.

A shudder traveled down her spine as she thought of that moment five years ago: silent running on the ship. Pitch-black, and the flare from the submarine illuminating the sky to direct the helicopter.

Another covert operation.

When she got to the helipad Thorne was there waiting, the helipad surrounded by armed military police.

"It's about time," Thorne snapped.

"Who's coming in? The president or something?"

"They didn't say. Just that it was covert. Most likely Special Ops."

The roar of the helicopter sounded in the distance and they braced themselves for the wind being stirred up as the helicopter landed. Once they had the all clear they ran forward with the gurney and loaded the patient, who was screaming in agony.

The patient's commanding officer leaped down beside the gurney and helped them wheel the man toward the hospital.

"Prepare for more incoming," the commanding officer said. "We had a few casualties, but he was by far the worst."

"Do we get any specifics?" Erica snapped. "Or do we refer to him as John Doe?"

"Commander Griffin!" Thorne warned.

"John Doe, Commander," the unit's commanding officer responded. "It's all classified."

"Understood," Thorne said. "We'll take care of your man. What happened to him?"

"Explosion. Shredded his arm. We packed it the best we could, but I think it's infected."

"Are you medical?" Erica asked sharply as they wheeled the John Doe into a triage room and began to undress him to get to the damage.

"I am."

"Maybe you can scrub in," Thorne suggested.

"I can't. As soon as the men are stable we have to ship to our meeting place."

Erica snorted and Thorne sent her a look to silence her.

The moment Erica came close to the man's left arm, he screamed in pain, and as soon as she got close to him she could see the infection. It was worse than Thorne's had been. She didn't know how long these men had been in the field, but this John Doe was lucky to be alive.

"He needs surgery," Erica said, turning quickly to start a central line to get antibiotics into the John Doe and sedate him.

"Agreed," Thorne said. "Don't worry, seaman, we'll take care of you."

Erica had the central line in as fast as she could and was pumping the medicine the John Doe needed. He was also severely dehydrated, by the way his lips were cracked, and she couldn't help but wonder how much blood loss he was suffering from.

Thorne sedated him and then was inserting tubes down the man's throat so that he could breathe.

After a few orders, the nurses who were in the know had the OR ready to go and they were wheeling their John Doe off to surgery.

Erica scrubbed alongside Thorne as the nurses prepped and draped the patient.

"Pretty basic, I think," she said.

"What's basic?" Thorne asked.

"Amputation of the arm."

Thorne stopped scrubbing for a moment. "If it's deemed necessary."

"I think it's necessary. Don't you?"

Thorne ignored her and walked into the OR where a nurse gowned him and put gloves on him.

Erica cursed under her breath and followed him, jamming her arms angrily down into the gown that was held out for her.

As she approached the table she could see the damage the IED had caused and this time she did curse out loud.

Thorne glanced at her quickly. "I know."

"He's lucky to have lived this long. Do you think it can still be saved, Captain?" The tone was sarcastic. It was meant to be, but then the scrub nurse beside Thorne gasped, and few others looked at her like she'd lost her mind.

She was being insubordinate to her commanding officer in his OR.

"Get out," Thorne said.

"What?" Erica asked.

"I said, get out."

"Why? He obviously needs an amputation. Are you telling me that you're going to work on his arm when it's clearly not salvageable?"

"That will be my decision as head surgeon. Now, Commander Griffin, if you'd kindly leave my OR and send in Ensign Benjamin. He's been cleared for this level of security and he can assist me in saving John Doe's life."

"With all due respect, Captain. I'm scrubbed in and ready to go. I've dealt with infections of this caliber before. I think I should be the one assisting."

"Do you?"

"I do." Erica held her ground. She had nothing to lose anyway, as she was heading to Annapolis.

"I don't think so, Commander. You wrote off his arm before you had X-rays done or even thoroughly examined the wound. Is that how you made your decision when you took my leg and ruined my career?"

The room was silent—at least, she assumed it was, since her head was filled with the thundering of her blood as it boiled.

She thought he'd forgiven her or didn't blame her for the decision she'd made five years ago, which had taken his leg, but apparently that wasn't true. He still resented her. Enough to bring up her competence in front of other staff members; he'd humiliated and embarrassed her.

Erica took a calming breath and stared at him across the OR.

"I saved your life."

"And I will save his. Now, get out of my OR, Commander. That's an order."

Erica didn't say anything but obeyed her commanding officer. She ripped off the gloves and gown and jammed them in the soiled bin and then scrubbed out as quickly as she could. When she was in the hall, she ripped off her surgical cap and tossed it against the wall.

She'd been so foolish to fall in love with her commanding officer, a former patient, even. She was stupid to think about trying to make it work, to think of having it all and settling down. She was weak for letting herself be momentarily ruled by her heart.

Well, it wouldn't happen again. She would never open her heart again.

She was tired of it being broken.

Thorne couldn't save the John Doe's arm. Erica had been right. He'd known from the moment he'd seen it briefly in the triage room, but instead of listening to her he'd been ruled by his emotions, by the feelings of betrayal he'd felt ever since she'd told him that she was leaving Okinawa to take a prestigious posting at Annapolis.

If it had been anyone else he would've been happier for them. He was happy for Erica, but the fact was she was leaving him, and he was acting like a fool.

She was leaving and he didn't want to let her go.

This is what you wanted, wasn't it?

He deserved this. He didn't deserve to be happy. It was fitting she was leaving.

He wanted her to leave Okinawa so he wouldn't be tempted, the only problem being he'd been tempted long before she'd decided to leave and now he didn't want her to go. He wanted her to stay with him. Only, she couldn't.

Thorne had to let her go.

It was for the best.

She would move on.

Erica wanted to advance her career: it was evident from the postings she'd chosen, by how far she'd come and what she'd endured to get to her position.

He couldn't be selfish, because he couldn't promise her anything.

Why not?

So he had to let her go. But first it was up to him to explain to the John Doe how his career was over and up to him to see the Special Ops team off to wherever they were going. Most likely San Diego.

As he headed out into the private room where the team was waiting, he caught sight of Erica in her uniform, her rucksack over her bag. She'd obviously cleared out her locker.

Let her go. She's mad at you and doesn't want to speak with you.

"Commander Griffin."

She turned and faced him. Her expression was unreadable as she dropped her bag and saluted him, holding herself at attention.

"Erica," he said.

"Captain." She would not look him in the eye.

"You're being ridiculous."

Her eyes narrowed and she looked at him, but wouldn't speak to him.

"You're at ease, Commander."

Erica relaxed her posture. "Can I help you, Captain?"

"I need to speak with you. Privately."

"I don't think that's wise, Captain. I think everything has been said."

"Please."

Erica sighed and picked up her rucksack, following Thorne into a small exam room. She shut the door behind her.

"What do you need to talk to me about? Whatever it is, make it quick. I'm catching the next transport back to the US."

"I know. I wanted to apologize."

"Apologize."

"I was out of line. You're right; the John Doe lost his arm. There was no way to salvage it."

Erica frowned. "I'm sorry that it couldn't be saved. I am."

Thorne nodded and then reached into his lab coat pocket for the small package he'd been carrying around since before she'd been leaving. Maybe because on some certain level he always knew she'd leave. "There was no excuse for my behavior. I wanted to clear the air before you left and give you this."

Erica glanced at the box with trepidation. "What is it?"

"Open it."

She shook her head and handed it back to him. "I can't accept this."

"You can. It's just a token, a reminder of your month here in Okinawa Prefecture."

Erica opened the box and pulled out the tiny bottle full of sand. "Sand?"

"It's from Iriomote Island, a bit of a distance from here, but it's *hoshizuna*—also known as star sand."

A brief smile passed on her face. "Thank you."

"Good luck."

She paused and then nodded. "Thank you, Captain."

Say something.

Only Thorne couldn't express what he wanted to say to her. He couldn't tell her how he felt; he just stood there frozen, numb, as she picked up her rucksack and turned to open the door. He moved quickly and held his hand against the door.

"Thorne, what're you doing?" she demanded. "I'll miss my transport."

"Stay," he said. "I'm sorry for kicking you out of my OR. That won't happen again. Just stay."

"Why should I?" she asked.

"You're my second in command. The best I've had since I took this posting."

"That's the only reason? Because I'm a good commander?"

No. That's not the only reason.

"Yes."

She shook her head. "I can't stay, Thorne. I'm being promoted to captain and to a position I've dreamed about holding for a long time. I'm sorry, but I have to go."

"What more do you want from me?" he snapped. "I can't give you any more than that. If you were expecting something more after our night together, I made it very clear."

"As did I," she said. "I should've known better than get involved with a commanding officer again."

"I'm not that man."

"You basically questioned my judgment in that OR."

"I apologized for that!" Thorne shouted. "What more do you want from me, Erica?"

"Nothing. There's nothing I want or need from you. Let me go, and please don't damage my professional reputation."

He clenched his fists. "Do you think I would damage your career out of spite?"

"You're not the first. It took me a long time to earn back what shred of respect I have and now I'm finally getting the promotion I deserve. I won't let anyone take that away from me."

"You obviously don't know me."

"I thought I did."

"You don't because you must think so little of me to think that I would stoop to Captain Seaton's level."

The blood drained from her face. "I never mentioned his name before."

"The name of your former commanding officer is on your record and, since I know you didn't have an affair with Dayton, I put two and two together. You really get around with your commanding officers, don't you?"

The sting of her slap rocked him. He deserved it. What he'd said was out of line and totally inappropriate.

"Goodbye, Captain Wilder."

And this time he didn't stop her from leaving.

He'd severed the tie and let her go.

CHAPTER FOURTEEN

IT WAS BEST to let her go.

Was it?

No, it wasn't. Erica had been gone a week and he missed her. The guilt ate at him for the things he'd said to her. It made him angry when he thought about it. If Liam had heard him speak that way he would've beat his butt. Day to day he just moved through the motions; sometimes he wasn't aware of the passing of the day. Another mistake he'd made, and he had to live with it, but it was difficult.

Things she'd brought alive were dull and gray in comparison now. He went to Scooby's every night and all he could hear was her laughter above the noise. When he glanced at the green shag carpet in the Jungle Room, and saw the booth they'd shared, his stomach would knot up.

And the pineapple pizza… He couldn't stomach it.

"You miss her."

Scooby had said that numerous times, but Thorne had never deigned to respond to him. He was trying to ignore the obvious, because if he ignored it, if he pretended it hadn't happened, then it wouldn't hurt so much.

The pain would go away.

Yeah, right.

Her quarters were still empty, waiting on the next commanding officer to take over. He walked by them daily, thinking about how she'd opened up to him about why she couldn't be in a relationship and he'd said nothing at all.

Just kept her out, because he'd thought it would be for the best.

A quick break.

Only, no matter how he tried to purge her from his system, he couldn't. She'd haunted him for five years before she'd come to the base. Now that he knew her, now that he'd touched, kissed and caressed the woman of his fantasies, he couldn't expel her to the dark corners of his mind.

She wasn't just a memory to look back on fondly. She was everywhere, even in his flesh. There was no way he could purge her from his system and he didn't want to.

Erica was so much more and he was too obtuse to see that.

"You look deep in thought," Scooby remarked, setting down a beer.

"What?" Thorne glanced around and didn't even realize that his walk had led him to Scooby's place or that he'd sat down at the bar. He rubbed his face and groaned.

"I said you look deep in thought, but not anymore. Sorry for interrupting your thoughts, Captain, but you looked a bit like a zombie."

"As long as I wasn't moaning." Thorne took a quick swig of beer, but it was flat in his mouth.

"How can I help you, Captain? I hate seeing you walking around here like some *deretto* fool."

"Deretto?"

"Love-struck."

Thorne snorted. "Who said I was love-struck?"

"The expression on your face speaks volumes. I may be old, Captain Wilder, but I'm not blind. You were in love with her."

"No. I'm not." Only he was, but he didn't deserve her. Because someone who was in love with someone didn't hurt them the way he'd hurt her. They didn't deserve to have a happy ending. He didn't deserve love.

"You're pulling my leg, Captain. You love Commander Griffin and she loves you."

Thorne chuckled. "She doesn't love me. Well, she may have, but not anymore. Not after the way I hurt her."

"Hurt her? What did you do to her?"

"I said some things I regret and she left." He touched the side of his face where she'd slapped him a week ago. It still hurt.

After he'd talked to the Navy SEALs about the John Doe, he'd gone out to arrange their transport and had seen Erica heading across the tarmac. Without thinking, he'd run after her, calling her name. She'd turned and looked, but ignored him as she boarded the plane.

He deserved it.

He didn't deserve her.

"You said things to her? What kind of things?"

"It doesn't matter. She's gone."

Scooby reached across the bar and gave him a quick smack upside the head. *"Baka!"*

"What? Why did you do that?"

"Idiot. You're an idiot, Captain Wilder." Scooby shook his head and uttered a few more choice swear words in Japanese. Probably all of which meant Thorne was an idiot or worse.

"What the heck have I done to you lately, Scooby?"

"Fuzakeru na! Stop being stupid, Captain Wilder. Go after her."

"Who?"

That earned him another cuff around the head and another oath in his direction. "Commander Griffin. You need to go to Minneapolis and get her back."

"You mean Annapolis."

"Isn't it the same?"

"No."

Scooby shrugged. "I've heard of Minneapolis. I've been to Minneapolis. Where is Annapolis?"

"Maryland."

"And that's not near Minneapolis?"

Thorne shook his head. "No."

"Then you need to go there. Tell her how you feel and apologize for your obtuseness. Apologize for driving her away, like you've always driven away people who try to become close to you."

"It's not that simple."

"*Fuzakeru na!* Of course it's simple. You love her, don't you?"

Yes. Still, he couldn't say it out loud.

He'd been hiding it from himself for so long, trying to suppress it, but, yes, he loved her. He was in love with Erica and he was an idiot for letting her go.

For so long he'd fought love, but maybe it was worth the risk. It was better than living a numbed existence. Still, he didn't deserve it. Not after what he'd done to Liam.

Liam never blamed you. Liam would want you to be happy. Stop blaming yourself.

But it was hard to let go of years of blame.

Tyler.

It went off like a lightbulb. Tyler had come to him a couple of years ago to apologize for his mistake which had cost Thorne his leg.

It had torn Tyler up inside to know he was responsible.

Thorne had sat him down and told Tyler that it wasn't his fault and that he didn't blame Tyler for the loss of his leg. It was part of serving. Thorne had told Tyler to let go of his guilt and get on with his life.

Yet, he hadn't done that.

He was a hypocrite.

The John Doe had been disappointed that he'd lost an

arm and could no longer serve, but he'd put a positive spin on it.

"At least my wife will be glad that I'll be home permanently."

Even the John Doe had someone waiting for him. Liam had had a wife and two beautiful kids. Neither of them had been afraid of serving their country and coming home to their families. Why was he so scared?

"I can't just leave my command. I have to arrange for a leave."

"Bah, you're making excuses."

"I'm not making excuses." He closed his eyes. "Maybe I am, Scooby. I don't know why I'm so…"

"Afraid?" Scooby shook his head. "Love, it sucks. It's hard and painful, but it's worth it."

"I've always said you're a man of many layers, Scooby."

He nodded. "Well, when you own a bar where a lot of different armed forces personnel move through, you pick up the odd thing. You all think the same thing: you're not afraid to lay down your life for your country, but when it comes to matters of the heart a lot of you are a bit more hesitant. Love is a powerful thing."

"Is it only the men?" Thorne asked.

"No, it's not. Commander Griffin is scared. I know she is. You two are the same and I believe I told you that when she first arrived here. You two are so volatile."

"I don't think you quite know what volatile means."

Scooby cursed under his breath. "Bah, you know what I mean. You two are both hotheaded, stubborn officers. You'll rub each other the wrong way, but you're meant to be together. Nobody else can put up with you."

"I'll arrange for a replacement and a transport."

"Good! You do that, Captain. Make the arrangements and go."

"And if she still doesn't want me?"

Scooby shrugged. "Then it's her loss, but at least you'll have closure."

"Thanks, Scooby. I think." Thorne set money down on the counter. "Though, you do know 'volatile' means something explosive?"

"Exactly my point, Captain. Now, get out of here."

Thorne chuckled. "Thanks."

"No problem." Scooby moved down the bar, muttering under his breath.

Even though he didn't deserve Erica, even though he'd messed it all up, he was going to try. He was brave enough to find out the answer—and if it was yes. If she loved him, he'd make it up to her even if it took him the rest of his life.

One month later, Annapolis, Maryland.

Erica had been paged by the recruitment office, something about a new plebe for the medical corps that they were eager to have at Annapolis.

She wasn't sure why they needed her there, but since it came from Admiral Greer she wasn't going to question anything, even though she was just about to head into class. Thankfully her second in command could take over the class while she dealt with this special request.

As she moved across the grounds, the trees were just starting to bloom with the first sign of spring and the red tulips in the center green were waving slightly in the warm breeze. It was familiar and, even though she was by the sea, she kind of missed being in Japan.

She absolutely loved her new position at Annapolis, but often there were times her mind drifted back to Okinawa.

There'd been a difference in the air there and it had been nice to see palm trees and white beaches. Not that Maryland wasn't beautiful, with the colonial charm and tall sails filling Chesapeake Bay; it was the company she missed.

Thorne.

She missed him and she didn't realize how much. Her day-to-day operations at Annapolis were just an existence.

Maybe it was because she was now a teacher at the most prestigious academy in the United States, but there was none of the familiarity or comraderie that she'd had when she'd been in Okinawa or serving on board the *Hope*.

Her commanding officer wasn't close to her age. He was older and didn't seem to have much of a sense of humor. Admiral Greer seemed to live on pomp, circumstance and regulations. So when she wasn't doing a shift at the base hospital where she could be in scrubs, the rest of the time she had to stay in her everyday dress uniform and heels.

She hated heels.

So, yeah, there was a lot to miss about Okinawa, but for the most part it was Thorne. When she'd left Ginowan she didn't realize how lonely she was until her companionship was gone.

It tore her heart out to leave him, but it was obvious that he didn't feel the same way as she did. Not after that fiasco in the OR when he'd made it quite clear that he still blamed her for the loss of his leg. When he'd thrown her out of his ER she'd tried to get him out of her mind—then he'd apologized and for a brief moment she'd thought he was going to open up to her. Instead he'd hurt her.

He'd expected her to give up on her dream so that she could stay with him. That was something she couldn't do.

Even though she was in love with him. Because there was no point in denying it: she loved Thorne. But she couldn't give up the life she'd mapped out for herself. Just like she didn't expect him to give up his life and his command posting in Okinawa.

It was cruel how love worked out that way sometimes. They were not meant to be together and she had to try and forget him.

Which was not easy.

She'd tried to do just that, but to no avail because, instead of the mysterious stranger with the intense blue eyes who had called her an angel, the Thorne she'd fallen for invaded her dreams. Every time she closed her eyes he was there.

So real and intense. She could recall his kisses, his touch. He was everywhere, his memory haunting her like a ghost. In the naval base hospital when she saw wounded warriors coming through, trying to heal themselves and continue to serve, she saw Thorne's determination to continue on.

Or, when watching a batch of plebes training to become Navy SEALs by drown proofing in the pool, all she had to do was close her eyes and picture him watching them, his arms crossed, assessing them.

Or when she went out and had a slice of pineapple pizza, which didn't hold a candle to Scooby's house specialty.

It pained her physically not be with him.

She'd grown numb.

Don't let him in now.

Right now she had a job to do. There was no room for Thorne in her mind. She didn't know why she was thinking of him constantly.

You miss him.

Erica took a deep breath and stopped to glance up at the blue spring sky. Yeah, she did miss him.

When she had started to unpack she'd found the star-shaped bottle with the sand. The one he'd given to her.

She'd almost thrown it out, trying to sever the tie, but she couldn't bring herself to do it. Because, even though he'd made it clear he didn't want her and didn't care for her, she loved him. She wished things between them had been different, but it was the way it was.

Besides, he didn't want her. He'd let her go.

He'd severed the ties long before she'd left Okinawa.

With a deep breath to ground herself, she headed up the white steps of the building she'd been asked to report to.

Before she headed into the recruitment office, she tidied her hair in a mirror and straightened her dress uniform jacket.

"Captain Griffin, the new recruit is waiting in room 407," Lieutenant Knox said, rising from his seat from behind his desk. He handed her the file.

"Thank you, Lieutenant." She flipped open the file. "A Navy SEAL?"

"Yes, Captain."

"His name is John Doe?" Erica asked, annoyed.

"Yes. I wasn't given specifics about why he stated his name was John Doe. He was quite unbending."

"He has to have a name. Why wouldn't he give you specifics?"

Lieutenant Knox shrugged. "Perhaps he's Special Ops. I don't know. I didn't see him. He was ushered in under a covert detail."

Erica was confused. "A covert detail? This doesn't make any sense."

"I'm sorry, Captain. That's all the intel I have."

Erica nodded and then headed to room 407. She didn't know what was going on here, but she was tired of covert operations and Navy SEALs. She'd taken this position at Annapolis to escape all that. There was only so much she could take in one lifetime of Special Ops, Navy SEALs and secrecy.

And she was tired of reminders of Thorne.

She knocked once and headed into the room. "Seaman, I understand you want to join the Med…"

She gasped and almost dropped the file in her hands, because they were shaking so bad. Standing in front of her in his dress whites was Thorne. He took off his white cap quickly and tucked it under his arm.

"Captain Griffin." He saluted her.

"C-Captain Wilder?"

He smiled. "Yes."

"What're you doing here? You're already a member of the Medical Corp."

"I know."

"Then why are you at the recruitment office?"

"I called in a favor from the admiral." Thorne set his cap down on the desk and took a step toward her.

"What kind of favor?" Her pulse began to race; he looked so good in his dress uniform. She'd never seen him in it. It suited him and made her weak in the knees.

Jerk. Remember what he did to you. How much it hurt.

"I told the admiral that I made a foolish error letting my second in command come to Annapolis."

"This is about getting me transferred back to Okinawa?" Rage boiled inside her. She threw the file at him, which he dodged. "Get out!"

"That's not why I'm here."

Only she wasn't going to listen to him. "How dare you? I'm not going to return to Okinawa as your commander. I can't believe you traveled halfway around the world to start up this old fight. You…you…."

"Erica, would you just calm down a minute and listen to me?" He tried to pull her to him, but she brushed off his embrace.

"Don't touch me—and it's Captain Griffin!"

"Erica," he said sternly. "I'm not here to take you back to Okinawa."

"You're not?"

"No, I'm not. Besides, that's not my posting any longer."

"What?" she asked in disbelief.

"I took an open position here at Annapolis."

"You what?" She took a step back and then leaned against the wall to collect herself. "You transferred here, but why?"

He smiled at her, those blue eyes twinkling. "Isn't it obvious?"

"No. It's not." Her voice shook as she braced herself. It was obvious, but she was in disbelief about it.

"I love you."

Erica's knees wobbled as the words sank in. "You love me?"

Thorne nodded. "I tried to resist you. I tried to wipe you from my mind, I tried not let you in. I told myself after my brother died in my arms and I saw the pain on his widow's face, the hole left in his children's hearts, that I wouldn't ever allow someone to mourn me. I joined the SEALs to fulfill my brother's dream and I blamed myself for Liam's death, and for that I felt I didn't deserve any kind of happiness."

"I don't understand what you're trying to tell me."

He ran his hands through his hair. "I was happy as a SEAL and then on a covert operation I was injured saving another man's life and I met you. You entranced me. My foggy memories had one bright spot and it was you. Of course, then I actually did meet you, and you weren't exactly as angelic as I thought you were in my fantasies."

Erica chuckled at that. "I'm not gentle. Must be the Cajun in me."

"I'm sorry for trying to shut you out, for embarrassing

you that day when the John Doe came in. You were right. He lost his arm. It was too far gone and, what I said? I was out of line."

Erica nodded. "I know. I saw his medical chart when he returned to San Diego. You did a good job with his amputation. As for the other things, well, I wasn't exactly easy on you."

"Thank you." Thorne closed the distance between them again. "Look, I just couldn't tell you how I felt about you, because I didn't think I deserved it. How could I be happy when I'm the reason Liam lost his life?"

"You deserve to be happy."

Thorne took a step closer. "So do you."

"Perhaps."

"I don't know what the future holds for me or you, but I know one thing: I love you and I can't live without you. It's worth the risk to be with you. I need to be with you, Erica."

She couldn't believe he was saying the words that she herself hadn't known she was longing to hear, but now that he was saying them she knew that she could have both her career and him. Something she never thought before. Most men had been intimidated by her rank, her career, except Thorne.

He was her match in every way.

Thorne ran his knuckles down her cheek. "I love you, Erica. I'm sorry for being such a…"

She suggested a word in Cajun and laughed at her secret joke.

"Sure, but I'm not sure I should admit to anything you say in Cajun."

"Then how about 'I forgive you'?"

Thorne smiled. "That I can live with."

He leaned forward and kissed her. His lips were gentle, urging, and she melted in his arms, totally forgetting that she was angry at him, that he'd hurt her, because he was sorry for what he'd done. He hadn't meant it. Thorne had tried to push her away just as much as she'd tried to push him away, but as Scooby had said they were "volatile" together.

Explosive. And, even though they were a combustible match, they were made for each other. They both had just been too stubborn to see it.

"What're you smiling about?" he asked.

"Something my *mamère* said."

"You better keep it to yourself."

"Why?" she asked.

"I don't want to be left in the dark with all the Cajun words."

Erica kissed him. "I promise to fill you in on Cajun when I can, but then again maybe not, as I have an advantage over you when you tick me off."

Thorne rolled his eyes, but laughed. "Well, I have to get used to living stateside again."

"Are you sorry you left Okinawa?" she asked.

"I'll miss it, I won't lie, but you're more important to me. I can get used to having soft-shell crab instead of pineapple pizza."

"Have you ever had soft-shell crab?"

"No."

She grinned. "Well, I hope you'll let me take you for your first time."

"Deal."

"I'm sorry too, for what it's worth."

"For what?" he asked.

"For walking away. For being insubordinate to my commanding officer on numerous occasions and for not telling you that I love you too."

He grinned. "Well, there are ways you can make it up to me."

"Is that so? Well, I can start off by giving you a massage."

"Oh, yes." He cupped her face and stroked her cheek. "That's a good start But first I have to check in officially."

"I'll take you there."

Hand in hand, they walked out of the recruitment office.

EPILOGUE

One year later, Annapolis, Maryland.

ERICA'S HEART RACED and she was shaking as she stood in a small anteroom off the side of the chapel on the naval base, a historic building. She thought if she was ever going to take the plunge and get married she was going to have her ceremony at the Naval Academy Chapel.

There were so many things architecturally about this chapel she loved. So much represented her core beliefs about being in the Navy. Like the stained glass window of Sir Galahad and his ideals which every Naval officer tried to live up to; and the domed ceiling, which reminded her of a cathedral in Florence, Italy, and was beautiful to look at.

Of course, when she'd originally had that thought when she was going for training here, she hadn't thought it would actually come to pass because she hadn't thought that she'd actually get married.

It hadn't mattered if she ever got married, until she'd met Thorne. Even if he'd never asked her, she'd have been happy with the life they were living in Annapolis. Both of them had been furthering their careers in the Navy, saving lives and training recruits when the proposal had happened. She hadn't been expecting it. They'd been walking along the shore a month ago, watching the sailboats with the colorful sails moving across the blue water, when he'd cried out in pain, dropping to his knee.

When she'd tried to see if he was okay, worried it was his phantom leg pain, he'd opened a small velvet box and proposed.

It was like something out of a dream; she still felt a bit dazed by it all.

And now she was standing in the antechamber, her knees knocking under the white silk of a very simple wedding dress.

"You could've worn your Navy uniform," Commander Rick Kettle, Regina's husband, whispered in her ear. "You are a captain."

"No, she's not!" Regina screeched and Erica chuckled.

"She's a captain, Regina. She has every right to wear her dress uniform."

Regina shot her husband the stink eye. "She looks beautiful and she's going to get married like a proper bride. This is a momentous occasion."

Rick shook his head and Erica glared at Regina, who was rocking back and forth, holding her newborn daughter named after Erica.

"If you weren't holding my goddaughter you would be in serious trouble, my friend."

Regina winked. "Well, at least it got your mind off your nerves, now, didn't it?"

Erica was going to say more when there was a knock at the door and Erica's mother stuck her head into the room. Erica had resolved things with her mother and, even though her mother didn't totally agree with Erica's career choice, she'd absolutely been won over by Thorne. The rift between her and her mom was healing and she was very excited to be a part of the wedding.

"It's time."

Regina came over and squeezed Erica's arm. "You can do this!"

Erica nodded, but she was still shaking.

Regina and her mother left the anteroom. Erica didn't have any bridesmaids because the only man Thorne had wanted to stand up with him was his brother and he couldn't have that. So they'd both opted to keep the wedding small.

The only people attending were close friends and family.

Erica would've liked Captain Dayton to walk her down the aisle, but he was out at sea on the *Hope,* so Regina's husband was stepping in, and he did look quite dashing in his white dress uniform.

"You ready to go?"

"Yes; if I linger too much longer I might bolt from sheer terror."

"As long as it's not Captain Wilder making you bolt."

"No," Erica said and then smiled. "No, not him."

Rick smiled and took her arm. "Left and then right, Captain Griffin. Just one foot in front of the other."

Erica nodded and he walked her out of the antechamber to the main chapel. The large pipe organ began to play the bridal song, but she couldn't hear it over the sound of her pulse thundering in her ears.

As she started walking up the aisle there was a call out and a salute, which caused her to gasp, as a group of Navy SEALs decked out in their dress uniforms stood at attention for her, their sabers hanging at their sides.

They were Thorne's old unit. She recognized Mick the commanding officer she'd stood up to all those years ago on the *Hope*—and then she got a glimpse of Thorne standing there in his dress uniform and suddenly she wasn't so nervous any longer.

She walked up the aisle and glanced at all their friends

and family; she welled up when she saw Bunny and Scooby in the aisle, smiling at her. Scooby bowed quickly, beaming at her. She stopped Rick, breaking rank, so she could hug them briefly, trying not to cry.

When she got to the front Thorne took her hand. She didn't even remember the ceremony, because all she could see was Thorne—the man who'd had no name when she'd first met him but was full of fight, spirit and a passion to serve his country.

He enchanted her and enraged her at times. They were volatile together, so explosive, and Erica loved every minute of it.

Before she knew it, she was kissing her husband to an audience that was cheering and clapping.

"Are you okay?" Thorne whispered in her ear.

"I'm fine, why?"

"You look a bit shocked."

"A deer trapped in barbed wire?"

Thorne chuckled. "Headlights. I'm buying a book of old sayings for our first anniversary."

Erica pinched him as they headed down the aisle. "If we survive that long."

"We will."

"How do you know?" she teased. They paused at the entrance of the chapel as his old unit raised their sabers in a salute. Erica and Thorne passed under them, kissing at the end.

"Because I love you and I'm never letting you go."

* * * * *

THE COURAGE TO LOVE HER ARMY DOC

KARIN BAINE

For the ladies who've shared this adventure with me—
Ann, Cherie, Donna, Doris, Heather, Joanne, Julia,
June, Kiru, Michelle, Rima, Sharon, Stacy, Stephanie,
Sukhi, Summerita, Suzy, Tammy, Teresa and Xandra.
UCW was where it all began.

With thanks also to the residents of Los Balcones
and the members of 'The Monday Club'
who bring a little sunshine into my life.

And to George—the other half of me.

CHAPTER ONE

PARADISE. IT WAS the only word to describe these sun-drenched islands that Emily Clifford hoped were going to change her life. Unfortunately, she hadn't accounted for the distance she would have to travel to find her solace.

Travel sickness wasn't something she'd ever suffered before or she would've had one of her colleagues at the GP practice prescribe her something before she'd left England. If she'd been thinking clearly she might have realised that accessing one of these remote Fijian islands would take more than a taxi ride. Her first day after landing at the airport on the main island, Viti Levu, walking through the markets, and her night at a luxurious five-star resort now seemed a lifetime ago.

Today's white-knuckle charter flight, followed by a bone-jangling cross-country drive and hours of sailing these waters, had taken their toll.

The only thing she was looking forward to more than a shower and bed was seeing Peter, her stepbrother, waiting for her. He was the reason she was even attempting this adventure. The chance to prove her ex-husband wrong about her being *boring* was simply a bonus.

She and Greg had been together since high school, married for ten years, but it hadn't been enough. She hadn't been enough.

When Peter had told her about the mission out here and how they were struggling to find medical professionals to volunteer, she'd jumped at the chance to help for a while. Not least because this fortnight away meant she'd be occupied while Greg and Little Miss Bit-on-the-Side held the wedding of the year.

Another swell of nausea rose as the boat bobbed again but this had to be better than sitting at home, crying over her wedding photographs and wondering where it had all gone wrong.

As they finally reached the far side of the island and prepared to go ashore, she could see a figure sitting cross-legged at the water's edge. She waved manically, desperate more than ever to get off this boat and find comfort in the arms of her big brother.

With her hand shielding her eyes from the glaring sun, she squinted at her welcome party of one slowly getting to his feet. He appeared to have grown in the two years since she'd last seen him, and he was leaner than she remembered, as though someone had stretched him like golden-coloured toffee.

Eventually she had to come to terms with the fact that no amount of sand, sea and sun could cause such a physical transformation. Disappointment settled in her belly as she realised it wasn't Peter at all. She was going to have to wait for her tea and sympathy for a bit longer.

She'd done her best to be strong over this past year and a half, holding it together as she'd moved out of her marital home and keeping a smile in place for all her patients when she'd been dying inside. For a short time she wanted to stop pretending she wasn't crushed by the rejection and it didn't take every ounce of strength just to get out of bed in the morning and face the world. Ten minutes of being the baby sister, crying out her pain to her big bro, would help reset the factory settings. Two weeks doing what she loved, what she was qualified to do, would remind her she was more than a redundant wife. She'd lasted this long for a shoulder to cry on so waiting a few extra minutes wouldn't kill her. Although she couldn't swear the pent-up anger and emotion she'd been gearing up to release wouldn't seep out somewhere along the way.

Her bejewelled sandals and floral maxi-dress flapped through the water as she stepped ashore. In hindsight, it hadn't been the ideal choice of travelling outfit. Her feet ached, her dress was creased and as she came face-to-face with the hunk on the beach she was pretty sure the flower in her hair was wilting. What had been an attempt to get into the holiday spirit had probably succeeded in making her appear even more ridiculous than usual, like a stereotypical tourist instead of a qualified professional hoping to fit effortlessly into society.

With his close-cropped brown hair and dressed in mid-length khaki shorts and navy T-shirt, her greeter looked more action man than island native. There was no sign of a grass skirt anywhere. Unfortunately.

'Hi. I'm Emily.' She held out her hand for him to shake but he bypassed the traditional greeting to head for the boat. The bit of research she'd done said they mostly spoke English here on Yasi island but perhaps she'd found the one local who didn't.

He began unloading her luggage, muscles flexing as he hurled her case and boxes of supplies onto the white sand.

'Bula.' She tried again, using the one Fijian word she'd picked up on her travels so far.

The Peter impostor waved off her last link to civilisation and came back to join her.

'Bula to you too.' The cut-glass British accent didn't fit with the swarthy skin but the familiar tongue and the glimpse of a smile put her mind at ease about being stranded here with an uncommunicative stranger.

'You're English?'

'Yeah. From Oxford, actually. I'm Joe. Joe Braden.' This time he did shake her hand, the firm grip showing the strength behind those muscles.

Emily shivered, regardless of the tropical heat. Clearly she'd been on her own too long when a single handshake was enough to get her excited. Not that she was ready for the dating game. In the day and age when physical attributes held more value than loyalty or commitment, she was in no rush to put herself through any more heartache.

'Joe Braden… Why does that name ring a bell?' They'd never met. She'd have remembered if they had.

'I served with Peter in Afghanistan.' The smile disappeared as quickly as it had formed.

That made sense of the military haircut and the no-nonsense attitude. She'd heard that name in conversation and she was sure there was an extra nugget of information tied to it that was just out of reach in her subconscious.

'Where is he? No offence, but I had hoped he'd be here to meet me.' She didn't want to get into a conversation about their time in combat and she doubted he'd be keen to rehash the whole experience either. It had been hell for all those involved, including the families waiting anxiously at home for their safe return. Peter's decision to leave the army and begin a life dedicated to his faith had been a relief to everyone who loved him.

'None taken. We couldn't be sure exactly what time to expect you and Peter had a service this evening. I volunteered for lookout duty.' He handed her a suitcase and a holdall while he hoisted the large box onto his shoulder.

She didn't dare ask how long he'd waited. His lips, drawn into a thin line and his apparent hurry to get moving, told her it had probably been too long. Not exactly the welcome she'd been hoping for.

Joe was already taking great strides across the beach,

so Emily traipsed after him as fast as she could with a holdall hooked over one shoulder and a suitcase in the other, waddling like a colourful penguin. There was no immediate sign of human habitation nearby and she didn't relish the thought of being left behind.

'What brings you out here anyway?' She caught up with him at the bottom of a steep, grassy slope. Their journey apparently wasn't going to be an easy or short one. Some small talk might help it pass quicker.

'Your stepbrother.'

'You're visiting Peter?' He hadn't mentioned having company in his emails. She hadn't counted on sharing his attention. As pitiful as that sounded, she hadn't seen him in two whole years and wanted to make up for lost time. Who knew where he'd be going next or how long he'd be gone? Quality time with him wasn't going to be quite the same with surly soldier dude tagging along.

'I'm here as a medical volunteer, the same as you. I'll be here for another month. Maybe. I prefer to keep on the move. What you would call a modern-day adventurer, I guess. This is the longest I've actually spent in one place since leaving the army, which is entirely down to your stepbrother's powers of persuasion.' He didn't even slow his pace to deliver the news, leaving her staring open-mouthed at him.

There were two things wrong with that statement. First of all, it meant he had personal intel on her already if he knew why she was there. She didn't have her stepbrother down as the gossipy type since he hadn't seen the need to share information concerning her new companion, so perhaps soldier boy had insisted on a debriefing before meeting his assigned target. Goodness knew what went on between ex-military buddies, they had a bro code mere mortals could never infiltrate, but she hoped any discussion about her arrival hadn't included details of her failed marriage. That shame was exactly what she was trying to escape.

Secondly, his introduction undoubtedly meant she'd be working alongside this man for the duration of her stay. Trying to get more than a few words out of him on this trek was proving hard enough.

In her version of this medical outreach programme she was simply transferring her cosy GP office to an exotic location without interference from third parties. Peter had sounded so delighted to hear she was coming she'd assumed she'd be the sole medical professional in residence. This Joe was stealing all her thunder.

'Do I call you Dr? Sergeant? Joe…?' She was going to have serious words with her stepbrother about dumping her on a complete stranger without a word of warning. It immediately put her on the back foot when Peter should have known how important it was for her to feel comfortable in her surroundings.

'Joe will do just fine.'

She couldn't work out if the reluctance to engage in conversation was personal or he was simply trying to conserve energy. The hike up this hill was a test of endurance in itself, never mind the heavy box he was balancing on his broad shoulders. She was starting to regret packing the weighty school books she'd brought with her as a gift.

'Isn't there someone who could give us a hand?' She was tired, achy and full of guilt, watching him shift the burden from one shoulder to the other.

'Did you bring the *yaqona*?' He ignored her question to stop and ask one of his own, as if hers wasn't important enough to deserve the few seconds it would take to answer it. With any luck this place was big enough to house two independent clinics. There was no way she was spending the duration of this trip with someone so rude.

'Yes. It's in this bag.' She, however, was polite enough

to answer him. Peter had at least given her the heads up about bringing gifts with her, including the root of this pepper plant. Apparently it was some sort of payment for her stay among the villagers, even though it did look kind of funky to her. She would have preferred to give him a pot plant or a nice bottle of wine with a thank-you card.

'Good. We'll go and make *sevusevu* now with the chief.'

'Can't we do that later? I really need to shower and freshen up.' By the time they reached their destination she wouldn't be fit to be seen in public.

'No can do. You have to show your respect to the tribal leader before you can integrate yourself into village life. If you respect the customs here it'll ensure you become part of the community.'

Right now, the heat and humidity were making her feel as though her face was melting. She was very wary of her potentially sliding make-up and the fact he was telling her she wouldn't get the chance to redo it. The heavy, thick concealer she wore to cover her birthmark was the one essential from home she couldn't do without.

She was self-conscious of the deep red port wine stain dominating the left side of her face, so noticeable against her otherwise pale skin. It was something that had caused her a great deal of distress over the years. And not only from uneducated, tactless strangers. Her own mother had been ashamed of her appearance. She'd told her that when she'd forced her through painful, ineffective laser treatment as a child. She'd shown it when she'd left the family home without her. In the end it had been the camouflage make-up and the love of her father's new family that had helped her live with it.

This was a big ask for her anyway, to come to foreign lands alone, never mind leaving herself exposed and open to scrutiny from strangers.

As they crested the hill she could see the settlement nestled below. It was now or never.

She stopped and dropped her bags. This trip was always going to be about improvising and making use of whatever resources she had at the time.

'What are you doing?' Joe raised an eyebrow at her as she rooted through her belongings for her mirror compact.

'I need to look my best if I'm going to meet someone of such great importance.' She made a few repairs before she scared small children and animals, ignoring Joe's shake of the head.

'You know, that's really not necessary. You should let your skin breathe and I'm sure you look just as amazing without it.'

There was no time to linger on the fact he'd paid her a compliment as he spun on his heel and started walking again. Besides, he'd be running if he knew what really lay beneath. She took one last glance in the mirror to check for any errant red patches shining through the layers of powder and paint and packed her precious cargo away again to follow him. Now she'd had a chance to boost her confidence again she could face any new challenge.

Joe couldn't hang about to watch her plaster that stuff over her face. He knew why she did it, of course, he'd seen the photographs of his kid sister Peter had kept with him out in Afghanistan. It simply irked him that someone had made her feel as though she had to use it to keep her real self from view. He knew how it was to have people devalue your worth so readily over a minor flaw.

Okay, his hearing had taken a hit along with the rest of him on the front line but that didn't mean he should have been written off altogether. The army might think all he was good for now was a desk job or teaching but he had no intention of sitting still. Fiji was just one stop on the list of adventures he'd embarked on since taking medical retirement.

According to Peter, Emily had had a rough time of it lately but Joe knew how empowering these trips abroad could be. His time trekking in Nepal, island hopping in the Philippines and swimming on the Great Barrier Reef had kept him from focusing on all the negatives in his past. With any luck she'd return at the end of this mission equally as upbeat, not caring a jot about other people's perceptions of her.

Although how she could think she was anything other than stunning he didn't know. The second she'd stepped ashore he'd known he was in trouble.

His decision to volunteer as official island greeter had been born of curiosity. He'd seen the worn photographs of her and Peter as kids, the shy Emily always hiding behind her stepbrother, and he'd wondered about the woman she'd become. The doctor he was going to be working alongside for the foreseeable future.

In the four weeks he'd already spent in this island paradise she was the most beautiful sight he'd seen yet. With the golden waves of her hair shining in the sunlight, her turquoise eyes the colour of the water and her slender form draped in azure, she could've stepped out of a shampoo advert. It was too bad she was his mate's little sister and nursing a broken heart. Two things that immediately put her off limits. Even if hearing-impaired ex-army docs were her thing.

He'd let enough of his army buddies down without failing Peter too. Neither was he in the market for any sort of emotional entanglements. Emily was literally carrying more baggage than he was prepared to take on. He was more of a backpacking guy, travelling light with no intention of setting down roots. Although he helped out with these outreach programmes now and then when people were in dire need, he was better off on his own. It meant no long-term responsibility to anyone but himself.

The last time he'd been charged with the welfare of people close to him, it had cost two of his colleagues their lives. When the IED had knocked him to kingdom come he'd failed to be there for the men he'd had a duty of care for. Next to the young families left without fathers, his loss seemed insignificant. These days he preferred to keep his wits about him rather than become too complacent and safe in his surroundings.

'Are we there yet?' Emily was smiling as she jogged to keep up with him.

At least when she was close he could hear her or interpret her facial expressions. He only had a six per cent loss of hearing but sometimes it meant he missed full conversations going on in the background. More often than not he chose to let people think he was an arrogant sod over revealing his weakness. He and Emily had their pride in common.

'Very nearly. Now, there are a few protocols to be aware of before presenting the *yaqona* for the kava ceremony. You're dressed modestly enough so that shouldn't be a problem.' He took the opportunity for a more in-depth study of her form, though he wasn't likely to forget in a hurry how she looked today.

'What's the kava ceremony?' She eyed him suspiciously, as if he might be luring her to the village as some sort of human sacrifice.

'Basically, it's a welcoming ceremony with the most senior tribal members present. They grind the *yaqona*, or kava, and make it into a drink for you to take with them in a traditional ceremony. All visitors are invited to take part when they first arrive on the island.'

'It's not one of those hallucinogenic substances you hear about, is it? I don't want to be seeing fairies dancing about all night in front of my eyes. I'm not even a big drinker because I don't enjoy that feeling of being out of control.' She was starting to get herself into a flap for no reason.

Joe hadn't even asked questions when he'd taken part in his first kava ceremony, he'd just gone with the flow. He embraced every new experience with gusto, whereas Emily seemed to fear it.

'Don't worry. It's nothing sinister, although the taste leaves a lot to be desired. There shouldn't be any fairy visions keeping you awake. If anything, it's known to aid sleep, among other things.' He kept the claims of its aphrodisiac properties to himself rather than freak her out any further.

'I don't think that's something I'm going to have a problem with tonight.' She set her case down and rubbed her palms on her dress before lifting it again. The heavy labour in less-than-ideal circumstances was something she was going to have to get used to and only time would tell if she was up to it.

He, on the other hand, had a feeling his peace of mind here had suddenly been thrown into chaos.

It was just as well he thrived on a challenge.

CHAPTER TWO

ALL EMILY WANTED was a familiar face and familiar things around her. It wasn't a lot to ask for and the sooner she got her bags unpacked and her clinic in the sun set up the better. Then she might be able to finally relax. She'd had all the excitement she needed just getting here.

Her pulse skittered faster as the ramshackle buildings with their corrugated-iron roofs came into view. This was as far from her humdrum life as she could get and a definite two-fingered salute to her ex.

'Can I refuse to take part in this kava thing?' She'd used up her quota of bravery already. Drinking unknown substances with strangers was the sort of thing that could make her the subject of one of those 'disappearances unsolved' programmes.

Her idea of living dangerously was putting an extra spoonful of sugar in her cuppa at bedtime, not imbibing a local brew of origin unknown to her. It wasn't that she'd heard anything but good things about these people, she was just scared of all this *newness*. This would've been so much easier if Peter was here with her instead of the scowling Joe.

'You have free will, of course you can refuse. It would, however, show a distinct lack of respect for your hosts.'

That would be a no, then. It was going to be difficult

enough fitting in here, without incurring the wrath of the community from the get-go.

Trust and respect were vital components between a doctor and her patients. It had taken her a long time to gain both from her colleagues and the locals when she'd first joined the GP practice at home. Only years of hard work, building her reputation, had moved her from being last option to first choice for her patients.

With only two weeks to re-create that success here she'd have to take every opportunity available to ingratiate herself. Even if she was breaking out in a cold sweat at what that meant she could be walking into.

They passed a white building, larger than the rest, which her tour guide informed her was the village school. Although lessons were surely over for the day, the children were congregated on the patch of green surrounding it, playing ball games. There was a chorus of '*Bula!*' as the youngsters waved in their direction.

Unfortunately, one boy by the volleyball net was too distracted by their arrival to see the ball coming straight for him. The loud smack as it connected full in his face even made Emily flinch. As the child crumpled to the ground, for a split second she wondered if there was some sort of protocol she should follow as she hadn't been officially introduced. Common sense quickly overrode her worry and she dropped her bags to run to him. It was only when she was battling through the throng of children to reach him that she realised Joe had followed too. They knelt on either side of the boy, who was thankfully still conscious but clearly winded.

'If you could just stay still for us, sweetheart, we want to give you a check over. That was quite a hit you took there.' She couldn't see any blood or bruising as yet but she wanted him to stay flat until they'd given him a quick examination.

'Hi, Joni. This is Emily, the new doctor. You know, Pastor Peter's sister?' Joe made the introduction she'd omitted to do herself, and was already checking the boy's pupils with a small torch he'd retrieved from one of his pockets.

She'd bet her life he had a Swiss Army knife and a compass somewhere in those cargo shorts too. He was the type of guy who was always prepared, like a rugged, muscly Boy Scout. The only survival essentials she carried were make-up, teabags and chocolate biscuits, none of which were particularly useful at present. The few medical supplies she had with her were packed somewhere in her abandoned luggage.

Life as an island doctor certainly wasn't going to run to the office hours she was used to. She was going to be permanently on call and if she didn't come equipped, deferring to her army medic colleague was going to become the norm. That feeling of inadequacy could defeat the purpose of her personal journey here if she didn't get with the programme. This trip was primarily to bring medical relief to the people of the island and she could do without uncovering any new flaws to obsess over.

'Do you know where you are, Joni? Or what happened?' She wrestled back some control, determined not to let the issue of a pocket torch spiral into a major meltdown in her neurotic brain.

That earned her an *Are you serious?* glare. 'I'm lying on the ground because you two won't let me get up after I got hit in the face with a ball.'

Joe snickered as she was educated by her first patient.

'Dr Emily's making sure the bump on the head hasn't caused any serious damage, smart guy.' He ruffled the boy's hair, clearly already acquainted with the child.

She figured he was using her first name to break the

ice a little because she was a stranger. Either that or he didn't know what surname she was currently going under.

It was a subject she hadn't fully resolved herself. Greg Clifford was going to be someone else's husband soon. She no longer had any claim over his name, or anything else. Yet reverting back to her maiden name of Jackson was confirmation that her marriage had failed. She'd been returned unwanted for a second time, like a mangy stray dog. The idea of going back on the singles market felt very much like waiting for someone to take pity on her and find her a forever home.

She tried to refocus her attention back from her ex to the present. He didn't deserve any more of her time since all the years she'd given him had apparently meant so little.

'Do you have any pain in your neck?'

Her choice of words had her patient sniggering at her again.

'Come on, Joni. We're trying to help you here. We need to know if you're hurting anywhere before we get you back on your feet.'

It was comforting to find Joe had her back this time, even if his apparent seniority here was irksome.

'I'm okay.' As if to try to prove their fears unwarranted, Joni jumped to his feet, only to have to reach out and steady himself by grabbing Joe's arm.

If Emily was honest, she'd have made a grab for the strong and sturdy desert island doc too in similar circumstances.

'Really?' Joe arched a dark eyebrow as he glanced down at his new small-child accessory.

Joni shrugged but made no further wisecracks.

'We should really get him checked out properly.' Although he bore no immediate signs of concussion, it didn't mean they should rule it out altogether.

As well as getting a cold compress to prevent swelling, she'd prefer to keep him under observation in case of headaches or vomiting. He'd taken quite a wallop and although the skull was there to protect the brain there was always a chance the knock could cause the brain to swell or bleed. She didn't like taking unnecessary chances.

'The best option for now is to get him to Miriama's.' Joe crouched down for the patient to jump on his back. A piggyback was apparently the equivalent of an ambulance around here.

'Isn't there a medical centre we can take him to?' A small bird of panic fluttered its wings in her chest. She'd been led to believe there'd be some sort of facility for her to practise from. He might be used to treating people in the field but she certainly wasn't.

'Of sorts, but Miriama is his grandmother and the closest thing they have to a medic. She can keep an eye on him until you make *sevusevu* and if his condition changes we'll only be a few minutes away.'

It didn't slip her attention that he intended coming with her. In the absence of her brother she supposed he was going to have to do as backup. At least this incident showed he could be a calming influence when the need arose and she trusted he would keep her grounded until she tracked down her sibling.

'What about my things?' As they followed the dirt trail further into the village she fretted over her worldly possessions abandoned on the hillside.

'No one's going to steal them. We'll come back for the *yaqona* and send someone to take the rest back to Miriama's later.' He strode on ahead, unconcerned with her petty worries or the weight strapped around his neck.

She could picture him in his army gear, bravely heading into battle with his kit on his back, and it gave her chills. The idea of her brother in a war zone had always freaked her out and there'd been no greater relief than when he'd left the army. She was glad he was no longer in danger. Joe too. Life here might be more unconventional than she was used to but she didn't have to worry about anyone getting shot or blown up.

With her imagination slowing her down, she was forced to run and catch up again. The sandals slapping against her bare feet really weren't suitable footwear for chasing fit men in a hurry.

'Why should my luggage end up at Miriama's?' That obscure snippet of information hadn't passed her by.

'That's where you're going to be staying for the next fortnight. Miriama's your host.'

Although she hadn't expected the luxury of last night's five-star resort, she'd imagined she'd be staying with her brother rather than another stranger.

'Peter's staying with the village chief. He's earned a great deal of respect from the community for his endeavours here.' Joe headed off her next question before she could ask it. She couldn't help but wonder what his own arrangements were.

'And you? Where do you lay your head at night?' Only when the words left her lips did she realise how nosy that sounded. She hadn't intended prying into his personal life but this was all new to her. She didn't know if he was presented with pretty young virgins and his own house to thank him for his services. It would certainly explain her brother's reluctance to leave the village.

He cocked his head to one side, his mouth twitching as he fought a smile. 'Well, there's a new arrival in my bed tonight—'

She held her hand up before he went into graphic detail. 'I shouldn't have asked. It's none of my business.'

'So I'm moving from Miriama's into the clinic.'

It took a second for the image of Joe cavorting with exotic beauties to clear and let his words sink in.

'I'm taking your bed? Honestly, that's not necessary. I'm more than willing to take your place at the clinic.' She didn't know what that entailed but she'd take it over the lack of privacy in someone else's house.

Joe shook his head. 'The clinic's a glorified hut with two camp beds and a supply cupboard. You'll find no comfort there. I, on the other hand, am used to kipping in ditches, or worse. It's no hardship for me. Besides, you'll be doing me a favour.' He gave a furtive glance back at his charge to make sure he wasn't listening. 'I don't want to offend Miriama but I prefer the peace and quiet of being alone. I'm not used to domesticity.'

Perhaps it was because he was the first man to get so close to her in well over a year or the picture he painted of himself as some wild creature who couldn't be tamed but the shivers were back, causing havoc along her spine and the back of her neck.

Okay, she wasn't happy with the arrangements made on her behalf but she couldn't deny him his bed choice when he'd gone so far out of his way for her already. She couldn't form a logical argument anyway when her brain was still stuck on a freeze frame of caveman Joe.

The smiling Miriama was as welcoming as anyone could hope for. Until she found out Emily had yet to meet with the tribal elders and shooed them both back out of the door. She'd unhitched her grandson with the promise of getting some ice for the bump on his forehead and accepted some paracetamol, which Joe had produced from his shorts of many pockets. This new informal approach to treatment would take some getting used to. Just like her new co-worker would.

They retrieved her gifts for the community on the way

back to the chief's house and dispatched the rest of her belongings back to her temporary lodgings with the children. Trust didn't come easily to her any more but she was willing to take a leap of faith safe in the knowledge there were few places on the island to hide. She'd found that out the minute she'd set foot on the beach.

Now she was standing on the doorstep of the most important man on Yasi as Joe entered into a dialogue she assumed involved her arrival. It was hard to tell because they were conversing in Fijian, another skill he'd apparently acquired in his short time here and one more advantage over her. Languages had never been her strong point. Along with keeping a husband.

She was hanging back as the menfolk discussed her business, still hoping for a way out, when a hand clamped down on her shoulder.

'Hey, sis. Long time no see.'

In her desire to be accepted she thought she'd imagined her stepbrother standing beside her in a garish pink hibiscus shirt but there was no mistaking the bear hug as anything but the real deal as the breath was almost squeezed out of her.

'Peter?' The tears were already welling in her eyes with relief to have finally found some comfort.

'I wouldn't miss this for the world. Now, Joe will be acting as our "chief" since he's the eldest of our group, or temporary tribe. It's his job to present the kava root to the elders. We'll talk you through everything else once we're inside.'

He instructed her to remove her sandals before they entered. Sandwiched between her brother and Joe was the safest she'd felt in an age. They sat down on woven mats strewn across the floor of the main room, surrounded by those she assumed were the elders of the village.

'I take it everything met with their approval?' She

leaned over to whisper to her unofficial leader sitting cross-legged beside her.

Joe kept his gaze straight ahead, completely ignoring her. She didn't know if pretending she didn't exist was part of the process until she was accepted into the community or if he was completely relinquishing all responsibility for her now Peter had appeared. Either way, it hurt.

She leaned back the other direction toward Peter. 'Am I persona non grata around here until the ceremony's over?'

He frowned at her. 'What makes you say that?'

She nodded at her silent partner. 'Your friend here can be a little cold when he wants. Thanks for landing me with a complete stranger, by the way. Just what I needed to make me feel at home. Not.'

The cheesy grin told her he'd done it on purpose. 'I thought you two could do with some team bonding since you'll be working together, and he volunteered in the first place. I should probably mention he's a bit hard of hearing, especially if you're whispering.'

'I had no idea!' Shame enveloped her. It had never entered her head that hearing impairment could've been an issue with Joe when he was so young and capable. She of all people should've known not to make assumptions based on people's appearances.

'Yeah. IED blast. The one where we lost Ste and Batesy.'

The pieces she'd been scrambling to put together slowly fitted into place. Of course, she'd heard of Sergeant Joe Braden. He'd been one of Peter's best friends and that blast had made her brother finally experience for himself the worry and fear of losing someone close. It hadn't been long after that he'd made the decision to change his career path completely. She hated it that his friends had suffered so much for him to reach that point and now she'd met the man behind the name, that blast held more significance than ever.

She sneaked a sideways peek at him. His strong profile gave no clue to his impairment. There was no physical evidence to provoke a discussion or sympathy. Unlike her, whose scars were there for the world to see and pass judgement on.

Over the years she'd heard all sorts of theories whispered behind her back. From being scalded as a baby to being the victim of a house fire or an acid attack, she'd heard them all. In the end it had been easier to simply cover the birthmark than to endure the constant rumours.

Joe came across as a stronger, more confident person than she could ever hope to be, but that kind of injury must've caused him the same level of anguish at one time or another. Someone like him would've seen it as a personal weakness when their whole career had been built on personal fitness and being the best. She barely knew him but she could tell that the word 'courage' was stamped all over his DNA. She was even more in awe of him now she knew something of his past.

As though he could sense her staring at the sharp lines of his jaw and the soft contours of his lips, Joe slowly turned to face her. 'There's a certain guide to drinking kava. You clap once with a cupped hand, making a hollow sound, and yell, *'Bula!'* Drink it in one gulp, clap three times and say, *'Mathe.'* You'll be offered the option of high tide or low tide. I strongly advise low tide for your first time.'

'Okay…' She might've put this down as some sort of elaborate practical joke if it wasn't for the twinkle in his eye and his excited-puppy enthusiasm while waiting for the ceremony to begin. In contrast to her reservations about the whole palaver, he clearly relished being a part of the culture.

He fell silent again as the villagers began to grind up the kava in the centre of the room. There were few women present but as the proceedings got under way she didn't feel intimidated at all. The relaxed atmosphere and the men playing guitar in the corner of the room gave it more of a party vibe. Despite her initial reservations, she was actually beginning to relax.

After they ground the kava, it was strained through a cloth bag into a large wooden bowl. It looked like muddy water to her but the chief drank it down without hesitation, as did Peter and Joe. She was thankful for the advice when it came to her turn. Requesting 'low tide' ensured the coconut shell she was offered was only half-full.

It didn't taste any better than it looked. Like mud. Bitter, peppery mud. Definitely an acquired taste but she drank it in one gulp and did the happy, clappy thing which seemed to please everyone. For unknown reasons the proud look from Joe was the one that gave her tingles.

In fact, it wasn't long before her mouth and tongue seemed to go completely numb.

'Whath happenin'?' she lisped to Peter as her tongue suddenly seemed to be too big for her mouth.

'That'll be the kava kicking in. It's a very mild narcotic but don't worry, it'll pass soon.' Something that wasn't bothering her God-fearing brother as he accepted another bowl.

She declined to partake in any further rounds, which her hosts accepted without any offence. Clearly she'd already proved herself as a worthy guest. Thank goodness. Any more and she'd either pass out or lose control of the rest of her faculties. All she wanted now was for Joe to take her to bed. Home. She meant home...

Joe had become accustomed to the bitter-tasting celebration drink to the point even a second bowl had had no effect. He was aware, however, that it might not be the same for Emily, especially as she was probably tired and hungry and currently running her fingertips across her lips. Numb no doubt from the small taste she'd had. He watched as she darted her tongue out to lick them, drawing his attention and thoughts to where they shouldn't go.

Emily was his best friend's sister and obviously running away from her demons to have come somewhere so clearly out of her comfort zone. She wasn't, and couldn't ever be, someone he could hook up with. Normally he didn't hesitate to act on his attraction to women on his travels. Life was too short and so was his stay in their company when he was always on the move. This was an entirely different situation. Peter would always be part of his life and he wouldn't jeopardise that friendship when he invariably moved on. There was no point thinking of her as anything other than a hindrance, a soft soul who'd probably never left her cosy office and would only get in his way. A liability he didn't want or need.

Now she had been fully accepted into the community the villagers soon let their curiosity shine through and asked the questions he already knew the answers to.

'Do you have a husband?'

'What about children?'

The first question had thrown her, he could see it in her wide aquamarine eyes and knew why. Peter had confided in him about her marital problems long before her arrival because he'd worried how she might've been affected by it all. He'd taken her acceptance to help out on the mission as the first step to her recovery and had sworn Joe to secrecy. Not that it was any of his business anyway and he'd no wish to embarrass her by answering for her now. This was her call.

She took her time in finding an answer she was happy to give them. 'No husband or children.'

It didn't surprise him to find her divorce wasn't a subject she intended to discuss. She wasn't the only one who

preferred to keep private matters out of the public domain. Only Peter knew about his past in the army and
the fallout from the IED, and that's the way it would stay.
Much like Emily, he'd decided he didn't need sympathy
or pitying looks.

The gathering and the kava seemed to relax her more
as the evening wore on, and she fielded their questions
about her work without giving away too much personal
information. A single, female doctor was something of a
novelty out here and he understood their fascination. He
was caught up in it too.

As usual, the evening ended with music and dancing, with both he and a yawning Emily watching from
the sidelines.

'You can go any time you're ready.'

'Really? They won't mind?' In contrast to her earlier
attempt to cry off from proceedings, she now seemed
apprehensive about potentially upsetting her hosts. That
was the beauty of the people here. They were so warm
and friendly it was impossible to feel like an outsider for
too long.

'Sure. You've done everything right and they'll understand you're tired. This could go on all night.' He got up
and helped her to her feet.

'Peter?' She waited for her brother to join her but he
wasn't as ready as his companions to leave.

Joe couldn't wait for some time out from the crowd.
Sometimes the white noise could be a bit overwhelming
when he couldn't pick out individual conversations.

'You could see Emily to Miriama's, couldn't you? It's
on the way back to the medical centre.'

He couldn't fault Peter's logic since he was staying
with the chief anyway but it meant prolonging his role as
escort a while longer. This was beyond the remit of his
volunteer medic/best friend duties and he didn't want it

to become a habit. He'd only known Emily a few hours and for someone who considered himself a lone wolf he'd already taken on too much responsibility.

'Fine.' He sighed with just enough sulkiness to let Peter know he wasn't happy playing babysitter any more.

The only thoughts in his head about Emily should be to do with the clinic and how they were going to make it work together. Now there was no chance of forgetting how beautiful she'd looked, sitting cross-legged, utterly transfixed with island life, if she was going to be the last thing he saw before going to sleep.

CHAPTER THREE

EMILY WAS STILL trying to shuffle back into her shoes as she trailed after Joe. If it wasn't for it being completely pitch-black outside without the streetlights she took for granted back home and the sense of direction that meant she shouldn't be allowed out of the house unsupervised, she'd totally have made her own way back without him. Joe's term as 'leader' had clearly ended given his reluctance to see her home. Not that she blamed him. She'd imposed long enough and as soon as she had five minutes alone with her brother she'd tear strips off him for palming her off on him all night.

Peter should have understood what a big deal it had been for her to come here and gone out of his way to look after her. She needed some TLC after everything she'd gone through, not being frog-marched home as if she'd broken curfew. This was supposed to build her confidence, not reaffirm that idea she spoiled everyone's fun.

'I'm sorry you've copped babysitting duties for the nuisance little sister again.' She made sure she spoke loudly and clearly for him to hear. She didn't know the full extent of his hearing loss. He wasn't wearing a hearing aid but he was the type of guy who wouldn't be seen with one even if he needed it.

'No problem. We can't have you stumbling about here

alone in the dark. It'll take a while for you to get your bearings but you'll be able to walk this island with your eyes shut in no time.'

She didn't correct him by admitting another of her weaknesses since he was probably pinning his hopes on it so he wouldn't have to do this again. However, without her chatter, the sound of his heavy footsteps dominated the night, reminding her he was trying to ditch her as soon as possible.

'So what was with all the questions back there? They're not planning on marrying me off to the chief's son, are they?' It was a pseudo-concern in an attempt at small talk. Mostly.

The footsteps stopped and she could hear him grinding the dirt underfoot as he spun round.

'You've watched way too many movies. These people are no different from you or me. They simply have a sense of tradition. They've accepted you as one of their own, there's no ulterior motive.'

She was caught so off balance by his passion as he spoke of his new friends that she stumbled. She made a grab for him in the dark to steady herself and found a nice sturdy bicep beneath her fingers.

'Sorry,' she mumbled, eventually letting go once the shock of coming into contact with bare male body parts wore off. Or at least when she thought the prolonged touching was entering the awkward and desperate phase. He may be lean but he was one hundred per cent solid hunk.

She was nodding her head and apologising as he defended his friends, in an attempt at a mature response, which probably shouldn't include going back for another squeeze.

'You're right. I…er…was thrown by the level of attention. I'm not used to it.' If anything she tried to avoid those kinds of situations where she was the focal point of interest in case people studied her too closely and spotted her secret shame.

She caught the glint of his smile in the moonlight as he looked down at her. Compared to her last port of call, she should've been more at ease under the cover of darkness but her birthmark may as well have been blazing under his night vision she felt so exposed here with him.

'You're beautiful and smart. Of course they want to know your story.' The tone of his voice was soft enough to snuggle into, never mind the unexpected compliment almost bringing her to a swoon.

Except he was back on the move again, not lingering for a romantic smooch under the stars. She definitely watched too many movies. Probably because reality was too damn anticlimactic. She sighed, forced to gather herself together and remember this was no holiday romance, as much as she wanted to get carried away as far from real life as possible.

He didn't elaborate on what had prompted the ego boost and she had to hold her tongue to stop herself from pushing for more praise. How had he reached the conclusion she was either of those things? And did he have any interest in her beyond work and doing favours for her brother? Would it matter if he did?

The resulting silence between them stretched out to Miriama's house, giving her time to get her head back out of the clouds. He hadn't seen her true, vivid, scarlet colours. His assessment of her looks and personality was based on a lie. He knew nothing of the scarred woman beneath who'd been rejected time and time again.

By the time they reached her doorstep she'd firmly landed her backside back on earth with a thud. All he'd been trying to do was illustrate how ridiculous her assumptions had been. He probably hadn't even meant what he'd said but it had been so long since a man had paid her a compliment she'd taken it and twisted it into something it wasn't. She blamed the kava. Apart from the numbness and the tingles, she'd add delusions to the list of side effects. She'd have to remember to ship a crate of the stuff back to England with her.

To Joe, the short walk to Miriama's seemed twice as long as usual. That was the trouble with island life. It was too easy to get caught up in the beauty of the surroundings. They should really think about investing in some streetlights here. The electric hum and fluorescent orange glare might have made this feel less like a walk home after a first date than the moonlight and the sound of the sea.

All he'd intended to do was put her mind at ease that the people here weren't perhaps as…duplicitous as those she may have encountered recently. Instead, those careless few words had given away his less-than-platonic thoughts about having her here. Now he was watching her in the dim light of the doorway, pouting and tracing the outline of her lips with her fingertips.

'What are you doing?' He cocked his head to one side, fixated by her fascinating courtship display. If this was designed to pique his interest even further, it was working. His whole body was standing to attention as he followed the soft lines of her mouth, envying the manicured nail that got to touch them.

'Just checking my lips are still there since I can't feel them any more.' She poked her pink tongue out, parting her lips to dampen them, leaving them moist and a temptation too great to ignore any longer.

He stepped forward to give her a soft peck on the lips. Enough to satisfy his curiosity but insufficient to quell the rising swell of desire inside.

If he didn't break away soon this would change from

a simple goodnight kiss into something steamier and liable to offend Miriama. Especially as Emily wasn't protesting against this.

'Yup. They're still there. Goodnight, Emily.' He turned his back on her and walked away so he couldn't see the dazed look in her eyes and her still-parted lips, although the sight and taste of her would probably be seared in his brain forever.

He ditched all thoughts of going to bed and chose the path back down to the beach instead. There was no point trying to go to sleep when adrenaline was pulsing through his whole body. That had been a dumb move, an impulsive one, one born of pure instinct and lack of judgement. He'd wanted to kiss her so he had, without any thought to the consequences of his actions. That spur-of-the-moment thinking was fine when it came to picking a new place to visit where no one but him would come a cropper if he made the wrong decision. When it came to kissing emotionally fragile divorcees related to his best friend it had the potential to get messy.

He lifted a pebble from the beach and threw it, watching it skim the surface of the water before disappearing into the darkness along with his common sense. He pitched another and another, venting his anger at himself in the only way possible without punching something. In the end he stripped off his clothes and chucked himself into the sea to cool off. Late-night skinny-dipping had often been a way for him to unwind but tonight it was his attempt to cleanse himself of his transgression. He didn't kiss women because he'd made an emotional connection with them, he kissed them because he wanted to. This was a woman he was going to be working with closely for the next two weeks and he was in serious trouble if he couldn't go one evening without controlling himself around her.

He dipped his head below the surface but even as he scrubbed his face with his hands he knew the cold salty water couldn't wipe away the taste and feel of her lips on his. The damage was already done. All he could do now was add it to the list of mistakes he carried with him and hope Emily didn't expect anything more from him than medical input and local knowledge. He'd hate to disappoint her as well as himself.

Emily suspected the local brew had a lot to do with her falling asleep the minute her head touched the pillow and the weird dreams that followed. She spent the night imagining she was stranded on a desert island with a hunky sea captain who looked suspiciously like Sgt Joe Braden coming to her rescue. There was no need to overanalyse it. It was simply her mind trying to make sense of the day's events, and better than spending all night worrying about what sort of creatures lurked in her small room, or thinking about that kiss.

Joe more than likely left dazed women in his wake with his throwaway kisses every day and would have no clue of the impact it had made on her. It was silly really to obsess over something so fleeting, but up until last night her husband had been the only man she'd ever kissed.

She remembered every tiny detail of the brief connection between her and Joe. The firm but tender pressure of his mouth on hers, the bitter taste of kava lingering on his lips and her body frozen while her veins burned with fire.

The past eighteen months had made her a jaded divorcee so she shouldn't have had her head turned so easily. She really needed to work on building up those walls if she was being a fangirl over a peck on the lips from a glorified babysitter.

Today was the start of her placement alongside last night's fantasy figure. There was no room for schoolgirl crushes when she was already on edge about working here. She'd risen with the sun, showered with the aid of a bucket of cold water, breakfasted on bread and jam with Miriama, and checked on Joni, but she couldn't put it off any longer. As she walked towards the medical centre she tried to focus on the positives instead of the nerves bundling in her stomach.

The sky was the brightest blue she'd ever seen, her skin was warmed by the sun and she'd swapped her usual restrictive formal attire for a strappy pink sundress and flats. She was confident in her work and her capabilities, it was more the personal aspects causing her anxieties. Last night she'd mixed well with the community but that had been in an informal setting. It hadn't escaped her attention that very few women had been present at the kava ceremony and they'd had to wait until the men had taken their fill before they'd been served. She hoped it was another nod to tradition rather than any prejudiced attitude towards women's role in society.

Joni had shown her the route back to the medical centre on his way to school and it really was nothing more than a glorified hut on the edge of the village. Thankfully the boy had shown no signs of concussion this morning but in her line of work it was always better to be safe than sorry when it could mean the difference between life and death. It was a shame that same adage had caused the end of her marriage. Playing it safe in her personal life had driven Greg away and made her sorrier than ever for the risks she hadn't taken.

Still, her love life, or lack of it, wasn't the sole reason she'd come all this way. Joe Braden certainly wasn't the risk she wanted to start with. She was here to help a community that didn't have immediate access to medical facilities, nothing more.

Once she set foot inside the designated workspace she

realised how difficult it was going to be to avoid further close contact with him.

'Welcome to your new clinic, Dr Emily.' A grinning Joe greeted her, his outstretched arms almost touching both sides of the hut.

The sun shone in behind him through the one window in the room, the rays outlining the tantalising V-shape of his torso through his loose white cotton shirt.

'You've got to be kidding.' She hadn't meant to vocalise her thoughts and for a shameful second she wished this was one time he hadn't heard her. No such luck.

'Hey, we gotta work with what we've got. I know you're used to all the mod cons at your practice but you have to remember the context here. Me, you and this equipment donated by the church is more than these people usually have.'

The good news was he thought her only concern was her new working conditions. The bad news was…her new working conditions.

There were two basic camp beds, not unlike the one she'd been put up in at Miriama's, a couple of medical storage lockers and chairs, some old IV stands and monitors and some sort of curtain on wheels she guessed was supposed to be a privacy screen. There were adequate facilities for routine health checks and not much else but enough to divide the workload and shared space.

'I think this will work best if we treat this as two different clinics and double the output. You do your thing and I'll do mine.' Never the twain to meet and make body contact ever again.

She moved one medical trolley to one side of the room and claimed her half by wheeling the screen between the two beds.

'If you say so…' Joe didn't sound convinced but at least he wasn't getting precious about this being his territory. Chances were he was happy to block her out anyway after being forced to lead her around by the hand all day yesterday.

'I do. This is going to work.' This new set-up enabled her to take back some control of her life here and already made her feel less nauseous about the days ahead.

This was never going to work. Joe had been here long enough to understand the logistical nightmare of putting her idea into practice. There simply wasn't enough room to create two viable working spaces, although he didn't try to dissuade her from attempting it. She'd work it out for herself eventually without him coming across as a tyrant by refusing to cooperate with her plans. It was his fault she felt the need to put a barrier between them in the first place.

After his antics last night he was lucky Peter hadn't rounded up a posse to turf him off the island for laying lips on his sister. He'd been beating himself up over it all night and this display of skittish behaviour wasn't easing his conscience at all. By all accounts Emily was recovering from an acrimonious split and definitely wasn't the sort of woman he should be kissing on a whim.

His one saving grace was their apparent mutual decision not to mention it. Perhaps his casual walk away had lessened the significance of the event. He might start kissing everyone goodbye and make it out to be more of a personal custom rather than the result of his attraction to her. Although there was something intimate about seeing her fuss around the bed where he'd been lying, thinking about her, last night.

He'd been honest when he'd said he preferred the quiet out here to Miriama's busy household. There was also the added benefit of being able to see the door from his bed. Combat had made him hypervigilant about his surroundings. He wasn't comfortable in a room where he couldn't see all entry points. Army life taught a man that concealed entrances were all potential ambushes where the enemy could attack. That level of paranoia had been essential in his survival but it hadn't left him even after his medical retirement to civilian life. It was simply part of his make-up now and another reason he took to the open road rather than remain cooped up in a two-up, two-down suburban prison.

'So, do we have any particular schedule, or is this more of an A and E department we're running?' Emily encroached on his half of the room, arms folded across her chest.

'I thought we'd break you in gently today and run more of a walk-in clinic. We can organise something more formal once you're settled, if you prefer.' He operated a casual open-door policy every day but he got the impression this GP would expect something more…structured.

Emily struck him as the type who preferred knowing exactly what she'd be doing from one day to the next without any disruption to her routine. The complete opposite of how he lived his life.

'I'd like to set up a few basic health checks. We could start with taking blood pressure, maybe even a family planning clinic.' She was drifting off into the realms of her own practice but it was a good idea.

Specific clinics might draw in more of the community for preventative check-ups as opposed to waiting until something serious occurred when it was too late to get help from the mainland.

'I think the female population might be more open to you too. Perhaps you could think about running a women's wellness clinic? It's not every day they have someone to talk to them about sensitive subjects such as sexual health or female-specific cancers.' It was as much about educating patients as treating them and he would happily defer to Emily in areas where she had more experience.

'That's a great idea. I'm sure I can put something to-gether for later this week.' Her eyes were shining with excitement rather than fear for the first time since they'd met. Well, if he didn't include last night on her doorstep.

His gaze dropped to her mouth as he relived the mem-ory and the adrenaline rush it had given him. Was giving him. Only her nervous cough snapped him out of his slide back into dangerous territory. He certainly didn't want to freak her out after they'd just established their boundaries.

'Good.'

'Glad we got that sorted.'

It was better all around if they kept their lips to them-selves, on different sides of that screen.

There'd been a steady influx of patients throughout the day, more minor ailments than emergency medicine to deal with. Not that she was complaining. Coughs and colds were manageable and it meant she didn't have to call on her colleague for an extra pair of hands. She had, however, handed out a vast amount of paracetamol and antibiotics, not to mention sticking plasters. It was prob-ably a combination of not having these drugs readily avail-able and the novelty of a new, female doctor in residence. At least it showed she'd been accepted in her role and she'd kept busy. That was better than sitting fretting in the corner with nothing but tumbleweeds straying into her section of the clinic. Worse, she'd have had time to over-analyse that kiss some more. Every time he so much as looked in her direction her body went up in flames at the memory. While she was investigating the swollen glands of a pensioner she wasn't thinking about Joe. Much.

'Say "Ah" for me.' She bent over the side of the bed

to peer into her patient's mouth and felt a nudge against her backside.

She turned around to read the Riot Act to whoever it was getting handsy with her when she saw the shadow on the other side of the curtain. Joe was innocently tending his patient too and proving that having little room to manoeuvre was going to be an issue if the butt-bumping became a regular occurrence. It mightn't faze him but she was finding it pretty distracting.

'Your tonsils are quite inflamed but it's nothing a course of antibiotics won't clear up.'

She heard Joe prescribe the same treatment she'd been dishing out all day. It wasn't unusual for viruses to spread like wildfire in such a small community and she was glad of the extra supplies she'd brought with her. They were going to need them, along with the hand sanitiser and vitamin tablets she'd be using to prevent succumbing to it herself. The last thing she needed was Joe having to tend her too.

If the claustrophobic room wasn't hot enough, the thought of her next-door neighbour mopping her fevered brow was enough to bring on the vapours.

Emily moved closer to the oscillating fan before the heat in her cheeks eroded her camouflage make-up and caught sight of a young woman running up the path with a baby in her arms.

'Help! She's not breathing!'

The baby, no more than nine or ten months, was conscious but not making a sound, even though her limbs were flailing in a panic. Not hearing a baby cry in this situation was heart-stopping for her too, indicating the child's airway was completely blocked.

'Give her to me. Quick.'

The child's lips and fingernails were already turning blue but there was no visible sign of obstruction in her mouth.

Joe was at her side in the blink of an eye. 'What happened?'

'She… We were eating breakfast. She grabbed some bread off my plate. Is she going to be okay?'

Emily slid one arm under the baby's back so her hand cradled the head. With her other arm placed on the baby's front, she gently flipped the tiny patient so she was lying face down along her other forearm. She kept the head supported and lower than the bottom and rested her arm against her thigh for added support. With the heel of her hand she hit the baby firmly on the back between the shoulder blades, trying to dislodge whatever was stuck in there.

Delivering a blow to such a small body wasn't easy to do without guilt but the pressure and vibration in the airway was often enough to clear it.

Unfortunately, after the recommended five back blows there was no progress. Time was of the essence as the lack of oxygen to the brain would soon become critical. She rushed over to lay the baby on the bed, paying no mind as Joe kicked the screen away so he had room to assist. He cradled the infant's head, murmuring soothing words for child and mother as Emily started chest thrusts.

With two fingertips she pushed inwards and upwards against the breastbone, trying to shift the blockage. She waited for the chest to return to its normal position before she repeated the action. Her skin was clammy with perspiration as she fought to help the child to breathe. If this didn't work they'd run out of options.

Joe reached out to touch her arm. 'I've done a few tracheostomies in my time if it comes to it.'

He was willing to step up to the plate with her and she found that reassuring. She'd never performed one and hoped it wouldn't come to that. The idea of making an incision for a tube into the windpipe of one so small was terrifying.

'Thank you.'

With her surgical inexperience and the primitive facilities she was glad to have the backup but it was absolutely the last resort. His calm demeanour in the face of a crisis helped her to centre herself again and deliver another chest thrust.

She checked inside the mouth again. If this didn't work she would repeat the cycle before letting Joe take over. After another chest thrust she felt movement beneath her fingers and heard a small cry.

'You've got it!' Joe's shout confirmed her success and she stopped so he could retrieve the chunk of bread causing the trouble.

The colour slowly returned to the baby's face and Emily had never been so relieved to hear a child cry.

'Thank you. Thank you.' The weeping mother alternated between hugging them and stroking her daughter's face.

'I just want to sound her chest.' Emily unhooked her stethoscope from around her neck so she could listen to the baby's heartbeat and make sure there was no resulting damage from the trauma. Her lungs were certainly in good order as she raged her disapproval.

Once she'd carried out her checks and made sure all was well, she gave the relieved mother the go-ahead to comfort her child.

'I think I need to keep you all under observation for a while. Emily, if you don't mind, I'm going to break into that stash of tea and biscuits I saw you put in your locker earlier. We all need it for shock.' Joe's worried frown had evened out into a relieved smile to match her own. She sat down on the bed and waited for the much-needed cup of tea, still feeling a tad shaky herself after the ordeal.

Having a partner here mightn't be all bad. He'd let her take the lead today while still providing support, and tea, when she'd needed it. It made practical sense for them to work together. If only she'd stop overreacting to the slightest body contact. And staring at his backside as he bent down to retrieve her precious cure-all.

CHAPTER FOUR

'I THINK WE deserve a break,' Joe waved off their first emergency patient and her mother at the door once they were sure she had fully recovered.

'I was under the impression we'd just had one.' While it had all been very dramatic and draining, saving lives was part of their job. It shouldn't be an excuse to shut up shop and act unprofessionally. If anything it highlighted the need for them to keep to a schedule so people knew where to reach them at any given time.

'Even busy doctors are entitled to a lunch break. Are you telling me you don't take one back home?' His raised eyebrow and smirk dared her to deny it.

'Of course I take my regulation breaks. Just not usually all at once.' She omitted to mention she took a packed lunch and did her paperwork through those breaks since it made her sound as if she had no life outside work.

He made a derisory '*pfft*' sound through his teeth. 'Ten minutes off our feet, keeping a baby under observation, isn't a real break. We need a proper time out to de-stress before our next patients, otherwise how can we do our jobs effectively? You need to learn how to go with the flow, Emily.'

His cheeky wink only served to irritate her further.

'I thought that's what I *was* doing.' The sigh of self-pity was entirely justified, she thought, after coming all the way out here and taking part in everything thrown at her thus far. If she let herself get carried away too much there was a danger she'd end up completely lost at sea.

'It's lunch, Emily. It's not a big deal.'

It *would* seem silly to him but in her head it translated to something much bigger—ditching their responsibilities for their own gratification. That was exactly what Greg had done and she'd been the one left to deal with the consequences. It wasn't a situation she intended to re-create any time soon.

'What about cover? We can't abandon our post here and leave people without adequate care.'

'We can put a note on the door but, honestly, we won't be that hard to track down if something happens. Yasi Island has survived all this time without us and I'm sure they'll cope over one lunchtime.' He was already scribbling on a piece of paper now he'd made her concerns seem ridiculous.

She was here for two weeks, had treated one emergency patient so far, and was trying to avoid a shared break under the cover of her 'they can't live without me' excuse. It was no wonder he wasn't buying it. This was about him, and her fear of spending time with him, and nothing else. She had to get over it or the next fortnight was going to be hell.

'Is there some place we can buy lunch? I don't recall seeing any fast-food restaurants nearby.' Her tongue-in-cheek comment was intended to make her seem less of a jobsworth but the practicalities of his proposal were no less important to her. While it was refreshing not to have a coffee shop or burger joint on every inch of land, there was also a distinct lack of grocery outlets. She had literally nothing to bring to the table and it wouldn't be polite to help herself to Miriama's meagre provisions.

'Lack of refrigeration is a problem on the island when the only electricity available is via the odd generator here and there so most of the food is fresh. There's none of your fast-frozen, pre-packed, no-taste, processed muck here. The gathering of food is a communal effort, as is eating it. There'll be no shortage of hosts to take lunch with.' He pinned the note to the door and hovered, clearly waiting for her to leave with him.

She was certain the idea of turning up at people's homes uninvited and unannounced was something he did all the time, given his nonchalance now, but she was used to a certain etiquette. Dinner parties and organised soirées were more her thing than breaking bread with strangers. Honestly, this man had no shame.

'Should we take a gift?' Something to break the ice and make it seem less like begging for food. She'd rather starve than face any humiliation.

'You've already donated supplies to the school and I thought we could head there first. The children will be thrilled to meet you. They enjoy showing off and I know for a fact this is their lunchtime too. So…' He gestured for her to make her way out in front of him but she wasn't entirely convinced by his argument. That 'first' comment alluded to the idea there'd be more than one stop.

'You could take your medical bag with you if that makes you any more comfortable about leaving.' He pre-empted her next attempt to back out.

'A mobile clinic?' It wasn't a bad idea to combine work and lunch, and accepting their hospitality in exchange for her medical skills was much more palatable than simply pulling up a chair and waiting to be served.

'If that's what you'd prefer.' His voice was a mixture of amusement and exasperation.

'It is.' She knew she could be hard work when people seemed to tire of her so easily but at least Joe nudged her with encouragement rather than criticism. It left her free to make decisions on her own terms.

Negotiations over, she grabbed her bag and followed him out the door. Despite her initial reservations, reaching this compromise felt like a win. With a little forward planning she could *do* spontaneity. Somewhere between Joe's laid-back attitude and her regimented approach to work they might find a way to actually make this work. Perhaps if she found that happy medium in her personal life, she might make that work again too.

Joe had been right again. It was becoming a habit. And very annoying. Every time his cool, calm and rational thinking was proved correct it made her fears seem all the more neurotic.

Their impromptu visit to the school had caused such a commotion the children had immediately abandoned their lessons. She would've felt terribly guilty about the disruption if their teacher hadn't been equally animated by their arrival.

'*Vanaku*. Thank you for coming to see the children.'

The pupils all stood to attention behind their desks as though someone of great importance had entered the room. It was difficult to come to terms with the fact that person could be her.

'I, er…we thought I should come and introduce myself. I'm Emily, the new doctor.' She shook hands with the pretty young teacher.

'I'm Keresi. We're so grateful for your wonderful gifts to the school. Aren't we, children?'

They were prompted into an enthusiastic chorus of agreement that managed to suffuse Emily's cheeks with heat.

'It's nothing, really.' She'd only brought a few stationery supplies at the last minute. Nothing that would've warranted such an outpouring of gratitude at home. It was humbling to be reminded how lucky she was in the grand scheme of things and how much she took for granted. Okay, her heart had taken a mauling recently but she'd had a university education that enabled her to live a life of luxury compared to many here.

'We would really like to do something for you.' The effusive teacher clapped her hands to assemble the kids along the back wall of the classroom.

Emily stepped further into the room to allow Joe in on whatever was about to happen. No matter how hard she tried to make this a solo adventure they were destined to share these experiences and if she was honest, everything seemed slightly less intimidating when he was close by. This morning had been a prime example. She'd coped with the emergency largely on her own but having him there had been a comfort when she was so far from the medical support she was used to. Joe had been the first person in a long time to make sure she hadn't felt alone.

The children launched into a repertoire of songs and dance, so well choreographed she understood this must be something they performed on a regular basis for tourists—and hungry doctors. It enabled her to stop over-analysing what people would think of her for turning up uninvited and enjoy the proud display of talent. Old and young alike had made it impossible not to be a part of the community here.

Once the show was over, she and Joe broke into applause.

'That was just...lovely.' The tears in her eyes and lump in her throat arrived unexpectedly.

'Yes, thanks, everybody.' Joe lifted his hands above his head and gave them another round of applause.

'We're going to take our lunch outside now, if you'd

care to join us.' Keresi motioned her class outside as she delivered the invitation Joe had prophesied.

'That's so kind of you. We'd be honoured. Wouldn't we, Emily?' He didn't even attempt to hide his glee at being proved right.

'Sure, and in return we'd be happy to do a free health check for everyone while we're here.'

She'd call that an even trade and a conscience salve all in one.

With everyone in accordance and no one beholden to anyone else, the trio of adults joined the rest of the class outside on the grass.

Joe had made it sound as though lunch would be some grand affair with buffet-style tables of food, or at least that's how she'd interpreted it. Instead, the children were cross-legged under the shade of the trees, tucking into their food boxes.

'What are we going to do? A lunch-box raid?' she murmured, before catching herself.

She cleared her throat to draw his attention and spoke again. 'I'm not taking food from the mouths of babes.'

'Will you chill out? I can guarantee you'll neither have to ask for food while you're here nor starve. Honestly, you put yourself through so much unnecessary stress you'll make yourself ill. You should take a leaf out of your brother's book and take this all in your stride.' He rested his large hand on her shoulder in an act that should've been easy for her to shrug off along with his advice, but his warmth on her bare skin stole away any snarky retort. His touch had distracted her even from the arrival of her stepbrother, who was strolling towards them.

'Hey, you two. I saw your note and figured you might want to share a bite to eat.' He held up a basket of fresh fruit and other foods not readily identifiable to Emily. At this moment she didn't care. Her stomach was rumbling and Peter was family. She was entitled to take food from him guilt-free.

'Oh, ye of little faith.'

Joe was really going to keep this gloating going all day.

Thankfully he did release her from his thrall, abandoning her shoulder in favour of a banana. There was definitely a happy vibe about him, her brother too, which was surprising given their previous life before Yasi. It showed a definite strength of character in both of them to have come through the darkness that time in Afghanistan had surely brought to their door.

She kind of envied this enlightened attitude they'd found where they no longer sweated the small stuff and trusted that everything would somehow work out in the end. Although not the path, or the losses they'd endured to reach this Zen place. A place that seemed so far beyond her reach when even the timely food delivery was causing concern.

'Er…what is this?' She prodded the leafy parcels that were apparently the main component of their meal.

'*Rourou* and cassava,' Peter declared, as though that helped her identify what he expected her to eat. Time apart had made him forget who he was dealing with here. This was the girl who'd taken a great deal of persuading to partake of the mildest curries when they'd gone to an Indian restaurant for the first time. She needed any new dish explained in simple layman's terms and a tasting demonstration before she ventured into new territory.

Joe had no such qualms as he dug in with his fingers to take a sample. 'They're *dalo* leaves with boiled tapioca.'

'Just like real school dinners, then?' With her food taster apparently unharmed, and Peter helping himself too, Emily braved the unknown. It wasn't as bad tasting as she'd imagined and the starchy snack would fuel her for the rest of the afternoon, along with the more familiar fruit she took for later.

'I know you'd rather have a pasta salad and a fruit smoothie but this is the next best thing. You'll get used to it. I have.' Peter took a second helping to prove his point.

'I see that.' She also saw the way his gaze kept drifting past her to watch the pretty Keresi in the background.

'Did you make these, bro?' Joe scooped up the last food bundle after she declined it.

Her taste buds had been enjoying the sweet and stodgy delights of comfort food these past months so it was going to take some time to adjust.

'No. The young mother whose baby you saved this morning sent them over to say thank-you. You two are her new heroes.'

'Hey, it was all your sister. This girl knows her stuff and I wouldn't want to get on the wrong side of her by claiming credit for what she did. She can hit pretty hard when she wants to.' Joe held his hands up and deflected the praise back to her.

'Oh, I know all about it. She can be vicious if you take her toys without permission and as for her chocolate stash, if you touch that your life won't be worth living.' Peter made it sound as though they'd had a tempestuous relationship growing up when nothing could be further from the truth. She'd been so happy to be accepted by him and his mum, Shirl, she'd followed him like a puppy. He'd have been justified in pushing his pesky shadow away but he'd never once made her feel like a nuisance or his ugly stepsister. She'd often thought how different her life could've been if Shirl had been her *actual* mother, avoiding all the unpleasantness of her early years.

Peter rubbed the invisible evidence of their imaginary argument on his leg but his eyes were still focused on something, someone else. That someone who was making her way over to their little group.

'Can I get you a drink?'

'That would be—'

'I'll help you.' Peter cut her off as he stumbled to his feet in a hurry.

'Could he be any more obvious?' Emily's eye-roll was born out of her irrational jealousy that there was now a third party competing for his attention. She may as well have been back in high school when he had been the popular kid and she'd been the newbie with no friends of her own.

'Give him a break.'

'I thought he was here to spread the word of God, not get romantically involved with his congregation.' She'd never seen him so smitten as he trailed after his love interest into the school, his tongue practically hanging out, but she shouldn't be a brat and put her own happiness above Peter's. This lovestruck bohemian was a far cry from the traumatised veteran she'd last encountered and his healing was all that mattered.

'He's a red-blooded, single man, not a monk, and this place is doing him the world of good. He'll be settled down with two point four kids before you know it.' Joe plucked a blade of grass from the ground and wound it around his finger until the circulation stopped and it turned white.

Despite his wise words on the subject he didn't look any more thrilled about that prospect than she did. He was supposed to be the fly-by-the-seat-of-his-pants adventurer, not a stick-in-the-mud who hated change like her.

'And you? Are you planning on settling down at some point?' Her heart fluttered as she asked the question, which had been on her mind since he'd kissed her.

His snort-laugh cut any hope dead that she could be

the one to make him think again about his nomadic life choice but it was better to face that truth now before she got carried away over the next few days and considered that a possibility.

'No chance. These itchy feet of mine don't let me hang around long enough to develop that kind of attachment.'

'Why's that?' It would've made more sense to her that someone who'd been in a war zone would've been glad of the normality and stability that a family could bring.

He was pulling the grass out in clumps now. 'Life's too short not to get out there and experience everything the world has to offer. I'm never going to be the pipe-and-slippers type to sit and vegetate in front of the telly with his missus.'

There was the crux of Emily's ill-judged attraction towards him. If you swapped the pipe for a bar of chocolate he'd just described her idea of a perfect night in.

He hadn't mentioned the events leading to his retirement from the army but she guessed that was part of the reason for his compulsion to live life to the full. In that sense he and her brother were very alike. The blast had had a profound impact on how they lived from day to day and she was in awe of their courage when any new experience brought her out in a cold sweat. If, on the other hand, this drifting from one place to the next had been the guys running away from dealing with what had happened, setting down roots was a huge step forward. Still, long-term relationships didn't always equal a happy-ever-after.

'Yeah, marriage sucks,' she said, trying to convince herself she didn't want or need it any more either.

Joe raised his eyebrows at her as he stood and brushed the grass from his hands. Now she was going to have to explain herself and confess she was one of those losers who'd tried and failed at it.

'I'm divorced. Greg left me for another woman.' Even

in the shade she was burning with the shame of her husband's rejection. Although it was almost a relief to say it out loud.

Colleagues and friends knew about the split but she hadn't divulged the gory details. Blurting it out to a man she'd only met and most likely would never see again was liberating. She could vent without fear of repercussions.

He held out his hand to help her up and without missing a beat said, 'He's an idiot.'

Those three simple words brought a smile to her lips and a lightness in her heart. There was no changing of the subject or querying the circumstances, he'd simply decided in her favour. Greg *was* an idiot and she should stop wasting any more of her life on him.

Joe's lifestyle sounded too lonely for her but she could appreciate its merits. There was an attraction in walking away from a relationship before things got too serious and certain expectations grew around it. Such as being together for ever. Avoiding love was the best way to protect your heart. Thank goodness she no longer trusted anyone with hers.

CHAPTER FIVE

JOE'S PLAN TO get outside of their confined workspace into the great outdoors to create some distance between him and Emily had backfired spectacularly. Somehow mingling with a large group of excited school children had led to lunch together discussing their private lives, or in his case a lack of one. Where Emily's was concerned he'd call it a lucky escape.

Peter didn't usually take against people without due cause but when he talked about his ex-brother-in-law it had never been with any degree of affection. It would take a certain kind of someone to get him offside when he was such a people person. The sort who imagined he could do better than Emily. *Idiot* wasn't a strong enough word to describe what Joe thought of the guy but it was the only tag he could give him in the presence of children.

Although it was early days to be thinking of Peter and the schoolteacher as being in a serious relationship, leading to something more permanent, it certainly seemed to be heading that way. It caused him mixed emotions. He was happy to see his friend in such a great place after struggling with his faith in the aftermath of Afghanistan and it meant he himself was no longer obligated to stick around as his sole support system. Peter settled down would give him the freedom to move on to his next adventure free from residual responsibility that kept him tied to his old army pal. It certainly shouldn't create the extra hole in his heart and a pang for the life he'd never have.

He couldn't afford to have a wife and children relying on him when he couldn't even depend on himself, on his own emotions. He'd heard somewhere that grief was the price you paid for loving someone but he really didn't want to go through it again. He'd loved Batesy and Ste like brothers, grieved for them as part of his army family, and shouldered responsibility for their loss as any other medic who'd lost patients would have. It was impossible not to become that close to anyone and not feel compassion again. He was risking his heart and his sanity by remaining in the medical field but it was still his calling. These pop-up clinics were a compromise, his answer to preventing further long-term damage to his soul while still being able to treat those in desperate need. Listening to Emily's tale of marriage woe was enough to strengthen his resolve on the matter. Commitment to anything beyond a casual arrangement did more harm than good.

Hence this afternoon's impromptu alfresco lunch. Working side by side in that hut had not only led to inadvertent body contact but a growing admiration for his co-worker. This morning had shone a light on her professionalism in what had been a highly emotive and dramatic case, the like of which she probably wasn't used to in her day job. He shouldn't be surprised, she was a qualified doctor after all, but he'd clearly been thinking about her in a less than professional manner.

Romantic picnics in the park weren't going to help get his mind back in the game but the clinic idea at the school had helped re-establish the boundaries of their relationship. For the past couple of hours they'd been busy chatting to the children and making sure they were all in tip-top health, with Emily on one side of the room and him on the other. Except now her queue of children had come to an end and she was making her way over to his table.

'Well, Dr Braden, anything to report?' She was totally at ease here. He could see it in her relaxed body language and the big smile on her lips.

He should really quit paying attention to what her lips were doing at any given moment. It wouldn't help him forget how they felt against his: soft, pliant, agreeable...

There was no way he trusted himself not to try and experience it again if they were holed up in that close space for another two weeks.

'Just another A-star pupil.' He gave his last patient a high five and watched him run off with his last excuse to hang around.

'They're a pretty happy, healthy bunch all round.'

'And more than willing to have a bit of fuss from the glamorous new doctor.' He hadn't missed the girls' fascination with her blonde hair, or the fact she'd let them braid it while she'd worked. The boys too had been more interested in what was going on at that side of the room, which had made their eye checks challenging.

Emily's laughter reached right in and twisted his insides. It was the first time he'd heard it since her arrival and he knew he wanted to hear more of it.

'*Glamorous* isn't the word I'd use right now.' She was finger-brushing the various plaits and knots her army of hairdressers had created, leaving her tresses wavy and unkempt and looking a lot like bed hair.

It conjured up images of her in the morning, in bed, and brought a lot more adjectives to describe her that weren't appropriate in a classroom. Joe had to turn away and pack away the ophthalmoscope and otoscope he'd been using to check the children's eyes and ears before he said or did something stupid. Again.

'Thank you for doing this.' Keresi interrupted Joe's wayward thoughts to shake hands with him and Emily.

'Thanks for letting us disrupt your lessons today. We're going to take our travelling sideshow further afield but I'm sure you could get Peter to track us down in an emergency.' He'd disappeared during their clinic but Joe had a hunch he'd return before the end of the school day.

'Since when?' Emily's mouth flattened out into an unimpressed line once they were alone again. Her mouth was puckered now, her turquoise eyes blazing with flecks of amber fire and her arms folded across her chest as she made her disapproval known. He supposed it would be totally out of order to comment on how hot she looked.

'We've had such a great response here I thought we could venture further around the village with our mobile clinic. A meet and greet with those who might be too busy to attend isn't a bad idea.' In the army he'd learned to think on his feet, and forced with their imminent return to the claustrophobic hub of medical operations he'd made an executive decision. Not to.

'You really need to stop making decisions for other people. You're not in the army now and you're certainly not my superior,' Emily huffed, as she made the scarily accurate call about his thought process. He was railroading her into taking a trail away from his temporary lodgings when they were supposed to be equal partners but separating her from his bed space would be beneficial to them both in the long run.

'Sorry, I'm not used to working with a partner. I should have asked if you would prefer to spend the afternoon bumping into each other and waiting for people to show up or go out and drum up some interest in your clinic.' He didn't think of it as emotional blackmail, more as forward planning. Once Emily had her own patients set up they could alternate between running both static and mobile practices. With some organisation he could engineer the rest of her stay so they spent minimal time in each other's company.

'When you put it like that I guess it's a no-brainer.' She stuck her tongue out at him in a manner more like that of a friend than a professional colleague. Definitely time to make that distinction between them. There wasn't room in his life even for a friend. He already had one more than he needed. It was the only reason he'd stayed on Yasi as long as he had. He would never have stood back and ignored Peter's pleas for help out here when he still felt as though he had a huge debt to repay. As soon as his stint here was over and all necessary referrals to the hospital on the mainland had been made, he was gone. Ready to disappear into anonymity again and start over somewhere where they didn't know his history.

Their stroll through the village in the daylight was taken at a more leisurely pace than last night's constitutional. Out here in public view with the sights and sounds of island life around them somehow felt less intense, safer. Even if it hadn't taken away the urge to kiss her.

'What's that growing on the roof up there?' Emily pointed at the rows of brown string covering which, to the untrained eye, could've been mistaken for decaying foliage.

'That's coconut husk. They dry the strands in the sun before they braid it. *Magimagi* is the main source of income here. Children are taught the skill from a very early age. Unfortunately, even with all the hard work that goes into it, it sells for a pittance. You're talking only a few dollars for about twenty-five yards of handmade rope.'

'Wow. I don't know whether to admire the work ethos or pity the folks who do it. I'll never complain about my long hours again. At least I get paid a living wage.'

'Both. It's part and parcel of living here. Unless you're a blow-in, of course, who's benefiting from the local hospitality.'

'Don't make me feel any guiltier about accepting food and lodging than I already do.'

Her genuine outrage made him chuckle. Emily would no more take advantage of people than her generous-spirited stepbrother. From what he'd gathered about her personal life, he suspected it was probably the other way around. It would be so easily for a manipulative sort to tie her soft heart into knots to suit their own agenda. She'd had enough of that in her life for him to do the same. His actions were merely to protect her as well as himself.

'I'm only joking. Everything given to you here is simply payment for all the work you're doing to help the community. Think of that as your wages, then there's no need to feel guilty.' At least, that's how he viewed it when the doubts crept in about accepting so much from those who had so little. It wasn't as though rejecting their gifts of friendship was an option when it would cause even greater offence.

'I'll try to remember that,' she said, a tad more brightly, clearly never having considered the work she was doing here as anything more than the job she was born to do. That humility made her all the more special.

She had that same warrior spirit of every man he'd ever fought alongside—selflessly giving of herself without expecting anything in return. Unfortunately she didn't recognise her own strengths, only her weaknesses. The sooner she found them herself, the sooner he'd be off the hook.

'You should. You'll definitely earn your keep over the next two weeks. The community as a whole will make the most of having qualified medical personnel, even if there are a few too busy trying to make a living to visit.'

'The *magimagi* weavers?'

'And the rest of the arts and crafts community. The economy here is based on the sale of handmade goods such as wooden sculptures and woven mats. If you're lucky you might get to try making some for yourself.' He was counting on it. Okay, so his service to the community wasn't as selfless as Emily's. He'd been part of the scenery here long enough to know that taking her out to that part of the island would be another excuse for a social gathering.

Not only was he spreading the word about the clinic by introducing her but it would certainly help them pass the afternoon. In company.

Emily knew exactly what Joe was up to. He was trying to get her out of his way, palm her off onto someone else. It was the only plausible explanation as to why he was so reluctant they return to what was supposed to be their base of operations. She didn't totally buy this notion of extending personal invitations to her practice when news seemed to travel so quickly across the island anyway.

The kava ceremony was supposed to have been her introduction to society and unless he was using this to ensure he had a dinner invitation too, it felt like a futile exercise. She was only going along with it so she could get a bearing on her surroundings and those she'd be potentially treating. Once she'd established her own list of patients and could manage a conversation without an introduction from her self-appointed leader, she could stop relying on him to get her through this. She wasn't swapping one man-sized crutch for another. This was no journey of self-discovery if Joe was always there showing her the way.

He was a man who craved excitement, thrived on it. The more he did for her, smoothed the way for her, the less interesting she would become to him. As they spent more time together the last thing she wanted was for him to find her just as boring as her husband had.

She'd come here with the idea of reinventing herself as a fearless trailblazer, an inspiration to life's other rejects too afraid to step back out into the sun, only to find herself falling into step behind Joe and following that safe path.

With the warmth of the islanders she was beginning to shed her nerves. There'd been nothing but support for her so far and this morning's drama, although traumatic, had proved her professional worth. The children had been wonderful too, and although another random house call could be seen as skiving she was kind of looking forward to it.

Ten-minute appointments with patients passing through her office on a conveyor belt was frustrating to say the least. At least here she wasn't restrained by time limits or budget; she was free to diagnose and treat anyone who needed her help.

The way of life here was so fascinating and such a far cry from the frantic digital age where she spent more time on the phone or answering emails than getting to know the people she was treating. Time out here had a different meaning, more significance, and gave her extra opportunities to be the best doctor she could be.

'They do say hobbies are a great way to relieve stress. Perhaps I'll find a new creative outlet for my frustrations and irritations.' She batted her eyelashes and smiled a saccharine-sweet smile, enjoying Joe's obvious bewilderment at her sudden compliance.

When it came to interpreting her thoughts and feelings regarding her chaperon she was just as confused. Apart from her own neuroses, he was the main stumbling block between her and her new super-identity. But she'd be lying if she said she didn't appreciate having him as a safety net at times, knowing she could rely on him if she needed support. Plus he was great eye candy. She might have put her heart under lock and key but that didn't mean she was made of stone. She could still appreciate the sight of a perfect male specimen. Especially one flashing his rippling torso as he lifted the hem of his shirt to wipe his brow.

Shallow. So very shallow. She of all people should've resisted objectifying another human being but that flat, toned body deserved recognition. Hell, it deserved its own social media account. She fanned herself with her hand. The heat was starting to get to her and it wasn't entirely down to the fires lining their path through the encampment.

When she managed to drag her gaze away from his midsection and back up to meet his eyes she could see he was more amused than appalled by her visual appreciation.

Busted.

'So, what do they do here?' She coughed away the stirrings his naked chest had caused with a question about the other sights of interest. Okay, steaming pans and bubbling pots weren't nearly as interesting as cheese-grater abs but were infinitely less likely to get her burned.

'This is where they boil the *pandanus* leaves to make them soft enough to weave. They fade from green to white once they're left to dry in the sun before the cloth they make is painted to make colourful mats. It's quite an art.' Joe gave her a quick run-down of the process, displaying more local knowledge than a mere tourist should be privy to.

He might claim to have no attachment to Yasi other than another pin tack on his wall map but it had already become a part of him. Emily wondered if its mystical healing powers would work on her too. Her brother had certainly found his peace on the island and Joe was way too involved in the way of life for someone who'd probably been strong-armed into volunteering here in the first place. If all her wishes came true too this magical isle would conjure up her own successful, independent practice and someone other than her stepbrother who loved her and accepted her for who she was.

The second of those was never going to happen since there was no way in hell she'd forgo her camouflage and let anyone see the *real* her. The best she could hope for was a holiday tan and a good time. After the last year she was willing to settle for that.

He introduced her to Sou and a few of her friends, sitting cross-legged on the floor painting the mats. They welcomed her and immediately invited her to stop clutching her medical bag as though she'd come to sell them encyclopaedias and join them.

Furniture was overrated anyway. Along with the internet and hot running water. And abs. A girl could live without all of them. If she had to.

She didn't want to interrupt their working day but they were keen to start a new mat in her honour and have her be a part of it.

'What kind of paint is this?' she asked as the ladies coloured black geometric shapes with earthy red tones.

'The black is made from ash and coal from the fire mixed with water. It can be messy.' Sou gave her a toothy smile as she prepared the primitive materials in a bowl with her hands.

'The red is actually from clay found on the island. It's scraped and rinsed with water to create various shades.' Although this activity appeared to be primarily women's work, Joe happily took up a place beside her on the floor.

'You've done this before?' Was there anything left for her to explore on the island that he hadn't already laid claim to? She wanted to be annoyed at the unintentional one-upmanship but it was impossible when he didn't have a bad bone in his body. And she'd thoroughly inspected it.

He didn't seem to care about losing face at sitting in the midst of all the women, when his joy at sharing his newly acquired skill with her was plain to see.

This mat-painting session was Yasi's equivalent to a coffee morning, as Emily soon found out. The ladies spent their time swapping anecdotes and chatting among themselves but she was finding it tough to pay attention to everything going on around her when her gaze was locked onto that of the smiling hunk next to her.

'You dip your finger in the clay mixture.' He took her hand in his and pressed her fingertip firmly into the red sludge. 'Then it's simply a matter of colouring between the lines.' He leaned across to guide her between the thick black outlines.

His breath was hot against her neck and her own was caught somewhere between a squeak and a squeal as it brought goose-bumps along her skin. Somehow she managed to daub enough paint on to fill the small triangle she'd been assigned. Amazing when his touch had turned her into a ragdoll with no control over her floppy limbs except by his hand.

Only when he excused himself from the group to go and visit the wood-carving menfolk outside was she able to breathe and move freely again. She could inhale a lungful of fresh air no longer contaminated by his spicy, exotic scent, which had made every breath feel as though she was taking part of him inside her.

'That man is handsome!' Sou's unlikely outburst was accompanied by the giggles of grown women with a girlish crush.

Emily gave a nervous laugh along with them, grateful she wasn't the only one finding his charms irresistible.

'And single!' There was another titter of female appreciation. Clearly, getting het up around this man was a normal reaction and nothing for Emily to worry about.

'Are you two together?'

It took a moment before Emily recognised they'd stopped gossiping among themselves and were addressing her directly. Four pairs of eyes were watching her unblinkingly and waiting for her answer.

'No. No.' She couldn't keep the hint of regret from her voice when she was still recovering from her up close and personal painting tutorial.

'Why not?' Sou tilted her head to one side and stared at her as though she was trying to work out what was wrong with her.

'We're colleagues and I only arrived twenty-four hours ago.' Emily dodged eye contact and concentrated on staying between the lines so no one would see the naked desire for him she was fighting with every breath.

As she stared at her discoloured fingertips and shuffled position so her legs didn't fall asleep, it struck her how off track her itinerary for this trip had gone. Other than the ladies promising to drop in at the clinic, this had nothing to do with her duties as a doctor.

Sou made a strange grunting noise, which sounded like something between disbelief and bewilderment. 'I can tell he likes you.'

The others nodded and clucked their agreement like hens around her.

'Really?' As much as Emily was uncomfortable about her and Joe being the topic of conversation, their reassurance created a warm glow inside her. She wanted him to like her, to see her as more than his mate's kid sister he was obliged to take under his wing, and to think of her as more than a colleague. The way she was doing about him.

There was more clucking.

'I can see it in the way he looks at you. The way he touches you.'

'Oh, yes!'

'Mmm-hmm.'

Another chorus of oohs and laughter sent Emily's temperature rising with the heat of being in the spotlight. Perhaps it hadn't simply been a case of wishful thinking after all.

She cast her mind back over their interaction with a different eye. Had there really been a need to hold her hand? Or sit that close? There was also the matter of that kiss. Dared she hope there'd been more to it than she'd convinced herself? And what if there was? Did she want to go there and start kissing a man she barely knew and wouldn't see again?

Every time she envisaged going through the same heartache Greg had caused her, she pictured Joe instead with his smile and gentle consideration. The answer was overwhelmingly yes, she wanted to kiss him again.

It was the possibility of rejection that frightened her, that abandonment she'd suffered too often, but at the end of this trip *she* would be the one walking away. The whole idea was that she went back to England a stronger person, a braver one for the risks she *should* take. It was time to woman up and live dangerously, and there was nothing more terrifying than the prospect of dipping a toe back into the dating pool. What better way to reintroduce herself than with a holiday romance?

She smiled to herself.

The room erupted into laughter around her.

'Just co-workers, huh?'

'Emily, you've got it bad.'

Yes, yes, she had and it was within her power to turn it into something good.

CHAPTER SIX

JOE SWUNG THE axe and brought it crashing down to split the timber in two. It was a powerful blow designed to be effective both physically and mentally. He'd needed to be in the company of men, doing manly things. Not more hand-holding and making memories with his pretty co-worker. It was all very well making sure they were in a public place but it kind of defeated the object of avoiding close contact if he couldn't leave her side.

He'd been carried away with the whole tour-guide demonstration with the *masi* process because she'd been so open to it. A complete attitude turnaround since the kava ceremony and he hadn't been able to resist capitalising on her new willingness to participate in the local culture. It wasn't often he got to share new experiences with anyone and showing her how to paint the mats had given him the same buzz as when he'd tried it for the first time.

So engrossed in that moment of her new discovery, he'd forgotten the reasons they were there in the first place. Patients. Work. Education. Definitely not taking part in couples' activities as if they were at a holiday camp together. He'd remembered that too late—after the touching and the quickening pulse as he'd leaned too close to the flame.

He'd made a bolt for it in an attempt to direct the adrenaline coursing through his body toward something more practical than neck-kissing his colleague in public. The sculptors had given him the job of sanding the wooden bowls they sold for mixing kava but the smooth, silky texture hadn't really detracted his thoughts away from Emily's skin beneath his touch. So he'd moved on to the more demanding task of preparing the raw material for them in the hope he'd be too exhausted to keep thinking about her. It clearly hadn't worked.

His time hadn't totally been wasted as he'd persuaded a few of the men to stop by the clinic before the end of the week for blood-pressure checks and a general 'MOT'. If Emily had stuck to the plan she'd have a few more recruits on her side too.

'I think we have enough now, Joe, and the light's starting to fade.' Tomasi, Sou's other half, was the one to finally call time.

Joe had been concentrating so hard on making sure he chopped the wood in half and not his foot, he hadn't noticed the sun beginning to set. In the name of health and safety he would have to call it a day. Besides, they had enough wood stacked now to last for weeks.

'I guess I was enjoying my workout too much.' He snatched up his shirt from the top of the wood pile where he'd thrown it after working up a sweat.

'Sou says we're welcome to stay for dinner...'

Joe glanced up as Emily's voice trailed off at the doorway to find her staring again, her mouth open but no further words forthcoming. Her eyes travelled up and down his body without ever reaching his. There was no other word for it. She was *ogling* him.

He made a bigger deal of unfolding his shirt and pulling it over his head than he really needed to, giving her more time to look. No woman had stared at him with such naked desire since the explosion, or if they had he hadn't noticed or found it quite so enjoyable.

He'd flirted and slept with women since leaving the army but a part of his male pride had died along with all his other losses. Although it was only his hearing that had been damaged in the blast he'd stopped thinking of himself as a 'whole' man. With Emily watching him dress as though he could've been the world's sexiest male model instead of a disabled ex-soldier, he made the most of every second of it. She was a doctor who'd probably seen better bodies than his over the space of her career but her apparent fascination was proof this attraction wasn't one-sided. Not that he knew what he should do about that, if anything, when it would only complicate everything.

'Sou has…er…invited us inside for a bite to eat.' Emily slowly came out of her trance now that those hypnotic abs of steel had been hidden from view. Thanks to the T-shirt's shield of invisibility, his hold on her was temporarily suspended. She pretended she was squinting into the semi-darkness, trying to see him, rather than getting her rocks off staring at him half-naked.

'Is that what you want to do?'

Damn him, he'd deployed that adorable smile to disguise his dirty tactics. He was forcing her to make the decision.

'It would be rude not to.' She'd spent the past couple of hours in their company, being part of their group, as Joe had done with the men. It wouldn't be right to shun their invitation now, especially when she had nothing to rush back to. Unlike her *real* life, she wasn't planning her evening to catch up on paperwork or binge-watch episodes of her favourite TV shows.

Dinner with friendly islanders and a hunky ex-serviceman could be the most exotic meal she'd ever have in her life.

Take that, boring old Emily Clifford!

It turned out to be every bit as extraordinary as she'd imagined. The men and women all gathered inside Sou and Tomasi's house and took up their places on the floor mats. The women had put together a feast while Emily had finished up her painting and Joe had been flexing his muscles outside. Although she remained wary about the contents of the dishes laid before her, she had Joe on hand to sample the menu for her first.

With no cutlery available she had no choice but to follow suit and eat with her hands. She chose a pork dish and something delicious called *palusami*, which Joe explained was spinach prepared in coconut cream, and washed it down with a cup of black tea. With her belly full she realised she was getting the hang of this immersion into Yasi society. The only times her nerves had bunched together to remind her this wasn't the norm for her had been when Joe had brushed against her and made her tingle with sexual awareness.

It was a blessing the others hadn't continued with their teasing because she was pretty sure she was doing a bang-up job of making a fool of herself without their help. She'd been positively drooling as she'd watched his topless axe work and tensed every time he leaned in to explain the menu to her, like some virgin schoolgirl with a crush on her teacher. Her emotions had been stretched to every conceivable extreme today and although she was glad to end it in such good company, the walk home was playing on her mind. Their last one had ended in *that* kiss and she was so tightly wound after this evening she might explode if she didn't get the release she'd been craving since his lips had first touched hers.

'Don't forget to take your *masi* with you.' Sou presented her with the finished mat, which already held so many memories for her, when she stood to leave.

'Thank you. That's so kind of you.' They'd spent hours working on it. Time that should have been channelled into their livelihood. It was a wonderful gesture that choked her up even though she should expect this level of kindness by now.

'A souvenir of your time here.'

Emily didn't miss Sou's gaze flicker between her and Joe, a silent insistence she attributed significance to *all* of tonight's events.

'I'll cherish the memories of everyone here,' she assured her with a wry smile. Tonight wouldn't easily be forgotten, with or without the satisfactory conclusion of a second, perhaps more passionate lip-lock.

Emily retrieved her long-forgotten medical bag from the corner of the room. If today had taught her anything apart from her apparent weakness for muscular medics, it was that an office and an appointment book was no substitute for getting out and experiencing life. It was no wonder Greg had grown tired of her if this was what he'd been doing while she'd remained stagnant.

After all the sweetness she'd tasted today, the thought that her inability to spread her wings beyond her own living room had killed her marriage left a sour taste in her mouth. The only consolation she had was that wherever Greg was, whatever he was doing, it couldn't compare with her current adventure.

'Is everything all right, Emily? I know you didn't particularly want to leave the clinic but, honestly, we'd have heard about any emergency.' Joe's concern as they waved their goodbyes reinforced the idea she spoiled everyone's fun by always playing by the rules.

She'd gambled a few times over this last couple of

days and the world hadn't stopped turning because she'd swapped her sensible shoes for some frivolous flip-flops. Far from creating a catastrophic shift in the universe, these spontaneous acts had added a new, fun dimension to her existence.

Each new accepted challenge had enriched her time here with new friends, new skills and tastes, and the new memories were starting to dim the unpleasant ones she'd accumulated recently. One of which topped them all. Every time Greg's cruel words came back to haunt her she'd replace the image of his mouth curled in a sneer as he turned her heart inside out with one of Joe. His lips soft and tender on hers and leaving her fuzzy inside instead of cold.

She sighed. 'It's not that. I just couldn't help thinking that perhaps if I'd been a different woman then, this woman, perhaps Greg wouldn't have left me for someone else.'

Joe frowned at her with a scorn she hadn't expected after their evening playing nice. 'Is that what you want? To waste your life on someone who doesn't appreciate you for who you are? Did you ever think that *he* should've been a different man, a better husband, someone you weren't afraid to try new things with?'

Someone like Joe.

She'd never considered that take on the situation and had simply accepted the blame for the breakdown in their relationship as she had when her mother had left. Neither had wanted to be with her any more and since she had been the common denominator it was logical to assume she had been the root cause. They had wanted her to be someone else to suit their needs but she hadn't found that out until it was too late.

The truth was she couldn't pinpoint one specific reason why Greg had cheated on her and effectively ended their marriage. Yes, he'd said she was boring but she'd been the same woman he'd married. She hadn't changed, he had. One morning he'd simply woken up and decided he could do better. He'd simply grown tired of her and decided he no longer wanted her in his life. That thought had kept her awake and tearful for a long time. It didn't do a lot for a girl who was faced with her own faults in the mirror every single morning. She didn't want to hold on to that negativity any more.

'No.' To all of it. Including Greg.

'Good.' Joe took the mat and helped share her load.

She'd been clinging to the idea of marriage, not the realities of it. Working long days and being expected to have dinner waiting for her husband the minute he walked through the door had been a juggling act. In order to be the perfect wife she hadn't even confronted him on those times he'd arrived home late without an explanation, food ruined and a complete waste of her time cooking it. After the shock of his infidelity those overrunning meetings and last-minute business trips had taken on a sinister new meaning. She'd taken his word his absences were work-related, too trusting to even contemplate it was all lies to cover his dalliances with another woman. Or women. Her trust had been shattered to the point she'd no longer known who it was she'd married.

She'd never forgive him for what he'd put her through, regardless of how much he'd insisted it was her fault he'd chased excitement elsewhere. A marriage was supposed to be a partnership based on love, trust and communication. None of which it turned out they'd had. He hadn't even given her the chance to fix anything when he'd ditched her rather than discuss their problems like a normal couple. Although it hadn't seemed like it up until now, being on her own was probably better than going through the motions of a sham marriage. It had only taken some good company and straight talking for her to finally see that.

She didn't want to waste another second on regrets. That included not acting on the sexual chemistry between her and Joe. Not that she was intending to seduce him or anything, that would be a step too far, but even initiating another kiss seemed such a thrilling prospect it was all she could think about. The spectre of rejection always haunted her actions but he'd kissed her first, looked at her the way she'd lusted after him and lessened the chances he'd spurn her. It was the next big step in becoming Emily Jackson again.

Except she'd spent so long overthinking how she should approach this they were almost back at her door. So much for being spontaneous. She'd never learned how to flirt, had never had reason to. The ugly duckling would've been laughed out of high school if she'd even attempted it and it had been Greg who'd done all the running after they'd first met. She tried to convince herself this was only carrying on from where they'd left things last night when Joe had started this chain reaction inside her. He'd lit the fuse so he'd have to take responsibility for the fallout.

'I had a good time today.' She stopped short of Miriama's house so they weren't under the porch light and reduced the pressure to make something happen there and then.

'Me too.' Joe's bright smile lit up the semi-darkness and took the chill off the evening air.

She reached out to take the mat from him and Joe brushed his thumb along her fingers in the handover. The only sound she could hear was her own breathing as he watched her intently with no sign of backing away. It was now or never. She swallowed hard as she took a step closer to him.

They were both holding onto the mat as she closed her eyes and offered her lips up to his.

For a heart-stopping moment there was only cold air to meet her. Then the weight of his mouth was on hers, accepting her, loving her and bringing her almost to tears with relief. Each caress of her lips, every flick of his tongue to match hers made her confidence stronger and her body weaker. She'd taken a gamble and this was her reward. In future she'd remember how utterly satisfying, and hot, victory tasted.

It was a triumph over her anxieties, her fears and, above all, her old self. This was anything but boring, as her fevered skin would testify.

'I don't want this.'

Her new fairy wings disappeared and left her plummeting back down to earth as Joe did the one thing she'd feared from the start.

'I, I…' She didn't know whether to apologise or say goodnight but either would be better than dissolving into a puddle of tears, which was exactly what she wanted to do. Her determination to prove she was still attractive to someone, that she could change, had obviously built this up into something Joe hadn't been expecting. The celebrations heralding the brave new Emily had been premature. Nobody wanted *her* either. The difference was she would no longer let other people's opinions define her.

Joe wanted Emily more than anything else in the world right now. That was the problem. It was one thing for him to snatch a kiss from her and walk away but quite another for her to initiate one. Double standards for sure but what was a moment of madness for him could mean something entirely different for her. They were already too close when every attempt to create some distance between them only succeeded in them spending more time together. To what end? She wasn't going to find peace with him when he couldn't find his own.

'Okay, I do want this, there's no point in denying it.' Not when he could see how much hurt he was causing her by doing so. That tilt of the chin didn't fool him when she was clutching her medical bag like a security blanket and her eyes were glassy with tears.

'So why do it? Why keep pretending there isn't something more than my brother or work binding us together?'

He admired her strong stance, facing him out over his cowardice despite her wobbly voice. She deserved the truth. He dug his nails into his palms to stop from reaching out to her. This was exactly why he should have avoided kissing her in the first place.

'I've told you, I'm not boyfriend material. You'll end up just another holiday memory when I move on and after everything you've been through you need more than that. I don't want the level of responsibility that comes with being the rebound guy. I'm not going to be the one to restore your faith in men or be your emotional crutch until you're over Greg, and I won't pretend to be.' Cards on the table, he braced himself for her reaction. He doubted any woman wanted to be told the man they were kissing was emotionally unavailable, and since he hadn't found it in himself to walk away he was counting on her to make that call.

Emily closed the gap he'd created between them. 'I don't remember saying I wanted any of those things from you but thank you for your honesty. I guess we both know where we stand.'

Too close for him to think straight. Alarm bells were ringing in his head with her breathy acceptance of his terms but it was no longer his head he was listening to.

'I don't want this,' he repeated, even as his lips inched towards hers.

'Neither do I.'

Their mouths collided in a crushing kiss as if they were trying to exorcise this need for one another. The very opposite happened to him as his brain short-circuited and erased the reason he shouldn't do this. Something about him being an idiot and Emily accepting it.

The medical bag and mat fell in the dirt as they clung to each other tighter, her hands around his neck, his around her waist, their legs entwined as they tied themselves into a love pretzel, obliterating all pretence for good.

There was so much fire as she came back time and time again for more, exploring him with her tongue, her passion took him completely by surprise. This naked display of desire for him from a woman who worried about every move she made was such an aphrodisiac his body was already racing on to the next stage. Neither of them were ready for that. At least, not here, not now.

He loosened his hold and gradually let the intensity of the embrace subside. Eventually he had to break free before the most demanding part of his anatomy wrestled sole charge of the situation.

'Glad we got that sorted. It stops any future misunderstanding.' The only way he could survive this was to make a joke of it and diffuse the crackling sexual tension for the moment. Neither of them wanted this but it was happening and there was clearly no escape from it on this tiny island.

'Yeah. We wouldn't want things getting awkward at work.' Emily teased him back but she was already collecting her things from the ground, the moment over.

'Goodnight, Emily.' He kissed her on the cheek, avoiding her lips in case his chivalry died altogether.

'Goodnight, Joe,' she whispered directly into his ear. Even if he hadn't heard it, the deliberately provocative breathy goodbye would still have had the same effect on his libido. Deadly.

This surge in Emily's confidence had the potential to be one of the greatest challenges of his life if he kept resisting his natural response to her. If she was really the sort of girl who could hook up with a stranger on a whim they'd have got it on as soon as she'd set foot on the beach. The attraction had been there from the start. She'd had no more casual flings than he'd had ex-wives. They were completely incompatible. Except where it counted.

He was a thrill-seeker because he needed that reminder he was still alive, and his life hadn't ended in that blast. There'd been no greater example of that than when he'd had Emily in his arms, his heartbeat thundering in his ears as she'd kissed him.

It would be madness to carry on with this reckless attraction, let it develop beyond stolen kisses in the moonlight and risk anyone getting hurt. Then again, he was an adrenaline junkie. Playing it safe simply wasn't his style and, it would seem, no longer Emily's.

CHAPTER SEVEN

'SOMEONE'S HAPPY THIS MORNING. I heard you up, singing with the birds.' Miriama peered at Emily over the breakfast of sweet rolls she'd provided.

Emily wolfed them down, ravenous after a good night's sleep and some very pleasant dreams.

'I'm loving my time here, that's all,' she said, washing her white lie down with some lemon tea. Whilst she was happy to be here, this morning's mood was solely down to one man on the island.

'And we love having you here. Perhaps you could stay a little while longer?' She had such hope in her eyes it was a shame to let her down. It wasn't everyone who would open their homes up to a complete stranger in the first place and it was lovely for Emily to hear someone wasn't sick of the sight of her. Not yet anyway.

'I wish I could but I've got my own clinic, my own patients, waiting for me at home.' There was no place she'd rather be than Yasi Island right now. It had made quite an impression on her.

She traced the outline of her mouth with her fingertips absent-mindedly, replaying the moment it had all been worth it to come here. It was no wonder Miriama was staring at her as if she was mad. She couldn't stop smiling.

There was no way of telling if it was down to this place

or merely being away from the toxic environment of a life she'd shared with her ex, but she was beginning to feel like a new person. A woman who could override her fears with a burst of courage when it was required. The benefits she'd received in doing so would only inspire her to keep challenging herself.

Until last night she would never have entertained the idea of making a move on a man but she was glad she had. A lovely shiver tickled the back of her neck at the thought of her reward. She didn't know if anything more would come of it and constantly worrying about it would only spoil things. As with any other holiday memory the kiss was simply something to look back on fondly. A fantasy designed to give her a boost when real life became a drudge, not take seriously.

'Oh, well. You're ours for a while at least, so you should go make the most of your time here. I'm sure Joe is waiting for you.'

She tried to block out her inner worrywart, who always did her best to sabotage the good things that came her way, and focus on the positives as she made her way to work. Such as the reserves of courage she hadn't known she'd had to make a move on him in the first place.

'Hey.' Her breakfast did a backflip in her belly at the first Joe sighting of the day.

'Hey,' he said back, every bit as bashful as they faced each other from either end of the hut.

It seemed they were back to yesterday's avoidance tactics again and although it was probably best when they had to work together, there was still that sinking feeling in her stomach that their moment had passed.

They kept themselves busy by setting up what minimal equipment they had and she was glad when Sou made an appearance to interrupt the awkward atmosphere.

'Hey, Sou. What can we do for you?' Joe asked.

'If it's a general health check you want we can start with your blood pressure.' Emily turned back to fetch the blood-pressure cuff, only to collide with that solid wall of muscle again.

'Excuse me,' she said, attempting to duck past Joe.

'Of course.' He moved aside but she promptly ran into him again.

'Sorry.'

'Sorry.'

'If you two have quite finished, is there somewhere I can set these before my arm drops off?' Sou shoved a plate of sweet desserts between Emily and Joe's clumsy tango.

'You can set them over here.' She cleared a space on the table for Sou's offering and prayed it wasn't completely obvious that she and Joe were dealing with personal issues. It was taking all her mental strength to relegate their ten minutes of sexy times to the past when she was still trying to regulate her breathing and her heart rate, but she would never bring her personal business into the workplace.

'I'll go…do something else.' Joe backed out of her personal space and her skittishness immediately began to dissipate.

Good. It would help her get back to the day job if she couldn't see him. They couldn't let things between them affect their work.

'Take a seat, Sou. I wasn't expecting to see you so soon. What can I do for you?'

Yasi Island, and Joe, were making her forget who she was *supposed* to be.

She wrapped the cuff around Sou's upper arm and watched the dial as she inflated it.

'I haven't been myself at all lately and I thought it was about time I saw about it. If I'm honest, it's only because you're here that I'm bothering at all.' Sou rested her hands on her lap and that sparkle she'd had in her eye when she'd first walked in began to dim. There was clearly something bothering her more than she wanted anyone to know.

'Well, your blood pressure's fine. We'll start with taking a few measurements and then we'll discuss whatever problems you're having.' Emily unfastened the cuff and started a file for her new patient. She plotted her height on the wall chart and pushed the scales out to get a quick weight reading.

Sou was fifty-eight, and very overweight, which could lead to all manner of health issues.

'I'm tired and thirsty all the time. I know I'm not getting any younger but I'm exhausted.'

'Are you passing urine more frequently too?' Alarm bells were already ringing in her doctor brain.

'I thought that was because of the extra drinks?'

'It could be but we have to look into all possibilities. Tell me, Sou, do you know if there's a history of diabetes in your family?' It would certainly explain the symptoms but Emily didn't have the means to treat it effectively here. She would have to refer Sou to hospital on the mainland for the kind of long-term care that would require and she'd have to be certain of her diagnosis before she started the ball rolling on that score.

'My mother had it but she hated the hospital. She didn't always do everything they advised. She was a stubborn lady and I miss her.' The fear in her voice came from someone who didn't want to follow that same path but neither did she want to face the scary truth. It was important for Emily to treat her with kid gloves so she didn't scare her off back into denial.

'If it is diabetes we're dealing with, we *can* manage it effectively. First things first. We'll do a wee sample to test your blood sugar levels. You'll feel a little prick in your finger as the needle draws the blood but it'll all be over in seconds. Okay?' She only had the small reading device at her disposal and any in-depth analysis would have to be done in the hospital labs but it should give her a good indication if there was a problem.

Sou nodded her head and slowly extended her hand. While Emily was used to this sort of test she understood this wasn't something her patient would be too familiar with and counted to three before she clicked the needle into the skin.

Unfortunately her hunch proved correct. The glucose levels exceeded those she'd hoped for.

'Going by the reading here, diabetes is a definite possibility. I'd like to repeat the test tomorrow if you could fast in the morning for me. We'll take a urine sample first thing too to make sure this isn't some sort of anomaly. If there's no change we're going to have to refer you to the hospital to arrange long-term care for the condition.'

She rested her hand on Sou's, wishing this lovely woman had better news coming to her. 'You can do a little something to help yourself in the meantime. If you could cut out the sweet stuff and take up even the smallest exercise, it can make all the difference.'

Sou's long stare was that of a woman who may as well have been handed a death sentence. Emily understood how much food was a part of the culture here but Sou needed to help herself when there wasn't immediate access to medical facilities and drugs on the island. Diabetes unchecked could lead to all sorts of other health complications, which were often more difficult to treat. Prevention was always better than cure.

'We can work together to come up with a healthy eating plan if it would help.'

'Yes, please.'

That would be her homework tonight, to try and devise a meal plan that could work in a place where food supplies were already limited. With any luck Joe would help her. Putting their heads together for the sake of their patients was the perfect excuse to cosy up this evening.

'I know it's easier said than done but try not to worry about it. Carry on as normal tonight. We'll do more tests tomorrow, then take it from there.' She'd get his advice on hospital referrals too when he'd finished with his own patient. Joni was currently monopolising his time with another sports injury of some sort.

'Can I still drink kava?'

If this had been a patient at home she wouldn't be encouraging alcohol but not overwhelming Sou with too much change was just as important. They'd take this one step at a time together.

'I'm not going to stop you partaking tonight but we will look into your alcohol intake as part of this lifestyle change at some point. Everything's possible in moderation. Now, go home, talk this over with Tomasi and I'll see you back here in the morning.'

Sou rose slowly from the bed. It was no wonder she was still in a daze after the bombshell she'd just had dropped on her.

'I'm here any time you need to talk or if you have any questions.'

'Thanks, Emily.'

'No problem. We'll get you back to your old self as soon as we can.' She wrapped Sou in a bear hug, another thing she'd never have dreamed of doing in her own practice. That line between patient and friend had been blurred around the same time as the one with Joe.

She made a note to call in and check on Sou later as she waved her off. It was a lot for her to take in and meant huge changes in her life, something that was always difficult to come to terms with even when it was for the best. She was a prime example herself of someone who'd resisted adapting to the new hand fate had dealt her and was only now reaping the benefits of that evolution. It would've been nice if she'd had someone to hold her hand and assure her things would be okay and her world wouldn't come to an end because of one event.

Perhaps she wouldn't have been in the right head space to hear those platitudes about life going on after Greg but it had, and in quite dramatic fashion. In those dark early days she'd never have imagined flying to a remote island, treating patients with rudimentary equipment and snogging the local totty. She was proud of herself for all of it. Sou would be too if she made a few simple changes to improve her lot. Although Joe was definitely out of bounds, she would find her courage rewarded in other ways.

Her attention inevitably returned to her army medic, who was patching up Joni's knee. She could hear the pair of them laughing and was automatically drawn towards the easy camaraderie after the difficult start to the day.

'Have you been in the wars again?' she asked the patient, who was lying on the bed with his hands behind his head as relaxed as could be.

'The perils of running and not paying attention.' Joe grinned at her over his shoulder, sending her pulse skipping off into the sunset with her common sense.

'It's as well you're made of tough stuff around here, huh?' Her attempt at playful banter fell flat as Joni was staring at her unblinkingly, clearly disturbed by her presence.

He sat up, his face screwed up as he peered closer into her face, his nose wrinkled in disgust. Emily moved away from the bedside taken aback by the boy's sudden change in demeanour. She could sense Joe tensing next to her too and she panicked she'd made a mistake in coming over and interrupting their male bonding.

'What happened to your face, Doc?'

It was the kind of blunt questioning she should've been used to by now but it still managed to knock the air out of her lungs. This was why she took great steps to make sure she kept her birthmark covered and avoid this sort of confrontation. Joni had reacted so strongly there had to be something wrong with her usually foolproof camouflage.

She'd been so high on life this morning she barely remembered anything before coming to work. Her routine never differed—shower, dress, make-up, breakfast. Except this wasn't any ordinary day and this certainly wasn't the usual running order. She'd swapped her hot showers for buckets of cold water, dressed according to the weather instead of her job title, and…she didn't recall performing her twenty-minute beauty regime while she'd been singing and daydreaming about the night before. That would teach her to get carried away with romance. Now stark reality was staring her right in the face. This fairy-tale was well and truly over.

'I…uh…' She scrabbled around for her bag. There should be an emergency compact in there and she'd handle this better if she wasn't so exposed.

She couldn't even look at Joe now her big secret had been revealed in its full gory glory. Goodness knew what he was thinking. Probably how much of a lucky escape he'd had.

'It's a birthmark. Just a different coloured patch of skin Emily was born with. We're lucky she feels comfortable enough with us to stop hiding it under her make-up.' Joe shot her a smile warm enough to thaw out her bones, which were chilled after being called out on her deception. Bless him, he was trying to make this easy on her when he'd been the one kept in the dark.

She was torn now between doing a last-minute cover-up, pretending this had never happened, or playing along that this had been a deliberate move on her part. Joe wasn't stupid, he'd have known she'd never have intentionally 'come out' and left herself open to such scrutiny. It was testament to his strength of character for trying to save her blushes when it must have been a shock to his system to see her like this. Greg wouldn't have been so accommodating. He would've escorted her to the nearest mirror to rectify her glaring blunder. Although he wouldn't have let her leave the house make-up-free in the first place, never mind make excuses for her. He'd always made her feel as though she earned more respect from people when she perpetuated the lie about her true appearance.

She was lucky to have met a man who didn't need to put her down and always did his best to make her comfortable in her surroundings. No matter what the circumstances. That total acceptance of her as a person was something rare in her world.

'Does it hurt?' Joni was still staring at her face, which was aflame with the continued line of questioning.

'No. I forget it's even there.' That wasn't strictly true. Apart from today when it had apparently gone completely out of her head, that wretched port wine stain was the bane of her existence.

It was a boring enough answer for the child to lose interest.

'Will I have a scar?' he asked as Joe finished dressing his knee.

'No. You should be all healed up in a day or two. Now, get yourself off to school before your teacher sends out a search party for you.'

Joni looked remarkably disappointed not to have a long-lasting reminder of his injury as he hopped down off the bed. 'I suppose I'll see you later, then.'

At least when he was engrossed in his own woes it stopped him gawping at her as though she was a side-show attraction. The novelty usually wore off but that initial shock and revulsion was always difficult to stomach. Sometimes children could be the worst, laughing and pointing at her affliction, too young to understand the pain it would cause, but Joni had been quite straightforward about the matter. He'd asked questions and once they'd been answered it was no longer an issue. He'd made no judgement on her as a person because of her physical disfigurement.

It suddenly struck her that Sou and Miriama had also seen her without her camouflage. That explained the curious stares that she'd put down to her Joe-enhanced mood but they'd just been too polite to comment.

A woman with a dark red birthmark apparently wasn't anything the people of Yasi were going to waste energy thinking about when they were working so hard to just get by themselves. Physical attractiveness didn't hold much meaning out here because it had no effect on their quality of life. That's the way it should be; the way Emily preferred it. Except when she was unashamedly ogling Joe, of course. She was aware of the irony.

Joe. He'd seen her long before Sou or Joni had come onto the scene and he hadn't blinked, hadn't felt the need to point it out to her.

She opened her mouth, trying to find the words she needed to express what that meant to her, and failing. His easy acceptance was already making her tear up.

'Is everything all right with Sou? I think Joni was only trying to avoid class. He spends so much time here we should probably find him a job.'

She couldn't believe he wasn't even going to mention her birthmark. Honestly, she was finding his nonchalance even more disturbing than the boy's reaction. It wasn't the norm and, as such, she didn't know how to handle it.

In the end she decided to go with honesty and straight

talking. Another new first when it came to relationships for her.

'Are you really going to stand there and pretend nothing's wrong?'

'What are you talking about?' His naivety on the subject was annoying her now. No one could possibly be that oblivious to her predicament.

'This.' She couldn't believe she was voluntarily pointing out her flaw.

'Oh, your birthmark? I see it. So what?' He shrugged, increasing the chances of her giving him a good shake.

'So what, he says. You could have given me a heads up I'd gone out in public like this.' She didn't know why she was taking her mistake out on him when he'd been nothing but supportive. Her lashing out might have had something to do with this being the most vulnerable she'd felt since arriving on the island.

'As I said to Joni, I'd assumed you were actually comfortable enough around us to stop hiding away.'

'You weren't shocked? I mean, this ugly big mess can take some getting used to.' Nearly thirty years of living with it hadn't made it any easier for her so she didn't expect anyone else to take it in their stride the way Joe had.

'If I'm honest, I knew about it. I've seen the family photos Peter carries around with him but even if I hadn't it doesn't make any difference to me.'

Emily had to admit that took the shine off his brilliance somewhat. He'd had time to prepare himself for the great revelation. Unlike her discovery about his hearing problem. Perhaps the knowledge of her struggles with defective body parts had been what had drawn him to her in the first place and had made her seem attractive as another damaged soul. If something appeared too good to be true, it usually was.

'Hey. Your birthmark is part of you. How could it be

anything other than beautiful?' He tilted her chin up so she had to look in his eyes and believe what she saw there—pure, undiluted desire.

Whether he'd had advance warning or not, whether she covered up or not, he always looked at her as though she was the sexiest woman alive. There was no greater compliment for a woman like her. When he'd said her birthmark didn't matter to him, holding her gaze this way, she was more inclined to believe it.

Joe leaned forward and placed a light kiss on the exact spot between her cheek and her nose where her greatest weakness blazed brightly. She held her breath. It was one of those moments she'd dreamed of, when someone would embrace her, warts and all, not shy away from any part of her. She'd never had that complete acceptance from Greg and, despite being together so long, she'd always been slightly on edge. With good reason, it had turned out.

Joe was different. He believed in qualities and causes that mattered, not superficial nonsense that held no significant meaning. He was a special person. One with whom her time was limited.

Typical.

If she was only to encounter this kind of acceptance once in her lifetime she should really immerse herself in the experience. No holding back. No regrets. Be herself without conditions.

For the first time in her life she was seriously considering ditching her camouflage on a permanent basis and really letting loose. It was a bold move she would never have undertaken without Joe's unconditional support, and she was keen to share the rest of the adventure with him.

CHAPTER EIGHT

THERE WERE TIMES when Joe needed his medical work to give his life meaning and other times it was something he felt compelled to do. Today it felt like the latter. He'd volunteered to come to Yasi because he'd genuinely wanted to help, and he still did, but the success of the clinic had curtailed his personal life. That hadn't been a problem up until now. He'd spent all day treating one patient after another with Emily almost within arm's reach. It was torture if he was expected to forget everything that had happened between them.

He shouldn't complain, though, when their outreach yesterday had garnered so many follow-up appointments. It would go a long way towards improving the long-term health of the inhabitants. At one point they'd had a queue outside of people waiting to be seen for check-ups, which hadn't happened since he'd set up the clinic. Such an influx could've been overwhelming for Emily, especially since she'd chosen not to cover up her birthmark again. Of course there'd been comments and stares but she'd dealt with them all without any upset or drama, as if she'd reconciled herself about living without the make-up.

When she'd turned up this morning, her natural beauty shining through, all he'd wanted to do was take her in his arms and kiss her. It didn't matter it had turned out to have been an oversight on her part, her actions since had established her bravery and made him want her more. Every inadvertent brush against each other since had simply increased his desire to act on that impulse—impossible given their circumstances, not to mention the room full of people between them for most of the day. He couldn't afford to let anyone else down when he was still coming to terms with the last time he'd failed people who had needed his help.

They were making a difference here and that's what was important. Along with minor ailments and a test of his suturing skills on one of the local craftsmen, who'd whittled his hand instead of the wood he was supposed to be carving, they'd uncovered a few more serious health issues in the older population. Emily had confided in him about Sou, but diabetes, along with hypertension, wasn't an uncommon problem in remote regions like Yasi. Without adequate primary health care access and education, the rates of non-communicable diseases were often high and many cardiovascular risk factors also went unchecked. He already had a list of patients who'd require further investigation and treatment in proper hospital facilities.

In turn, the island was also doing Emily the power of good. That creep of an ex-husband had taken a sledgehammer to her confidence with his callous behaviour but she was flourishing out here. The same woman who forty-eight hours ago had been unable to walk more than twenty paces without touching up her make-up and had wanted to hide from company was fresh-faced and joking about with the locals.

She'd told all manner of tall tales to explain the birthmark, making light of it to avoid any awkwardness. He'd even heard her tell one curious patient it was the result of dodgy suncream application. By the time she revealed the truth it didn't seem to matter any more. Talking about it somehow made it less of a big deal and it was great to see Emily comfortable in her own skin. She didn't need him to wrap her in cotton wool when she was making such great progress on her own. It made his life easier too if she wasn't relying on him to act as intermediary any more.

'I've got another patient to add to the list of referrals. His heartbeat is irregular and he's out of breath. I'd be happier if he had an ECG to see what's going on in there.' Emily was all business as she approached him during a lull. She'd wound her hair up into a topknot and Joe's hand twitched to reach out and pluck out the pen holding it in place.

He gave himself a shake to rid himself of the image of her shaking her hair loose and showed her he could be just as professional. 'If you jot down all his details I'm going to make a few calls on the satellite phone later to the medical outreach co-ordinator and the hospital to get people here as soon as possible. Perhaps they can arrange communal transport to save money and effort in the transfer.'

'Like a community day trip? I suppose they could take a picnic and do some sightseeing on the way.' The corner of her mouth curved up as she teased him.

'Careful or I'll appoint you as tour rep.'

'I'd say you're the man for the job, not me. I imagine you'd be really good.'

He knew she was referring to the introductions he'd made for her around the island, yet the unintended innuendo immediately brought a groan from his inner Neanderthal. Given the chance with Emily he'd show her just how good he could be.

Her cheeks flushed scarlet as though she was reading his X-rated thoughts. The only thing more frustrating than not being able to act on his attraction to Emily was being aware that she wanted him too.

She made a move towards the new batch of patients hovering nearby, but Joe was finding it hard to let the moment pass without recognising the frisson of sexual energy they'd created in the space of a few seconds. Despite the buzz and whirr of the neon danger signs around her, he enjoyed Emily's company and the adrenaline rush he got simply from being around her.

He leaned down to whisper in her ear as she passed by. 'Why don't we get together tonight?'

Her eyes nearly popped out of her head at the suggestion. Clearly her thoughts were as muddled as his own about his motives. 'I, er…'

'You know, to catch up on that patient transfer list.' They could play it safe, didn't have to do anything other than chat about their working day. It would be novelty enough for him to entertain a guest, without getting into trouble with Peter's sibling and causing all manner of problems.

'Oh, yes. Of course. I'd also appreciate your help in devising some sort of healthy eating plan for Sou. We could even draw up an easy-to-read guide on healthier living for everyone to explain the basics.'

'Why don't we do it over dinner?'

'Here?'

'Sure. Leave it with me. As soon as we wrap up here you go and get freshened up and I'll rustle up some food for us. Just a quiet dinner for two.' So far, all their meals had been very public affairs where she'd found it difficult to relax. He wanted to change that for her without the pressure of structured proceedings. Just work talk and chill.

'That would be nice.'

'So it's a date, then?' He couldn't stop himself from teasing her one last time.

'It's a date,' she confirmed, before resuming her work

duties. The smile on her face eased the sense of loss as she turned away, knowing he'd been the one to put it there.

He had no expectations for anything beyond a nice evening together. A working dinner sounded more manageable for both of them long-term than an appointment for hot, unforgettable sex. Although he imagined that's exactly what would happen if they ever gave in to temptation.

That thought wasn't going to help this day go any faster.

The butterflies in her stomach might be older and more cynical than they had been fifteen years ago when she'd gone on her first date to the cinema, but they weren't any less mobile on this *non-date*. She was playing with fire tonight and she knew it. Joe had made it clear he didn't intend anything other than work-related conversation, but their apparent chemistry had a way of throwing them off track. She took full responsibility for last night's descent into madness and she wasn't ashamed of it. Taking the initiative had given her a confidence boost, especially when he'd been so responsive to her advances, but she wasn't sure she wanted to take things any further than that. Joe was an experienced man of the world who'd invariably expect more than a kiss in the moonlight.

Although she'd initially been disappointed they hadn't carried on where they'd left off, it was probably better they let things cool off. As much as she wanted to exorcise her demons once and for all, she wasn't ready to sleep with anyone yet, not even someone who was so accepting of her, flaws and all. While the idea of sharing Joe's bed was appealing on the surface, it would probably only give her more issues to worry about. Including all the ways in which he could find her lacking as a lover, given her limited experience.

Until she fully overcame her personal issues she'd have

to make do with the exhilaration of anticipation instead. This was the most alive she'd felt since the divorce, when all hope inside her for the future had seemed to have died along with her marriage. Even the idea he might want to sleep with her had definitely got the blood pumping back in her veins and that was enough for now.

She'd come armed as she entered the battlefield tonight where hormones would fight against her battered heart for supremacy. Flowers and chocolates were usually the gifts to bring on such an auspicious occasion but stationery was her particular weapon of choice this evening. An armful of paper, glue and coloured markers seemed like a good distraction from the beds that would dominate tonight's dinner venue.

She'd informed Miriama she'd be working late and wouldn't be around for supper when she'd gone back to change. There wasn't much to choose from in her limited wardrobe but she'd gone with Capri pants and a navy and white polka-dot halterneck for what she hoped was a touch of vintage glamour. It had taken longer for her decide on her make-up for the evening. While using her thick foundation could be seen as taking a step backwards, there weren't many women who'd get ready for an evening in male company without a little extra help. After much debate she'd decided a sweep of mascara over her eyelashes and a dab of lip-gloss would do just fine.

She'd taken so much time and care over her appearance she hadn't given a thought to how Joe would look tonight. When he opened the door to her she hadn't expected to see him in anything other than his casual T-shirt and shorts combo. So the more formal cream-coloured linen trousers and unbuttoned white shirt he was rocking had her eyes out on stalks.

'What? You don't think I can scrub up well too?'

'You look great.' She appreciated the effort he'd gone

to for her and that appreciation had reached deep inside and touched somewhere that definitely went beyond the friendship realm.

'So do you.' He leaned in to give her a welcome peck on the cheek, his skin smooth against hers and smelling of aftershave and soap.

She closed her eyes and breathed him in, the combination of familiar citrus tones and spicy musk seeming to complement his personality perfectly. Like him, his cologne was comforting with a dangerous hint of the exotic. Not to mention so very moreish. But standing on the doorstep, sniffing him, wasn't supposed to be the highlight of her evening.

'I'm intrigued to find out what you have planned for dinner.' She didn't have much of an appetite, at least not for food, but she was curious about how he'd sourced it, or if he'd cooked it himself.

'Come in and be prepared to be blown away. I can guarantee you the best meal you've had on the island, all cooked by my own fair hand.' He ushered her inside with the urgency of a man keen to show off said cooking skills.

'Bold claims. You're going to have to go a long way to top Sou's spread last night. I hope you've had some training.' She was still battling her fear of new foods, especially when not all of them here were to her taste. Except the coconut spinach thing.

Please, let it be the coconut spinach thing.

'I'll have you know I've cooked this very same meal while trekking through the Amazon rainforest. I'm a very capable chef who has whipped up a veritable feast even in the most trying circumstances.'

'In that case, I'm most honoured to be your guest.' And impressed with the casual mention of what must have been the most epic of adventures. Time spent in the jungle put her island escape well and truly in the shade.

Conditions here were probably luxurious compared to what he'd endured and she was panicking about what was on the menu. She should think herself lucky people were happy to keep feeding her. If left to her own devices she'd probably starve once her biscuit stash ran out.

'Take a seat and make yourself comfortable. You can set your things over there in the corner.'

She thought it was his idea of a joke when her bones were still protesting against this tradition of sitting on hard wood floors until she saw what he'd done with the place. The room was lit with the lanterns she'd seen in all the other houses, which somehow here they took on that air of intimacy a candlelit dinner for two demanded. He'd pushed all the medical equipment to the side and pulled the table, now covered with one of the painted *masa* mats, into the middle of the room. There were even two crude wooden chairs, one either side of the makeshift dining table. Bliss!

'I thought we were doing paperwork.' She clutched her armful of stationery closer. It was her security blanket, supposed to keep her grounded and stop her from getting carried away with the idea of romance.

'We are but we'll think better on a full stomach.' He eased the supplies from her grasp and set them on top of the medicine cabinet.

'It might be an idea to make a food pyramid to explain the basic principles of healthy living at a glance. You know, one of those colour-coded posters that starts with a small amounts of fatty foods bad for the body and ends with encouraging more fruit and veg in the diet.'

'Sure. I'm no artist but I'm sure we can manage a simple pictograph between us. Now, if you'll excuse me I must go and check on dinner cooking on my camping stove out the back.' It was only when he padded away from her that Emily noticed he was barefoot. He had his very own brand of sophistication that, while traditionally handsome, still paid homage to his bohemian nature. The best of both worlds from a spectator's point of view.

He gave a half-bow before ducking back outside. Emily took the seat facing the door in order to see this spectacle as it unfolded. He'd certainly gone to a lot of trouble but nothing so far indicated what she should expect on her plate. Her suspense was prolonged even further when dinner did arrive as he kept it covered, using an upturned wooden bowl as an improvised cloche.

'Ta-da!' He lifted the cover with a flourish.

Emily released the breath she'd been holding in a splutter of disbelief. 'Beans on toast? Where on earth did you get that?'

The welcome sight of an old British favourite, baked beans in tomato sauce, was a little piece of home that immediately brought her comfort. He'd even taken the care to toast the rustic bread to keep it authentic.

'We explorers always carry a few emergency supplies.' He produced an empty tin, which he'd obviously brought with him from England.

'This beats a fancy restaurant any day of the week.'

'Wait. You haven't seen anything yet.' He disappeared again, returning with two tin cups full of what looked suspiciously like English tea.

She took a sip of sweet heaven. 'But how…?'

Joe sat down too. 'I told you, I have a few essentials and I called in a few favours for the rest.'

She wanted to tell him he shouldn't have gone to so much trouble for her but she was too grateful to him for sacrificing his supplies for her. And her mouth was watering to taste something familiar.

'I've never eaten beans and toast with my fingers.'

'You don't have to. Unless you want to.' He reached into his pocket and pulled out a set of small stainless-steel cutlery. The kind no good Boy Scout would ever leave home without. It also proved his commitment to being part of the community here when he'd chosen to forgo using them until now.

Emily reached out and snatched a knife and fork from him. 'It's the little things that mean the most.'

That first bite of hearty nostalgia seemed to go in slow motion as she savoured the taste of home, enjoying the textures and flavours she knew so well. After that, she practically devoured her plate in hunger. When she was done she wiped her chin to make sure she hadn't embarrassed herself by dripping tomato sauce down herself.

'I aim to please.' He set down his cutlery on his clean plate with every reason to look smug after pulling out all the stops tonight. She wouldn't have been more pleased if he'd wined and dined her at The Ritz.

'I can't believe you did this. More to the point, I can't believe you wore white, knowing this was what we were eating. That's a laundry nightmare waiting to happen.'

He leaned forward, his intense gaze holding her captive in her seat, that desire they'd been trying to swerve all day flaring back into life. 'What can I say? I live right on the edge of danger.'

They both did if the sparks between them were anything to go by.

'Maybe we should get started on our craft project?' Before they cleared the table and lunged at each other in a fit of passion.

'There's no rush. Now, I hope you have room for dessert?'

'Always.' It was usually her favourite part of a meal but there wasn't much that could possibly top that main course.

Except the two chocolate bars he was waving in her face. All her Christmases had come at once.

'I was saving them for a special occasion.'

'Well, now's not the time to be selfish,' she said, holding out a hand for her share, secretly pleased he deemed an evening in her company 'special' when she was thinking exactly the same thing about him.

He was good-looking, generous, thoughtful and funny. Everything a woman could want in a man.

Joe Braden spelled trouble with a capital 'T'.

'Hmm, I don't think I'll ever make it as an artist.' Emily chewed the end of her pen and squinted at her depiction of Fijian desserts in the 'Eat Less' section at the top of the food pyramid. The only reason she didn't feel a hypocrite after scoffing down that chocolate was because it was the only indulgence she'd had in three days.

After their feast on comfort foods they'd got their heads together to create a diet plan for Sou and had now taken up residence on the floor to work on their healthy eating poster. The idea that there'd be more room to spread out had actually led to the two of them sitting almost on top of each other as they drew on the same piece of paper.

Joe glanced up from his scribbling to see her efforts for himself. 'Don't put yourself down. That's an excellent cheese wedge.'

'It's supposed to be coconut cake.'

'Maybe we should label everything.'

She gave him a dig with her elbow, making him give his perfectly drawn apple an extra-long stalk on the 'Eat More' shelf as he laughed at his own joke.

'I think they'll get the gist of the message and we'll explain it as part of the general physical exam anyway.'

'I'm only messing with you. I reckon we've done a great job. This artwork will still be hanging here displaying the info long after we've gone, essentially doing our job in our absence.' Joe hammered his fist on the sheet of A4 paper in passionate defence of their initiative.

'That's a scary thought,' she said with a giggle. He did make her laugh. And swoon.

'Which bit? The quality of our legacy or the idea of us leaving this place?'

Just like that the jovial mood gave way to something more serious, something more intense. Leaving Yasi meant leaving Joe behind too and she wasn't ready for that. He held her gaze and right there and then she knew she didn't want this to be over. She wanted this to be the beginning.

'Both.'

It was impossible to tell who'd made the first move when they'd both leaned in for the kiss.

Joe fastened his lips to hers with such stunning conviction she knew he'd been waiting for this too. She was starting to forget why she shouldn't let this happen when he knew her secret already and embraced it with more passion than she'd ever expected. He hadn't looked at her with any kind of pity today, only desire. Unless he was a very good actor or did charity work as a self-esteem booster for unfortunates, he didn't seem bothered by her *au naturel* appearance.

She scooted closer to deepen their connection and sample the best course of the evening in her opinion. Kissing him was even better than chocolate but every bit as delicious. Every romantic bone in her body melted as he pulled her close and reached out to cup her face in his hands, possessing her completely. It could've been a scene taken directly from one of those over-sentimental chick flicks she'd overindulged in recently. It was perfect.

Too perfect, that small voice of doom piped up.

It wasn't real; they weren't going to run off into the sunset together at the end of this.

Shut up, Miss Stick-in-the-Mud, and let me enjoy my wild side for once.

While the inner debate went on in her head, her body was making the next move for her. With her arms snaked around his neck and the rest of her draped over him like a silk scarf she was getting the full Joe Braden experience. He was all hard lines and smooth planes, the ideal structure to support her melty bones. They fitted together so well, felt so natural together, she didn't know why she'd worried so much. This dance around each other since her arrival had only been delaying the inevitable and they didn't have much time left together to waste. From now on she was going to take his advice and go with the flow, whatever direction it carried her.

Emily's knees were sliding from under her as he lowered her back onto the floor; their project quickly becoming a victim of their desire beneath their entangled limbs. Joe's body was heavy against hers but she'd never felt more secure, either with herself or another. Despite all her earlier anxieties, anticipating this moment, there was nowhere she'd rather be than here lying with him.

That didn't mean she wasn't a little skittish. She gasped at that first intimate touch as Joe slid his hand under her top to caress her breast, the skin-on-skin contact a shock to her system after all this time.

'You okay?' He immediately withdrew, leaving her feeling cold without the warmth of his touch.

'Mmm-hmm.' She nodded, keen to reconnect before she lost her bottle. It was better if she didn't have time to overthink and when his hands were on her she couldn't think about anything other than how good he made her feel.

'Tell me if this is going too fast,' he whispered against her neck, nuzzling that sensitive skin and stealing any potential argument from her.

'No.' Her breathy impatience saw him seek her out once more, kneading that soft mound into a hardened peak. Far from her usual cautious nature, she wanted to throw herself completely into the moment. She was too busy *feeling* to think or worry and it made her positively wanton, grinding her body against Joe's, aching for more.

His shirt came away easily beneath her busy fingers to reveal the well-defined torso she'd only ogled from afar until now. Up close it was even more impressive as she slid her hands over the bumps and contours of his body. It was amazing that one man was in possession of so much inner and outer beauty and she counted herself lucky she got to experience all of it.

The cool air puckered her nipple ever harder as Joe exposed her fully to his gaze. And his tongue. She moaned and arched up off the floor as he drove her to the brink of insanity with every flick. That little bud seemed to contain every nerve ending in her body, tightened with complete arousal and straining for his touch.

Eyes closed as she surrendered to her needs, she let her hands survey the rest of Joe's body. They slipped easily along his smooth skin until they met that trail of hair leading into the waistband of his trousers. Suddenly her nakedness didn't matter as much as his. She wanted to see all of him, feel all of him pressed against her. Into her.

He sucked in a breath as she unfastened the button and dared to go ever lower to trace the hard ridge of his erection. It was her turn to gasp. There was no denying the strength of his desire for her when the steely evidence was right there beneath her fingertips. The knowledge that the flawed Emily still had the ability to turn him on to this extent was a powerful motivator.

She explored his length and self-control through the fabric of his briefs, enjoying the groans of pleasure and frustration she drew from him with every feathery stroke along his shaft. However, teasing him also meant she was testing the limits of her own restraint and she was never one to inflict unnecessary pain on herself.

She squeezed his taut backside and Joe closed his eyes and tilted his head back in ecstasy. This shameless need to follow her desire and to hell with the consequences was new, exciting, and though she wanted to reach that final peak she didn't want this feeling to end. Although she might spontaneously combust if they didn't bring this to its natural conclusion soon.

She was scrabbling to undo the zip on her own trousers when the door burst open.

'We need your help!'

Emily screamed.

Joe swore.

'Get out!' he shouted, throwing himself on top of her to save what was left of her modesty.

'I'm sorry. Holy—'

She didn't hear the rest as the door closed again but she imagined there was probably an expletive missing at the end of the sentence.

'Was that—?'

'Yeah,' Joe confirmed her worst fears as he leaned his forehead on her chest and swore again.

The best moment of her life had transformed into one of the worst. Her own stepbrother had just walked in on her about to have sex with his best friend.

Lying here half-undressed with an almost naked Joe spread-eagled across the top of her suddenly became tawdry when she viewed it from Peter's perspective. The cold dose of reality brought back all the reasons this should have remained nothing more than a bad idea.

'I need to get up.' She pushed Joe off and covered herself up again, the thrill of the evening well and truly having worn off. It was unfortunate that after everything she'd gone through to reach this point she was back to being a disappointment.

Emily was hunched over, hugging her knees and almost rocking with the trauma of having Peter catch them at it on the floor. Joe knew he was going to have to man up and face the consequences with her stepbrother. The thought of that had killed his arousal stone-dead.

Once he'd relocated his shirt and pulled his trousers back up, he crouched down beside her.

'We didn't do anything wrong,' he whispered, desperate for her to come back to him. They'd acted on their mutual attraction, not committed a crime.

'I know.' She said it so softly and with so little conviction he'd had to read her lips. He could see the shame clouding her face and curling her body into a ball.

If it had been anybody else who'd burst in uninvited he would've read them the Riot Act, but on this occasion Peter had claim on the victim role. He needed to go and do some damage control but he was reluctant to leave Emily there, reflecting on the embarrassment she'd been subjected to because of him. He should've taken better care of her.

He dipped his head to drop a kiss on her lips, hoping to keep that connection alive. They'd come this far and risked so much to get to this point that it would be a shame to take two steps back now, but she remained motionless, unresponsive to the gesture. This sudden impassiveness wasn't something he was simply going to accept after the fire he'd just witnessed from her. He wanted her to stay with him and not give in to unnecessary guilt. She'd had enough of that recently.

With her face cradled in his hands, he teased her lips apart with the tip of his tongue, searching for that woman who'd had her hands down his pants not five minutes ago. Slowly but surely she began to respond, tentatively meeting his tongue with hers and opening her mouth to invite him further. He wanted to scoop her up and carry her off somewhere peaceful and private, preferably with carpet on the floor and a king-size bed. They needed somewhere with no distractions, no outside influences interfering in how they expressed their feelings for one another. Emotionally they mightn't have it all figured out, but until Peter had arrived they'd been happy for their bodies to make their decisions for them.

The sound of banging on the door reverberated around the room.

'Guys, I know this is…er…bad timing but we really have an emergency out here. So if you could postpone this for now and get your clothes on, I'd really appreciate it.' Peter was shouting so loudly it wasn't hard to figure out what he thought of this match. Seeing Joe rolling around half-naked with his stepsister might have played a part in colouring that judgement.

'We have to go. Peter definitely wouldn't be hanging around unless he really had to. It must be serious.' It was Emily who finally became the voice of reason. Someone needed their help, and everything else would have to wait.

Joe was dreading coming face-to-face with Peter more than whatever crisis was going on beyond this one.

'Are we good?' He wanted confirmation before they took this outside.

Emily nodded and attempted a smile. It would have to do until they were alone again and able to speak freely.

There was no putting this off any longer. They couldn't afford to let any awkwardness take precedence over someone's health. Joe opened the door to a scowling Peter.

'It's the chief's son. You'd better come and see him.' He turned on his heel, barely able to look at either of them.

Joe could hardly blame him. He was lucky he hadn't been on the receiving end of a fist. Although there was still time. He quickened his pace to keep up with his probably now ex-mate, aware that Emily was content to hang back.

'What's wrong with him?'

'He's running a fever, vomiting, and generally in a really bad way.'

In this region there was always a chance those symptoms could be more serious than a run-of-the-mill stomach bug. Malaria, typhoid and dengue fever were also commonplace alongside the usual culprits. They were also potentially deadly. He'd seen them all on his travels, along with the variable outcomes.

Joe stopped abruptly.

'We'll need medical supplies if he's too weak to come here for treatment.' It was the first thing he should have checked before heading off, and showed how far his focus had strayed over the course of the evening. This wasn't a typical nine-to-five job where he could clock off and have romantic nights in when he felt like it.

'Of course. There's no way he'd make it back here.' Peter slowed too as if he should also take the blame for the oversight. They were obviously all a little shaken up and not thinking as rationally as they should in their rush to get away from the scene of the alleged crime.

'I'll go back and get them,' Emily piped up from the back.

'Pardon me?' He wasn't sure he'd heard her correctly. Volunteering to go back meant she would have to find her way out to the chief's house alone, in the dark. It was a clear sign how much she was dreading being left with her stepbrother, trying to make conversation. He wasn't looking forward to it much himself.

'I said I'll get what we need and meet you both out there.' She spoke louder, with a determination he couldn't very well object to.

'Will you be able to find your way in the dark?' It was one thing for two ex-soldiers who'd been living here for weeks to track their way back with very little illumination and quite another for Emily, who was still getting to know her way around.

'I'll be fine. I'll grab a lantern from the clinic.'

Oh, yeah, that made sense. He might have done that himself if he hadn't thought he'd need both hands to fend off an irate stepbrother. Peter was keeping it together for now but he knew him well enough to know that rage was bubbling somewhere under that apparently calm surface.

'We're probably going to need antibiotics, paracetamol, a blood-pressure cuff, maybe an IV line—'

'I'm sure I can handle it.' Emily wasted no more time as she spun round and walked towards the light coming from the clinic.

He'd been so busy trying to cover all possibilities he'd neglected to give her any credit as his medically qualified equal in the process. That was another member of the Jackson family he was going to have to try and make amends with later. It wasn't that he was *trying* to tick everyone off tonight, it had simply happened organically.

'You heard her. We'll go on without her.' There was the tone of a big brother/kid sister talk waiting to happen and it wasn't as if Joe could walk away and let them get on with it. He was very much a part of it.

'Mate, I know what that must've looked like.' He was literally cringing at having to remind Peter of what he'd just witnessed but he didn't want to ignore the obvious tension and have their friendship fester because of it.

'Unless I'm wrong, it looked like you were seducing my sister on the floor.' Peter's teeth were a glistening vision of naked aggression in the moonlight and Joe braced himself for imminent attack.

'You're partially right. Although I wouldn't have said

it was all one-sided. Emily's a woman who knows her own mind—'

'I don't want to know the details, thanks.'

'Right. I just mean we both like each other. We're having some fun together.'

They'd been having a lot of fun right up until real life had barged in on them and burst their bubble. Up until the moment his love interest's protective big brother had come looking for her, they had been discovering their own little piece of paradise. Alone in that room, in each other's company, in each other's arms it had been easy to forget their lives outside that door and not consider the consequences of their actions. Such as protection. They hadn't discussed it and Joe had definitely been too carried away in the moment to think about it. Although his body had protested at Peter's interruption perhaps it hadn't been as ill-timed as he'd first thought.

A pregnancy would not have been a souvenir either of them would want to take away from this holiday romance. Emily was just getting her life back on track after her ex-husband's betrayal and her bravery today was proof of that. She didn't need to be tied to him for the rest of her days and vice versa. His personal issues would forever cloud any sort of long-term relationship and while this was still only a fling there was no reason to start trying to explain them. Unlike Emily, he wasn't ready to share them publicly.

'I thought I could trust you, man. You know what she's been through.'

'Yeah, and she needs this time away to try and forget it. I promise I won't do anything to hurt her.' He wouldn't be able to live with himself if he did. There'd be no trek long enough, or climb high enough to help him forget intentionally hurting either of them.

'You'd better not. I'd hate to have to hand back my halo

and take up arms again.' At least there was a hint of humour in the thinly veiled threat.

Joe held his hand up. 'Hey, I don't want to be the one responsible for sending you back to the dark side.'

'Then stay away from my sister.'

Okay, there wasn't a trace of a veil hiding that one. If only it was as easy as keeping his distance. Been there, done that, ended up rolling around on the floor with her.

'Sorry, bro, but I'm not going to do that. I don't want any bad blood between us but I like Emily a lot.' Joe waited for the explosions to start as he defiantly went against his friend's wishes. He only hoped Emily was as steadfast in continuing the relationship after this or else putting his friendship with Peter in jeopardy was all for nothing.

Instead of further threats of fisticuffs, Peter let out a sigh. The resigned sound of his disappointment was almost as devastating to Joe's equilibrium as the right hook he'd been expecting. Although he didn't want to examine his feelings for Emily too deeply for fear of what he'd discover, it spoke volumes that he was willing to risk upsetting the very guy he'd come here to help.

'I guess it's my fault for pushing you two together but I thought I could trust you not to take advantage of her.'

Another blow where it hurt the most.

'I would never do that. I respect her too much.'

'It didn't look that way to me.'

Joe's insides shrivelled up with shame. It would be easy to misinterpret what had been happening between him and Emily as something tawdry when it had evolved so naturally and beautifully. He regretted Peter walking in on them but not a second of the evening up until then.

'I'm sorry if you saw anything untoward but at the end of the day Emily's a grown woman who makes her own decisions.' There it was, the comment that could finally break their bromance. He was effectively telling the guy to butt out.

'That lack of judgement is the reason she ran out here in the first place.' Another sigh. 'I could use a cup of kava right about now, and a bucket of eye bleach. Your bare backside is not an image I want to go to sleep with tonight.'

Joe exhaled a nervous laugh. 'In that case, what do you say we forget it ever happened? I promise not to hurt your sister and keep my backside covered at all times.' It was the best compromise he could come to and mean it. Anything more than that and he knew he'd have difficulty keeping his word. He and Emily still had unfinished business.

'Hmm. I guess that'll have to do but the first sign of Joe-related tears from my little sister—'

'I know, I know, I should start swimming.'

'As long as we're clear.'

'Crystal.'

It wasn't anything Joe hadn't expected. All things considered, he'd got off lightly. Yasi Island really had mellowed Peter out. In another time and place he wouldn't have thought twice about knocking him out and Joe wouldn't have blamed him. He'd spent many a long night on training exercises talking about his family, shared all the big achievements in Emily's life with Joe as he'd read about them in cherished letters he'd received in Afghanistan. It was only natural tonight would seem like a betrayal and only time would let him prove otherwise.

As they reached the chief's house he was glad they'd kind of cleared the air. Whatever was ailing the patient inside was undoubtedly going to be difficult enough to manage, without the added stress of a duel over Emily's honour. He glanced back, checking for signs of her following, and could just about make out a bobbing flicker of light snaking through the village in the distance. Whatever the rest of the night had in store for him, he knew he would get through it better with her at his side.

CHAPTER NINE

EMILY KNEW JOE would have everything under control until she got there. At least as far as the medical emergency went. There were no obvious signs of a scuffle as she followed in their wake to the chief's house. She hadn't stumbled over any bodies so she'd take that as a sign he and Peter had either worked things out or chosen to ignore the humiliation they'd all just endured. It was going to take her longer to get over it.

She prayed Joe's quick actions had covered most of her blushes but it hadn't been enough to disguise what they'd been up to. Peter definitely would not approve, not because he was a prude, he was an ex-soldier after all, but because she'd chosen his best friend to get over her break-up. At the same time she realised Joe wasn't something she was willing to give up. Not yet. That time would come soon enough and she didn't want to miss out on anything he had to offer.

Tonight had only been a taster of what they could have together and not something she would easily forget when her body was still thrumming with sexual awareness. As long as she remembered this wasn't real, that they were never going to be part of each other's lives away from here, she shouldn't have to worry about anything other than enjoying the moment with Joe. Well, apart from her stepbrother walking in on them after passion had taken hold.

A shudder ripped through her. She was an adult, one who'd gone through an acrimonious split from her husband and deserved some fun and excitement in her life. That didn't mean one frowning look from her stepbrother wouldn't regress her back to that role of naughty kid sister, even when she hadn't done anything other than let loose for once. They were going to have to discuss what had happened, what was happening, between her and Joe so she could reassure him she knew what she was doing. Even when it seemed so far removed from her normal behaviour.

Joe and Peter already had proceedings under way when she caught up with them at either side of the patient's bedside.

'We thought he'd be more comfortable in my bed and we've stripped him down to try and bring down the fever.' Her stepbrother didn't waste any time on small talk, which suited her fine. They could discuss personal matters later in private, or not at all—either worked for her.

The small room was cramped with the chief and the three of them crowded inside, so she stood back, trying to remain invisible until she was needed. No such luck when Joe had anything to do with it.

'I need a thermometer if you have one in there.'

She rummaged around her bag and produced one while he stood with his hand out, waiting, as if he was the lead surgeon and she was the theatre nurse. It wasn't much of a stretch, she supposed, in this scenario where she was a spectator rather than the one taking readings.

'You've got a temperature of forty degrees, so we really need to get that down. I'll need plenty of water to keep him hydrated and we could use something to keep him sponged down. It would really help if we could clear as many people out of here as possible. Emily, I'm going to need your help to get this under control.' The crowd parted like the Red Sea to make a clear path between her and Joe, everyone watching for her reaction. Probably for different reasons.

'I'll get the water.' Peter's gaze flitted suspiciously between them as though they were trying to engineer another reason to be alone.

He shouldn't have worried. Emily needed time to process what had taken place tonight before they ended up back in the same scenario. It seemed neither of them were able to control themselves when left to their own devices and as yet she hadn't decided if that was detrimental to her well-being or not. Physically, there was no doubt they were compatible. It was the more *personal* aspects of getting involved that caused her concern. Her emotions were still in recovery and she didn't think they could cope with another mauling, no matter how unintentional.

Eventually Peter made a move towards the door, with the chief soon following behind.

Although it didn't make the room any less suffocating as she had to face Joe and try not to mention the incredible time they'd had together before fate had intervened.

'Nete is presenting with fever, along with muscle and joint pain. Did you bring some paracetamol?' He put her to shame with his thoughts being solely for his patient and not lingering back at their love shack. From here on they were merely medical colleagues working together to treat their patient. Everything beyond that could wait until their patient was back on track.

'Yes. That should help bring that temperature down too.' Important in preventing fits and further complications.

'Can you sit up for me?' He put a hand on the young

man's back and eased him up from the bed amid a lot of wincing.

Joe gestured for her to stand beside him. It was only then that she noticed the rash dotted across Nete's flushed skin, little islands of white in a sea of red.

'Have you been near any stagnant water recently?'

Emily's mind had instantly gone to all of those childhood illnesses mostly eradicated via the vaccination programme back home, but Joe obviously had different ideas about the source of the rash.

'I was down by the river a few days ago.'

Joe frowned, clearly disturbed by the information.

She knew herself that areas of stagnant water were a breeding ground for mosquitoes, airborne viruses and bad news.

'Could you get me the blood-pressure cuff, Emily?'

'I'm just going to wrap this around your arm,' she said to Nete. 'There will be a tightening sensation as we inflate the cuff but there's no need to panic. It's just how we test your blood pressure.' She knew the patient was too lethargic to really pay attention to what they were doing but it was important for her to have a role here and not fall back into the old pattern of feeling surplus to requirements. Joe had specifically asked her to assist him and this kind of emergency was exactly why she was here.

The lines on Joe's forehead grew deeper with the low reading she recorded. Although low blood pressure could be a sign of good health and fitness in someone of this age, coupled with the other symptoms it could be an indicator of heart or neurological disorders.

Joe loosened the cuff, squinting at the arm beneath as he did so and refastening it. 'I'm just going to do something called a tourniquet test. This means the cuff will tighten again for a few minutes.'

Emily watched in silence as he inflated it to the midpoint between the systolic and diastolic blood pressures, unease snaking through her body. She'd read up on tropical illnesses before venturing out here to practise and the tourniquet test was used to diagnose something far more serious than gastroenteritis. Dengue fever, also known as break-bone fever because of the associated joint pain. It was no wonder he was whimpering with pain even in his dazed state or that Joe was becoming increasingly concerned.

There was the threat of potentially fatal dengue haemorrhagic fever or dengue shock syndrome, neither of which they were equipped to treat. There was no intensive care unit in which to treat him if he needed it. Neither was there access to laboratory tests to confirm the initial diagnosis, which was why they would have to rely on this tourniquet test. With more than twenty petechial red spots from broken capillary blood vessels visible per square inch of skin, Joe's hunch was proved right.

There was no part of that diagnosis she found positive. Not only had she missed it, they were going to have a fight on their hands if his condition worsened.

'Okay, we'll let you rest again but you're going to have to sit up and make sure you drink plenty. Emily and I will go and see where Peter got to with that water.' Joe undid the cuff and tried to make him comfortable again before gesturing for Emily to join him outside.

'How did you know it was dengue?' It would probably have been well down her list of possibilities causing the patient so much discomfort and she could've wasted precious time in reaching the same diagnosis.

'I've seen it a few times on my travels. It's a nasty one. The rash and the joint pain are usually the main indicators, along with the more common symptoms.'

'What's the best way to approach this?' She wasn't

afraid to defer to him on this subject since it wasn't something she'd ever come across before.

'We need to keep an eye on him through the night in case his condition worsens. For now the paracetamol and tepid sponging should help control the fever at least, and if need be we can hook up an IV to make sure his fluid levels are balanced. We don't want to give any NSAIDs, such as ibuprofen or aspirin, in case they aggravate the risk of bleeding.'

Peter arrived back to meet them outside the room with the water and cloths. 'Bad news?'

Their faces must've expressed their concerns that a secondary infection could complicate matters beyond their capabilities with the limited medical supplies they had available.

'Dengue.' Joe shared their suspicions with Peter, then went back into the house to break it to the rest of the family, leaving her alone with her stepbrother and an awkward silence.

In the end Emily decided in the spirit of her new bolder persona she should be the one to broach the subject causing the tension. Except she didn't know how to appropriately rephrase, 'I know you're mad at me for getting jiggy with your mate but I literally fancy the pants off him.'

'I really like him. Joe, that is.' She went with inarticulate phrasing in the end.

Peter screwed his eyes tightly shut as though he was still trying to rid himself of the memory. 'I think I got that.'

'I mean, we didn't plan anything but we're, er, enjoying each other's company while we're here.' Her cheeks were burning as she tried to explain her outrageous behaviour to her religious sibling.

'As it was pointed out to me earlier, it's your life, Emily. But I would hate to see you get hurt. I've known Joe a long time. He's a good guy but he's not the commitment type. You've only just come out of a long-term relationship, your only relationship, and I don't want you to think he's the answer to being on your own. He'll be back on his travels in another couple of weeks.'

'So will I. You don't have to worry, I'm going into this with my eyes fully open. I know you're all loved up with Keresi at the minute, but the last thing I want is to be tied to another man.' However this progressed she was under no illusion that she was going home as part of a couple. The most this could ever be was a fling, a temporary arrangement, if that's what they both wanted.

'It's that obvious, huh?' It was refreshing to see her stepbrother take his turn at blushing. This woman clearly meant a lot to him. On the plus side, it took the onus off her and Joe.

'Well, not in the "found half-naked together" sense of obvious, but, yeah, I can tell. Is it serious?'

'We've been hanging out a lot and, yeah, I think I'm in deep.' His bashful smile said as much.

Emily gave him a playful punch on the arm, careful not to spill any of the water he was carrying. 'I'm so happy for you. For us.' She wanted him to understand they were both where they wanted to be in terms of relationships, or non-relationship in her case. The jury was still out on the official classification of her status.

'I haven't decided if I'll be leaving with you at the end of the month. I might stick around a while longer.'

'You do whatever feels right. I can always come back and visit when I need a bro-fix.' She smiled for his benefit, even though her heart broke a little more at the thought of losing him to Yasi permanently. Not that she would begrudge him this island paradise or a chance at happiness. She envied it.

'I haven't made any decision yet.'

'Something tells me you'll find it hard to leave.' She knew she would. If she had the choice between her lonely existence, bound by the rules of her position and the confinement of her office, or the freedom to help people out here with Joe by her side, she knew which one she'd take now.

'All I can do is take each day as it comes.'

'Is that the island motto or something? They should print that on T-shirts and sell them as souvenirs,' she said with a touch of bitterness. It was easier to do that when your days weren't limited to double digits.

He gave a hearty laugh, which did nothing to alleviate this particular case of the green-eyed monster. The clock was ticking on whatever this was with Joe, and she didn't have the luxury of deciding its fate. Peter didn't know how lucky he was. For her the dream would all be over too soon.

With the pressure of time weighing heavily on her mind, she thought of her patient, to whom it mattered most tonight. The next hours would be crucial in determining the severity of his illness and how effectively they'd be able to manage it.

'I should get back to work and take this water in before it reaches room temperature.'

'I'll give you a hand.'

True to his word, Peter helped her to get Nete upright and helped him drink the water, while she sponged him down. It wasn't long before Joe came back to join them and sent at least one temperature in the room soaring back up again.

'Isn't there a drug or something we can give him to counteract this?' Peter quizzed them, as he struggled to keep the lethargic patient upright.

'If only.' There was nothing she wanted more than to be able to give this boy a tablet and fix everything that ailed him. That was the kind of medicine she was used to—diagnosis, treatment, cure. Rare illnesses such as dengue weren't something she came across very often and when they did crop up the patients were invariably referred elsewhere. That wasn't an option out here. Even if they could get him transported to hospital, the journey alone could kill him. Seeing Nete in pain, following his progress right through, somehow made it real and personal. It was down to her and Joe to get him through this and out the other side.

Joe took another temperature reading and shook his head. 'There might be one thing we can try…'

As Emily took a peek at the thermometer she knew they needed to try something more than they were already doing. 'What is it?'

Joe exhaled a hard breath and it was a few heartbeats before he spoke as if he was debating whether or not his idea was even worth sharing. 'I mean, it's not scientifically proven or anything but when I was in India I saw them use the juice from papaya leaves to treat dengue.'

'Papaya leaves?' Although it wouldn't do any harm to try, Emily wasn't convinced that would really make much difference to his condition.

'I know it sounds ridiculous but I did do some follow up research into the properties of papaya leaves after seeing them used. Apparently they are packed with enzymes that are supposed to help clot the blood and normalise platelet count. It's worth a shot, right?' He was the only one offering a blink of hope, no matter how far away it appeared from the current reality of the situation.

'Definitely, but where do we get them and what do we do with them?' It was at times like this she missed the luxury of twenty-four-hour supermarkets and smoothie bars. She was too used to the convenience of modern life, and making simple requests like this without them seem impossible.

'I'm sure someone will know where to find them, then all we have to do is crush them.' Joe made it sound so simple when it scared Emily to put her faith in anything other than conventional medicine. That was probably the beauty of them working together and combining their so very different experiences.

'I know where we can find some. I'll go. I'm sure you can manage without me.' Peter gave a wry smile as he left on his mission. He clearly wasn't about to let go of her embarrassment any time soon but a nod and a wink was better than a frowny face and a half-battered Joe.

The patient gave a soft snore, oblivious to events unfolding all around him. They'd let him sleep through the pain until Joe concocted his marvellous medicine. In the meantime, Emily took the small battery-operated fan she kept in her bag and set it by the bed. Every little bit helped.

'Are things okay with you two, then?' She figured it was safe to ask now the initial awkwardness appeared to have passed.

'Yeah. We're good. You?'

She nodded. They'd known their actions would complicate all manner of things and yet that hadn't mattered at the time. It shouldn't matter now either since they'd addressed Peter's concerns. 'I can't say he's ecstatic about it but he knows where we're coming from. I think he's dodging Cupid's arrows himself at the minute.'

'I would say that little sucker struck his target long ago.' Joe's laugh reached across the bed to her and all the way down to curl her toes. She was already missing that carefree couple of hours they'd had. Who knew when they'd get to spend time together again? Or if it would ever be quite the same now they'd always be on their guard?

'Well, I hope he didn't give you too much of a hard time.'

'Nothing I couldn't handle,' he said, with the sexy smile of a man secure in his own skin. He could look after himself but Emily knew he would never have lifted a hand to do anything against his best friend except in defence. Even then, she suspected, he might've let Peter vent his anger unchecked if it made him feel better.

'There wasn't any blood spilled so I'd call that a win. I wouldn't want to be the cause of any unpleasantness between you.' She was fully aware of the special bond they had and, as far as she could see, the only real friend each of them had. It would be selfish of her to think a holiday fling should mean more to Joe than everything he'd gone through with Peter.

Joe carefully laid the cold cloth he was holding across Nete's forehead and walked around to the side of the bed where she was standing. There was definitely a shift in the atmosphere as he took her hand and turned her to face him, as if by entering her personal space he'd pushed out all the negative space around her and replaced it with crackling sexual energy.

'For the record, it would've been totally worth it.' His voice was a gravelly aphrodisiac, taking her right back to that moment before Peter had interrupted them. She'd been hovering on the brink of something amazing and she knew she wanted to go back there some time soon once they knew their patient was out of danger.

'I'm glad you think so.' Her mouth was suddenly dry and she had to moisten her lips with her tongue before she was able to speak. It hadn't been intended as a provocative action but she didn't miss the flare of desire in Joe's eyes as he watched her. They'd better get a move on with that miracle cure.

'I know so.' He dipped his head and left the ghost of a kiss on her lips; too quick to make a solid physical impact but with enough intention to stop her fretting that their time had already passed. There was still hope they could explore this chemistry if and when the opportunity arose again. Despite all the obstacles, Joe still wanted her and that was the best medicine in the world for her.

Joe hated it that they were pinning everything on this bowl of green mush on his say-so. Perhaps he should have kept it to himself and simply passed this off as an energy drink. That way the consequences of its failure wouldn't rest entirely on his shoulders. If this didn't work, the boy's condition was entirely down to the fates. Best-case scenario, he would recover on his own anyway. Worst-case scenario could lead to organ dysfunction, toxic shock and other life-threatening complications that required hospital intervention. Not two travelling doctors with little more than a first-aid kit.

He crushed the leaves with the wooden pestle and mortar he'd borrowed and ground away his fears before anyone could see them. As he'd watched the medicine men in India do, he squeezed the juice out into a bowl with his bare, clean hands. They didn't dilute the juice with water or add salt or sugar so neither did he, unwilling to take the chance of reducing its benefits.

'We need you to sit up and drink this.'

Peter and Emily took one arm each to help Nete sit up while Joe tilted the bowl to his lips for him to sip at. He hadn't tasted the juice himself but the sight of it and the patient's puckered mouth told him it didn't have the sweet, palatable taste of commercial medicines.

It had taken Peter a good couple of hours to source the papaya leaves for him, during which time he and Emily had managed to set aside their unresolved personal feelings for one another and focus on their patient's recovery. They'd seen a small decrease in his temperature as a result of the course of treatment provided already but not enough to sit back. The fever itself, he knew, could be biphasic, breaking and returning, and any sudden disappearance could be one of the warning signs of dengue haemorrhagic fever, the next critical level of the condition.

'When will we know if this is working?' Nete was understandably anxious for an instant cure for his pain but Joe didn't want to make any definite promises.

'You'll have to keep taking the juice at regular intervals through the night, I'm afraid.' He shot Emily a look of apology too since this was the first time she was hearing the news.

'We're all in for a long night by the sound of it.' Emily threw her hat in the ring to become part of the night watch alongside him.

Peter, on the other hand, already looked dead on his feet after his mad dash across the island, to retrieve the precious foliage. He'd done his part and keeping him here wouldn't serve any real practical purpose.

'I think you could use a few hours' sleep, mate. If you want to grab forty winks while you can, we'll give you a shout if we need your help.'

'I'll be fine,' Peter protested, blinking his eyes open wide.

'The last thing we need is to be another man down because you've overdone it. Now, take the advice of *two* doctors and get some sleep. You can take the next shift. Scoot.' Emily was the one to finally shoo him away so they could concentrate on the one patient they already had.

They'd do that better without the spectre of their indiscretion lingering in the room between them. Peter's reluctance to leave them alone again was proof enough that he hadn't got over it yet, even if they'd decided to leave it behind them until they had time and space to deal with it. Or carry on where they'd left off.

When it came to Emily all his common sense seemed to go out of the window and he could no longer predict his own actions from one minute to the next. Ordinarily he thrived on that level of excitement but tonight's events had shown him just how destructive that lapse in judgement could be. By continuing relations with Emily he was playing a dangerous game but he didn't think it was one he could quit any time soon.

'I don't know how you managed to keep control of an entire regiment. One pig-headed male is more than enough to deal with,' Emily huffed, as she won the battle of wills and common sense with her stepbrother.

To her it was a throwaway comment more about man's inability to admit personal weakness, something he knew a lot about. To him, any reference to his role in the military was a stark reminder of all the people he'd let down when they'd needed him most.

'I'm not sure I did.'

'There's no need for modesty. I'm sure you saved the lives of countless men on the front line and I know you pulled Peter out of a few tight spots.'

The patient was sleeping soundly now between them, dosed with papaya leaf juice and paracetamol and as cool as they could get him for now, so Joe stepped back from the bed for a little more space. He took a seat on the floor in the corner of the room and sipped at the cool water the chief had provided for them. Unfortunately, Emily followed him, apparently determined to carry on this conversation.

He'd probably played a part in saving lives in close-quarter combat. There were fleeting memories of bullet-ridden and shattered men he'd patched up and sent back in Chinooks to the base hospital, who he knew had later recovered from their injuries, but those faded against the vivid images of the last ambush he'd been caught up in.

He'd had to rely on the expertise of other medical personnel through that one when he'd *become* one of the casualties instead of being the one helping them.

'I did what I had to.' Mostly.

He took another sip of water, even the thought of the desert heat and that feeling of powerlessness making his mouth dry. Emily was oblivious to his discomfort, leaning forward, her head resting on her chin, listening intently as though he was telling her a bedtime story and not recounting the horrors of war.

'Do you miss it? I mean, I know Peter found it hard to adjust to civilian life again. I imagine it must be harder still if you were battling to save lives every day and suddenly no longer practising medicine. That must have been a huge departure for you.'

'It wasn't my choice.' The injustice of the situation forced its way to his lips before he could stop the words forming.

Emily cocked her head to one side, no doubt waiting for an explanation. He sighed, resigned to the fact he was going to have to reveal his biggest shame. Worse than that, he'd have to watch her reaction to it. Details of his hearing loss weren't something he often discussed. Generally he didn't stay in company long enough for it to become apparent. Asking people to repeat themselves, or missing snippets of conversation altogether, only became an issue if it was an ongoing problem. He didn't see the need to highlight his weakness and face more discrimination, decisions made on his behalf because of a perceived disability. The only reason he was considering telling her about it now was because she'd been brave enough to face her demons in his presence. Now it was his turn.

He took a deep breath.

'I had to take medical retirement after the IED that killed Batesy and Ste.' He debated whether or not to go as far as spilling his guts over the guilt he felt over the incident but decided against it. No one would ever understand how much his failing had affected him, still affected him, and he didn't expect them to. That was his own personal wallowing pool.

When Emily didn't launch into her usual line of questioning, which he'd expected to draw the information out gradually, he was forced to elaborate.

'The explosion damaged my hearing and the army decided they didn't want to take the chance of having a partially deaf soldier on the front line who couldn't hear the enemy coming.' The irony was that it was the stealth of the insurgents that had done the damage in the first place.

'Couldn't you have continued your medical expertise in one of the hospitals or in some sort of training capacity?'

There had been no gasp of shock as he broke the news. Although he wasn't looking for sympathy, he had expected some sort of emotional reaction. Here he was, spilling a secret so easily to her that usually only came out when circumstances forced it from him, and she was treating it as a minor ailment that could've been remedied with some paperwork shuffling. She should've understood how great the loss of his career had been when she was so tied to her own. If it wasn't for her own medical expertise keeping her afloat in the aftermath of her marriage she might have felt just as lost as he had when he'd first left the army.

'I was a soldier as well as a medic. I belonged in the field, not cooped up in some *safe* place while the rest of my colleagues were risking their lives. That blast stole my career from me and left me half the man I used to be.' There, he'd spelled it out to her in case she was missing the bit about him essentially being worthless to the army.

'It may have felt like that at the time but you're so much

more than the army. You've proved that with the work you've done here, and everywhere else on your travels.'

Joe wasn't sure if he imagined her flinching at the picture he'd painted since she spoke so coolly. Too coolly. Too precisely. Now he thought about it, he hadn't once had to ask her to repeat herself or speak up since they'd first met. She always spoke clearly, facing him, so he could read her lips, even if he couldn't hear her every word.

'You already knew.' The realisation hit him hard. All this time he'd been trying to impress her and she'd probably been aware of his inadequacy all along.

'Sorry?'

'Peter told you why I had to leave the army?'

The blush gave her away even before she confirmed his hunch. 'Only because I thought you were being rude by ignoring me.'

'I get that a lot.' He managed a half-smile at the thought of how riled she must've been at him for Peter to have told her. It was some consolation he hadn't simply been the subject of gossip between them but telling Emily was a big deal for him. It should have been his decision, his privilege to tell her.

'I think that makes us even. My secret for yours.' Emily nudged him, trying to make light of the moment.

It would be easy for him to lose his rag and tell her it was none of her business but she wasn't to blame for his inability to deal with this. No one was, not even Peter. He couldn't hide away from his hearing issue for ever and if he took a leaf out of her book he'd front it out and people would simply have to accept it. The strength of her courage became even more apparent when he thought of shining a spotlight on his insecurity for the whole world to see. Still, he'd share details of his deafness before he'd let anyone in on the events of that fateful day and his responsibility for it.

'How about a pact never to mention either?'

'Done.'

'And in answer to your original question, yes, I do miss it. Not the heat or the injuries my friends suffered, but the excitement and that sense of belonging. I had a role, a reason to be.' He shut his mouth before he said anything more. It wasn't in his nature to take a dip in self-pity, and especially not with spectators. Coming across as a sad sack certainly wasn't going to improve his chances of finishing what he'd started with Emily tonight. He was supposed to be the fun, uncomplicated side of this partnership. A traumatised ex-vet who needed sex to justify his existence probably wouldn't seem as attractive.

'You have a role out here. You're needed here. But I guess that's why you don't stick around. It never gets dull for you if you're always moving from one place to another.' Emily hugged her knees against her chest as she psychoanalysed him. Joe guessed she found that harder to understand than him hiding his disability when stability and security seemed to be what she craved most in her life. Things she would never find with him.

'Exactly. New places, new people get the adrenaline pumping for me.' The closest he came to that without leaving the island was when he and Emily were alone together. That was when he felt most alive, most validated as a person.

Once she left Yasi there would be absolutely no reason for him to stick around.

CHAPTER TEN

'MORNING.' EMILY YAWNED a greeting to Peter and Miriama as she passed them in the hallway. She and Joe had managed to grab a few hours' sleep on a couple of makeshift mattresses close by when they'd volunteered to take over the early morning shift. She thought all was well since she'd been left to wake up in her own time, until she saw that Joe had already vacated his bed.

'Morning.' Peter handed her some lemon tea, its bitter zing guaranteed to wake her up.

She cradled the cup in her hands, letting the comforting warmth spread through her weary body before she took a sip. 'How is Nete?'

'He's a bit brighter today. Joe's with him if you want a professional assessment.'

She trusted Peter's word but she did want to see for herself. An early morning Joe fix might just set her up for the day too.

'Hey,' she said when she saw Joe, thinking how unfair it was that he still looked devastatingly handsome on so little sleep. No doubt she had the world's worst bed hair and panda eyes, while his crumpled clothes and morning stubble simply elevated his hunk status.

'Hi, sleepyhead.' He had the bright eyes and cheerful

demeanour of someone who'd been awake for a while, or had somehow got his hands on a shot of *actual* caffeine.

Either way, she would have preferred to have been included than not. 'You should have woken me.'

'You were sleeping so soundly I hated to disturb you. Besides, you probably wouldn't have heard me above your snoring.' He shared the joke with their patient, who was now sitting up unassisted and laughing at her expense.

'I do not snore!' At least, she didn't think she did, unless a year of sleeping alone had somehow caused it to manifest. She was sure Greg would've told her if it had ever been a problem. He'd never been shy about pointing out her faults and not in such a jokey fashion either. In fact, she could see now that he'd been downright cruel at times, playing on her insecurities until she'd hated herself for not being the woman he'd obviously wanted.

At least now she was beginning to see she wasn't the only one who'd failed at that relationship. If Greg had accepted her as unconditionally as Joe seemed to, there would never have been a need to constantly belittle her. In hindsight that was probably what had made her cling to stability as much as she had. She'd needed something to make her feel safe and secure, with her husband constantly undermining her. Now that she'd moved on, found herself at peace with who she was, she didn't intend to return to that dark, uncertain place.

'I'm only messing with you. You needed the rest. I'm used to getting by on very little sleep.'

She faked a smile as he reminded her of their contrasting lifestyles. He was always going to be the drifter, content to take life one day at a time, when all she wanted was her own bed and job security. If she was realistic they'd probably only made a connection because they'd been thrown together on this tiny island and she didn't want to be with another man for all the wrong reasons.

'So, how are we getting on?' She glanced over the readings Peter had jotted down during the night, keeping track of his progress.

'Fever's broken, fluid intake is steady, as is urine output, and he's hungry, which is always a good sign.' Relief was etched all over Joe's smiling face, even though he hadn't once given in to panic during their stint last night.

'I'm so glad to hear that.' At times it had been touch-and-go whether or not they'd get to this apparent recovery phase. They'd sweated right along with the patient through every painful stage of the illness. Not that it was over yet, but Joe was right, the outcome was looking more favourable now than it had done at certain low points of the night. It had been a long shift and she had a new-found respect for hospital workers for whom the long hours and clean-up were simply part of the job. All worth it, though, if it meant the worst had passed.

'I think it's safe for us to nip home and get freshened up, if Peter and Miriama don't mind taking over here a bit longer?' Joe was able to put his question directly to the other volunteers as they entered the room on cue.

'No problem at all,' Miriama assured them both.

Emily would never dream of taking advantage but even a bucket of cold water seemed like a luxury right now to someone in last night's clothes who'd spent most of the last twelve hours mopping fevered brows and vomit.

'Er...the chief might have other ideas for you.'

Peter interrupted her immediate plans with a worrying comment. If there was some sort of ceremony to celebrate renewed health, Emily hoped she could still grab five minutes' privacy for a wash and change of clothes.

'We won't be long. Tell him we'll be back in our rightful places in no time at all.' Joe added his support to her cause, clearly with the same need to feel human again. They couldn't possibly be taken seriously as medical professionals dressed in wrinkled date-night clothes as if they'd just stumbled in from a club.

'Yeah, yeah, you can still go and get changed. I mean he has plans for the rest of your day. He wants to throw a beach picnic in your honour for saving his son.'

'That sounds lovely.'

'There's really no need. Besides, we're not completely out of the woods yet.' Joe talked over her acceptance with some uncharacteristic reluctance to take part on one of the spontaneous gatherings.

Emily pouted as the menfolk battled to plan her day for her. 'I haven't seen the beach since the day I arrived. You're the one who's always telling me to chill, take time out for me and stop stressing about deserting my post. Or is that only when it suits you?'

This was coming close to their first real argument, but while she was bracing herself for a showdown, Joe clenched his jaw and bit back whatever retort was on his tongue.

'He really wants to show you his gratitude and we can hold the fort for you here until you get back. You both need the break.' Peter was so insistent it would be a shame to send him back to the chief with bad news.

'We'd love to, wouldn't we, Joe?' She pushed her luck that tiny bit further. Once he had time to think about it he'd see some fresh air, a paddle in the sea and a picnic lunch might be the best medicine to revitalise two weary medics.

Neither his scowl nor his grunt were in keeping with that theory but he didn't object verbally and she took that as an uneasy acceptance. A complete role reversal from their usual power play. This time she was the one pushing him to try something different. Emily understood his concerns but the others were well versed in the treatment to give in their absence. Bar chartering a private plane to get their patient to a hospital, there was little more any of them could do if his condition worsened. The next time this illness struck the island it was entirely possible Miriama would be the only person here to treat it anyway. At least, that's how Emily justified this time out to herself.

It wasn't long before she and Joe were heading back to get ready for their lunch date, regardless of his reluctance to join the 'keep calm and carry on' party.

'You shouldn't have done that.'

'Why not? I think we earned a break. Anyway, aren't you the one always reminding me how much I'll offend people by not participating in these things? It's lunch, not a mutiny. I'm still coming back to resume my doctor duties once I've been fed. It might not be up to the culinary standards of your beans on toast feast but I'm hungry, sleep-deprived and generally in need of some me time. That might sound selfish but I think a less grouchy me will benefit everyone in the long run. We'll be back before you know it.'

She could see why he was so concerned about leaving their patient but she genuinely believed Nete was over the worst of it and they wouldn't be gone for too long. It was never going to be a continuation of their ruined date with so many others in attendance but it would do them good to get out of there for a while.

'That won't be as soon as you think.'

'What makes you say that?'

'Their idea of a beach picnic is on another island. It's a beautiful place but not very practical for getting back to a patient in the event of an emergency.'

'Why on earth didn't you tell me?' She wanted to scream at him for standing back while she'd blathered on about what *she* needed. If she'd known it would come at the possible cost of their patient's welfare she never would've pursued this.

He shrugged, increasing the chances of her giving those shoulders a shake herself. 'You didn't give me much of a chance. You seemed so determined to accept and I didn't want to worry the others unnecessarily.'

But it was apparently okay to make her more anxious by keeping the details to himself until it was too late to do anything. She ground her teeth, stifling her exasperation.

'Now what do we do?' She'd landed them in a tricky situation, caught between offending the chief and potentially jeopardising his son's health.

'Now we go and put on our beach clothes and graciously accept our host's invitation. We'll leave instructions for the treatment we would've carried out ourselves and keep our fingers crossed this works out.' His smile didn't travel any further than his lips and Emily knew it was only to placate her.

She'd messed up but something told her Joe would be the one to accept responsibility should the worst happen.

So much for acting spontaneously. It never ended well for her.

CHAPTER ELEVEN

AFTER HER LONGED-FOR freshen-up, Emily decided to go with the outfit she'd worn when she'd first arrived on the island. The maxi-dress wasn't any more practical than the last time but it was comfortable and put her back in holiday mode. The deed was done, they were leaving the island, so she may as well enjoy it.

She met up with Joe where they'd had that initial encounter at the water's edge, although there were a few more island greeters this time. He was wearing the same outfit as he had that day too, which she put down to their strong connection—or karma. Or the distinct lack of wardrobe choices available to them on the island.

At least he was smiling properly this time as he walked towards her. 'I've left the locum doctors with enough papaya leaves to paper the room with and a promise we'll be back before nightfall.'

'I'm sure everything will be fine.' She was trying to convince herself since it was too late to undo her mistake without causing panic.

They joined the small band of locals weighed down with armfuls of food for their day out. It seemed an age since she'd landed here with no knowledge of what she'd been getting herself into. Only a few days later she had friends who wanted to throw her a celebratory lunch, and

a man who seemed to like her. If they ever found themselves alone again they might actually get to explore what
that meant.

'You look beautiful, by the way,' he said, and pressed
a kiss to her cheek, drawing a few giggles from the kids
in the assembled crowd.

'I'm actually quite excited about this.' She meant about
their island hopping but it worked for Joe kisses too. No
matter how chaste, or not, the second his lips touched her
she was on fire with desire for him. Sooner or later she
was going to have to let it burn itself out or extinguish the
flames altogether. In the end there would be nothing but
ashes left anyway and a memory of what could have been.

'So are they.' He nodded in the direction of their happy
travelling companions who'd come together in their honour. Those who could afford to take some time out of their
busy day, at least. She and Joe really were very privileged
to have such generosity bestowed on them when resources
were so limited out here. That kind of respect and appreciation meant more to her than monetary bonuses or
finishing work on time every night. There was a definite
attraction to the laid-back lifestyle out here that wasn't
just about her co-worker.

'Where is this place we're going to?' Her adventurous
spirit hadn't completely run away with her. On seeing
their mode of transport, a couple of dinghies that looked
as though they'd been washed ashore during the last hurri-
cane, she was suddenly keen to remain within swimming
distance of Yasi. They definitely weren't in any condition
to go out on the open sea but the chief was beaming with
so much pride as he ushered them on board he could've
been giving them a tour of the islands on his private yacht.

'Not too far. There's a small uninhabited island just
across the bay.'

'A *real* desert island?' That was something she'd only

seen in the movies, usually involving starving cast-aways driven mad by heatstroke and loneliness. It wasn't a thought she relished on her own but with food and company, and the means to leave again, she knew it could turn out to be one of the highlights of her trip. Once she stopped imagining falling overboard and being stranded with nothing to eat but coconuts, she was able to focus on the merits of such a setting. Sand, sea and a sexy side-kick were the makings of a very different kind of film.

They all piled into the two boats, with the majority of the islanders in one dinghy, and Emily, Joe, the chief and the food in the other. This was obviously a treat for everyone and not something they did on a whim, given the level of excitement as the engine spluttered into life. It seemed this was the Yasi equivalent of first class and she should feel honoured, not clutching the side of the boat and praying.

'Stop worrying.' Joe prised her fingers loose and set her hand back in her lap, with his resting on top.

She closed her eyes and did her best not to imagine a watery grave as he gave her hand a reassuring squeeze, and she knew he'd keep her safe no matter what. The wind whipped through her hair, blowing away her residual fears as they skimmed the waves towards sanctuary. It was easy to imagine this was all an illusion created by her lack of sleep but the sea spray splashed her face, reminding her this *was* real even when it seemed too fantastic to be true. Nonetheless, when they cut the engine and came ashore, she had to restrain herself from jumping overboard and kissing the sandy ground. She took off her sandals as Joe helped her off the boat so her footprints were the first to mark the untouched beach.

Not for the first time she wished she'd brought a camera to document her travels. At the time of leaving England she'd been so eager to distance herself from reality she'd left all traces of the modern world behind her, including her phone. There was something so symbolic about that single track of footprints in the sand, marking her bold journey into the unknown, she'd never forget it.

When she reached a line of trees and looked back to see Joe making his way across the beach, leaving a second set of prints alongside hers, it didn't lessen the powerful image. He'd been very much a part of this adventure with her, coaxing this slightly braver Emily to explore beautiful new vistas. She didn't want to leave any of it behind in case she forgot it, or vice versa. Everything here had made such an impact on her for the better and she hoped she'd made some sort of lasting impression on Yasi, on Joe. It didn't seem fair to be falling so heavily for someone if she turned out to be nothing more than a side note in his travel journal.

She knew that's what was happening when she was so conflicted about what she wanted from this trip and from him. If he hadn't already claimed a piece of her heart she wouldn't be overanalysing every move about how it would affect her and simply go with her natural urges. It almost didn't matter if they took that next step together when the damage had already been done. He'd breached her defences and left her vulnerable.

'It's beautiful here.' She tried to keep upbeat even though the shock of her discovery was enough to bring her to tears. The sky might be bluer than she thought naturally possible, the white sand warm under her feet, but she was still a fool when it came to men.

Joe had warned her off against getting into anything she couldn't handle but she'd convinced herself she was tough enough to deal with whatever happened. Now, after little more than a few snatched kisses, she knew her heart had lied to her. It hadn't been broken beyond all repair after Greg, or why else would it ache so much for another man?

'I've been here a few times. It's a good spot to unwind. Mind you, there's work to be done if we're going to eat any time soon.' He pointed down at the rest of the islanders coming ashore in single file, carrying the food supplies, like an army of ants.

'I'm so sorry. I was so pleased to get here I didn't even think about helping to unload the boats.' She must seem so shallow and privileged to everyone else, used to mucking in and doing their bit as part of the community. She'd been living alone too long, concerned with nothing but her own survival until now.

'It's okay. Everyone is assigned jobs to do. Ours is to collect palm leaves.'

'Palm leaves? That's not lunch, is it?'

His laughter calmed her new food fears before they fully formed. 'No. They're used for weaving into plates for the food and as a makeshift picnic table. It means there's no litter left behind when we're finished here.'

They carried out their new duties in silence, with Joe cutting the leaves while she gathered them. She should have known this would be more than the tartan rug and plastic accessories she was used to in a basket. Then again, lunch here was bound to be more than a soggy sandwich and a packet of crisps. Even a simple picnic turned into something exotic and exciting when it was on one of these islands.

Never more so than when she saw how they were preparing the food. The *lovo*, as Joe explained to her, was an oven built in the sand. Emily watched with fascination as the men set a fire in the small pit and stacked rocks on top until they were hot enough to cook the food on. Banana leaves were then placed on top as insulation to keep the stones hot and moisture in the food while it cooked.

Emily sat with several of the women and children plaiting the palm fronds into primitive mats for the food and Joe waded out into the water with the others for a spot of net fishing. Part of her wished he was still wearing the translucent white shirt from yesterday as his wet clothes clung to him so she could have her very own Mr Darcy moment. At least she had first-hand experience of every solid inch of that torso to enable her imagination to bypass that dark perv-proof fabric. She fanned herself with one of the long palm fronds as he strode from the sea, water sluicing from his body as if he'd just walked out of a dream. An erotic fantasy she'd take back to keep her warm at night in her luxurious, but empty, bed.

'You'll be feasting today,' he promised her as they brought their catch in. Soldier, medic, lumberjack, fisherman—there seemed no end to his talents, or else he never grew tired of acquiring them.

She supposed she'd managed to add mat weaver and painter to her CV over the course of a couple of days too. That was the thing about the island, a person never seemed to be pigeonholed into one area of their life. It was all about working together and sharing jobs and skills to make sure the traditions never died out. One more thing she would miss when she returned home. Little wonder Joe couldn't see himself tied to a desk somewhere, shuffling paperwork, after trying his hand at so many new experiences. She wasn't looking forward to it herself after roaming free in the big wide world beyond her office walls.

It took a couple of hours for the food to cook, during which time she managed to cobble together a couple of flat mats to keep their lunch sand-proof. She was starting to see why the time frame for this meal had been such an issue for Joe. It wasn't the forty-five-minute lunch break she'd been expecting either, but it was worth it when the banana leaves were lifted off to reveal the feast Joe had promised her.

As well as the *dalo* and cassava root vegetables she'd become accustomed to, today saw the addition of fresh fish and crab. It tasted all the better knowing Joe had provided it for her.

'At least I know I won't starve if we get shipwrecked here,' she said, scooping up another piece of crab meat with her fingers.

'I might not be perfect but I'll always make sure you're looked after.' He grinned and helped himself to another chunk of fish, oblivious to the thrill he'd given her with a few simple words.

A whoosh of something powerful shot through her veins, immediately revitalising her previously weary body. It was only a figure of speech but deep down she knew that promise was true. Joe was the only man other than her stepbrother she could trust not to hurt her. Her soft heart was trying to convince her she should be with him even if a few days together was all that was on offer. There was a chance she'd regret missing out on that time more than walking away from him at the end of this trip.

It didn't take long to clear away the evidence of their beach invasion and, lovely though it was, she was getting kind of antsy to return to Yasi. Once they'd checked in on their patient and made sure there was no medical emergency, she and Joe might actually get some privacy. If it took barricading the clinic door with the furniture she was willing to do it if it meant getting to explore the next level with him. Although she wasn't sure if that would make it better or worse when the time came to leave.

She and Joe made their way to the boat they'd arrived in, only to find the chief barring their way. 'I want to thank you for helping my son.'

'You already did that. This was lovely.' Every future

picnic was going to be held up to this standard. A blanket on wet grass with a basket full of cold cuts simply wasn't going to cut it any more when it would be up against an afternoon on a desert island with present company.

They tried again to step on board but the chief sidestepped in front of them again. 'We want to give you a gift. Some time alone. You can keep the boat until you're ready to return to Yasi. There is enough room in this one for all of us.'

'That's really not necessary—'

'We couldn't ask you to do that—'

They stumbled over each other's words in their hurry to get back on the boat. It was a lovely gesture that would've been very welcome in other circumstances but this gift of time didn't stop the clock elsewhere.

'It's very, very kind of you but we must see to your son.' Her heart was in her throat as she dared to refuse his generosity but she knew how anxious Joe had been about coming out here in the first place. She didn't want to prolong his agony, or have him more ticked off at her if she could help it. Their fragile relationship would splinter completely if it became the reason a patient had suffered.

The chief held his hand up. 'I insist.'

His authority dictated they comply or run the risk of upsetting the entire tribe by declining this huge privilege bestowed on them. She was going to leave the next move up to Joe since he knew them better than she did and she didn't want to be the one to make the final call.

The rest of the group were watching them anxiously and he could see Emily's silent plea for help in her wide eyes. As doctors they both wanted to do what was best for their patient but as a seasoned traveller he understood the importance of maintaining good relations with their hosts. To his knowledge, he, Peter and Emily had been the first

Westerners to ever set foot on this island owned by the Yasi-based tribe. It was a greater honour still for them to be offered use of their only transport for his and Emily's enjoyment. They were a conservative race when it came to personal relationships, especially outside marriage, but they were clearly giving them some space to be together without any interference, something he would've grabbed with both hands last night.

Now, going against everything he'd worked so hard to avoid, he was making decisions that could affect so many people. It was going to be up to him to get Emily back to Yasi in one piece, without upsetting anyone and making sure it was done in a timely fashion to prevent any further medical emergencies. He took a deep breath and girded himself for the challenge.

'We'll make sure we're back before sunset.'

He could already feel Emily's gaze burning into the back of his head so he did what any man would do and pretended not to notice. She was polite enough to wait until company was out of earshot before saying anything.

'I hope you know how to get us home. I'm putting all my faith in you,' she said, without taking her eyes off the dinghy sailing away, now full to capacity.

Dread settled in the pit of his stomach. That's what he was afraid of. It was one thing puttering out here on his own but quite another when he was responsible for Emily too. One could never plan for any unexpected catastrophes but that didn't mean you weren't left carrying the resulting guilt for the rest of your life. He was becoming too emotionally attached to these people being continually left in his charge and soon he was going to have to think about moving on.

If things weren't so complicated he would've used this time to his advantage to seduce Emily. The setting, if not the current mood, was the ideal place for them to finally consummate this attraction. Unfortunately, sex wasn't the only thing on his mind. It was having to wrestle with the dangers of the open water and the potential consequences of their absence on Yasi for prominence. For now they'd simply have to wait this out until an acceptable amount of time had passed to pacify their friends.

'Don't worry, I've done this before.' Although it was usually out of a necessity to have some space to himself rather than with enforced company.

'Oh. You mean you and the chief have some sort of understanding where he'll help you kidnap unsuspecting female tourists so you can hold them hostage here until you get your wicked way with them?' Emily folded her arms across her chest as she mocked him, stretching the light fabric of her dress taut across her bust and really not helping to take Joe's mind off the idea of seduction.

'Yeah. You got a problem with that?' They exchanged cheesy grins as their sense of humour thankfully took over from that initial urge to panic.

Emily laughed and shook her head. 'Nope. Except maybe next time you could give me some warning.'

'You're right. The timing was a little off on this one. In future I'll make sure we're better organised.' His mind flitted towards a day here together with no worries dragging them back to civilisation. They certainly wouldn't be standing here, fully dressed, counting the minutes until they could leave.

The sound of the waves lapping at their feet punctuated the sudden silence between them as what-might-have-beens stole away any further chat. It would be selfish of them to act on impulse now and get lost in each other. One taste of paradise and he knew he'd never want to leave.

With one quick movement he stripped off his shirt and his shorts to wade out into the water in nothing but his boxers. He needed to cool off.

'What are you doing?'

'Going for a swim. Come on in. The water's lovely.' He lay on his back, making small circles with his hands in the sea to keep him afloat, tempted to let the gentle current carry him away.

Emily dipped a toe in the water and stepped back again. 'Are there sharks in there?'

'I haven't seen any but they're not likely to come this close to the shore anyway.' He flicked his fingers, soaking her with spray.

She walked forward until the sea was swirling around her feet and lifting the hem of her dress. Joe held his breath as she revealed every sensual curve of her figure. It barely mattered she was wearing a pretty pink bikini beneath, she may as well have been naked the way his body was responding. She tossed the dress onto the sand and slowly waded out towards him.

Joe spluttered as water covered his face and filled his nostrils. He gulped a mouthful as he struggled to stand upright. He'd been so engrossed in the sight of her stripping off he'd forgotten he needed to work to stay afloat.

'You okay?'

He could hear the flicker of amusement in her voice even though he couldn't see her clearly as he scrubbed the water from his eyes. 'Sure. I think I just forgot to breathe there for a second.'

'How come?' Emily was a little breathy, treading water deeper out into the sea.

Joe swam out to meet her, gravitating towards her like she was his life raft in raging stormy seas. They faced each other, only their heads bobbing on the surface of the water, and he knew he couldn't lie. Either to her or himself.

'Because you're so beautiful.'

Emily immediately cast her eyes down, reluctant to

accept the truth of his compliment. If she wasn't going to listen to him then he was simply going to have to show her. He waded closer and captured her mouth with his, the salty and sweet taste of her lips a feast for his senses.

She wound her arms around his neck and he was happy to anchor her legs around his waist and take her weight. In fact, with her body pressed tightly to his, if they sank to the bottom of the sea and drowned he'd die happy. Denying themselves any longer when everyone already assumed they were together seemed futile, and by giving in to his urges he was finally able to breathe again. It seemed as though he'd been holding his breath since last night, waiting for permission to exhale, and Emily had granted him that the second she'd kissed him back.

There was a flash of light and it took a while for him to figure out it was coming from above and wasn't fireworks going off in his head. He opened his eyes to see clouds rolling in, the sky now a palette of murky greys and purples. A rumble sounded in the distance, just after a charge of electricity that seemed to reach up to the heavens.

'We need to get back to the beach and find shelter.'

'Hmm?' Emily was still nuzzling into him, oblivious to the danger around them, which was either a sign of how far she'd come or how great a kisser he was to make her overcome her natural worry state.

'There's. A. Storm. Coming.' It was difficult to get the sentence out when she insisted on kissing him between words and scrambling his brain. In the end he simply carried her ashore, still clinging to him like a limpet on the rocks. Not that he was complaining. It simply made it harder for him to care what was going on out there too.

He laid her down on the sand but she refused to release her hold, bringing him down with her. Making love to Emily here, with the waves drifting in and out between their naked bodies, was the stuff of fantasies but tropical storms came in hard and fast. That wasn't how he wanted their first sexual encounter to go just because they were in a race against the elements.

Another roar of thunder reverberated around them then the rain came down in sheets and poured cold water on their ardour. Emily shrieked and jumped to her feet.

'I did try to tell you,' he said, rolling onto his back to let the rain cool his fevered skin.

'What will we do?' Emily was already back in panic mode, grabbing up her clothes and looking to him for answers.

Joe donned his shorts and T-shirt with more urgency as the gap between the flashes of light and crashes of thunder became ever smaller. The storm was coming closer… the rain was reaching saturation point. If they didn't get struck by lightning first, their cold, wet clothes sticking to their bodies might lead to pneumonia. They needed to get somewhere that would shelter them from the elements and keep them safe and dry.

'I know somewhere.' He grabbed her hand and made a dash for higher ground. There was a recess cut into the rocks that he knew from experience would provide everything they needed until this storm passed. His secret until now.

They clambered up the boulders in the rain and Joe kept hold of Emily's hand until they made it to the rocky hidey-hole in case she slipped in her no-longer-practical sandals. It was dark inside but at least it was dry.

Emily was watching the storm from the entrance, her shoulders shaking from the cold.

'I'll start a fire to get us warmed up.' He wasn't as eager to have a ringside seat for the fireworks. Loud noises and bright lights weren't as attractive to him as they once might have been.

'How do you propose to do that?' Apparently man creating fire was more interesting than nature's fury as she turned her attention back to him.

'I could sit here half the night trying to get a spark from rubbing a couple of pieces of wood together, or we could just use these.' He was almost sorry to disappoint her with the kindling and box of matches he'd left after his last visit here instead of showing off his caveman skills. Modern fire-making methods were quicker but they weren't as manly as starting one from little more than sticks and friction.

'Wait, is this your *actual* man cave?' She said it as though it was something he should be ashamed of but this place had been his salvation at times, not merely some whimsical notion of reliving his youth.

'Sometimes a guy needs a little time out.' He shrugged it off. It was difficult to explain his need for time out now and again, away from even the small population of Yasi.

This retreat enabled him to maintain a physical and emotional distance when he was in danger of getting too close to the people he was working alongside. By bringing Emily here with him, he'd totally screwed with that idea. Now there was nothing keeping his heart out of matters. He was past the point of no return and the damage was done. There was no way he was going to walk away from this without collecting a new battle scar.

He hadn't even told Peter, his oldest friend, about this place. Peter, who, up until a few days ago, had been the closest person in his life, the only one keeping him out here. Somehow Emily had crept in and hijacked his affection. Why else would he be holed up here with her instead of doing his job back on Yasi?

He got to work setting the fire and Emily came to kneel beside him. 'You know, if this trip has taught me anything it's that it's more fun being around people than sitting moping on your own.'

'I spend plenty of time in company, have made acquaintances all around the world. I'm simply happier in my own company.' That wasn't necessarily true. *Safer* was the word he'd been searching for but he didn't want to get into that with Emily and have to explain why he didn't get involved with people. That meant sharing the most painful part of his life with her and publicly owning the part he'd played in the deaths of his friends. Something he'd never done with anyone.

'Would you prefer it if I left you alone?' Emily made a half-hearted attempt to leave but they both knew she wasn't going anywhere. Neither of them were until this storm had passed and it was safe for them to take the boat out again. Matters outside this cave were completely beyond their control.

'No.' He stood up to block her exit. 'I want you here with me.'

He meant it in every sense. He wanted her company, to share this space, and most of all to help him forget everything going on in the outside world. This was their time together when they were free to relax and be themselves, without any outside influence bursting their bubble.

Emily shivered as he reached for her.

'You know, it's going to take a while for this place to heat up. We should really get out of these wet clothes.'

He slipped one strap of Emily's dress over her shoulder, then the other, and watched the garment pool at her feet. She stood proudly before him, making no move to cover the rest of her body from view. In fact, she was already reaching up to undo her bikini top.

'I've heard the best way to fight hypothermia is to share body heat.'

'I've heard that theory.' He peeled off his T-shirt, eager to put it to the test.

Emily slowly and silently removed the last of her

clothes and time stood still for Joe. She was a goddess with a body worthy of being immortalised in marble to epitomise the beauty of woman. Her soft curves and perfect proportions deserved love sonnets written in her honour but he wasn't a sculptor or a poet. All he had to offer her was himself. So he unwrapped her gift as quickly as he could.

There was something very primitive about standing in a cave with a naked woman and his body responded accordingly. Thankfully his brain was still capable of making some of his decisions. If this was to be the only private time they were to have together, he wanted it to be truly memorable for both of them. They needed more than a frantic coupling on a cold floor.

He reached out to brush her wet hair from her shoulders and felt her tremble beneath his fingers.

'Are you still cold?' The blood pounding through his body had warmed him from the inside out so he'd assumed the same was true for her. He was relieved when she shook her head or else he really would have to start trying to get heat back into her body.

'Nervous.'

Her answer was full of her characteristic honesty. It didn't take a genius to work out he was probably the first man she'd done this with since her husband. Joe ignored all the warning signs flashing in his head about what that meant and accepted it as his privilege, not his downfall.

'There's no need. I won't do anything to hurt you.' All he wanted to do was please her, love her, make her feel as special as she deserved. He was going to be the one hurting when this fantasy ended. Emily would go home and probably find a new love, whereas he knew he'd never be this open again. She'd stolen a piece of his heart he'd never intended to give to anyone and would never, ever get it back.

It was his turn to tremble at the enormity of the revelation. They didn't have a future together when she couldn't rely on him to keep her safe when she needed him most. He would only let her down and he couldn't bear to disappoint her or, worse, face the agony of losing her because of his actions. He was in love with Emily but he couldn't tell her, couldn't do anything about it other than show her.

CHAPTER TWELVE

THERE WAS SOMETHING different about kissing a woman he was in love with. Something familiar, as if he'd found a missing part of himself, yet with an element of danger attached. He was used to living life on the edge but for once he was actually afraid of what was going to happen to him at the end of this. There was no stopping this now when the momentum was carrying him ever forward into new territory, but that didn't mean he wasn't going to get hurt somewhere along the line.

There were reasons he didn't get close to people and falling in love was probably the worst thing he could've done. It made him weak, susceptible to more heartache. Before going to the army he'd been too young to get serious with a girl, too single-minded about his career. After his retirement the layers of guilt and self-pity had been too dense for anyone to fight through them to reach his heart. Somehow Emily had found a path straight to that vulnerable spot and it was too late to plug that hole in his defences now.

He'd spent too long running from any form of affection, pre-empting the possibility when there was a chance he'd have his insides ripped apart again. The woman he loved was giving herself to him and now there was nowhere left to run. No reason to run. Any other man wouldn't think twice about letting this play out and enjoy this experience, instead of fearing it. He wanted to be that man, for himself and for Emily, and listen to his heart instead of his head for once. They both deserved a bit of honesty in their feelings for each other, even if they couldn't find the words to express it. He would deal with the consequences later. They couldn't be any more painful than ending this here and not knowing what they could've had. Even for the briefest time.

He could feel goosebumps on her skin under his fingers; the hard points of her nipples pressing against his chest. There was no denying she was as turned on as he was but she was still tense. It was his job, his pleasure to help her relax and enjoy this time with him.

He already knew how responsive she was to his touch so he cupped her breast in his hand and rolled her tight nipple between his finger and thumb. Her gasp of pleasure strengthened his resolve, and his erection. Soon they'd be so consumed with need and lust that nothing else would matter except coming together, and that's exactly how he wanted it.

He wrapped his lips around that sensitive pink nub, teased her with the tip of his tongue to claim his breathy reward. She clung to his shoulders, her nails digging further into his skin with every lap of his tongue. The sharp pain was worth it to see the ecstasy on her face and feel the tension leave her body. It was addictive.

He slid his hand down between her legs and into her wet heat. She was ready for him, her body trembling from need now with every stroke.

'What about protection?' Emily gasped as he lowered her to the floor.

Joe scrabbled for his shorts and pulled a condom from his pocket.

'I always carry one. They're an essential part of a survival kit. You can use them for carrying water and keeping tinder dry.' He didn't want her to think sex was nothing special to him, something he took for granted. Tonight it was everything.

'I think we should probably go down the traditional route and use them as they were intended.' She giggled and took the packet from him to rip it open.

Joe sheathed himself and settled himself between her thighs, slightly nervous himself now since they'd been building toward this moment for so long. Emily lifted her head and kissed him, bringing him back down to the ground with her. Sliding into her, forging their two bodies together was the most natural thing in the world. Nothing was ever going to come close to replacing this feeling of complete happiness. Part of him didn't think he deserved it, while another part never wanted it to end.

He moved slowly inside her, each second of her tight heat a gift he intended to treasure.

He loved her. He couldn't have her. The unfairness of it all drove him to find his peace, every thrust inside her bringing him closer to finding it. She was his sanctuary and he wanted to be hers too. Her body rocked against his, rising and falling in perfect time with him, climbing towards that peak. Every bite of her lip, every moan, every clench and release of her internal muscles charted her journey and Joe wanted to be the one to help her reach that final destination. He braced himself on the cold, hard floor, not caring about anything except watching that bliss play out over her features, and slammed into her again. Emily cried out, clutched him closer and he felt her break apart beneath him. Only then did he give in to his own climax, the primal roar of his release echoing around the walls.

There was a lump in his throat as he looked down at Emily, so beautifully serene beneath him. If he were a different person, in a different life, they could've had this every day. Instead, all they had was until the end of this storm. For both their sakes there was no choice but to let his love die with the embers of the fire. Forever wasn't an option.

Emily lay quietly while Joe spooned in behind her, afraid to speak in case she burst into tears and ruined the mood. This was a monumental moment for her, though she hadn't realised until just now. She had finally moved on from Greg, from her marriage, in the most spectacular fashion—by giving herself completely to someone else. She'd held nothing back here with Joe and perhaps for the first time in her life had truly been at peace, with herself, with him and with what they were doing. Hidden away here, they no longer had to be concerned about outside influences. For this snapshot in time they were able to be true to themselves and each other. When insecurities and obstacles were stripped away they were simply two people who had a very special connection. One that had sparked to life and delivered more than she'd ever dreamed of.

This had been more than sex, even though that was all it ever *could* be. It didn't matter how great they were together or how they felt about each other because it wasn't going to last. This was probably the last time she would ever feel complete happiness because when this was over she'd have to return to her world of playing it safe. It was the only way she could survive.

Joe snuggled into her neck, his warmth reminding her he was still hers for now. She closed her eyes and clung to the thick forearm wrapped around her waist. It wouldn't do any harm to let the fantasy go on a little longer. After all, she was good at this pretending lark.

Emily was jolted from a peaceful slumber by a shout and Joe thrashing on the ground beside her. He tossed and turned, mumbling incoherently as he battled some un-known force in his sleep. She couldn't see his face as it was dark outside and the fire barely more than a glow. It was chilly now they didn't have the heat of passion keep-ing them warm.

She pulled on her now dry clothes and knelt to add more kindling to the fire. A smile played on her lips as she hugged her knees, watching the embers catch and res-urrect the flames. It was representative of what Joe had done for her—taking her dying heart and sparking it back to life. She knew he felt it too, and she'd be lying if she said she wasn't hoping they could do this again. Okay, a long-term relationship might not be viable, given his life-style, but he was a traveller and there was no reason he couldn't add England to his list of places to visit. Right now hooking up a couple of times a year seemed prefer-able to never having this again.

Another flash of lightning illuminated the cave, the crack of thunder ripping through the air after it. Joe was sitting upright, naked, panting and sweating. He was star-ing off into the distance almost in a trance, his face a mask of utter terror. This was more than a nightmare, he was living this horror right here and now. She moved slowly to his side and rested her hand on his arm, his skin clammy beneath her touch.

'Joe? It's all right. You're here with me.' She tried not to spook him but gently coax him back into the present.

He turned his head slowly towards her but he wasn't really focusing.

'It's me, Emily.' She took a risk by pressing her lips to his. In his current agitated state there was a possibility he'd lash out but she hoped the bond they had was special enough to bring him back to her.

It took a few seconds but he did finally respond, kissing her with a hunger that could only come from the Joe she knew.

'How come you're dressed?' he asked, apparently now wide awake and aware of his surroundings.

'It got cold and look how late it is.' She handed him his own clothes, pity though it was to have him cover up.

'I guess we're here for the night.'

The storm had struck again and Emily saw him flinch, the sight and sounds clearly part of whatever was bothering him.

'That was some bad dream you were having. I was getting worried I wouldn't be able to pull you out of it.'

'I didn't hurt you, did I?' The scowl on his face was more out of concern for her than himself and she guessed this wasn't the first time it had happened.

'No. A lot of shouting and tossing and turning but you didn't lash out.'

'Good.' That seemed enough reassurance for him but that sort of sleep disruption shouldn't be taken lightly. He could do himself serious damage in that trance state in an unfamiliar place, not to mention the exhaustion and lack of concentration that could result from lack of proper sleep—two things that could impair his judgement when it came to treating his own patients.

'Does it happen a lot?' It was in her nature to be inquisitive when it came to people's well-being and Joe was no exception, regardless of his reluctance to talk about it. Doctors often made the worst patients, refusing to accept they were human and fallible just like everyone else.

'Every now and then.' He pulled on his T-shirt so she wasn't able to read his expression. She guessed it happened more than he was prepared to admit since he'd been so quick to move into the clinic on his own.

'Afghanistan?' She took a stab in the dark. By all accounts from her parents it had taken Peter some time to readjust after everything he'd witnessed out there, along with medication, counselling and his faith. Things she was pretty sure Joe hadn't availed himself of since leaving the army. He was too stubborn and tirelessly independent to turn to anyone for help.

'There are a few things that can take me back there in a heartbeat. The senses get a little messed up after being on high alert for so long. One loud bang, a flash of light and I'm back in that tank, helpless, powerless. The mind can play cruel tricks on you when you least expect it.'

'But it's over. I know what happened must've been terrible for all of you but that life is in the past. You still have a future.' With or without her. As long as he was running away from dealing with this he was never going to have the life he deserved—in one place surrounded by people who loved him.

'Batesy and Ste don't. I was the medic, the one who was supposed to be there to save them. I failed to do the one thing I was trained to do. It's my fault they're not here today with their families. How can I expect anyone to rely on me when I can't even trust myself to do the right thing? I mean, the chief's son is lying sick back on Yasi and I'm here, carrying on as if we're on a dirty weekend away.' He wasn't looking at her any more but was staring out at somewhere beyond the ever-changing skies, caught between the past and the present.

Emily knew the rage was directed at himself, fuelled by guilt and grief, but she still took a hit. This was more to her than sex and she certainly would never have intentionally put a patient in jeopardy just to spend some time with Joe. Even if she'd had an inkling of how phenomenal it would be.

'You were injured, you couldn't help what happened to your friends. The only ones to blame are those who planted the bomb. You can't spend the rest of your life afraid of getting close to people in case you let them down. What kind of tribute is that to those who aren't here any more? Taking risks and experiencing things most of us can only imagine is one thing, but shouldn't you be embracing all aspects of life? Including love?' She swallowed hard, catching herself before she blurted out the three words guaranteed to send him running.

Joe was emotionally stripped bare before her, still reeling from his trauma. She didn't need to add more by revealing her feelings for him. He hadn't asked her to fall for him or promised her anything in return. It wasn't fair to expect anything from him now and she knew if she told him she loved him he would feel under pressure to act on it. That's the type of man he was. One who always wanted to do right by others, even if it cost him peace of mind.

There was no way she wanted to increase his burden now she knew that happy-go-lucky façade was hiding his true pain from the rest of the world. Telling him now would only be for selfish reasons, voicing that small hope he would reciprocate her feelings, while all the while knowing nothing could come of it anyway. He'd spelled out the very reasons he couldn't be with her, even if by some miracle he thought of her as more than a holiday romance.

Like her, he was damaged goods. She knew how it was to fake a smile when you were crying on the inside and it was good for him to finally be honest about what he was still going through. The day she'd revealed her birthmark to him had lifted the stress of keeping her secret from her. She hoped this breakthrough tonight would do the same for him in some way. It had taken a great deal of trust from him to confide in her as much as he had, and she was privileged she was getting to know the *real* Joe Braden.

His eyes shimmered in the darkness but he was still refusing to give in to the grief he was obviously suffering. Instead, he ended the conversation by moving in for another kiss. Emily knew he was avoiding further discussion on the subject but she was powerless to resist him when this could be their last opportunity to be together.

They lunged at each other with the urgency of two lovers soon to be separated, possibly for ever.

This time the slow burn of passion was replaced with a fierce need to block out reality and get back to that place of utter contentment as soon as possible when they were both struggling to keep it together. They tore at each other's clothes in their need for a hit of those feel-good endorphins only hot sex could provide. Clinging to each other as though they were adrift at sea, holding on to one another for survival, they joined together in one frantic thrust. For a moment that was all Emily needed, to know he wanted her, that they were together. Then he was moving inside her, turning her thoughts to more primitive needs and how quickly he could take her back to that pinnacle of utter bliss.

Her mind and body were completely consumed by the frenetic pace of their lovemaking as Joe drove into her again and again, chasing away his own demons. There was a moment when their eyes locked, that connection stronger than ever, knowing they both needed this release to free them from their inner turmoil. They came together, their combined cries drowning out the sound of thunder in the distance.

Emily had never known such pleasure and pain, knowing this was the only time they'd have this freedom together. A true passion she'd probably never experience again.

They lay in each other's arms, watching the flames dance in the corner of the cave until Joe's soft snore broke the comfortable silence as he finally seemed to find some peace.

Emily turned on her side and whispered, 'I love you,' safe in the knowledge he wouldn't hear her.

She knew it was the last time she'd ever say it.

'It's time to go.' Joe was gently shaking her awake but she didn't want to open her eyes because that meant facing the truth. The dream was over.

He tried again, a little more forcefully this time. 'We need to get moving before they send a search party out for us.'

She groaned like a truculent teenager forced to get out of bed on a school morning. 'Do we have to?'

'Yes.' He dropped a kiss on her nose.

She supposed food and a warm bed were a good incentive. Plus, if he was brave enough to get that close to her morning breath he must really want to be out of here.

Despite fighting his own demons half the night, Joe clearly hadn't put thoughts of his patient out of his mind. Now it was daylight and their return was inevitable, Emily's concern grew too over what might have occurred in their absence. A more in-depth discussion about Joe's past and his thoughts on a future with her could wait until after they'd checked in with Peter and Miriama.

There was a tad more urgency to her movements now she'd stopped thinking only of herself. She got up but there was no bed to make, no post-coital lazy breakfast together or reason to dilly-dally. Joe kicked some dirt over the fire to make sure it was out and then it was time to leave their little love nest.

They made their way back down to the beach to retrieve the boat from where it had been stashed the night before and pulled it to the edge of the water. The sea was calm today, like flat blue glass for them to slip effortlessly across to Yasi; the sky was as calm as the water. It was almost as if yesterday's drama had never happened.

That wasn't what she wanted at all. Last night with Joe had been the best night of her life. They'd connected in every way imaginable and she didn't want to lose that as soon as they stepped off the island. She still had a few days left before she went home and believed that, given time, they could make this something more than a holiday fling. He'd already started to open up to her and she was willing to risk her heart by giving this a shot.

'What's wrong? Are you sad to be leaving?' Joe didn't seem to understand her attachment to this place, which didn't bode well for a budding romance.

Sleeping with Joe had marked a new chapter in her life. It had put an end to her marriage once and for all. The divorce papers had made it official, but it hadn't been until she'd fallen in love with another man that it had become real to her. She would remember this island for ever as the place where she'd become Emily Jackson again, a single woman living her own life, making her own decisions. She kind of hoped it—she—meant as much to Joe.

He was waiting for her to answer and she thought about laughing it off, pretend last night had been nothing more than sex. But she'd spent too much of her life lying about who she was. If he couldn't handle her feelings, well, she'd simply have to live with the repercussions.

'I don't want this to end. Once we go back to Yasi we're doctors, somebody's family, somebody's friend. Here we're just Emily and Joe, with no expectations from anyone other than ourselves.' A night with Joe had exceeded any expectations she might have had and given her a taste of something special. It wasn't something she was in any hurry to abandon in favour of cool reality. Yasi now seemed like the first step back towards her actual life, where there was no hunky man to spoon with her at night and a whole lot more besides.

With his hands on his hips, his gaze cast down at the

waves washing in and out on the sand, Joe let out a heavy sigh. For a moment Emily worried he might jump in the boat and sail off into the blue without her. Instead, he splashed along the water's edge towards her and wrapped his arms around her waist.

'This won't end until we're both ready.' His words didn't bring her as much comfort as he probably intended because he was still stamping their relationship with a use-by date. It *was* going to end, albeit on a different island with more than swaying palm trees to witness her eventual heartbreak. This might be the new Emily but she still had the same old soft heart. Tears burned the back of her eyelids as Joe gave her one last castaway kiss. She doubted she'd ever be ready. No matter how much notice she had, when the end came it was going to come hard and fast. Joe had left a mark on her soul that wasn't likely to fade any time soon. She knew she'd be thinking of him every time she stepped into the sun.

Joe's head was scrambled, his troubling memories of Afghanistan mixed with those of last night and Emily comforting him. Loving him. He'd spent so long battling the nightmares on his own that he didn't know how to cope with sharing them. Nothing made sense to him any more except kissing her. In some ways he could understand her reluctance to leave. It was easier to stay here wrapped up in each other's arms and ignore everything else outside this slice of paradise. Except hiding wouldn't solve anyone's problems, his least of all.

Even if they chose to push the boat out into the ocean minus its passengers and purposefully strand themselves on this island for ever, it still wouldn't help him reconcile with his faults, or make him the right man for Emily. If something happened out here she'd be dependent on him and that was too much to contemplate for someone who couldn't be trusted with that level of responsibility. Someone who didn't want that level of responsibility again after losing two people he'd loved who were supposedly under his care. Last night, making love to Emily with complete abandon for the first time since leaving the army, had been wonderful but their status couldn't be any more permanent than his stay on this island. As much as he loved her and had probably been searching for her all his life, his wants and needs would have to come second to hers. She deserved more than him.

'Ready?' he said with a forced laugh, making a joke of his last comment before Emily read too much into it. She'd been let down too often. There was no point in leading her on with false promises into believing any of this was real. They had no chance of being together and living happily ever after. That was for heroes, strong men who'd given everything of themselves for others, not those who'd failed in their duty.

'Okay.' Her smile was as fake as his attempt at humour but at least she seemed to understand this need to stop lying to themselves. They had to go back and pick up the reins at the clinic again. It was their job, their calling, their reason for being out here, and it wouldn't do them any good to get too caught up in this fantasy when people depended on them.

As he pushed the boat into the water with Emily on board it was all he could do to jump in beside her, knowing they were sailing towards the end of this romance. The sands of time were shifting ever faster as the sea breeze carried them closer to Yasi and further away from their own personal love island—the only place they could ever truly be together.

When they came ashore on Yasi there was no singing, dancing welcome party to greet them. On the plus side, there wasn't an angry stepbrother waiting for him with a shotgun either. It was going to be pretty obvious what had happened between them left alone on that island all this time when they'd barely been able to keep their hands off each other in company. Peter had already warned him off hurting Emily and that was another promise he knew he was probably going to break when the thought of leaving was already causing him pain. Although she hadn't spoken the exact words, her every look, every touch said she loved him as much as he loved her.

They hauled the boat up onto the beach, where it could be retrieved later. Depending on what they were going back to, it might be used for another voyage soon. There was no point in dragging this out and causing more suffering. If all was well back at the clinic and the chief's house they should probably quit while they were ahead and cherish the happy memories of their night together rather than wait a week for the tears and recriminations to start.

He strode ahead on their walk back into the village in a scene reminiscent of their first meeting. A different couple would have marched along, not caring who knew what had happened or what came next. He couldn't afford that luxury and neither could Emily, though she didn't know it. It was almost inconceivable to think that a few days after their first meeting his whole world would be upside down and he'd broken every one of his relationship rules because of this woman. If Emily expected a loved-up stroll, hand in hand, making the most of their last minutes alone, she didn't say anything. At least nothing he heard.

He paused at the top of the hill to take a breath and a mental snapshot of the view he'd called home for too long. It gave his walking companion time to catch up.

'You seem in an awful hurry to get back.' She moved directly in front of him so there was no escaping the sound of disappointment in her voice.

'I'm sure it's been a long night for everyone. They'll be wondering what's keeping us with the storm long past and half the morning gone already. It's not fair to make them wait any longer than necessary.' They'd had their fun and now it was time to face the consequences.

'Joe? Is everything all right? Between us, I mean?'

This was his opportunity to tell her the truth. Everything between them was far from all right. It was crazy and messed up and scaring the hell out of him enough to consider getting the next boat off the island. Instead he slung an arm around her shoulders as if she was an old mate seeking reassurance on a trivial matter, not a lover asking him about his feelings for her.

'Sure,' he said, his confidence failing him. Going back into the community with shattered hearts suddenly seemed crueller than letting this play out until he had his bag packed.

'I guess we do need time to acclimatise again, give Peter some warning that we were together before he figures it out for himself.' She gave credence to his explanation, increasing his uneasiness by expanding on it until it became her truth. This trust in him was exactly the reason he should leave. He couldn't live up to her expectations and when the blinkers came off it would be in the most humiliating fashion.

'Right,' he said, picking up the pace and carrying the lie away with him.

'The wanderers have returned!' Peter and Miriama were every bit as exhausted and pleased to see them as he'd expected. The guilt slammed into Joe's chest harder than the group hug in which he and Emily were swamped.

'Sorry you had to hold down the fort for so long but we thought it best to wait out the storm.' He immediately felt the need to justify their long delay, even though the reason would've been obvious to anyone who'd witnessed Mother Nature's rage last night.

'I'm just glad you didn't get caught up in it. Did you find somewhere to shelter?' Peter rubbed Emily's arm as if he was trying to generate some heat for her even now. It was a reminder she still had someone to turn to, come what may. Her stepbrother was that person, not someone who was already planning to run away before they reached the first hurdle.

'Joe knew somewhere—'

'We found a place up in the rocks out of the rain.' He cut Emily off before she gave Peter the idea he'd somehow pre-planned all of it.

Besides, the cave had been his secret and it wasn't something he wanted to share with anyone but her even now. Revealing its whereabouts, leaving it open to future visitors, would defile the time they'd spent there together. He wanted them to be the last two inhabitants; the ghosts of their pasts and never-to-be-had future doomed to haunt the stony cavern for ever.

'Good. I had enough to worry about here and figured years of survival training would see you right. Although I would've thought a desert island in a tropical storm was a doddle compared to rain-soaked ditches in the English countryside.'

'You bet. I hope you didn't have too tough a night here without us.' He'd spent the night cuddled up with the most beautiful woman in the world while her stepbrother had been doing the job *he* was supposed to be doing.

'All the delights you'd expect but nothing we couldn't handle. He seems to be through the worst of it for real this time.'

'Thanks, mate. I really appreciate you stepping up to the plate for me. I'm just sorry we put you in that position in the first place.'

'I would say you shouldn't make a habit of it but I reckon we can spare you another couple of hours if you want to have a kip or get changed.'

'That would be great. Cheers.' All of a sudden Peter's generosity made Joe want that space all the more. So no one had died this time, but he had still let his friends down. He could've said no to going in the first place and saved everyone a lot of trouble. He could've insisted on leaving the island at the same time as the others or come back sooner. It had been his selfish wish to spend some alone time with Emily that had put so many people in jeopardy. Pure luck had kept them all from serious harm during his negligence.

He was distracted and unfocused, everything he'd feared would happen if he forged relationships with people. If he hung around here much longer the worst was bound to happen. There was always going to be dengue fever, diabetes, choking babies and people relying on him to save them. Without a local hospital or access to crucial medication the people he'd grown to love were someday going to need more than he could give them. He'd barely come out the other side of grief the last time and he couldn't face it again. He couldn't face these people again knowing he'd failed them. His heart wouldn't survive losing Emily if he failed her too. He'd had a lucky escape this time and it was time to check out while the going was good.

He took off out the door without a backward glance for Emily, afraid that if he looked at her he'd bottle out of this altogether.

'Hey, wait for me.' She'd really got this ninja frontal attack down pat. He didn't even know she was following him until she was there blocking his path.

'Look, Emily, I need some time on my own. Sorry.' He started walking again, unable to offer her a proper explanation when he didn't fully understand why he was throwing this away himself.

'Joe?' Another stealth move and he was faced with those doe eyes pleading with him not to do this.

He had to swallow the ball of emotion lodged in his throat. It was never easy ending a relationship and he was effectively ending two of the most important ones in his life by leaving Yasi. He didn't want to do this out here in the open. Hell, he didn't want to have to do this at all but he was supposed to be a drifter and the difficulty level of ending this was proof he'd already stayed too long.

'I never said I'd be here for ever. Last night proved to me it's time I moved on. I should never have let things get this far and I'm going now before I do any more damage. There are enough of you to carry on what I started. You don't need me any more.' They didn't need him but it was becoming clear that he was starting to lean on them too much and that was equally as dangerous. Spilling his guts to her last night in the wake of his latest nightmare had shown how weak he'd become in getting close to Emily and everyone else on the island. It was only a matter of time before someone got hurt. More hurt.

'I don't suppose the fact I *want* you to stay makes any difference?' She was killing him but this was going to take tough love to make sure she didn't end up mooning after him and ruining the rest of her trip.

'You know I can't stay still. I get bored too easily. I'm grateful for this adventure but, really, I'm ready for the next one.' He saw Emily flinch at his choice of words out of the corner of his eye.

'Joe?' Another plaintive cry for an explanation he couldn't give her.

It broke his heart to ignore it.

'I don't have much to pack so if I can get the chief to agree, I'll be taking the boat out again soon.' He didn't care how he got back to the mainland or how long it took as long as he put some distance between him and Yasi Island fast. It wouldn't take much for his resolve to weaken.

'If that's what you really want…'

'It is.' He was almost gasping for air as the lie choked him. What he wanted was a life with Emily but that was as impossible as Batesy and Ste having theirs back.

'Is that it? You got what you wanted and now you're running out on me?'

'You knew this wasn't for ever. One night together doesn't mean I've changed who I am. I was upfront from the start about my intentions. All I'm doing is putting an end to it sooner than planned. Chalk this up to part of the adventure package.'

He couldn't bear to look at her any more as he stumbled away. Ripping the sticking plaster off with a short, sharp shock was supposed to alleviate the pain more quickly but that expression of betrayal he saw welling up in her eyes was going to stay with him for a long time. He needed to get off this island. Now.

Emily couldn't breathe, the shock of Joe's words sucking the air from her lungs. After last night he knew this was more to her than a holiday fling and she'd hoped he'd felt the same. This sudden coolness and what seemed like unnecessary cruelty was difficult to get her head around when they'd shared so much, grown so close.

Frozen to the spot, all she could do was watch him go. Even the tears she needed to shed for their short-lived relationship refused to fall in her confusion. If she were a stronger person she might have given chase and demanded answers but part of her already knew the answers. He was bored with her. He'd said as much. All of that anxiety she'd felt when Greg had told her the same thing came whooshing back and left her gasping for air. This was re-affirming that idea she wasn't good enough for anyone.

The energy seemed to drain from her body as the implications of his words sank in, leaving her limp and unsteady on her feet. She reached out to brace herself against one of the palm trees that once upon a time had held so many good memories. Now she would always associate everything she loved on this island with this utterly overwhelming sense of desolation. She sank down onto the grass, her body only upright with the support of the solid trunk of the tree. This was how she was going to spend the rest of her days—alone, broken-hearted, unwanted.

Hard-hitting rejection wasn't new to her but it wasn't any less painful the third time around. If anything, it hurt even more than losing her mother or her husband when Joe had appeared so much more supportive and accepting of her for who she was. Last night she'd held him through his night terrors, made love as if they'd been embarking on the start of an exciting journey, and now he was saying it was over? It was hard for her to accept she wasn't anything more to him than any of the other women he'd spent time with on his travels when he'd come to mean so much to her. He was part of her now. He'd helped her learn to love herself again and she'd fallen head over heels for him in the process.

She couldn't imagine going back to her old life as if this had never happened. Neither could she face the rest of her stay here without him. There were memories liable to start a monsoon of tears at every turn. Even from her tragic position here on the ground she could see the hill they'd marched down laden down with her luggage and the school where they'd had so much fun with the children. Her lip began to wobble as she realised this was probably the very tree they'd sat under and shared lunch. If she was expected to forget him she was going to have to leave early too.

She struggled to her feet and resolved to make her way

back to Miriama's before she gave in to the big fat tears threatening to fall. Once she was behind closed doors she could mourn properly—cry, rage and eventually decide where to go from here. Whatever happened next was entirely down to her. From now on she was on her own.

Emily had spent more than enough time moping in her room like an angsty adolescent. Her throat was raw from sobbing, her eyes puffy and red from crying, but she knew she still had to face up to her responsibilities. Just because her life was falling apart it didn't mean she should neglect the inhabitants of Yasi. With Joe gone she was the only doctor left in residence.

She splashed her face with cold water and pulled her hair up into a ponytail. There were always going to be patients to treat and her job was the one constant in her life. At least she was always going to be in demand professionally, if not romantically. In some ways she felt sorry for Joe. The transient life he led to ensure he didn't get close to people also meant he never got to fully experience that feeling of belonging.

With her mind clearer now the initial shock of his rejection had passed, she began to analyse that last conversation. He'd given her the impression he'd tired of life here, that she'd bored him. If this had been England and she was back in her office with nothing to look forward to than a cup of tea while watching the soaps on TV she'd buy it. But not when she'd spent the last days throwing herself into local customs that ordinarily would have terrified her. She wasn't that same meek divorcee who'd set foot on the island and she was ticked off he'd made out she was. After everything he'd told her she began to wonder if it wasn't his insecurities he was running away from. He'd been so locked into his grief and guilt he'd become a martyr to it, denying himself, and her, any chance of happiness.

She found herself veering towards the clinic. If she didn't try to make sense of this now she knew she'd come to regret it. Whether he was leaving because of her or his own demons, she wanted closure before returning home so she was free to start the next chapter of her life. With or without him.

Her once weak limbs now carried with renewed strength. She'd never taken the opportunity to confront Greg about ending their relationship and had simply walked away with her tail between her legs. Not this time. Good or bad, she wanted honesty about why this was over so she wouldn't be left in limbo.

Unfortunately, by the time she reached the clinic all traces of Joe were gone. All that was left was a scribbled note on the door.

Thanks for everything.
Joe x

That was it? After everything they'd been through together all she deserved was an impersonal message that could've been directed at anyone on the island. She crumpled it in her hand in disgust. He hadn't even managed a proper goodbye to her, to Peter, or anyone else who loved him. She wasn't usually prone to violent outbursts of temper but this all seemed such a waste she wanted to punch things or scream out her frustration.

The hub of the village wasn't the place to do it and she knew she couldn't focus on work until she'd worked through this part of the grieving process. She took the path to the beach instead. The same one Joe would had to have taken to make his escape. She wondered what kind of mindset he'd been in when he'd walked this route. Sad? Relieved? Excited to be starting a new adventure?

Perhaps, instead of spending the last hours weeping

and wailing she should've been finding out. There was a small chance he might even have counted on her coming after him and begging him to stay. After all, she hadn't been honest about the strength of her feelings for him. It was too late to find out if that would have stopped him from leaving.

Her eyes were burning again with those useless tears as she reached the top of the hill. Somewhere in the distance she swore she heard a boat splutter into life. She blinked away the tears to see two figures launching the boat from shore. Joe was there, sailing away for good. This was the last time they'd probably ever see each other and she wanted to make sure there was no way back before she moved on. She raced towards the beach like a woman possessed. He didn't look back, probably because he couldn't hear her yelling over the death rattle of the diesel engine. It was up to her to make him listen.

She kicked off her shoes and didn't think twice before wading out into the water. Joe had taught her not to overthink and complicate matters but to simply jump right in and see where she ended up. Soon the boat would be too far out for her to reach. She gulped in one last breath before diving into the unknown.

Swimming out to a lover who'd jumped on a boat to escape her was either the most romantic gesture ever or the action of a desperate woman who had serious issues about letting go. It was impossible to gauge which way he'd take her action but hopefully he'd spot her soon before she drowned and became some sort of tragic folklore story. She didn't really want to spend eternity wailing for her lost love when she still had a life to get back to at the end of all this.

When she'd expelled all the oxygen in her lungs trying to reach him, she popped her head above the water and waved. The last thing she saw before she sank under the water again was Joe getting to his feet. At least she'd had one final look before she went to her watery grave. That would make the soulful songs about the lonely English-woman who drowned chasing the handsome traveller all the more poignant.

'What the hell are you doing?' Joe was reaching down through the water to grab hold of her. A hero truly worthy of becoming part of Yasi folklore.

She climbed into the boat with the help of two pairs of male hands. Excellent, she had a local to regale the rest of the island with tales of her daring escapade. Which was fine if she benefited somehow from this recklessness and didn't make a complete ass of herself. The latter seemed the more likely outcome as she was sitting between two bemused men like a bedraggled mermaid they'd accidentally caught in their fishing net.

'I. Thought. You'd. Gone.' Her teeth were chattering with the shock of what she'd just done more than from the cold.

Joe pulled a sweater from his bag and draped it around her shoulders. 'I had to wait until we could take the boat out again. It's stormy out there.'

Only now he'd pointed it out did she realise the skies had clouded over again, matching her unsettled heart.

'I want to know the real reason you're leaving now.'

'You're crazy. *This* is crazy!'

'You drove me to it so the least you can do is be honest with me.' It was true in every sense. She'd never have done anything so impulsive before meeting him, never have felt the need if she hadn't have fallen so hard for him.

He stood up, rubbed his hands over his scalp and sat down again. 'I can't believe you did something so stupid.'

'You're the one running away from this when we both know we have something special. In my book that's equally idiotic.'

His sigh came from somewhere deep inside him. Somewhere the truth was probably hiding. 'I told you what happened in Afghanistan. I don't get close, I don't get hurt. Simple.'

He wasn't saying he didn't love her, didn't want to be with her. Reading between the lines, it was because of those reasons he was leaving. Her big brave army doc was afraid to admit to his feelings because of things that might never happen. It was something she could relate to when she'd spent her whole life trying to pre-empt the negative outcome of every situation.

'That's not living. Loving someone, being loved, is part of life. You're the one playing it safe when you know sometimes the biggest risk brings the greatest rewards. What happened to going with the flow? Unless you missed it, things were flowing pretty great until you jumped into this boat and headed out to sea.' A destination that hadn't yet been corrected. If she didn't get through to him soon she'd be making the return journey with only a very tactful islander pretending not to notice her pouring her heart out.

'I don't want you to get hurt.' He took her hand and rubbed the heat back into her fingers, showing he was always tending to her needs without even thinking about it.

'You couldn't hurt me any more than you did by walking out on me without giving us a chance. I want to be with you. Beyond that we'll just see what happens.'

'Damn. You got really bossy in the space of just a few days.' He was smiling as he linked his fingers through hers but she could see the turmoil in his eyes. It was going to be down to her to convince him to take a chance on love. The knowledge he wanted to be with her was powerful enough motivation for her.

'I prefer to think of it as becoming more decisive. I'm taking charge of my life and I want you to be part of it.

I love you, Joe Braden.' Her heart was pounding like a drum as she put it all on the line for him. Joe wasn't the only one taking a risk here. After everything she'd been through, starting a new relationship was like setting foot on Yasi all over again. She had no clue what she was letting herself in for and could only cross her fingers and hope that it would all turn out good in the end.

'And I love this crazy, impulsive Emily. She sounds like the ideal travelling companion for lots of fun new adventures.'

Her heart felt as though it was beating for the first time it was so full of happiness to hear those words and know he meant them.

'So what's the plan from here?' She wanted to go with the momentum, wherever it took them.

'Well, there's a little place I know where we can reconnect and take some time out before we commit to that next step. Perhaps we could take a detour and get our captain to drop us off across the bay before the storm moves in.'

Another shiver rippled up and down Emily's spine, this time with anticipation. It was the ideal place to truly get to know each other and make plans for a future.

One thing was sure, with Joe in her life she'd never be boring again.

EPILOGUE

EMILY WOULD NEVER have believed she'd be back on Yasi Island within a year, much less for a wedding. Her wedding. She looked across at Joe, her husband-to-be, so handsome standing barefoot next to her on the beach. They were never going to have a traditional ceremony and had decided to incorporate elements from Fijian culture into their day.

'Dearly beloved, we are gathered here today to join this man and this woman in holy matrimony.' Peter give them both a smile. Having him officiate made this day truly special, as did having the rest of her family here with them. There was quite a crowd assembled on the beach, all dressed in their finery.

Her wedding dress was a simple, white, strapless gown and Joe had gone with his white shirt and linen trousers. The festive garlands the islanders had bestowed on them, including the ring of flowers in her hair, brought a bright splash of colour to proceedings. Sou, Miriama, her step-mother, and all the other women from the village wore the traditional dresses made from tapa cloth and decorated with the red clay paint that had brought her and Joe so close that special day. The men, bar her father in his Hawaiian-style shirt, were in full warrior costume—she finally got to see the grass skirts! It was all so exotic and exciting it was no wonder she'd found it so hard to settle back home.

After she and Joe had spent the second week of her trip together almost twenty-four hours a day, it hadn't taken much persuading for him to go back to England with her. They'd tried to make it work there but ultimately she'd been the one craving everything Yasi had brought into her life. The regimented schedule had suddenly become too stifling for her and she'd seen Joe's relief when she'd finally admitted it. They didn't have to box themselves into a suburban life in order to be together and he'd proposed when she'd uttered those very words to him.

It had taken a few months to get their affairs in order but they'd both agreed they wanted their new start to begin where they'd first fallen in love. She was looking forward to spending time with Peter again but they hadn't made definite plans to make the island their permanent home. There was a whole world waiting for them out there.

'I do.' Joe gave his promise to love, honour and comfort her, and Emily did the same in return. They'd been there for each other through so much already, to the point she wasn't even wearing her cover-up for her wedding day and his nightmares were becoming rarer with every passing night they spent in each other's arms.

They exchanged simple gold wedding bands as a token of their pledge of love for one another before her stepbrother pronounced them husband and wife and gave them permission to kiss in front of everyone.

'I've never kissed a married woman before,' Joe said when they finally came up for air.

'Well, make sure it's only *your* wife you're kissing,' she said with a grin to match his. 'Wife' was a title she'd worn before but it no longer defined her. She was still Emily. This ring simply meant she was privileged to be sharing the rest of her life with Joe, and vice versa.

'There's no one else I would want to do this with.' He took her hand and kissed her wedding finger, a sign he was talking about his next great adventure and not just a snog here and there. They were in this together.

As the *vakatara*—the orchestra—struck up their percussion instruments and the *matana*—dancers— assembled to begin the celebrations, Emily counted every one of her blessings. The biggest one of all she was yet to share with her new husband. She rested her hand on her slightly rounded belly. In seven months they would embark on a new chapter of their lives and all the new adventures parenthood would bring them.

* * * * *

COMING SOON!

We really hope you enjoyed reading this book. If you're looking for more romance, be sure to head to the shops when new books are available on

Thursday
18th October

To see which titles are coming soon, please visit
millsandboon.co.uk